Georgia Bockoven is an award-winning author who began writing fiction after a successful career as a freelance journalist and photographer. Her books have sold more than four million copies worldwide. She is a former winner of the prestigious RITA from the Romance Writers of America as well as the Reviewer's Choice Award for Best Contemporary Novel. Georgia Bockoven's work has also been translated onto the screen. The mother of two, she resides in Northern California with her husband, John.

BLESSING IN DISGUISE

When Lynda Miller is injured in a tragic accident, her single mother, Catherine, is wracked by guilt and doubts. Her happy-go-lucky daughter has gone from being a good student and cheerleader to a virtual recluse. Robbed of her self-confidence at such a critical stage in her life, Catherine doesn't know how best to help her. Support for both of them is at hand in the form of Rick Sawyer. A fire-fighter and counsellor used to working with families in distress, he has been assigned to help the Millers. But, having been deserted by one man too many, winning their trust isn't going to be easy . . .

GEORGIA BOCKOVEN

BLESSING IN DISGUISE

Complete and Unabridged

ULVERSCROFT
Leicester

First published in Great Britain in 2000 by
Judy Piatkus (Publishers) Limited
London

First Large Print Edition
published 2003
by arrangement with
Judy Piatkus (Publishers) Limited
London

British Library CIP Data

Bockoven, Georgia
  Blessing in disguise.—Large print ed.—
Ulverscroft large print series: romance
1. Mothers and daughters—Fiction
2. Accident victims—Fiction 3. Large type books
I. Title II. Disguised blessing
813.5′4 [F]

ISBN 0–7089–4784–0

Published by
F. A. Thorpe (Publishing)
Anstey, Leicestershire

Set by Words & Graphics Ltd.
Anstey, Leicestershire
Printed and bound in Great Britain by
T. J. International Ltd., Padstow, Cornwall

This book is printed on acid-free paper

1

Catherine Miller stood at the cabin's kitchen window and watched a squirrel stretch from one branch of a fir tree to the next in an effort to reach the bird feeder she'd put up less than an hour ago. On the dock, a Steller's jay sat on a pillar, its head cocked to one side, intently eyeing the unfolding scene.

Abruptly, as if everything had been choreographed and timed, the feeder tipped, the jay took off to capture the spilled prize, and Tom Adams came up behind her to slip his arms around her waist. He pulled her against his chest, fitting her back and buttocks into his long torso. His breath hot and moist against her ear, he whispered the plans he'd made for later when they were alone. Catherine caught her breath at her body's immediate, powerful response.

Tom Adams could do more to arouse her with words than Jack had managed with his peculiar brand of foreplay during their entire marriage. Feeling a familiar guilt at their intimate display, Catherine sent a furtive glance in her daughter's direction. Thankfully, as usual, Lynda was caught up in her compulsive need to be in touch with the members of her own fifteen-year-old world, and was as oblivious to them as she was to the suitcase she'd promised to take to her room and unpack an hour ago.

'We really need to be more careful when Lynda is around,' she reminded him. Tom could be led, but balked at being pushed. She maneuvered out of his arms, took his hand, and moved to the far side of the kitchen.

Tom followed, caught Catherine, and pulled her into his arms again. 'Stop worrying. I made sure she wasn't looking. I always do.' He kissed the base of her throat, then her mouth, touching and tasting her lips with his tongue before leaning back and grinning seductively. 'Besides, what we're doing isn't anything she hasn't seen already or doesn't imagine. She's a lot more savvy about what goes on between us than you want to think she is.'

'Even if that's true, I'd rather leave it to her imagination than lay it out for her.'

At that he held up his arms in surrender. 'Whatever you say.'

'Please don't do that.' She put a conciliatory hand on his chest. 'Let's not spoil the day by fighting.'

He took another step backward, leaving her hand suspended in air. 'Who's fighting? I'm simply giving you what you want.'

She knew if she didn't do something to smooth things over they really would get into an argument. She'd put too much work into arranging this vacation for the three of them to let that happen. She wanted this to be a time to look back on and reminisce about, a memory that would get better and better with each telling. She had her camera and five rolls of film, and the determination to see that every shot was a memorable one. She even had the album ready — one she'd found at a card shop that had FAMILY PHOTOS stamped in gold on the green leather cover.

Before Catherine could find the words to appease Tom, Lynda hung up and came into the kitchen. She took a bottle of water out of the refrigerator, studied her mother as she opened it, and asked, 'Are you mad at me about something?'

Lynda had uncanny perceptions; but in typical teenage fashion, she invariably believed herself to be the source of any conflict. 'What makes you think that?'

'You look like you're upset.' She started to take a drink and paused. 'You're not thinking of changing your mind about letting me go to the party, are you?'

'No. But I don't want you making any

3

more plans this week without checking with me first.'

'By 'making plans,' would that mean inviting Patty to go bicycling with us tomorrow?'

'Oh, Lynda, you didn't.' Lynda's friends were the veins she needed to supply her with social oxygen. She collected them wherever she went, like seashells and pinecones, with a natural, uncomplicated ease.

'I thought you liked Patty.'

'I do, but this vacation was supposed to be just the three of us doing things together.'

'We've got the rest of our lives to do things together,' Tom said as he put his arm around Lynda's shoulders and gave her a quick hug. 'Lynda only has one summer to be fifteen. She should be with her friends.'

Catherine was stunned. And angry. Tom knew how much this vacation meant to her. Now, with the two of them lined up against her, she didn't stand a chance. 'We'll talk about this later.'

'Does that mean it's okay about Patty?' Lynda asked.

'Do I have a choice?'

'No . . . ' Lynda grinned, breaking the tension between them. 'But I'd like you to think you do.'

They were Catherine's own words, ones

she'd used in a half dozen disagreements they'd had that past month. 'I'm going to give you this one, but no more commitments without checking with me first, okay?'

'Okay.'

'Promise?'

'Cross my heart.'

'What time is Brian going to pick you up?'

'Twelve thirty.'

Catherine glanced at the clock on the microwave. They'd been there less than an hour and Lynda had already made two dates to be with friends. 'How did he even know you were here?'

'He saw us drive in.'

'From across the lake?'

'What difference does it make?' Tom asked in a get-off-the-kid's-back tone.

Catherine bristled but didn't say anything. To Lynda, she said, 'Why so early?'

'I volunteered to help set up. He's having a ton of people — even some of the renters. Can you believe it? Nobody ever invites renters to parties.'

The social circle at Rainbow Lake went back generations and rarely included anyone who'd owned their cabin less than ten years. Catherine's grandfather had acquired their place as partial payment for a business debt during the depression. Now it belonged to

Catherine's mother. Eventually — possibly very soon — if her mother really did move to Arizona, it would be passed on to Catherine and her brother, Gene.

'Is Brian coming here or are you meeting him at the store?' Catherine asked.

'The store. Jody's coming, too. I told her we'd pick her up on the way. I hope that's all right.' Lynda drank the last of her water and put the empty bottle on the counter.

Isolated years earlier from the main road by a rock slide too massive to clear, Brian's family's house was one of three on the lake that could now be accessed only by boat.

Tom didn't give her a chance to answer. 'I'll drive you,' he said. 'I think your mother could use a little time alone to unwind from the trip up here.'

Catherine let the odd comment pass. 'How late is the party supposed to last?'

'It's open-ended. But don't worry. Brian said he would bring me home when it was over.'

'I want you here by midnight.'

'*Mom,*' Lynda groaned. 'That's so unfair.'

'Twelve thirty, then. No later.' She gave Lynda her I-mean-it-this-time look that still magically worked.

'All right. But I'm going to feel like a jerk

asking him to leave his own party before it's over.'

Lynda left to change clothes and Tom leaned against the counter and reached for Catherine. She stepped into his embrace, loosely wrapping her arms around his neck. 'I didn't mean you couldn't come with us,' he said. 'I just thought that you might want to stay here and relax for a while.'

If she'd missed the look he gave her, she would have picked up his meaning in the low, throaty way he said the words. Rarely did they have three uninterrupted hours alone together, let alone twelve. She could hardly blame him for being excited at the prospect.

Catherine ran her hands through his thick dark hair and came forward for a kiss. 'I think I just might use the time for a nice, long bubble bath.' She was still coming down from the every-minute-must-be-accounted-for life she'd led before quitting her job two months ago and had to remind herself that a bubble bath was not something she had to schedule anymore.

He pressed his cheek to hers and whispered into her ear, 'With that to think about on the way home, I may wind up in the lake.'

She laughed. 'How is it you always know the right things to say?'

'Simple. I have the right woman to say them to.'

When Catherine heard Lynda coming down the hall, she moved to free herself from Tom's arms. He loosened his grip but refused to let her go. Catherine made one more attempt before Lynda appeared in the doorway and it became a moot point.

'Ready?' Tom said.

Lynda nodded. She'd put her shoulder-length hair up with a clip and changed into khaki shorts and a bright red chemise top.

A half dozen warnings and reminders danced in Catherine's mind as they always did when Lynda was ready to go somewhere, everything from applying sunscreen to not swimming immediately after eating. She managed to control them all save one. 'Don't forget to take a jacket.'

'All I have is that great big one Dad gave me. I forgot to pack anything else.'

'Then take my sweater.'

'I'll be okay. It's — '

'Indulge me.'

With a groan, she asked, 'Where is it?'

'In the hall closet.'

Lynda opened the door. 'You mean this green thing?' She held the sweater out in front of her. Big and bulky with a rolled collar and dangling belt, it looked like a garage sale reject from the sixties.

'It may not be beautiful, but it's warm. You'll thank me when you're out on the lake tonight.'

Lynda made a face. 'You're kidding, right? You don't really expect me to let anyone see me wearing this.'

Tom took the sweater from Lynda and put it across her shoulders. 'You want to stand here and argue or you want to meet Brian at the store?'

For a second, it seemed Lynda might actually be considering her options. Then, sighing again, she took off the sweater and stuffed it in her bag.

Catherine walked them to the car. 'Remember — twelve thirty.'

'Uh-huh.' Four graduated gold rings reflected the sun from her right ear; two more and a small diamond stud decorated her left — compromises from Catherine for a promise they would be the only parts of her body she would pierce.

'Have a good time.'

'I will.'

'And don't make any more plans for the week,' she couldn't resist adding.

'I won't.' Lynda got in and waited for Tom to start the engine on Catherine's Lincoln Navigator. She rolled down the window as they backed out of the narrow driveway. 'If Jody calls, tell her we're on our way and that I decided not to take my swimsuit after all.'

Catherine waved and waited until they were out of sight before she headed back to the house. She veered off at the last minute to check the status of the bird feeder. Rounding the corner, she heard a chirped warning. An irate squirrel dashed past, its cheeks stuffed with pilfered sunflower seeds.

A breeze swept a yellow cloud of pine pollen off the wooden dock and into the lake. For a month every summer the pollen coated everything with a fine dust. Viewed from the top of one of the surrounding mountain's peaks, the lake itself took on a yellowish cast and looked like a giant, swirling pot of blue and yellow finger paints.

June was not Catherine's favorite month here. As an adult, she much preferred May, before the summer crowds settled in, or September, after Labor Day, when most of the cabins were closed for the winter. Of course, when she'd been Lynda's age and she and her brother had spent the entire summer at the lake, she'd counted the days until her friends arrived and bemoaned the day or two they stayed after everyone had gone. Those were the days of stay-at-home mothers who had their summers free and fathers willing to commute from as far away as San Francisco on weekends.

Only six miles from Lake Tahoe, where lakefront property was as pricey as oceanfront property in Malibu, the snows at Rainbow Lake were too heavy and the roads too narrow for winter access, which kept cabin prices down. The lower prices made it possible to pass the vacation homes from one generation to the next, helping to keep the small community stable.

If her mother did move to Arizona, Catherine and her brother would find themselves responsible for the upkeep of a cabin neither of them used more than a few weeks each summer.

Which was one of the reasons she'd decided to bring Tom there instead of somewhere more private for their pre-wedding family get-together. She wanted to see how he felt about the lake, and whether she could count on his support if she decided to buy Gene's share should he want to sell.

On impulse, Catherine slipped out of her loafers, cleared the pollen from a spot on the end of the dock, and sat down, dangling her feet in the cold water. The sun-heated wood stung the backs of her bare thighs. She rocked from side to side until the burning became a comfortable, welcoming warmth. Settling, she

11

closed her eyes, listened to the wind slip through the pines, and tried to remind herself not to luxuriate too deeply in her newfound happiness.

Her austere German grandmother had instilled a fear of tempting the Fates with a show of too much joy. There'd been little danger of that happening before she met Tom. She'd been content with the job she'd taken to fill her days after her divorce from Jack, and she loved being Lynda's mother, but joy wasn't a coin she spent in her realm.

When Tom came into her life, he reminded her how much she liked being with a man. And Lynda actually gave Tom a chance, something she never did with the other men Catherine dated. He didn't try to parent her, and she responded with a hesitant, developing friendship that Catherine was convinced grew stronger every time they were together.

Her life couldn't be better.

There, she'd said it. She'd actually challenged the Fates. Instead of cowering in fear, she felt free and alive and powerful. Happiness as complete as hers was its own shield.

2

Catherine was in bubbles up to her chin when Tom returned. He came into the bathroom with a bottle of champagne in one hand and two long-stemmed glasses in the other. She leaned languorously against the back of the enormous clawfoot tub and smiled. 'A little early, don't you think?'

'For us, opportunities like this don't come along very often. There's no way I'm going to let this one go uncelebrated.' He put the glasses on the tile counter, uncorked the bottle, and poured them each a glass before coming to sit on the edge of the tub next to her. Before offering a toast, he came forward and gave her a lingering kiss. 'To a lifetime of opportunities.'

She touched her glass to his. 'And to you to share them with me.'

'Until I'm too old to recognize how much more intoxicating the bubbles that you're sitting in are than the ones in this glass.'

She took a sip and licked the moisture from her lip. 'And here I was beginning to think you hadn't noticed.'

He gave her a look that let her know he'd

missed nothing. Slowly, deliberately, he began removing small, crucial clusters of foam from her body, never touching her directly but sending an electric, unmistakable message. Her skin flushed pink with anticipation. Her breathing grew shallow. In response, in encouragement, she arched her back and moved her legs, placing one foot on the faucet, the other on the drain.

Tom was an inventive, imaginative lover, reveling as much in the pleasure he gave as in the pleasure he received. There had never been an awkward moment in their lovemaking, a miscue or a time when she hadn't been ready. He sensed and understood her moods, unerringly choosing his approach when she was most receptive.

If she wondered about him at all, if she admitted to the slightest doubt, it was that he seemed too perfect to be real. Or maybe it was that she didn't understand why he'd chosen her when he'd had his pick of any single woman, and a lot of the married ones, in their circle of friends. It was almost as if he'd come to the dance at the country club just to meet her. She'd spotted him looking at her the minute she walked in. Later, he told her that he'd decided at that very moment that she was the woman he'd waited his entire life to meet. He'd pursued her with single-minded dedication and determination, and won her with his charm, humor, and easy acceptance of Lynda as an integral part of the equation — something no other man she'd dated since her divorce had even attempted.

'Stand up,' he ordered.

She struggled to surface from a sensuous depth she didn't want to abandon. Handing him her glass, she rose from the water and stood before him, clusters of foam still attached to her body.

When she moved to step from the tub, he said, 'No, stay where you are.' He reached for the bottle of champagne and poured a splash into his hand. When it was warmed, he let his hand slip over her shoulder and down the length of her body. He repeated the process until she was shimmering with the small, intoxicating bubbles, then put the bottle aside, helped her from the tub, and began drying her with his tongue.

Catherine shuddered, caught her breath, and held it for long seconds before releasing it with a sigh. He lingered at the cup of her shoulder, lapping her skin with the tip of his tongue, taking in her essence along with the champagne and traces of water. Slowly he moved lower, negotiating a path to her breast and its passion-hardened nipple. She let out a soft moan of anticipation, urging him on, seeking a release while delighting in the journey.

He looked at her, smiled, and lifted her into his arms.

'From now on, every time you think about this cabin, you're going to think about this moment, this entire day.'

'Just this one day? What about all the others that will follow? We have a lot of years ahead of us.'

He laughed deeply. 'I like the way your mind works.'

Pulling her close to fit them through the doorway, he swung her around in a circle in the bedroom before placing her gently on the bed.

'Fates, are you watching?' she whispered. 'Are you jealous?'

Tom looked up from unbuttoning his shirt. 'What?'

'I'm tired of being afraid. From now on I'm going to revel in my happiness. As a matter of fact, I'm going to shout it from a mountaintop tomorrow for the whole world to hear.'

'What brought that on?'

'I'm in love — can't you tell?' And there was something else, something she would never admit to him, something she barely admitted to herself: She wasn't bone-achingly lonely anymore.

He tossed his shirt and jeans onto the chair by the window and joined her on the bed, grabbing her by the waist and pulling her on top of him. 'I don't know. Maybe you should show me. I've always been more physical than verbal.'

She sat up and straddled him, slowly pulling the pins from her hair and then shaking it free. Fully aware of the effect her deliberate movements had on him, she delayed even longer to look at him through hooded eyes, her mouth slightly open, her tongue touching her lip.

He put his hand on the back of her neck and pulled her down for a deep, plundering kiss, beginning the day he'd promised she would remember for the rest of her life.

★   ★   ★

Fresh from a second bath to rid herself of the sticky champagne residue, Catherine snuggled into Tom's side and ran her hand over his chest. He was two months shy of his fortieth birthday and had the body of a twenty-year-old. No, that wasn't right. He had the body of a man who put effort into the way he looked. A lot of effort. Muscles rippled when he moved. His stomach stayed as flat when a beautiful woman looked away as it did when she looked at him. Physical fitness was important to Tom and through his gentle prodding, it had become important to her.

But how he looked and the way others looked at him were inconsequential parts of her love. Even if he couldn't understand why things were important to her, he believed they were when she told him so, and acted accordingly.

This trip was a test of sorts. For all of them. Which was why it was so important that it went well. Until now, she and Tom had never spent an entire night together. Catherine wanted to give Lynda the mental shelter of believing whatever she wanted to believe about her and Tom's relationship. By having Tom come with them without sharing Catherine's bedroom, they'd taken a step. Not one so large Lynda would be stripped of her security; but it was time she understood what it would mean to have him with them at breakfast as well as dinner.

The battle for them to sleep in separate bedrooms had been hard-won. Tom was convinced Lynda was not only ready for her mother to take that step, she didn't care. In the end he'd given in, although reluctantly.

Tom took her wandering hand and brought it to his lips for a kiss. 'There's something we need to discuss.'

'You sound so serious.'

'Sorry — I didn't mean to. But it is serious, in a way. It's about Lynda. I know I told you I wouldn't interfere, and I'm not, it's just that I want to offer another viewpoint.'

'About?'

'Making her be with us every second she's here. I know what you want to accomplish this week, but I think you're going after something you already have. She already thinks of us as a family, Catherine. To her it's no big deal for the three of us to be together all the time. We love each other, she loves you and accepts me, and I think that's a whole lot more than we had a right to expect at this point.'

He rolled to his side to look at her, as if to gauge her reaction and form his argument from that. 'I'm afraid if we make her miss this time with her friends she's going to resent being with us, not go home thinking what a great time she had.'

'I don't — '

'Didn't you tell me she only gets to see this set of friends when she's here?'

'For the most part.'

'And that she's been looking forward to this for weeks?'

'Yes,' Catherine admitted. Maybe she had made a mistake coming here. If she'd wanted Lynda to herself, they should have gone to another resort.

'Now put yourself in her place. How would you feel about the people who — '

'I get your point.'

'Besides, this is our vacation, too. We have a right to some time alone, the same as Lynda.'

He'd had her up to that moment. She tried to ignore the flicker of disappointment she felt. After all, his first consideration had been Lynda. Of course he would think about spending time alone with the woman he loved, maybe even feel a little selfish about it. Would she really want it any other way?

'I don't know. Maybe you're right,' she said. 'It's just that you and Lynda have spent so little time together.'

'All right. Let's say she woke up one morning and decided she didn't like me. What would you do?'

'That's not going to happen.'

'But what if it did?'

She wasn't sure what he was after. 'I'd have to find another way to make her see what a wonderful man you are.'

'And if that didn't work?'

Catherine propped herself up on her elbow. 'You can't be asking me who I would choose if it came down to you and Lynda.'

'What if I were?'

'What good does it do for us to discuss something that isn't going to happen?'

He rolled onto his back and sat up. 'Maybe I just want to know where I stand with you. Sometimes I get the feeling it's pretty far down the line.'

'You know that's not true.'

'Okay. Maybe not far down the line — but definitely second place.'

How had they gone from lovemaking to the verge of an argument? Had she missed a step somewhere? 'Did I say something wrong? Did I do something? I don't understand what's going on here.'

Tom stared at her for several seconds before shaking his head in defeat. 'It isn't you, it's me.' He tenderly tucked her hair over her shoulder. 'I've never been this happy with anyone. I can't seem to keep myself from looking for something that would tell me it isn't real. Self-protection, I guess. I'm just afraid of being hurt.'

They were words to melt her heart. 'I'm here. And I'm real. And I'm not going to go away. If there's a problem, we'll find a way through it. I promise.'

He kissed her, his mouth hungry and demanding, his body instantly ready for her again. She responded with an equal intensity, eager to have him understand the depth of her commitment in his body as well as his mind.

★ ★ ★

They had dinner on the deck that night: Brie and sesame crackers; tart, sliced apples; plump, succulent grapes; and an exquisite cabernet sauvignon that Tom had been saving in his wine locker for a special occasion. They leaned back in their chairs to let the last of the day's sun warm them, and talked about the pollen and the office building that Tom's company had built in Roseville and the guest list for the wedding.

She wanted a small wedding. He wanted her to invite everyone she knew, including most of the membership of the country club. His request had confused her until he reminded her that being new to the area put him at a disadvantage, and he considered the reception an opportunity to meet people as well as celebrate their marriage. She couldn't fault his ambition — overcoming a background of neglect and poverty to become a vice president for LandCo was one of the things she admired most about him. Still, she would have liked to save their wedding for them.

When they were sated with food, they took the last of the wine inside and made love with as much passion and enthusiasm as before. Then, just before Tom slipped into a contented sleep, he toasted Catherine and told her that she'd made him realize there were no problems the two of them together could not solve. She was the woman he'd been looking for his entire life, the woman he'd given up hope of ever finding.

Catherine stayed in bed with Tom until she was sure she wouldn't disturb him by leaving. Slipping into her father's old flannel robe, a fixture at the cabin as old and worn as the carved wooden bear beside the front door, she tiptoed into the kitchen to fix a cup of hot cider.

Cider was a treat she reserved for the cabin. Except for wine and an occasional glass of milk, she never drank anything that had calories. But even with watching her diet and regular workouts with Tom, she still couldn't shed the eight pounds she'd put on in her thirties. One pound for every year. Her friends worried about their birthdays because they hated the idea of getting older. She worried how many more years and accompanying pounds it would take before she had to move up another dress size.

Taking her cider outside, she lifted a cushion off a deck chair and took it with her to the dock. The night air wrapped her in a cool, fragrant embrace. She looked at the sky, a black quilt embroidered with stars in wondrous, mysterious patterns.

Tom was right. Lynda only had a few more summers of freedom, and even fewer of childhood. It was wrong to take even part of one away from her. There would be lots of time for Lynda and Tom to get to know each other better. A lifetime. He would be a grandfather to her children, undoubtedly seeing them more often than Jack saw his own daughter. But then, Jack had never been much of a father, and there was no reason to believe he'd be much of a grandfather. Catherine had no doubt that Jack would abdicate this future role to Tom, too.

Catherine sat and propped the cushion against a post, leaning back, savoring the smell and then the taste of the cider, taking small, luxurious sips as she stared at the stars. At moments like these she mentally resisted Tom's gentle nudging for her to get back into the kind of projects that had consumed her life when she was married to Jack. She'd become a volunteer for any and all organizations he'd felt were important for their social standing. She did the work, he made appearances at the functions where he would be seen and could network.

At the time, she'd been as caught up in building his career, in doing her part to see he met the right people, as he had been. Then, when he left and she went to work and didn't have time to keep up with everything she'd committed herself to when they were married, she'd discovered most of the friends she'd made over the years were connected by a common thread she no longer held.

She understood Tom's desire for her to be the partner she'd been to Jack, saw the benefit it would bring, but couldn't summon the enthusiasm she'd once held.

Which, she knew, wasn't fair to Tom. And, basically, she was a fair person. No doubt she would rejoin the organizations she'd once led that had gone on very successfully without her.

She studied the lights across the lake, trying to pick out the Winslow house, finally deciding it was the one with the open, flickering fire out front. She hadn't been to the house in years but remembered the large parties the Winslows had put on and the enormous barbecue pit where they'd cooked dinner for over fifty people at a time.

The Winslow boys were the wild ones at the lake when Catherine was growing up. At least one out of the three of them was in some kind of trouble at all times. The youngest was four years older than Catherine, old enough for her to have had a crush on, too old for him to have paid her anything other than cursory attention.

Brian's father was the middle Winslow boy, the only one who'd actually ended up in jail for one of his pranks. Now he owned his own real estate development company, was happily married to his high school girlfriend, and lived in a two-million-dollar house in Carmichael.

Catherine finished her cider and put the cup aside. A mosquito buzzed near her head. She swatted it away and leaned back against the post again. For several seconds she sat perfectly still and simply listened, to the sounds of water against the shore, the call of an owl, the faint, bass beat of music being played at one of the distant cabins.

At that moment Catherine knew that if her mother moved to Arizona and left the cabin to her and Gene, no matter how much trouble it might be, she could never let it be sold away from the family. She felt at peace here.

Not until she'd made her decision did she realize how much it had been bothering her. Now she felt free to think about and plan future summers for her and Tom and Lynda — the trips they would take to Lake Tahoe in July to watch the fireworks, the hikes into Desolation Valley. This place would provide another link to hold them together, another love they had in common. Tom might not be as enthusiastic about the cabin as she'd like, but she had no doubt it would grow on him. Especially when they updated things a little. The formica countertops in the kitchen had never bothered her, but she could understand Tom's feelings about them. He liked to be surrounded by nice things. They were important to him. In reality, it was a very small thing to ask.

Her meandering thoughts abruptly ended. Something in her ordered, familiar world wasn't right. It was as if the stars had shifted or the crickets had stopped chirping or . . . the fire she'd been watching at the Winslows had grown larger and moved.

She leaned forward, staring intently at what she convinced herself had to be an optical illusion.

Until it moved again.

3

The shifting flame flared brightly, conspicuously consuming its fuel in a burst of energy. It flickered and flashed, as if playing a bizarre game of hide-and-seek in the trees.

Fire didn't move. It was rooted to its base. The only way it could move was if its source moved.

She held her breath until her lungs screamed for air. The moving flame had to be an optical illusion — or someone whose clothing had caught fire.

Precious moments passed and still she didn't move. She couldn't. As long as she stayed where she was, as long as she didn't go inside and call, she could escape in the search for yet another explanation.

A mocking voice emerged from the recesses of her mind, echoing the foolishly brave thoughts she'd allowed herself that afternoon. She'd known she was taking a chance expressing such complete and utter happiness. What ego had tempted her to do something like that?

Stop, she told herself. She stood and picked up the cushion. If fear didn't turn her into a basket case, head games would.

Lynda had said dozens of kids would be at the party. Why would she automatically assume Lynda was the one whose clothing had caught fire — if, indeed, anyone's had caught fire?

The pep talk almost worked. She was ready to accept that she'd imagined the whole thing when she heard the choking sounds of a boat motor starting. She hugged the cushion and waited and told herself the sound could be coming from any one of the fifty houses on the far side of the lake. Even now, she sought a safe explanation. When had she become such a coward?

Running lights appeared — at the Winslows' dock. The motor changed to a low roar; the lights moved. And finally, Catherine moved. She hurried along the dirt path to the cabin. A siren cut the air, drowning the boat motor, calling the volunteer fire-fighters to gather at their station behind the store.

She moved faster, murmuring a prayer. *Please, God. Let Lynda be safe.* Her toe hit a rock and she stumbled, catching the hem of her father's robe on her heel. The fabric made a tearing sound and she let out a small cry at the loss.

She couldn't think about it now. She had no time for small regrets. It was just a robe, a piece of flannel, cut from a bolt of cloth and stitched together on an assembly line, special only because it had once belonged to her father.

What was she thinking? How could she be concerned about a robe when — *Dear God, it couldn't be Lynda who'd been burned*. Not her beautiful little girl. Lynda was fine. She was always fine. When she and her father were rear-ended in his car, she'd come through without a scratch. She was lucky. She'd always been lucky. She'd played soccer and softball and hiked and swam and rollerbladed. She'd even participated in a hundred-mile bicycle race and she'd never been hurt. Not once.

And she was sensible. She didn't take chances. She thought skateboards were dangerous and didn't like snowboards.

It wasn't Lynda.

It couldn't be.

Catherine slammed the kitchen door against the cupboard as she ran into the house. She grabbed a pair of jeans out of her bedroom closet and stumbled down the hall to Tom's room as she put them on.

'Tom — wake up. Something's happened.' She hit the light switch and went to the dresser to get his clothes. 'We have to get to the store.'

Climbing from the depths of sleep, he was slow to respond. She expected more and lost patience. '*Right now.*'

'What are you talking about?' He rubbed his eyes and sat up in bed. 'What's happened?'

'I think one of the kids at the party got burned.' She couldn't tell him she was afraid that it was Lynda. He wouldn't understand and she didn't have time to explain. 'I'm not sure, but that's the way it looked. I saw the fire — and then I heard the boat and the sirens.' She flung underwear and socks in his direction and went to the closet for pants and a shirt.

'Catherine, calm down and think about this for a minute. Obviously you believe Lynda is involved, but if that were true, don't you think someone would have called us by now? The Winslows must have your number.'

They were words she needed to hear, the logic that controlled emotion. 'Yes . . . *no.* I don't know. Even if Lynda isn't the one who was burned, she's going to need us.' Her anger flared when she saw that he still wasn't moving. 'Goddamn it, Tom. Are you coming with me, or do I have to go by myself?'

'I don't even know where we're going.' He swung his legs over the side of the bed.

'To the store to meet the boat.'

The tone of the alarm changed from a summons for the firefighters to the siren on a piece of emergency equipment. Catherine stopped to listen more closely. 'Something's wrong. The boat couldn't be at the store already. Why are the firefighters leaving?'

She threw his shirt at him and raced back through the house, this time going out the front door, where she could get a better look at the road. Flashing red lights reflected off houses and trees as the fire engine made its way along the narrow, twisting road. She whipped around to look at the lake. The boat was still there, slowly moving across the water as if time were as abundant as the pollen.

Could they see the flashing red lights from the boat? Did they understand the men on the fire equipment had received the wrong information and hadn't waited for them at the store? She mentally reached out to the driver of the boat, begging him to pay attention. Only then did she realize the reason the boat appeared to be going so slow: It wasn't headed for the store, it was coming in her direction. It had been all along.

She reached for the porch railing to steady herself. Tom joined her, still buttoning his shirt. She pointed to the boat. 'They're coming here. It's Lynda. They're bringing her home.'

Tom looked at the boat and the fire engine. 'They're meeting here,' he said. 'We're twenty minutes closer to town.'

Grateful for his calm reasoning, she put her hand on his arm and admitted, 'That didn't even occur to me.'

'Standing around trying to guess what happened is crazy. I'm going to call the Winslows. Where's their number?'

'There's a local phone book for the lake residents in the drawer under the microwave.'

'You should have thought of this yourself, Catherine,' he gently chided. 'Somehow I thought you'd be better in a crisis.'

His words stung, not so much from their accusation as from his lack of understanding. 'Find out if Lynda is with them on the boat.'

He came back to the doorway. 'And if she isn't?'

'I want to talk to her.'

Alone, she listened to the siren and boat motor grow louder and realized she was cold, not only on the surface, but bone-deep. She hugged herself and stared at the running lights across the black lake. In the distance she heard the faint wail of a second siren. They must have called for an ambulance to meet them. Was it standard practice? Precaution? Or was it necessity?

She didn't wait well. She was a do-something kind of person.

Tom came back just as Catherine decided to go after him. 'Well?'

Instead of saying anything, he reached to take her in his arms. She backed away. She wasn't a child who needed a hug. She was a mother in need of answers. 'What did you find out?'

Foolishly, he reached for her again. She knocked his arm away. 'Goddamn it, tell me what happened.'

'What's the matter with you? I'm only trying to help.'

'*Then tell me.*'

'You were right,' he snapped. 'Lynda's the one who was burned.'

She stood perfectly still, her arms at her sides, her hands curled into tight fists. 'How bad?'

'They don't know for sure. Someone said they thought they saw the tie on her sweater catch on the barbecue grate. It caught fire before she could get it free and she panicked. When she couldn't get the sweater off, she ran. Brian chased her and managed to get the fire out — but not before she was burned.

'According to the kid who was telling me this, Lynda's in a lot of pain. Which was why they didn't wait for the firemen to come to them. My guess is that she'll probably have to go to the hospital to get checked out.'

'It wasn't her sweater,' she said numbly. 'It was mine. I made her wear it. You heard me. I told her she had to take it.' Lightheaded with worry, she started shaking, just a slight trembling at first, and then violently. She put her hand against the side of the house to keep from falling. 'It's my fault.'

'It's not even that cold. She really didn't need a sweater.'

Instead of feeding her guilt, Tom's words made Catherine realize she didn't have time for the luxury of indulging in self-doubt or pity. The seeds were planted. The feelings would take root and grow later.

When he looked at her she didn't see the expected sorrow or concern in his eyes, she saw fear. She immediately assumed he was holding something back. But that wasn't Tom's style. He never protected her that way.

Peripherally, it came to her that the boat motor had slowed. They were approaching the dock. She took off without saying anything more. He could follow or stay; at that moment, she didn't care.

Catherine had expected Peter or Julianne Winslow to be driving. Instead it was one of the kids from the party, someone she didn't recognize. It took a second to sort through the other worried faces in the open bow boat, all of them teenagers, before she spotted Brian in the back. He had Lynda cradled in his arms, her face tucked against his neck, her body covered with a blanket.

Catherine reached for the line one of the boys threw but Tom got to it first. She'd been so focused on Lynda, she hadn't realized he'd joined her.

The motor stopped, leaving the sirens to synchronize in an urgent rhythm, their shrill sound echoing off the surrounding mountains, fueling the sense of urgency.

Of the half dozen kids in the boat, only one looked at Catherine: Brian. She tried to swallow the lump of fear in her throat and almost choked on its size.

Flashing red lights slashed through the moonless night. First the fire engine and then the ambulance pulled into the driveway. Tom anchored the line, then clasped extended hands. Catherine found herself surrounded by young people whose immediate job had come to an end and who now had no idea what to do with themselves. Tom directed them off of the dock and up to the house. Only Brian and Lynda remained on the boat, isolated, abandoned.

Look at me. Say something, Catherine

silently commanded her daughter. *Let me see that you are all right. Give me this one thing to hang on to.*

'She's in a lot of pain,' Brian said. 'I don't think we should move her until the ambulance gets here.'

Catherine nodded, yielding to his request, grateful for the caring tone in his voice. In the background she heard rescue equipment being unloaded and the low sounds of men talking to each other. Help was only seconds away. She should wait; she'd be in the way if she got in the boat now. But she couldn't wait. She had to let Lynda know she was there.

She stepped into the boat and knelt beside Brian. He and Lynda were soaked. His face was white, his lips blue, his teeth chattering.

'I read somewhere that cold water stops a burn from going deeper,' he said, responding to her confused look. 'I carried her into the lake. It was the best I could do.' He looked at Catherine, a desperate need in his eyes.

She didn't understand his need, but her heart went out to him. 'Thank you,' was all she could think to say. She gently touched her daughter's hair. A long strand broke off and crumbled to coarse dust in her hand. An acrid smell she refused to let her mind identify filled her nostrils.

'I'm here, sweetheart,' she whispered, afraid to trust her voice with anything more. Lynda needed to believe Catherine was in control and that she was safe.

Finally Lynda lifted her head, gasping at the effort. 'I'm sorry, Mommy. I'm so sorry.' She caught her breath. 'Help me. Please help me. I hurt so bad.'

A powerful spotlight stole the night and created a tunnel for the rescuers to follow. Lynda blinked and turned away. The boat rocked. Catherine heard voices and felt someone take her arms and lift her onto the dock where a man wearing a firefighter's helmet and yellow canvas jacket questioned her, quietly but persistently. She answered automatically, giving names and addresses by rote.

She stopped listening when she heard Lynda scream. The sound cut through Catherine like acid through cloth, leaving a jagged, gaping hole that terror rushed to fill.

'Be careful,' she begged them. 'Please . . . be careful.'

'Why don't you come to the house with me?' the man with the clipboard said. 'They're going to take her out of the boat in a minute and we'll just be in the way.'

What was wrong with him? How could he even suggest such a thing? What if Lynda wanted her and she wasn't there? 'I can't leave.' She looked past him to her daughter. 'She might need me.'

'Is there someone who can drive you to the hospital?'

'My fiancé.' She looked for Tom. He should have been easy to spot in the hushed, anxious crowd standing around the house, but she couldn't see him. 'Which hospital?'

'Barton Memorial. They'll want to stabilize her there before lifeflight takes her to Sacramento.'

'Lifeflight?' The word hit like a first. Lifeflight was something they talked about on the news, a last-ditch effort to save someone grievously injured in an accident. How could it have anything to do with her daughter? Frantic, Catherine searched the faces of the men taking Lynda from the boat, looking for a sign that they believed their job hopeless.

'I'm sorry — I didn't mean to scare you. Lifeflight is what we use to transport people who need more care than we can give them. Your daughter needs to be in a burn unit and we don't have one here.'

'What about Reno? Isn't it closer?'

'By air, it's about the same.' He guided her out of the way of the arriving rescue workers. 'Besides, there's that new Shriner's hospital in Sacramento.'

Lynda screamed again when she was taken from the boat and placed on the gurney. 'They're putting her on her back — that's where she was burned. Someone should tell — '

'As soon as the morphine takes effect, she won't feel the pain.'

'But what about her back? Shouldn't they — '

'They have to keep her airway open and they can't do it if she's on her stomach.'

'Her airway?'

'It's just a precaution.'

Two firefighters stood at each end of the gurney and guided it off the dock and up the hill. Lynda rolled her head from side to side, looking for a familiar face. 'Mommy? Where are you?'

Catherine ran after them, calling, 'I'm right here.' She made it to Lynda's side and reached for her hand. 'I'm coming with you.' She looked to one of the men in white for confirmation.

'Are you the mother?'

'Yes.'

'You'll have to ride in the front — and there's only room for one.'

Again, Catherine looked for Tom. She found him standing on the porch talking to a firefighter. 'I'll be right back,' she told Lynda.

To the man in white she said, 'Don't leave without me.'

She ran to Tom and grabbed his arm to get his attention. 'I'm going to the hospital with Lynda. Get my purse and meet me there with the car.'

'Now?' He glanced around at the assembled people as if he were the host of a party and couldn't leave.

'Yes — now.' Instantly she went from being furious to contrite. He had no way of knowing Lynda was being flown to Sacramento and that they had to drive there to meet her. 'Don't forget my purse,' she said in a conciliatory tone. 'I'll need the insurance card.'

'How do I get to the hospital?'

The question dumbfounded her. Tom was a take-charge person. A man who gave orders, not took them. 'I don't know. Ask someone.'

He said something more, but she was halfway to the ambulance and couldn't hear him over the sound of the engine. She had her hand on the door handle when she realized Brian had come up beside her.

He held out his hand and then turned it over. Lynda's earrings filled his palm. 'They were hot. I took them off so they couldn't burn her anymore.'

He looked lost and devastated. He needed reassurance, but she had none to give. She put the earrings in her pocket and then gave him a quick hug. 'Thank you — for everything.'

Two men, a firefighter and an ambulance attendant, climbed in back with Lynda. They worked with quiet efficiency in the cramped space, one cutting off her clothes, the other hanging an IV.

'How is the pain now?' Catherine heard one of them ask.

'Better,' Lynda murmured.

'There aren't any medals for bravery around here. I want you to tell me when it hurts so I can do something about it.'

'I will.'

The depth of relief in Lynda's voice made Catherine flinch. Lynda never gave in to pain. She'd even refused aspirin when she'd broken a tooth and exposed the nerve.

Catherine felt something in her hand and looked down at flecks of Lynda's hair caught between her fingers. She rolled them in her palm until they turned into a fine powder.

She tried, but couldn't stop her tears. What was to become of her beautiful, carefree daughter?

4

Rick Sawyer spotted the roiling black smoke from the car fire six blocks away. He tapped his engineer's arm and pointed. Steve McMahon nodded.

'Looks like it's been going for a while,' Rick said. The fire was in the middle of an apartment complex in the poorer section of their district, and was most likely set by someone covering a theft. Car fires with bodies inside were rarely set in public places.

Steve slowed and hit the air horn as they neared an intersection, then swung the fire engine into the turn lane to go around the stopped traffic. Although bored with being at a slow firehouse, Rick liked his crew, especially his engineer. Steve knew his district and wasn't a frustrated race car driver. He handled the fire engine with such finesse it could have been a sports car, and he had the uncanny knack of knowing precisely how Rick wanted to fight a fire from the moment they arrived on the scene.

'Hey, Captain — look over there,' Paul Murdoch said over the intercom.

Rick twisted in his seat to look out the back

where the rookie pointed. Paul had spotted the fire. His grin of anticipation at responding to his first fire exposed every tooth in his mouth.

'That's it all right.' Rick gave him a thumbs-up signal and turned back around, shaking his head.

Steve laughed. He'd heard the exchange through the headset that connected the cab to the rear-facing back seat. To Rick, he said, 'You forget what it was like when you first came on until you get a rookie to remind you.'

Rick had been with the Sacramento Fire Department for eighteen years and could remember his first fire as clearly as if it had happened his last shift. His baptism had been more memorable than most — a warehouse fire where he'd found a transient still alive when every rule of medicine said he should have been long dead. Nothing in the intervening years had come close to the horror he'd felt that night. Now the ones he remembered were the saves. The man whose heart had stopped beating, who brought a cake to the firehouse three weeks later; the five-year-old girl they'd pulled from the bottom of a swimming pool, whose mother now brought her to the firehouse every year on the day she was rescued to celebrate her rebirth day; the thirteen-year-old who wrote them a letter thanking them for rescuing his dog from a burning garage.

Steve pulled into the apartment complex and around the back where they were greeted by an excited man waving his arms. The car was an Oldsmobile, a '74 or '75, lowered, with junk rims and small tires used for spares in a lot of new cars. Rick called dispatch and told them that there were no structures involved and that their engine could handle the call, then climbed out of the cab and went over to the man.

'I got everybody out,' he said. 'I told them they had to leave or they were going to be trapped inside when this thing blew and I couldn't be responsible for getting to them if that happened. Figured it was my job being I'm the manager and all.'

Rick checked to see that his firefighter, Janet Clausen, had taken the hose off the rig and that the rookie wasn't standing around with his hands in his pockets. 'There were people inside the car?'

'No, inside the apartments. The car's been here for weeks. Dumped one night with the insides gutted so it wasn't no good to nobody. We called the cops. They said they'd come out but they never did.'

'So you cleared the apartments?'

45

'Got everybody over there.' He pointed to a group of men and women and kids, from toddlers to teens, intently watching the action from the sidewalk.

'Thanks.' He shook the man's hand. 'We appreciate your help. It makes our job a lot easier.'

The man lit up like a flashlight in a blackout. 'Hey, no problem. I seen how these cars can go up when they start burning and I didn't want no one hurt. I take care of the people who live here.'

'I'll be sure and put what you did in my report.' Gently, he maneuvered the man away from the engine. 'Now I think it would be better if you stayed over there with the others and let us take care of this.'

'Yeah, right.' He grinned. 'Wouldn't want to become no statistic after I went and saved everybody else.'

They had the fire out, the stolen car report to the police department, and the hose reloaded, and were back at the station cooking dinner — barbecued chicken, potato salad, and green beans — within forty-five minutes.

Paul looked up from dicing an onion for the salad. 'Hey, Capt'n, mind if I ask a couple of questions about the fire?'

'Ask as many as you want.' Rick added a

46

couple of shakes of garlic powder to the mayonnaise mixture and set the bowl aside.

'They taught us at the tower that burning cars don't explode. And yet you told — '

'Do they explode on television?'

'Yeah, all the time. But — '

'Then they explode in real life. You're never going to convince anyone Hollywood got it wrong, so you might as well save your breath.'

'So you were just shittin' the guy?'

'I was thanking him. He did what he did believing he could be blown up at any moment. No way was I going to take that away from him.'

'Then they were right at the tower? Cars don't explode?'

Rick didn't mind the questions. The rookies that scared him were the ones who came out of the tower convinced they knew it all. 'I didn't say that. And the minute you believe it, you'll have one go up on you.'

He opened the pickle jar and handed half a dozen to Paul to chop. 'For an explosion to happen the tank has to be pressurized. If the vent got plugged somehow or the fill tube got closed off, theoretically, you could have it blow. In an accident, you're more likely to be working with a ruptured tank and a rapid burn.

'What you have to remember is that to the

layperson, there's not even a fine line between an explosion and a rapid burn. While nothing goes flying through the air with a rapid burn, it's impressive as hell to see gasoline pouring out and burning everything in sight.'

The captain's phone rang in Rick's office, interrupting the lesson. He wiped his hands. 'I'll be right back.'

Lyn Cassidy from the Firefighters' Burn Association skipped her usual meandering path to the reason for her call and got right to the point. 'I have a big favor. I know I promised you could have the summer off, but I'm desperate. We had a girl come in a couple of days ago and no one is available to take her case until August.'

Rick had graduated his last burn patient that past spring, a difficult case that had lasted four months past the prescribed twelve. The boy had years of treatment ahead of him, but was finally strong enough emotionally for Rick to step back and let him reach out to others.

'What about Faith?' Both of the kids they'd taken care of last had graduated from the program at the same time.

The Burn Association assigned member firefighters as mentors for burned children and their families. They acted as guides through the tangle of agencies and programs available to patients, and as sympathetic listeners when the child or parent simply needed someone to talk to. Rick was convinced the program worked as well as it did because of the care taken with the pairings. With few exceptions, they'd found that children related best to someone of the same sex.

'She's leaving for France next week.'

'Sydney?'

'Pregnant.'

He hadn't heard the news, and he put it in the back of his mind to call and congratulate her and Manuel when he got off the phone with Lyn. 'How old is this girl?' The age made a big difference. There wasn't as much psychological damage when the patient's body image hadn't been set mentally. The younger the kids were, the more readily they accepted the scars as part of their makeup. Once the image was set, the change could be, and often was, devastating.

'Fifteen.'

Rick flinched. 'How bad is she?'

'Twenty percent. Her back mostly. Some upper arm involvement, some neck, one forearm, but no buttocks or head.'

'I've never worked with a girl that age. Would that be a problem?'

'I don't know. It may be,' she added with

49

reluctant honesty. 'You're the only man I even considered asking. If you can't take her, I'll wait until Faith can.'

'Tell me about her.'

'Her mother says she's outgoing and gregarious. Very pretty. A cheerleader, and an athlete. Good student. Popular. No steady boyfriend. Goes out a lot with friends but isn't into the one-on-one yet.'

'What happened?'

'She was at a party at their vacation home near Tahoe with friends and her sweater caught on fire. She panicked and ran. She got quite a ways before one of the boys caught her. Her mom's single, but there's a fiancé. I'm not sure how much help he's going to be, though. He seems a little skittish to me.'

'What do you mean?'

'Not the kind who comes through in a crisis. Every time I've been at the hospital, he's off somewhere and the mother is looking for him.'

'How is the mom handling it?'

'She's still in shock. I have a feeling there's some guilt working in the mix, but she's not talking about it. At least not to me.'

'Can you give me a couple of hours to think about this?' He knew how to reach fifteen-year-old boys; he didn't pretend to understand the first thing about girls that age.

'I know I promised you the summer off . . . '

He'd been remodeling his house for eight years. Somehow, despite his best intentions, life kept getting in the way. 'That's not it,' he said. 'I just don't want to step into something where I might do more harm than good.'

'So you can't talk boyfriends with her. You're a hell of a lot better than no one being there at all. And if you think she needs to talk to a woman later, I'm sure Faith will give you a hand.'

'I'd like to think about it tonight at least.'

'That's fine. But could you get back to me first thing in the morning?'

'Why then?'

'I have an appointment with the mother at ten. I'd like to be able to tell her when and if she can count on us.'

'And if I say yes?'

'Then I'll call and tell her you'll be taking the meeting.'

Rick hesitated. 'Actually, it might help me decide what to do if I talked to her and got a feel for the situation. Tell her to expect me, but don't say anything about my being officially assigned yet.'

'What if I tell her that you're there for the initial hospital stay and let it go at that?'

'Sounds good.' Rick hung up and immediately dialed his neighbor, Sandra Brahams. He'd scheduled a delivery from the lumberyard for the next morning and someone had to be there to sign the receipt.

'You going to be home tomorrow morning — say, until around noon?' he said at her hello.

She laughed. 'It's a good thing I know your voice. Yes, as a matter of fact, I am. Who's delivering what?'

'Meeks Lumber is bringing a load of drywall and the redwood for the back deck.'

'Where do you want it unloaded?'

'The garage is okay.' He had someone coming that weekend to help him hang the drywall in the dining room and kitchen or he would have postponed the delivery.

'Overtime?'

Sandra knew his schedule almost as well as he did. They shared a golden-Lab mix named Blue that lived at her and Walt's house when Rick was working and at Rick's whenever the dog saw his truck in the driveway. 'A new kid came into the hospital a couple of nights ago. I have a meeting with the mother and her fiancé at ten.'

'I thought you said you were taking a couple of months off.'

'Yeah, well, you know how that goes.' In the

background Rick saw the hall lights go on, the precursor to the bells going off for an alarm. 'Gotta go, Sandra. There's a run coming in.'

'See you tomorrow.'

Rick headed for the kitchen to help put the food away. The rookie sported a grin, the rest of the crew a look of acceptance. Rick shoved the potato salad in the refrigerator and went to the computer for the printout of the details of the call. He gave the address to Steve and told his crew that they were responding to a woman locked out of her car.

Steve pulled into the parking lot of the Bel Air Supermarket, the one where they shopped for the firehouse. Rick looked around for a blue Acura and spotted it on the far side by the cleaners.

'Did you get the chicken off the barbecue?' Steve asked Rick.

'Not me.' Rick opened his microphone and looked at the back seat. 'Either one of you get the chicken?'

'Uh-uh,' Janet said.

'What chicken?' Paul asked.

'Maybe we'd better order a pizza before we leave,' Rick said.

'Shit — not again.' Steve groaned. 'I hate pizza.'

'Let's see . . . ' Rick held up his hands and

moved them as if weighing the options. 'Burned chicken . . . pizza. It's your call.'

'What about Chinese?'

'Not enough money in the food fund.'

'Jesus — what happened to it? We were fifty dollars to the good last time I looked.'

'That standing rib roast we had last shift wiped us out.'

'Uh . . . Capt'n . . . ,' Paul said. 'I think there's someone trying to get your attention.'

Rick looked up to see a woman standing beside the blue Acura. He assumed she was the owner. She glared at him, her hands on her hips, her mouth rapidly moving, her eyes full of fire. To Steve he said, 'You suppose she's telling us we're not moving fast enough to suit her?'

'Nah — she's probably saying she left a chicken on the barbecue and wants to get home before it burns.'

Rick laughed. 'Only an idiot would do something like that.'

5

Rick nodded to the receptionist as he entered the lobby of the Shriner's hospital and headed for the elevators. He loved this building. Where most hospitals were closed and cramped, here the architect had provided a wall of windows six stories high that made the trees and clouds seem a part of the enormous second-floor playroom, and gave the children's minds freedom while their injuries kept them confined.

He stopped by the nurses' break room and grabbed a cup of coffee — a prop to give a comfortable, relaxed impression when he first met Catherine Miller and her fiancé, Tom Adams. He wanted them to see him as an insider, a part of the hospital routine, someone they could trust without hesitation in an emergency. He'd discovered years earlier that it was the simple things that made a difference where trust was involved, the sense of belonging that came with a ceramic mug instead of a paper cup, the confidence to perch on the corner of a desk in a physician's office rather than a chair. By breaking down that initial barrier as quickly as possible, he could get down to his real job — helping Lynda get on with her life.

Today the meeting was scheduled in Marcia Randolph's office. She was the chief of plastic surgery and a long-time friend. Marcia's assistant, a young woman just beginning to show her pregnancy, smiled when she saw Rick.

'She's waiting for you.'

Rick glanced at the clock on the back wall. He was ten minutes early. 'Has she been here long?'

'About five minutes.'

Indicating her expanding stomach, he asked, 'Did you get Marcia's approval for that?'

She laughed. 'She did make me promise I'd be back. She even told me she'd get me a raise so Mike could stay home and take care of the baby.'

His hand on the office door, he added, 'See what happens when you make yourself indispensable?'

'Think I should start goofing off?'

'Sure — just don't tell Marcia I said so.' He was careful to lose the smile before he went inside.

A woman he guessed to be in her late thirties stood at the window, so lost in her own thoughts that she didn't hear him enter.

She was dressed in white linen slacks and a soft yellow sleeveless top that looked more like a vest than a shirt. She wore her hair in a sleek cut that skimmed shoulders tanned an unnatural shade of brown. The tan surprised Rick. She was obviously from money and at an age when a woman worried more about wrinkles than golden skin.

'Excuse me,' he said in a soft voice, trying not to startle her.

She turned to him and forced a polite smile, her eyes hollow and sunken from lack of sleep. 'Are you the firefighter?'

He came forward and extended his hand. 'Rick Sawyer.'

'Catherine Miller.'

'Beautiful, isn't it?'

He'd confused her. 'What?'

'The view. I saw you looking out the window when I came in.'

She turned to look again as if seeing the view for the first time. 'Yes, it is.'

'Can I get you something while we're waiting? A cup of coffee? Tea?'

'Someone else is coming?'

Over the years Rick had dealt with a lot of parents of burned children, had seen every degree of grief, yet the initial meeting still had the same sobering effect on him. Their fear and doubt, often laced with a pervasive guilt, were palpable, impossible to ignore.

He used to try to ease the families through the worst times by assuring them it would get better, that it always did. Finally he'd understood the journey itself was part of the healing process and could only be understood in hindsight.

'I thought your fiancé wanted to be here, too.'

'He said not to wait for him — that he could get tied up this morning.'

Rick gave her a moment to elaborate, to let her know he would listen to anything she wanted to tell him. When she chose not to say anything more, he said, 'Then why don't we get started.'

She moved from the window to a chair at the desk. Instead of sitting on the other side, or on the desk itself, which would have put him above her, Rick took the chair next to hers. 'I'm not sure how much you've been told about my role in Lynda's recovery, so I'll give you a quick rundown.' He told her in simple terms, leaving out the names of the agencies and people who would help her while letting her know she was not alone.

'Have you met Lynda?'

'I thought I'd stop by when we're through here.'

'She's having her dressings changed. That's

why I came upstairs early.' Catherine folded her hands in her lap and stared at them. 'They give her something for pain and a drug that induces temporary amnesia . . . ' She stopped and took a deep breath before going on. 'She'll ask me about it someday, but I don't think I'll tell her what it was like. For either of us.'

Rick had heard enough. He didn't need to know anything more about Catherine to know he could work with her. She was the kind of woman who would be there for her daughter in the hard times ahead.

'I understand Lynda is on the honor roll,' he said, purposely changing the subject.

The quick answering smile transformed her face. Rick was taken aback at the difference. A little sleep, a little makeup, and Catherine Miller wouldn't just be a pretty woman, she'd be someone people turned to look at twice when she passed. 'She's made it every year since third grade.'

Catherine leaned forward and for the first time looked at Rick as if she were actually seeing him. 'She's a remarkable young woman. I'll do whatever it takes to make her whole again. And I mean that — *whatever it takes*.'

'What do you mean by *whole*?' Rick asked carefully. If Catherine believed she could bargain or buy her way into returning Lynda to the girl she'd once been, she was in for a crushing disappointment. Lynda could be as smart, as funny, as personable as before, but she could not have her body restored. She would always be scarred. How those scars affected her mind depended in large part on Catherine.

'I want her to be as confident as she was before she was burned. She has to know that her scars don't matter. And not just in her mind, but in her heart.'

A fierceness accompanied Catherine's words. She was helpless to do anything to help Lynda now, but that didn't keep her from mapping their future. Rick not only liked this woman, he admired her.

'It won't be easy,' he said. 'Lynda has a set body image and it's going to be hard for her to accept a new one.' Pimples created a crisis in a teen's life; the scars from a burn could be devastating and often created a personality change.

A sound in the outer office distracted Catherine. She waited expectantly, hopefully, and then with a small shrug said, 'I'm sorry, I thought it might be Tom.'

'We can finish this later when he's here,' Rick offered. 'I have this afternoon free. I could come back then.'

'I couldn't ask you to do that.'

'I don't mind. Just give me a time.'

She considered his request. 'Is there a number where I could reach you? I really would like Tom to hear what you have to say and I don't want you to have to say it twice.'

He dug a card out of his wallet and gave it to her. 'My station number, home number, and pager number are on there. I'll bring a firefighter calendar that will let you know when you can reach me at work. I'm available whenever you want to call, day or night.'

'Goodness — you make it sound as if we'll be taking over your life.' She looked at the card. 'You're a captain? What does that mean?'

He smiled. 'I get to sit in the front of the fire engine instead of the back and I don't have to drive.'

'I'm sure it's a little more demanding than that.' She stared at the card as if memorizing it. 'I see by your home phone that you live in Placer County.'

'Loomis.'

'We're in Granite Bay.'

'Is that where Lynda goes to high school?' He was there to find out about her, not talk about himself.

Catherine nodded. 'She'll be a junior this fall.'

'Did she skip a grade?'

'She'll be sixteen in November.'

Six months away. That would be a rough birthday. 'Is she active in school?'

Catherine tucked a strand of hair behind her ear, recoiling at its silky feel, so different from Lynda's . . . not the way it had once been, but the way it was now. But how had it been? Three days wasn't enough time to forget. The immediacy of the moment, no matter how compelling its nature, couldn't erase the lifetime that had gone before. She would remember. She just needed a little time.

'She's into everything — choir, soccer, drama, cheerleading.' Catherine heard the pride in her voice, and under ordinary circumstances would have added something about how messy Lynda kept her room or the countless battles they fought over the telephone. Catherine would clean up after Lynda the rest of their lives, she would give up her elaborate wedding and elope, live on a desert island, *anything,* if she could just go back and change one thing: the sweater.

If only she hadn't made Lynda take the sweater. The memory snatched her out of the present and brought her into a world on a different plane, one she would inhabit in her mind forever. She shook herself free and forced a smile, unable to tell if it reached her lips until she saw Rick respond.

'With all that activity, she must have a strong network of friends.'

'The answering machine tape is full every time I go home, even if I've only been gone a couple of hours.' Tom had suggested they put medical updates in place of a message and it seemed to be working. Last night there had been as many hang-ups as requests for a return call, some from friends she hadn't heard from in years.

Again she heard a sound in the outer office. Even though Catherine knew it wasn't Tom — she still looked toward the door. This time it opened. It wasn't Tom but Gene, her brother, who appeared. She let out a welcoming cry and jumped up to greet him.

'What are you doing here? I told Mom not to call you.' She was ecstatic that her mother hadn't listened.

Gene was six-foot-four to her five-foot-seven. When he hugged her and she put her cheek against his chest, she could feel his strong, steady heartbeat and knew a familial security that was a balm to her own wounded heart.

'She knew I'd never forgive her if she waited until I got home to tell me. I'm just sorry I couldn't get here sooner. I snagged the first empty seat on the first flight I could find out of Tokyo.' He let her go and studied her. 'You look like hell. Where's Tom? Someone needs to tell him that he should be taking better care of you.'

She sidestepped the question, using Rick to divert him. 'Gene, I'd like you to meet — '

'*Rick Sawyer*. Well, I'll be damned. What has it been — fifteen, twenty years?'

Rick shook Gene's hand. 'At least twenty.'

Catherine looked from Gene to Rick and then back again. 'You know each other?'

'We were in the same fraternity at USC.' To Rick he said, 'I had no idea you went into medicine.'

'Not even close,' Rick said. 'I'm a firefighter.'

'Oh . . . ' He was plainly embarrassed by the mistake. 'I assumed Catherine was in here with one of Lynda's doctors.'

'He's here to help me — ' She tried but couldn't remember what Rick was supposed to help her with. 'To answer questions.'

'What kind of questions?' Gene asked.

'Anything and everything that isn't medical,' Rick answered for her.

'And you do this because . . . ?'

Rick liked this protective streak in Gene. He'd been a champion for the underdog in college, too. 'Firefighters are traditionally involved with helping burn survivors and in the support of burn units in hospitals. In Sacramento we take it a step further and assign volunteers to burn-survivor families. We stay in contact with them for the first year of recovery, doing whatever we can to make the process easier.'

'Sounds like a good idea to me,' Gene said.

'Yes — it does,' Catherine agreed, politely.

Rick knew it would take several more contacts before Catherine was ready to think about anything but the immediate future and that he'd done what he could for that day. 'I'm going to leave now,' he told Catherine. 'If you need me for anything, you have my number.' He nodded to Gene. 'Good seeing you again. Catch you later.'

'Yeah, I'd like that.'

Rick left and went downstairs to the intensive care unit to check in with the nurses before going home. The nurses dealt with the kids and their parents on a more intimate basis than the doctors, and he often got a better feel for the nuances of a case from them.

As much as he liked Catherine Miller and felt he could work with her, he still wasn't convinced he was the right person for her daughter — from all accounts a girl accustomed to being the center of attention.

Rick's sister, Cindy, had been a cheerleader in high school. A bad hair day was tantamount to going out on a date with the class geek. Rick hadn't understood her then and — with her trips to Los Angeles every three years to have something lifted or tucked by her favorite plastic surgeon — didn't understand her any better now.

He'd seen too many kids without ears or noses, too many mouths that couldn't form a smile, too many hands without fingers to feel sympathy for a woman whose mirror reflected mere wrinkles.

The intensive care unit was formed like a half wheel with the nurses' station as the hub. The rooms were large and filled with light. Each had brightly colored curtains and matching bedspreads, televisions, VCRs, video games, and whatever else might be requested to engage the mind in something other than pain and loss.

A nurse in her midfifties with hair the shade of red that only came from bottles looked up and smiled when she saw Rick. 'Hey, long time no see. You here for the boy they just brought in?' She rolled her chair back and reached for a chart.

'I didn't hear about the boy.' He leaned over the counter, saw an open box of See's chocolates, and took a caramel. 'I'm with Lynda Miller.'

'Going to work that special magic you do with a girl this time, huh?'

'Going to try.' The caramel stuck to his tooth. He pried it off with his tongue, making a sucking sound.

'Well, keep that up and you're a shoo-in. Nothing gets to us girls like slurping sounds.'

Rick laughed. 'If that's true, I think I need a little more practice.' He took another candy.

The phone rang. She picked it up, put her hand over the receiver and mouthed to Rick, 'She's in C unit.'

He nodded and waved his thanks.

He wasn't there to introduce himself to Lynda. He doubted she'd remember the meeting anyway. Even if she hadn't just had her dressing changed, at this point in her recovery the pain medication was still strong enough that only odd moments would be permanently imprinted.

The curtain to Unit C hung half-closed, and Rick had to pass the door to see inside. Lynda looked as he'd expected — terrifyingly wounded to a parent, perfectly normal to an objective, knowledgeable observer. The machines and monitors were standard stuff, as were the tubes that put things in and took others out. His only surprise was the teenage boy sitting in the corner of the room, his head propped against the wall, sleeping.

'Who's the kid in the chair?' Rick asked the nurse when she hung up the phone.

'His name's Brian Winslow.'

The name registered, but it took a second to connect. And then he remembered Lyn mentioning him that morning when he'd called her to make sure the appointment was still on. 'Isn't he the boy who was with her when she was burned?'

She nodded. 'He's been here every day and most of the nights.'

'Boyfriend?' Catherine had said Lynda didn't have one, but mothers had been known to be a step or two behind their kids when it came to things like that.

'I don't think so. At least that's not the impression I've gotten.'

Rick looked at him again. He'd slept on the tailboards and hose beds of fire engines during forest fires, but he'd never been able to fall asleep in a hospital chair. You had to be bone-deep tired and young enough not to worry about a stiff neck to do something like that.

'Has she had a lot of friends come to see her?'

'She told her mother she didn't want anyone here — including Brian. He sat out in the lobby until Catherine talked Lynda into letting him come back in her room.'

Rick admired loyalty in a friend, and hoped that was all it was. Guilt was a heavy and futile burden for someone Brian's age. Without the years and wisdom to know that sometimes shit just happens, the long-term consequences were devastating. Someone needed to be looking out for Brian, too.

And that someone might as well be him.

6

'Should we go downstairs?' Gene asked.

'We have to talk first.' Catherine couldn't let him see Lynda without preparing him. She would still be drugged and unlikely to remember Gene coming in to see her, but Catherine didn't want to take any chances. With Lynda's face pink and swollen, her body wrapped in bandages, a feeding tube taped to her nose, her hair a crude shag on the sides and missing in the back, and her eyes wary and frightened, even Catherine had to look hard to find the old Lynda. Gene would be devastated no matter how well she prepared him; Catherine just didn't want it to show. Lynda already had enough to deal with without worrying about upsetting her uncle.

'How about some coffee? Have you had breakfast?' He glanced at his watch. 'Make that an early lunch.'

She wasn't hungry but knew Gene needed something to do, something he believed would help her. They were alike that way. Inactivity was her enemy. It left her too much time to think. Before her divorce, she'd spent a year agonizing over what it would be like to

70

live without Jack and the next three years living what she'd imagined. At first the loneliness had been like a knife in her chest, reminding her with every breath that she slept alone, woke alone, and went out alone. Eventually the pain became as familiar as two place settings at the table instead of three; so familiar, she failed to realize the moment it wasn't there anymore.

'A cup of coffee would be nice,' she said. 'There's a cafeteria downstairs.'

He picked up her purse and handed it to her. 'I know I'm repeating myself, but I really am going to have to talk to Tom about taking better care of you.'

'If you can find him.' She was sorry the minute she said it.

'What do you mean?'

'Nothing. I'm just a little out of sorts today. Tom went up to the lake yesterday to close the cabin. I haven't heard from him since. At least not directly. He left a message on the machine saying he wasn't going to make it home last night. But I expected him long before now. He was here when I made the appointment to meet Rick and he knew I wanted him to be with me. At least I thought he did.'

'Did you try his cell phone?'

She nodded. 'And his pager — at least a

dozen times. He's not answering either of them.'

'That doesn't sound like Tom.'

'He's not taking this very well,' she admitted. 'He's disappeared on me a couple of times since we've been here. Turns out he's one of those people who doesn't like hospitals.'

'Please tell me he's not using that as an excuse.'

'Of course not.' At least not in those exact words. Tom had found ways to keep himself busy, all of them away from the hospital and always in the guise of helping. She'd gone from being grateful to confused to hurt. She wasn't sure what she felt anymore.

'Do you want me to talk to him?'

Confined in the sanctuary of the cherry wood-lined elevator, Catherine was tempted to dump her frustration and fear on her brother as she had during her divorce. Only the promise she'd made to Gene and herself never to do that to him again stopped her. 'I can take care of it,' she said.

They picked up coffee and, at Gene's insistence, sandwiches, and took them into the atrium, settling into a window seat that faced west.

'So tell me how she's doing,' Gene said. 'I

assume that's why we're here instead of in her room.'

Catherine took a sip of coffee and put the cup aside. Even a swallow was too much for her stomach to handle. 'She has what the doctors call a twenty-percent burn. They calculate these things to figure the medications and treatment and something else I can't remember.

'The second degree burns will heal on their own, but the third degree areas have to be grafted. The worst places are where her camisole melted and stuck to her skin.' Catherine remembered the day Lynda bought the bright red camisole. They'd been at Sunrise Shopping Center looking for a birthday present for Lynda's best friend, Wendy. After wandering the mall for four hours, they'd left with a new pair of pants for Catherine, the camisole for Lynda, and nothing for Wendy.

'You can actually see the outline of her bra across her back where it protected her for awhile.'

'Does she know what happened?'

'She remembers everything up to being put in the ambulance. After that it's bits and pieces. Now she's drowsy and sick to her stomach from the pain medication, and drifts in and out of sleep so I never know what she's

73

seeing or hearing.'

Gene took a bite from the corner of his sandwich and then set it aside, too. He leaned forward, his elbows on his knees. 'How long do the doctors think she'll be in the hospital?'

'Three to four weeks. She's scheduled for her first grafting operation in a couple of days. They want to see how much of her back is going to heal on its own before they go in.'

'Where will they get the grafts?'

'Her head and her buttocks. She'll have to put up with being bald for awhile and having her backside sore, but this way they won't be creating scars by taking tissue from more exposed places.' At Gene's encouragement, Catherine tried a bite of sandwich and almost gagged.

He gave up and put her sandwich with his. 'Her beautiful hair . . . '

'It's not so beautiful anymore,' Catherine said softly. 'She lost most of it in the fire.'

'Will it grow back all right after the grafting?'

'Eventually. They don't take the skin deep enough to affect the hair follicles. If she were a boy and went bald as a man you'd be able to see the scars from the surgery, but it won't affect her.'

'Does Lynda know?'

'I know she's heard me talking to the

doctors, but I don't know how much of it registered.' Catherine didn't mind the barrage of questions. It was Gene's way of coping with stress.

'How is Mom taking all of this?'

'She's getting through it, but I'm worried about her. I finally had to ask a friend to come and get her last night. She was so tired she couldn't walk straight.'

'At least you weren't alone,' he said cryptically.

Gene took his big brother role seriously. He'd been her protector from the time she was six months old and a neighborhood dog tried to steal her bottle.

'Tom's been here, Gene. He didn't completely abandon us.'

'It just looks that way, huh?'

She would have to be more careful. Gene might be slow to anger, but he was slower still to forgive. 'Actually, I've had more people wanting to help than I have things for them to do. I had Mom answer the messages on the machine at home and tell everyone that Lynda couldn't have flowers or visitors but cards were okay. Brian volunteered to call some friends and have them call everyone they thought would want to know.'

'Brian?'

'Brian Winslow. The accident happened at

his parents' house at the lake. If it weren't for him, Lynda would have been burned a lot worse.'

'All right, you've warned me about what to expect. When can I see her?'

'Now, if you want. She should be back in her room.'

'Is there anything else I should know? Anything I shouldn't say or do?'

'Don't try to con her. She knows how badly she's burned.'

'She must be scared out of her mind.'

Catherine leaned into his shoulder. 'Just like her mom.' Her cell phone interrupted them. 'I'd better get that,' she said, and reached inside her purse. 'It could be Tom.'

He stood and picked up their plates and coffee cups. 'I'll get rid of this stuff.'

'Would you mind going downstairs and seeing if Lynda really is back in her room?' She didn't want him listening if it was Tom on the phone.

'And if she is?'

'Come and get me.' The phone rang again, intrusive, promising, annoying. 'Oh, I almost forgot. You have to put on a gown before you go in,' she called to him. 'Ask one of the nurses to help you.'

She pressed the Send button on the phone. 'I'm at your house,' Tom answered cheerfully at her hello. 'Is there anything you want me to bring when I come down?'

'What are you doing there?' She made no effort to hide her irritation.

'What did you think I was going to do with all the stuff I brought back?'

'Where have you been all this time? And why haven't you been answering your pager? Jesus, Tom, you had to know that I'd be worried sick about you. You promised you'd be here this morning for the meeting.'

'I must have left my pager in the car.'

He was lying. She could tell by the tone in his voice. But why? 'That's a first. What about your cell phone?'

'What about it?'

'Why didn't you have it with you?'

'I did. Don't tell me it's not working again.'

'Funny, it was working when you called about the golf tournament at the club before you left.'

'There's been a lot going on outside that hospital, Catherine,' he said defensively. 'It may seem the world stopped turning to you, but the rest of us have had to keep going despite Lynda being burned.'

'I'm aware of that.' The last thing she needed or wanted was a fight. She didn't have the energy for the battle, let alone the reconciliation.

'You're obviously mad at me about something. Why don't you just tell me what it is?'

'I'm not mad, Tom. I'm worn out.'

'It's more than that.'

'All right, maybe I am a little upset.' She walked to the window and stood in the sunlight, closing her eyes against the brightness. She wished she'd known Tom longer. She needed him to be more than her lover; she needed him to be her best friend, the kind it took years to become. 'Can you blame me? When you left for the cabin yesterday you said you'd be back by ten, no later. You should have at least called to let me know you were tied up — or whatever it was that kept you from being here this morning.'

'You're right. I'll try to be more considerate from now on. It's just that I'm not used to reporting my comings and goings to anyone. Until I met you, my time was my own.'

It was such an odd thing for him to say she didn't know how to answer. Was she supposed to forgive him or apologize for being a burden? 'It's been so long since I had that kind of freedom I guess I've forgotten what it was like.'

'Don't worry about it — I understand how that can happen.'

'You asked if I needed anything. I could

use a change of clothes.'

'You're not doing Lynda or yourself any good spending every single minute in that hospital. Why don't you take some time off and come home for a couple of hours?'

They'd already had this discussion. She side-stepped a replay by saying, 'Gene is here.'

'I thought you said he wasn't due back from Japan for another two weeks.'

'Mom told him about Lynda and he flew home to see if he could help.'

'That's insane. The trip put him in line for a promotion. Your mother shouldn't have called him. I sure as hell wouldn't have. There's nothing he can do here. Besides, Lynda's doing fine.'

'She isn't fine, Tom,' Catherine snapped. 'She's a long way from being fine.'

'You know that's not what I meant. And you know if there was something, anything I could do to make her better I would do it. I just don't see how having a crowd of people sitting around the hospital is helping.'

It was one of those things she didn't want to have to tell him, that she wanted him to see for himself. But she'd given up on the possibility that he ever would. 'I need you as much as Lynda does.'

'Make up your mind, Catherine. Either I

do the running around you ask me to do or I'm at the hospital. You can't have it both ways.'

'I shouldn't have said anything. Are you leaving the house now?'

'I have to stop by the office first.'

'I thought you were still on vacation.' When would she learn? 'Never mind. Just come when you can.'

'Do you need the clothes right away? I can try to get there sooner if you do.'

'I'll have my mother stop by and pick up something on her way.'

'If you're sure.'

'I'm sure.'

'Say hello to Gene for me.'

'I will.'

He hung up without saying good-bye.

Catherine met Gene in the hallway outside the intensive care unit where he was leaning against the wall waiting for her. 'How is she?'

'Out of it. I tried talking to her but I don't think she even knew who I was.'

'It's the drugs.'

'How long will that go on?'

'For as long as she needs them. They believe in pain control around here.'

'Have you been able to talk to her at all?'

'Some. The worst time is after a dressing change. She'll be more lucid later on.'

'Is Tom on his way?'

She shifted her gaze to the floor and knew immediately that it was a mistake. Gene read body language as well as he did Japanese. 'He has to stop by the office first.' She'd sworn she was through making excuses for anyone. When had she started again?

'I assume he's all right.'

'What do you mean?'

'That he wasn't in a wreck or some other disaster that kept him from calling you.'

'He got tied up and forgot. I had him running from — '

'It's okay, Catherine. You don't have to explain.'

'He doesn't like hospitals.' She'd already told him that.

'Still . . . '

'I know. But he's so good to us in every other way. I feel judgmental complaining about this one thing.'

'Don't worry. I've had too many stones thrown at me. I'm not about to start throwing them at someone else.' Gene put his arm around her and gave her shoulders a squeeze. 'Speaking of stone throwing, what do you hear from Jack?'

'He met us here the night she came in, and he was here yesterday. He's in Dallas now and will be for the next week. One of the nurses told me he's called several times from there.'

'Is Jack coming around a problem with Tom?'

She wished it were that simple. 'The only time they saw each other was the first night, and it was pretty rough on all of us.' Gene didn't say anything, but she could feel his disapproval. How could Tom hope to build a relationship with Lynda if he wasn't around when she really needed him? 'I'm going inside. Do you want to come with me?'

'I'm here until you throw me out.'

She put her head on his shoulder and squeezed her eyes shut against a sudden, unexpected onslaught of tears. Why was it she could be strong until someone was nice to her? 'I'm sorry Mom called you and pulled you away from your meetings, but I'm so glad you came.'

'Of course I came. I had to. It's in the big brother's handbook under what to do if something terrible happens to your favorite sister's daughter.'

'I'm your only sister.'

'Which made it a real no-brainer.' He pressed a kiss to the top of her head. 'Now I need to find a phone and let Mom know I got here before she adds me to her list of things to worry about.'

Catherine dug her cell phone out of her purse. 'You can use my phone.' He reached for it but she didn't give it to him right away. 'First you have to promise to tell her that I look great and that you're surprised how well I'm holding up.'

He shook his head. 'Only for you would I tell such blatant lies.'

7

Rick arrived home in time to see the delivery truck pulling out of his driveway. He waited for it to pass on the narrow road, nodding to the driver and absently wondering which neighbor had ordered the remaining redwood on the flatbed. The telltale sign of summer in the foothills: fresh building material. Seemed everyone had a project going. Even Sandra and Walt, who'd sworn they were taking the year off, were talking about putting up a greenhouse.

Blue came trotting toward him. He barked a laconic greeting, his tail whipping in excited half circles. Rick climbed out of the truck and spent a few minutes scratching the dog's ears. He spoiled Blue, giving him free run of the house, letting him sleep wherever he wanted — including on the bed on cold nights — sharing his dinner with him, and even giving him an occasional contraband sip of beer. Rick believed it was little enough compared to the companionship Blue gave in return. When Rick was home, there was no question that Blue was his dog. When he was at the firehouse, Blue belonged to Sandra and

Walt. The arrangement was Blue's, worked out a couple of months after Sandra and Walt rescued him from the pound, and refined over the past two years.

Rick rounded the house looking for Sandra and found her in the combination garage-workshop. In square footage almost the size of the rest of the house, it was the first thing Rick had built. He'd lived there for two years before he completed enough work on the attached, half-burned shell to move in there.

Sandra had the delivery slip in one hand, a pencil in the other. 'Oh, hi,' she said, spotting him. 'Just making sure it's all here. How'd it go at the hospital?'

'I think it was a little soon for me to be there. The mother needs more time to adjust to what's happened before I start loading her up with information about support groups and therapy meetings.'

'Girl or boy?'

'Girl — fifteen.'

She grimaced. 'Bad?'

'Bad enough. Nothing facial, but she won't appreciate that until she's a lot further into her treatment.' Rick frequently discussed his assignments with Sandra. When it came to figuring out the mind of a teenager, he'd found no better resource or sounding board. She insisted the knack came from her twenty years of teaching high school. Rick was inclined to believe it came from her ability to see beyond the obvious.

'If she ever does,' he added. 'It's all relative. Telling someone he or she should be grateful they only lost a hand by showing them someone who lost an arm doesn't make it easier to pick up a piece of paper when it's dropped on the floor.'

Blue came into the garage and immediately jumped on top of the sheetrock, sat down, and swept an arc with his tail. 'Get down from there,' Sandra told him.

He looked at Rick for confirmation. 'Yeah, she's right,' he told the dog. 'It's going to be days before I can get this stuff hung and I don't want to be cleaning off your paw prints when I do.'

'Walt has a tarp you can borrow.'

'Thanks. I think I'd just as soon have this staring me in the face every time I come out here or I might be tempted to postpone this weekend to a more convenient time. Lately it's been out of sight, out of mind.'

'If having things stare you in the face worked, you'd have those closet shelves up by now.'

He chuckled. 'Point taken.'

'Well, I'm outta here. I promised Walt I'd get some prices on greenhouse heaters today.

He's still trying to pretend he's just thinking about it, but he made up his mind the minute he realized how early he could harvest tomatoes if he started them in a greenhouse first.'

'Thanks for taking care of the delivery for me.'

'No problem.' She looked at Blue. 'You coming?'

He sat as if following orders.

'I didn't think so, you ungrateful beast.'

Rick walked with her to the opening in the fence that separated their properties. When she was gone, he turned to Blue. 'Let's go see what we can scrounge up for lunch.'

He took a lot of teasing about his half-finished home — the never ending project, the new Winchester House, the champagne craftsman home on the beer income. He didn't care, because he was doing what he wanted to do exactly the way he wanted to do it. He drove a ten-year-old truck and had a ten-thousand-dollar bathroom in his master bedroom. He'd personally gathered every stone for the fireplace in the living room and spent six months making all the raised panel doors throughout the house. He cooked in a portable microwave or on the gas barbecue on the patio, and ate off a door suspended between two sawhorses. When finished, the kitchen would have granite counters, a tile floor, and washed pine cupboards, constructed from wood he'd rescued when he'd happened upon a barn being torn down.

The new cupboards, completed over the past two winters, stood in a corner of the garage, covered with sheets of plastic, protected from accidental bumping and scratching by a specially built frame. All he needed was some hardware, money, and time for the installation and the pieces would come together. The hardware was easy. The money was almost there — a couple more paychecks and he'd be at his budgeted goal for the granite countertops and tile floor. The time he'd think about later.

The house was his hobby, the only one he'd been able to afford once he and Barbara came to the conclusion they'd given a hopeless situation their best effort and decided to go their separate ways.

With an intense dislike of apartments as his guiding factor, he'd taken his share of their accumulated assets and bought a partially burned house on five acres in the foothills. *Rundown* would have been a kind description of both the house and property. He'd rented the largest Dumpster he could find and had it emptied weekly. Even at that, it took three months to clear the lot.

Now, after eight years, all he had left to do were the kitchen, dining room, and some odds and ends like the closet in his bedroom. Last Christmas, at their annual neighborhood get-together, Sandra had wondered aloud if Rick had slowed the work because he was reluctant to see it come to an end. He'd laughed at the idea, but had given it a lot of thought since. What was he going to do with himself once he finished the house?

Standing at the refrigerator waiting for inspiration, he absently broke off a piece of hot dog and gave it to Blue. The dog took it as if it were ice and he had a toothache, carrying it to the middle of the room and looking back at Rick with a disheartened expression.

'All right, so it's not steak. Bring it back and I'll see what else I can find.'

Blue dropped it on the exposed plywood floor.

'What part of 'bring it back' didn't you understand?' Rick picked up the offending piece of processed meat and tossed it into the freestanding sink. 'How about a tuna fish sandwich?'

This brought a soft whine and frustrated bark. 'Okay, dog biscuit it is.' He took the box from the single kitchen cupboard he'd left standing and tossed Blue one of the bone-shaped biscuits. 'Not even going to offer to share, huh?'

Blue ignored him and headed outside with his prize. His toenails clicked on the metal weather stripping on the garage doorsill and then the concrete floor. Rick listened closely, timing the steps. Sure enough, they stopped at the wallboard.

He was on his way to remind Blue that the wallboard was off limits when the phone rang.

'Rick — it's Lyn. How did the meeting go?'

'Not as well as I would have liked, but I'm going to give it another try tomorrow. Her brother came in from Japan and I took off to let them talk. I got the impression there's something going on with the fiancé that could cause some family problems down the line, but I might have read it wrong.'

'We had another boy come in a couple of hours ago. He's in pretty bad shape, but right now they're saying they think he'll make it.'

'The one from Fairfield?' Rick had heard about the fire on the news coming home and wondered if it was the same boy the nurse had mentioned.

'He's the only survivor out of a family of seven. Looks like the fire was arson.

Something to do with the brother being in a gang.'

Lyn didn't gossip and rarely had time for casual conversation. She was leading up to something. 'Did you want me to take this kid instead of the Miller girl?'

'Actually, I was hoping you could stop by to visit him when you're there with Lynda. At least until I can find someone in Fairfield to take his case. According to the police, he doesn't have any family left in the area and I thought it might help if he had someone to talk to.'

Rick had stopped looking for fairness in life, or believing good people were rewarded and bad punished, a long time ago. It didn't happen that way. There was nothing this kid could have done, no crime big enough, no sin bad enough to bring something like this on himself. 'What's his name?'

'Ray Tatum. He's seventeen and should be easy to talk to — when he can talk, that is. He's a candidate for valedictorian at his high school and, according to one of his teachers I saw interviewed on the news, he's being considered by both Harvard and Stanford.'

'Jesus, what a waste. Did you hear whether they know who did it?'

'Supposedly they have a couple of eyewitnesses.'

91

'Who'll develop amnesia before the case comes to trial,' Rick said.

'I don't know. The people in the neighborhood are pretty shaken by this. They're tired of having their lives controlled by a bunch of thugs.'

'Even if some of them are their own children? The changes they need to make are ones that are a lot easier said than done.'

'Granted.'

Rick stared at the hole in the dining room wall that he'd been staring at for the past eight years and decided today was the day he was going to do something about it. Tearing down wallboard would be a good way to vent his frustration, and if he had it out of the way, putting the new stuff up would go a lot faster. 'I'll call you tomorrow and let you know how things go with Lynda's mother. Right now I hear a hammer calling my name.'

8

Lynda woke to the now familiar beeps and humming sounds of the equipment around her bed. She opened her eyes to small slits, ready to close them again should she discover someone in the room with her. It seemed the only place she could be alone anymore was in her mind, and she escaped there whenever possible.

She didn't see anyone. Even ever present Brian wasn't there.

As much as she loved her mother and uncle and grandmother, she'd reached the point where she wanted to scream at the sight of them. For over a week now they'd all had the same look in their eyes, that 'oh, poor, poor Lynda' expression of pity. Only Brian treated her the way he had before. Which she didn't understand or trust. He should have checked out the first day when he saw that she was going to live and that there was nothing more he could do to help.

She couldn't figure out why he was there all the time, especially with the way she looked and the things he saw done to her. For a while she'd thought maybe he felt guilty, but he was the one who'd saved her from being a total matchstick, so he should have felt pretty good about himself.

Sometimes she liked having him there, especially when she needed to vent. He would listen and nod once in a while like he understood. Everyone else she tried to talk to would say things they thought would make her feel better, whether they made sense or not.

How could they think that was possible? Couldn't they see? Her life was over. At least the one she used to have, the one she wanted back more than she'd ever wanted anything in her life.

She didn't need people feeling sorry for her. And if she heard one more time how everything was going to be all right, or how good the doctor was, or how lucky she was that it was her back and not her face that had been burned, she was going to tell them that they didn't have a goddamned clue and to leave her alone.

Words never spoken aloud, they were her secret escape from being the perfect daughter, the perfect niece, the perfect granddaughter.

Damn. She was crying again. On display all night and all day, she couldn't hide her tears. Someone always saw when she was crying and made a big deal out of getting a tissue and holding her hand and saying something stupid like it was all right to cry.

'Your lunch is here,' a deep male voice announced.

Lynda startled at the sound. She hadn't heard anyone come in, so he must have been there the whole time. She opened her eyes and found him sitting by the window. He got up and came over to the bed. She realized she'd seen him before, but only briefly and only since she'd come to the hospital.

She shifted to move her good arm — actually her better arm — so that she could wipe her eyes with the corner of the sheet. 'Who are you?'

'Rick Sawyer.'

She didn't want his name, she wanted to know why he was there. 'That's not what I mean.'

'I'm a firefighter with the Firefighters' Burn Association.'

'From the lake?' The men who'd helped her there were indistinguishable in her mind. All she remembered were uniforms, lots of them.

He shook his head. 'We're local.'

'Why are you here?'

'To help you and your mother — if I can.'

'Are you asking permission or questioning

your ability?' The words came out slurred and sloppy, the way comedians sounded imitating drunks. She tried moving her tongue around to ease the dryness but it didn't help. It never did.

His lips formed a slow smile. 'Pretty feisty today, I see. Does that mean you're feeling better?'

She remembered him now. He'd been in to see her several times but had never stayed very long. 'Where's my mother?'

'She went to the cafeteria with your uncle to get a cup of coffee.'

Lynda brought her foot out from under the sheet and gave the tray table, and her lunch, a shove.

'Not hungry?'

'Not for that stuff.'

'Then ask for something else. They'll bring you anything you want.'

'Oh, yeah? Then why the milkshake when I told them I wanted a salad?'

Rick pulled up a chair and sat next to her, settling back and propping his feet on the bedframe. 'You drink the milkshake and I'll see that you get your salad.'

'I don't *want* the milkshake.'

'Look — there are only a couple of battles you have any chance of winning around here. The number of calories you have to eat every day isn't one of them, so you might as well yield that one and pick something else.'

'I can't eat all the stuff they give me.'

'Why?'

She considered giving him the same answers she'd been giving her mother but knew he wouldn't believe her. 'I'll get fat.'

'If you weren't burned, and you ate this way all the time, you're right. You would get fat. But now your body has different needs. It's using the extra calories for healing and if you don't replace them, you're going to end up in big trouble.'

'How?'

'You know that stuff oozing out of your skin — the yellow fluid that's on your dressing every time they change it?'

She looked at him, hating that this stranger knew so much about her when she knew nothing about him.

'It's the same stuff that comes out when you scrape your knee, pure protein. Only with you, it's coming out all over your back and arms. If you don't replace it with the food you eat, the organs that need protein to function are going to shut down.' He leaned in closer and lowered his voice to a conspiratorial whisper. 'You don't even want to know what they'll have to do to you if that happens.'

'I don't care.' She didn't believe him. They

were treating her like a little kid. All of them. Even her mother. No one listened to anything she said. No matter what it was, they always won. Whatever they told her to do she had to do. They poked and prodded and measured everything that went in and came out. They even told her when to sleep and when to wake up. Just this once she wanted the right to say no.

'Yes, you do,' he said with scary confidence.

Instead of taking it further, she went on the attack. 'Who told you that you could be here?'

'I'm a fixture in this place. I come and go as I please.'

'Not if I tell the nurses I don't want you here.' She was bluffing. It didn't matter what she wanted; no one paid attention, especially not the nurses. No one cared what she wanted.

Rick moved his chair closer and leaned an elbow on the bed. 'I know you feel as if you've lost control over everything that matters to you and that there's always someone telling you what you can and can't do, but the food thing is something they'll push to the limit. If you don't eat on your own, they're going to shove that tube back down your nose and pour it into your stomach.'

He sounded so damn sure of himself. 'Why should I believe you? You're just a fireman.' He'd finally succeeded in scaring her. She didn't want him to see how much.

She went on before he could answer. 'I'll be fine. Everyone says so.' But always a little too cheerfully, especially Tom. When he said it, she had the feeling he needed convincing as much as she did.

'And they're right. But it's a combined effort. It's time you started doing your share.' He reached for the milkshake and handed it to her.

She hesitated. 'Is that why you're here — to get me to eat this stuff?'

'I heard you were giving the nurses a hard time,' he admitted. 'And I figured you could use some straight talk about what's happening around here. This is the way it is, pure and simple. You can keep on being a little shit with everyone who's trying to help you — which you have to know by now is making what you're going through twice as hard on everyone — or you can cooperate and get the rules bent your way once in a while.'

'Some choice.'

'That's the way I see it, too.'

She took the glass and stirred the thick chocolate-flavored liquid with the straw. She preferred strawberry, but had refused to answer when they'd asked.

Tentatively, she took a sip. Even though giving in was hard, the same way apologizing when you knew you hadn't done anything wrong was hard, she didn't want them putting that tube back in her nose. Just the thought of how it made her feel made her want to scream or throw something or hit someone. Most of all she wanted this nightmare to end. She wanted to wake up and have her life back.

Damn, she was crying again. How stupid. And in front of him, no less. He probably thought he was the reason. She didn't want him thinking he had that much power over her, but she didn't know how to change his mind without telling him more than she wanted him to know.

Rick handed her another tissue. 'Brian tells me you're a cheerleader.'

'I was.'

'He has the impression you still are.'

'Like this? Not likely.' Not wanting to give him the opportunity to tell her she should take another drink, she did so before he had the chance.

'So you've quit but haven't gotten around to telling anyone yet?'

'What business is it of yours?'

'None.'

His answer caught her by surprise. 'I had my mom do it for me.'

'I see.'

'No, you don't. You don't see anything. You come in here and act like you know me and know what I'm going through but you don't.' Finally, she had a target for her anger, someone she didn't care about, someone she wouldn't have to apologize to later. 'You're just like everyone else who comes in here — telling me what to do and what to think, how I should feel and when I should feel it. You don't have any idea what it's like to be me.'

'You're right. I don't know you. But I do understand what you're going through.'

'Yeah. Sure you do.'

Instead of answering her with words, Rick rolled up his sleeve and showed her his arm. 'Does this give me a little credibility?'

Both fascinated and horrified, she stared at the patchwork of glossy skin and ribbed scars that ran from the inside of his wrist to his elbow. Was this the way her back would look?

Somewhere in her mind she'd always been aware that she was pretty. People told her so all the time. But until this happened she'd never really thought about it. It was just something she knew, like her lungs knew to pull in air after pushing it out. Now everything was different. She wasn't pretty anymore. She never would be again.

She saw that Rick was waiting for her to say something. 'How did it happen?'

'A firefighter fell through a roof and I reached in to pull him out.'

'Did you? Pull him out, I mean.'

'Eventually.'

'Did he make it?'

'No.'

The question had been automatic. The answer shook her. Sometimes her back hurt so bad she told herself dying would be better. She knew now she was wrong. She didn't want people talking about her in past tense. She wanted to see her friends again.

And her mother . . . how would she feel? Her father wouldn't even notice she was gone. But her Uncle Gene and Grandma Phyllis would miss her. Tom wouldn't care. That should have bothered her, but it didn't.

'I wondered why you were wearing long sleeves in the middle of summer,' she said.

Rick smiled and rolled back his other sleeve until it matched the first. There were burn scars there, too. 'I'm wearing this shirt because it was the only clean one in the closet. Laundry isn't high on my list of priorities.'

'What about your wife?'

'Don't have one. And when I did, I didn't take care of my clothes any better than I do now.'

No wonder he wasn't married anymore. 'Do people stare at you when they see your arms?'

'Sometimes — the way I stare at kids with spiked orange hair. It's human nature, Lynda. Curiosity is part of our makeup.'

'I don't want people to look at me.'

'Yes, you do. You just want it to be for the right reasons. And it will be again.'

'Tom said if I dressed right, no one would see the scars. He's going to buy me a whole new wardrobe when I get out of here. He said I could have his credit card and that he didn't want me to pay attention to the price of anything.'

'That's very generous of him,' Rick said carefully.

'It's no big deal really. He has lots of money.'

'I haven't met your father yet. Does he live in Sacramento?'

'Carmichael. But he travels a lot for his business, so he's gone more than he's home.' She didn't want him thinking her father didn't care. Lynda finished the milkshake and put the empty glass on the tray.

Rick surveyed the remaining food. 'If you

eat half the hamburger, I'll talk them into leaving you alone until dinner.'

She made a face. 'What if I eat the cookies instead?'

'All of them?'

She hesitated. 'I better taste one first.'

'They're not bad. I ate one while I was waiting for you to wake up.'

'Isn't that against the rules? How are they going to know how much I eat?'

'I'm going to tell them.'

'Snitch.' She took a bite. As chocolate chip cookies went, it wasn't bad. 'Can I really have anything I want? I don't have to eat this stuff as long as I eat something?'

'Within reason.'

'What about crab cakes — from California Cafe?'

'That could probably be arranged.'

She started to sit up and was savagely reminded why she was there. With a startled cry, she lowered herself back to the mattress.

'Do you want me to get the nurse?'

The pain stole her ability to speak. She nodded.

He motioned through the window. 'She's coming,' he said.

'My mom — would you find her for me? Please?'

As soon as the nurse came in the room,

Rick left to find Catherine. With each contact he became more confident that he could work with Lynda and her mother. He had reservations about Tom, but they ran along lines that had nothing to do with Lynda's care. Tom could be a problem down the line. But then Rick would be surprised if Tom was around too much longer, so he wasn't going to spend a lot of time worrying about it.

9

Tom reached across the table and adjusted Catherine's collar. 'That's been bothering me since I got here. You must have been in a hurry when you left home this morning. You know what you need? A mirror by the back door so you can check how you look before you leave the house.'

'You're right. I was in a hurry.' She'd slept through the alarm. If not for the garbage truck grinding its way through the neighborhood on its weekly pickup, she might still be in bed. 'I wanted to see Lynda before they changed her dressings.'

'We have an appointment with Roger Chapman this afternoon. He's squeezing us in as a personal favor to me and I don't want to be late.'

'Who's Roger Chapman?'

He made a frustrated sound and shook his head. 'Catherine, you have to start paying more attention. I told you about him a couple of days ago. He's the best litigator in the city. We're damned lucky that he's agreed to take Lynda's case.'

Finally, everything clicked. 'I told you I

didn't want to sue the Winslows, Tom. I don't understand why you thought I'd changed my mind.'

'I figured if I gave you a couple of days, you'd come to your senses.'

'It was an accident, Tom.' Somehow she'd failed to get across to him how she felt. 'How could I possibly sue anyone for an accident?'

'Grow up, Catherine. It happens all the time. It's the way the world operates. Why do you think there are so many insurance companies?'

'Well, it's not the way I operate.' She picked up her cup and took a sip of the now-cold coffee. Her stomach spasmed in protest. 'I need something to eat.'

Tom stood. 'I'll get it for you. What do you want?'

She tried to remember what she'd last eaten that had gone down without forcing. 'Toast — whole wheat.'

'Dry?'

'Jelly. Grape if they have it. And some milk.' He started to walk away. 'Wait. Get me a doughnut. A maple bar. One with lots of frosting.'

He reacted as if she'd asked for hemlock. 'Are you sure?'

'One doughnut isn't going to hurt me, Tom.' She should have known better than to ask. Tom equated sweets with drugs — equally destructive addictions.

'At your age — at *our* age,' he quickly corrected, 'every calorie counts.'

'Never mind.' He was a sentence away from becoming her broken shoelace on a frantic morning. 'The toast is fine.'

He smiled, his good deed accomplished. 'I'll be right back.'

As usual this time of day, the atrium was filled with the sounds of children at play: laughter, shouts of triumph at a well-played game, groans at losing. Normal sounds. Deceiving sounds.

Here what was normal became an oddity a step away from the entrance. The laughing little girl riding her father's shoulders seemed like little girls everywhere until you noticed she had no feet. With unimaginable determination, a boy in a wheelchair had learned to operate the controls without fingers. A tottering two-year-old wore flesh-colored pressure garments as if they were a playsuit.

Two weeks ago, Catherine could not have imagined herself a part of this world. She certainly couldn't have conceived how easily she would adjust. She didn't know whether to give herself credit for adaptability or to wonder about her lack of sensibility.

She'd changed so readily, at times she had

trouble understanding how hard it was for Tom. When he expressed pity instead of joy at one of Lynda's small triumphs, Catherine was torn between understanding, making excuses for him, and feeling angry.

'Here you go.' Tom took the toast and milk off the tray. 'I'm sorry about the doughnut thing, Catherine. I didn't express myself very well and I'm afraid I may have hurt your feelings.' He sat down next to her and possessively put his hand on her thigh. 'It's just that every time I see your mother, it reminds me that you and Lynda have her genes. I know you don't want to end up looking like her and I feel it's up to me to help you any way I can.'

Her mother was sixty-two years old, swam every day, led treks in the mountains for the Nature Conservancy, helped rescue sick and stranded marine mammals every spring, and wore a size eighteen. 'Did it ever occur to you that you might be a little hung up on this weight thing?'

'It's been proven time and time again that the thinner you are, the longer you live. I want us to have a long, long life together.'

'So how you feel has nothing to do with fashion?' She was purposely picking a fight with him and had no idea why. Only that morning she'd been thinking how much she missed him, their intimate conversations, their shared laughter, the quiet moments, the touching, the tenderness. She needed the man who cleared the clouds with a smile, and longed for the one who could make her heart soar with a word.

'Of course it does. I'm a man. Any man who tells you he doesn't care about a woman's weight is lying.'

'What if I did turn out to be like my mother? Would you leave me?' Why was she doing this?

'You're after something, Catherine. Why don't you just come out with it?'

'What if I were the one who was burned, not Lynda?' The question surprised her as much as it did him.

'You want an honest answer?' he asked after taking time to think.

'Yes.'

'I don't know.'

She couldn't imagine a knife hurting more than his words. 'I see,' she said softly.

'No, you don't. You just think you do. There's no way I could predict how I would feel about something like that and it wouldn't be honest to pretend it wouldn't matter. All you should care about is whether I would stick around long enough to make a real effort to get past my feelings.'

She started to say something when she looked up and saw Rick coming toward them. 'We need to talk about this some more,' she said. 'I don't want Lynda knowing how you feel.'

'It's not just me, Catherine. I'm not the one out of step here, you are. You're not helping Lynda by protecting her.' He saw Rick and groaned. 'Jesus, doesn't that guy ever work?'

Rick had spotted Catherine and Tom as soon as he stepped off the elevator, but they were so intent on their conversation he'd hesitated interrupting them. Tom appeared defensive, his body language closed and guarded. Catherine looked the way she had since Rick first met her, exhausted, hanging on with her fingertips to her world gone mad.

When she looked up and saw him she sent a smile that touched a protective chord in Rick.

'I didn't know you were here.' She moved to make room for him at the table. 'Have you seen Lynda?'

'I just came from her room.' For an instant, he considered waiting to tell Catherine that Lynda needed her. But it wasn't a few minutes free of crisis she needed, it was days. 'She asked me to find you.'

'Is she all right?'

'She will be as soon as she gets her shot. And she's eating.' He wanted her to have something positive to think about on the way to Lynda's room.

'How in the world did you manage that?'

'I told you the nurses would make her come around if you got out of there and let them do their work,' Tom said, looking to Rick for confirmation.

'Sorry, I don't agree.' Rick had a feeling they weren't words Tom was used to hearing. 'Lynda needs all the support she can get, even if she acts a little unappreciative at times.'

His hair fell across his forehead, almost into his eyes, not exactly the professional image he tried to project when Tom was around. He reached up to comb it back with his fingers. If he didn't get a haircut soon, he was going to have to glue it in place.

Catherine stared at his arm. 'I didn't know . . . '

He'd shown Lynda his scars to prove a point, one Catherine didn't need. 'It happened a long time ago,' he said. 'And has nothing to do with what I do or why I'm here.'

'Just part of the job, I suppose,' Tom said dismissively.

Rick wasn't about to get into a pissing

112

contest with Tom Adams. He didn't like the man and hadn't from the beginning, but Tom was an integral part of Lynda's recovery. If Rick couldn't neutralize his animosity, he couldn't be an effective agent for Lynda or Catherine. 'Not one we like to think about too much.'

Catherine stood. 'Gene is supposed to be here in a few minutes,' she said to Rick. 'Would you mind intercepting him and telling him where we've gone?'

'He doesn't have to do that,' Tom interjected. 'I'll wait for Gene.'

Normally Rick took whatever path necessary to steer clear of family dynamics. Perversely, this time he waded into the middle. 'Actually, I've been meaning to catch up with Gene anyway.'

Tom slipped his arm around Catherine in a blatantly possessive, if puzzling move. Rick almost laughed out loud.

'I'm not clear what your job is around here, but it's nice to know you're available for things like this,' Tom said.

Catherine folded into herself at Tom's condescending statement. The look she gave Rick held a plea for understanding. 'Will I see you later?'

Rick pointedly ignored Tom. 'I'll try to stop by tonight — around dinner.' He'd check with Lynda's doctor to clear bringing her the crab cakes and put in a standing order at the restaurant until she'd had her fill.

'Thank you.' For a moment, her face lit up with a smile. Tom immediately turned her toward the elevator and she had to call over her shoulder, 'For everything.'

'You're welcome.'

Rick shook his head and stuffed his hands in his pockets. What in the hell did a woman like Catherine see in a man like Tom? He'd known women who'd traded their souls for wealth and social position and were comfortable with the bargain. They were a type easily recognized. Nothing like Catherine. But then, what did he really know about her?

'Rick — ,' Gene called. 'I was hoping we'd run into each other before I had to leave.'

Rick shook Gene's outstretched hand. 'When are you taking off?'

'My flight leaves in the morning. I tried to get out of going, but the board insists they want me there for the final round of negotiation.'

'Catherine said you went into banking.'

'Long way from engineering, huh?' Gene sat in Catherine's vacated chair. 'Like everyone else, I went where the jobs were. How about you?'

'I was working in the state legislator's office when I stopped by a firehouse to pick up a friend for a fishing trip. That one visit was all it took and I knew I'd found what I wanted to do.'

'And you still like it?'

Gene had phrased the question better than most, but Rick had been through the drill often enough with his old college buddies to know what he was really asking. How could someone who'd graduated with honors from USC be satisfied with a blue-collar job? Where was the mental challenge, the advancement? Bottom line: Where was the money?

He'd stopped trying to explain what he loved about being a firefighter a long time ago. It was one of those things that if someone had to ask, there was no way he would understand the answer.

'I love it,' Rick told him.

'Wish I could say that about my job. There are some days all I can think about is finding a way to retire early.'

Gene's candid reply surprised Rick. 'I take it you don't get much time for fishing anymore.' In college he and Gene had been part of a group of guys that pooled their money two or three times a year to hire a boat to take them ocean fishing.

'I golf now, but it's for the business contacts, not for recreation.'

'I have a buddy who runs a charter service

out of Bodega Bay. I've never come home empty-handed when I've gone out with him. Give me a call when you get back and we'll work something out.'

'How do I get in touch with you?'

He reached for his wallet and remembered he'd left it in the truck. 'Catherine has my number.'

Gene seemed confused. 'I thought Tom told me she'd changed her mind about working with your organization.'

'If she has, she hasn't said anything to me about it. Which is odd, because I just arranged for her and Tom to attend a parents' support meeting in Stockton next Wednesday. And she has an appointment to meet with the director of the association to see whether she wants Lynda to attend burn camp this summer.'

'Burn camp?'

'We bring in burned kids from all over the state for a week in the mountains. They get to be around other kids who have the same kinds of problems and face the same surgeries, but most of all they just get to be kids.'

'I'm glad to hear she's considering it for Lynda. I was worried she was going to try to handle this on her own the way she's done with everything else since her divorce.' Gene's expression changed from open to angry.

'Have you met Jack yet?'

'He was here and gone before I arrived.'

'The son of a bitch told Catherine that he had to leave town on business and I ran into him at the bank yesterday.'

'Jack is Lynda's father?' He assumed as much but had been wrong about that kind of thing too many times to take anything for granted.

'Yeah — regrettably. He doesn't deserve her any more than he deserved Catherine. Everything Jack does is for show. If Lynda were allowed flowers, he'd have every surface covered. He'll spend money on her, but not time.'

Gene looked at his watch. 'Speaking of time, I should be spending what I have left with Lynda.' He stood. 'I'll be in touch about that fishing trip. Maybe we can get Catherine and Lynda to come along.'

Rick noted he didn't mention Tom and wondered whether it was a mental lapse or wishful thinking. He cleared the cups from the table, then went to the window to look at the Sacramento skyline, thinking that family dynamics were a lot like a city, filled with hidden surprises and dangerous alleys. At least cities came with maps. With Lynda and Catherine he was on his own.

10

'Are you alright?' Catherine asked.

'Of course I am,' Tom answered too quickly. 'What makes you think I'm not?'

'We've been in the car a half hour and you haven't spoken except to say yes or no to my questions.'

'I guess I'm all talked out. Or maybe I'm all listened out. I thought you said the meeting was only going to last an hour. Do you realize we were there over two?'

How could she not have noticed the way Tom had looked at his watch every five minutes? 'There were so many new people this time. They just wanted to make sure we felt comfortable with each other. That takes time.'

'I have to be honest with you, Catherine. I'm not sure how many of these meetings I can sit through. When that woman started talking about how the doctors were going to attach her daughter's new ears, it was everything I could do not to get up and walk out of there.'

'I admit it was a little hard to hear, but — '

'I don't understand how subjecting ourselves to this kind of thing is supposed to help

Lynda. What she needs is to get out of the hospital and go shopping. It's going to be damn hard to find something that will hide those awful suits she's supposed to wear. What is listening to a horror story about some stupid woman who let her kid play with matches supposed to do for us?'

'She didn't *let* her son play with matches, Tom. He found them in a drawer.'

'If she would have put them someplace where he couldn't get his hands on them, she would still have her cute little boy, not some kid the doctors have to try to reconstruct into something that doesn't scare all the other kids on the playground.'

'That's not fair.'

'And you can bet that's exactly what that little boy is going to say to himself every day for the rest of his life.' He stiffened his arms and pressed himself back in the seat, his desire to be anywhere else, talking about anything else, as evident as the bugs hitting the windshield. 'I'm sorry he was burned, and I'm sorry his mother has to deal with it, but that doesn't mean I want to hear about it every month for the next year. I have better things, certainly more constructive things, to do with my time.' He relaxed his arms, but not his posture. 'And so do you.'

She folded her arms across her chest and

gazed at the rows of grapevines that appeared to open and close like fans in the hands of a frenetic dancer as they passed outside her window. 'There's something I've been meaning to talk to you about. I know you were only trying to be helpful when you told Lynda that you would buy her new clothes, but — '

'You should have seen her light up. I felt like Santa Claus on Christmas morning.'

'Did you actually tell her that you were buying her new clothes so that she could hide her pressure suit?'

'Of course I did.'

'I spend all my time telling her she's perfect the way she is and you take it all away by telling her you'll pay for new clothes so she can hide.'

'That's a shitty thing to say, Catherine. You make it sound as if I'm ashamed of her.'

'That's the impression you give, Tom. You're a wonderful man, generous to a fault, but sometimes you say things without thinking them through. We have to be careful where Lynda is concerned. She's already made up her mind that she isn't pretty anymore. We have to convince her that she's wrong, not do things that will reinforce those feelings.'

'Do you want me to lie to her?'

The question took Catherine's breath away, leaving her agape. 'Don't you see? That's exactly what I mean. I know you don't think Lynda's burns make a difference, but you make it sound as if you do.'

He didn't say anything for a long time. 'This is going to hurt you, and I'm sorry, but if you're going to help Lynda, you have to face some facts about men and how they feel about women. Looks matter. If you tell her they don't and get her to believe you, you're setting her up to get hurt over and over again. Let's say she does find some oddball who really doesn't care. What kind of guy do you think he'll be? Not anyone of her class, certainly. Personally, I think she deserves more.'

'You can't mean that.' He couldn't. She searched her memory for the reasons she'd fallen in love with him, remembering his caring and tenderness, the way he'd accepted Lynda. Before Tom, the men she'd dated had made it plain they wanted nothing to do with being father to another man's child.

He'd admitted this was the first crisis he'd ever faced. Until now, his life had been as unextraordinary as white bread, his decisions free of emotion. She had no right to expect him to get it right the first time.

'It isn't just me; all men feel this way,

whether they want to admit it or not. Think about it, Catherine. What man, or woman for that matter, wants to be seen with someone who draws attention to themselves because of their handicap? It might not be fair, it might not be right, but looks matter. If we can help Lynda hide what's happened to her now, she'll figure out the rest for herself when she's older.'

'Did seeing Rick's scars change your mind about him?'

Her question took a second to register. 'You mean the fireman?' He laughed. 'Nothing could make me change my mind about him. I deal with his type all the time on construction sites. I know what to expect.'

'How long have we known each other?' she wondered aloud.

'What has that got to do with anything?'

'I'm confused — how could we have been together all this time and know so little about each other?'

'It's a difference of opinion, Catherine, not world peace.'

She was encouraged that he saw his view as opinion, not fact. Opinion was easier to work with. 'We've come full circle. Now you see why I think it's critical for us to go to these meetings, even if they do make us uncomfortable. It's important to find out what other people have gone through with their kids and how they handled it, so we don't make the same mistakes.'

'I can see your mind is already made up. Since it doesn't matter what I say or how I feel, there's only one thing left for me to do — lay some ground rules. From now on, I won't try to stop you from going to the meetings — just don't ask me to go with you. And don't talk to me about what went on when you get home. I don't want to hear it.'

She waited a long time before answering him. 'This isn't going to work, Tom.'

He turned to her, unsure at first, and then with a look of utter relief. 'Thank God. I've been thinking the same thing but didn't want to be the one to bring it up — not with all you've been going through.'

Her stomach did a slow, acid-filled roll that made her throat burn. He couldn't be suggesting what she thought he was. She had to have heard him wrong. Her heart raced as she considered the possibility. Finally, carefully, she asked, 'What are you saying?'

'The same thing you are. I never understood that expression about it being an ill wind that blows no good until this happened. I hate to think that it took Lynda getting burned to make us see how basically different we are, but there it is. She's saved us a lot of heartache down the road.'

Pride, pure and self-protective, kept Catherine from telling him that she'd been talking about doing things together in their relationship, not dissolving it. But that pride couldn't keep her from saying, 'This is it then? The engagement is off? You have no interest in seeing me or Lynda again?'

As if realizing he'd gone too far too fast, he began a new, slower dance. 'All I'm saying is that we should give ourselves more time — back off a little. Give each other more space.'

'I thought that term went out in the eighties.'

'You see what I mean? You never would have talked to me like that before the accident.'

She couldn't deny it. 'It's the stress.' Why was she defending herself?

'Stress doesn't change you, it brings out who you really are.'

She thought about his comment. 'Do you honestly believe that?'

'Yes, I do.' Attempting to offer her comfort, he put his hand on her thigh. He looked at her, this time long enough to see that he'd made a mistake. 'Oh, my God. I got it wrong, didn't I? You weren't breaking up with me. I'm sorry, Catherine. The last thing I wanted to do was hurt you.'

She pushed his hand aside. 'Your timing really stinks, Tom. How am I going to explain this to Lynda? She's going to think it's her fault.'

The pained look disappeared. 'Did you hear what you just said?'

'What are you talking about?'

'Maybe that's the real problem, Catherine. With you, Lynda always comes first. If you'd put me in that position once in a while, this might not have happened.'

'Trade places with Lynda, Tom, and I'd be happy to put you first.' Her fingers wrapped around the door handle. She'd give a year's salary to be in town and free to get out of the car instead of stuck with him on an isolated section of freeway with nothing but farmland for miles on either side. She didn't want him to see how much he'd hurt her. 'If you're right about stress bringing out someone's true nature, then I guess that makes you a coward.'

'Just because I don't like hospitals doesn't make me a coward.'

'I've been so stupid. I made excuses for you. To everyone. So many times I actually started believing them myself.'

'Go ahead, blame me if it makes you feel better. I can take it.'

The words sounded rehearsed. 'How long have you known you wanted out?'

He shifted position. 'Why does it matter?'

'Because it's important to me.' This was the man who had promised to love her forever, who listened to her hopes and dreams and vowed to make them come true. How could they have gone from that to this in less than six months? Was that the shelf life of his love?

Still he hesitated.

'Tell me.'

'You won't understand.'

'What possible difference does that make?'

'I want us to stay friends.'

'*Friends?* This isn't high school, Tom.'

'There's no way we can avoid running into each other. We go to the same parties, belong to the same club, know the same people.' His voice dropped to a pained whisper. 'Why make this any more difficult than it has to be?'

'I introduced you to those friends.' Tom was new to the area when they met, recently transferred from Southern California and in need of social and business contacts. 'You were accepted at those parties because of me.'

'Which is why I don't want anyone to have to choose between us. They may have been your friends first, Catherine, but they get things from me now that you can't give. I'm

126

an important part of the business community now.'

Could he really be threatening her? Did he honestly believe the friends who had stayed with her through her and Jack's divorce would abandon her now? 'You still haven't answered me. How long have you known you wanted out?'

'Since the doctors told us that Lynda was going to be permanently scarred.' Catherine started to say something. He held up his hand to stop her. 'Don't bother. I know how terrible that sounds. And don't think I haven't agonized over it. I've hardly been able to think of anything else since it happened. But I know myself and I know how I feel about being around handicapped people. They make me uncomfortable. Sooner or later Lynda would figure it out and it would only make things worse.'

'So what you're telling me is that you're really doing this for Lynda. Is that it?' The son of a bitch could twist anything to make himself look better. Was she so blind — or had she been so desperate to have a man in her life again — that she hadn't seen this trait before? How could she know this now and still feel as if her heart was breaking?

'I knew you wouldn't understand. How could you?' He made it sound as if she were incapable of complex thought. 'But before you condemn me too much, I want to say something in my own defense. You have an advantage with Lynda. She's your own flesh and blood. It's easier for you to make allowances about the way she looks. And you're a woman. You have no idea what it's like when important people judge you not for your own worth, but by the person at your side.'

The saddest part was that he believed what he was saying.

'Everywhere we went, every time we met someone new, I'd be put in the position of having to explain Lynda. Then I'd have to listen to men tell me they were sorry, when what they really meant was they were glad it wasn't them.'

'You're full of shit.' He could say what he wanted about her, but not Lynda. 'I don't know one other man who thinks the way you do.'

'Oh? Then why didn't Jack stick around? Lynda is his own daughter and he was in and out of her hospital room even faster than I was.'

'Jack has never stuck around for anything.'

'It's the way we are. I'm not saying it's right, but you can no more change how men think about this kind of thing than you can change the number of days in a week. Stick a Victoria's Secret catalog in front of any straight man — I don't care who that man is — and he's going to react the same way.'

'Not that it makes any difference, but what has any of that got to do with you and me?'

'I didn't sign on for this kind of problem. When I asked you to marry me, I figured Lynda would be off to college in a couple of years and we'd be on our own. Now with her being burned, everything has changed.'

'But you still want to be friends.'

'When I said everything has changed, I didn't mean how I feel about you. I still love you. I'm sure a part of me always will.'

'I can't believe you just said that.'

'I didn't just say it, I meant it.'

Afraid of what she would see in Tom's eyes if she chanced a look at him, she stared at the taillights on the Mustang they'd been following since leaving Stockton. She wanted to believe he'd turned into someone she wouldn't recognize, someone he'd kept hidden from her. She'd believed in him. She'd trusted he would be a good father to the daughter she loved more than her own life. How could she have been so wrong? What was it about her and men? First Jack and now Tom.

Finally she looked at him. Her chest

tightened; tears burned her eyes. Dear God, what was wrong with her? *I love this man.* Even after everything that had happened, everything he'd said to her, her feelings were in the present tense.

It took time to stop loving someone. For her it always had. She'd had to come home from the lake early one Sunday and find Jack in bed with another woman before the hurt became more powerful than the love.

An inner voice told her that it wouldn't take as long with Tom. She would stop loving him, soon. Eventually she would even hate him for the things he'd said and felt about Lynda. She just needed a little time.

'We won't be friends,' she said softly.

'I understand it might be hard right away.'

'It will never happen.'

'Why would you want to make this harder than it has to be?'

'You don't give a damn about how hard this is on me. You're worried how it will look when the word gets out that you dumped me while Lynda was still in the hospital.' She would not let him manipulate her again. 'I want you to take me to the hospital — now.'

'How will you get home?'

'You're not paying attention, Tom. This is my car. The question is, how will you get home?'

'It doesn't have to be this way.'

'Oh yes, it does.' Finally she looked at him. 'And about 'our' friends? I'd start making new ones if I were you. I have no doubt the men will still be happy to play a round of golf at the club and to take the money you lose so freely, but their wives are the ones who issue the invitations to parties. None of the women I know shop at Victoria's Secret. They're not likely to be impressed with the analogy.'

'The mouse roars, is that it?'

'I'm a Leo, Tom. You might do well to remember that.'

11

Catherine stood outside Lynda's hospital room, undecided whether she should tell her about Tom that night or wait until her daughter was home. Lynda was sure to notice that something was wrong. Now that she was taking less pain medication, she'd started picking up on the subtleties of the world around her again.

'Mom?' Lynda came out of Ray Tatum's room, Brian in tow. 'What are you doing here? I thought you and Tom were going home after your meeting.'

'I decided to come by to see how the new hat looked,' she said far too brightly. When Lynda's head was shaved to take the skin for transplant, the doctor left a fringe of hair along the front and sides that she could wear in curling wisps outside a floppy hat or baseball cap. After the first surgery, Rick presented her with a cap from his fire department. Now he brought one with every visit, each sporting a logo from a different fire department in the area.

Lynda self-consciously touched the brim and her hair as if assuring herself both were still in place. Discovering the bandage exposed in the back, she tugged on the cap to pull it lower.

'I think I like this one the best,' Brian said. 'The blue brings out the color of her eyes.'

Lynda looked at him and gave him a shy smile.

Every night, Catherine said a little prayer that Brian would be at the hospital the next day. In this, her prayers were answered. He had become Lynda's link to the outside world, the world of teenagers and music and fast food. When she'd finally had her fill of crab cakes from California Cafe, Brian stepped in to supply hamburgers and french fries, pizza, and tacos, matching her consumption down to the last french fry, refusing to let her quit until the calorie intake for the day was satisfied.

'How's Ray tonight?' Catherine asked.

'Okay,' Lynda said. 'The police found a relative in Kansas. An aunt, I think. She's supposed to be on her way here to see him.'

They moved into Lynda's room. 'Does he talk to you about what happened?'

'He's said some things to me,' Brian said. 'But it's the same stuff over and over again. He keeps telling me how he tried to save his little sister. It's like he's trying to convince himself he did everything he could. I don't

133

know if anyone told him that she didn't make it, so I don't say anything. I just listen.'

'He's pretty out of it most of the time,' Lynda said. 'He knows he's burned, but I don't think he knows how bad. At least he never says anything.'

'They had to take another part of his hand yesterday,' Brian said.

'His fingers are all gone now,' Lynda added. 'That's so awful. He's the quarterback of his . . . at least he was the quarterback.' She stopped in front of the mirror over the sink and looked at herself. 'I'm so lucky nothing like that happened to me,' she said softly.

Catherine had waited for the moment when Lynda would show a self-awareness that put her injuries into perspective. It was something she couldn't be told, something she had to feel for herself. Now the mental healing as well as the physical healing could begin. 'I have a sudden craving for ice cream. Anyone care to join me?'

Lynda sat on the edge of her bed. 'You're so obvious, Mom.'

'Sounds good to me,' Brian said.

Lynda looked from Brian to her mother and then back again. 'When I get out of here I'm never going to eat ice cream again.'

'Marshmallow sundae it is,' Brian told her.

'What about you, Mrs. Mil — Catherine?'

She smiled. 'Nice catch, Brian.' She'd been after him for days to stop calling her Mrs. Miller. 'You might as well make it three.' On the grand scale of things what were another thousand or so calories? A month of marshmallow sundaes and Tom could tell their friends he'd had to leave her because she'd let herself go. That was something they would have no trouble understanding. At least according to him.

'I'm going to the Baskin-Robbins, but I'll be right back,' Brian said at the door.

Catherine didn't have to search for her answering smile. She really liked this kid. 'We'll be here.'

Lynda left the bed and sat in the rocker. Catherine put her purse in the cupboard and joined her, taking her place on the bed. 'How does your head feel?'

'Worse than my back, but it's okay.'

'I tried calling Grandma this afternoon, but she wasn't home.' Catherine's mother was the only person she knew who didn't have a cell phone. 'Did you see her today?'

'She and Uncle Gene came by on the way home from the airport. He brought me those scarves.' She pointed to a stack of neatly folded, brightly colored scarves on the shelf by the television. 'But he said he thinks the

135

caps Rick gave me look better.'

'I'm glad he's home.' For more reasons than Lynda needed to know right then.

'Me too. He said Rick is going to take him ocean fishing and that I could come along if I wanted.'

'Oh?' She wasn't sure why it surprised her that Gene would be interested in doing something with Rick. Other than being alumni of the same school, they seemed to have so little in common. 'And what did you tell him?'

'No way.'

From somewhere in the middle of the dark cloud that Tom had created that night, Catherine found a smile. 'You never know, you might like it.'

Lynda made a face and shuddered at the suggestion. 'Brian's mom and dad came by, too. They want to know if they can do anything for me. It doesn't matter what I say, they just keep asking. Maybe I should make something up.'

'They feel bad about what happened.'

'It wasn't their fault.'

'That doesn't make any difference. They're nice people and that's what nice people do.'

'How was your meeting?'

The question seemed innocent enough, but Catherine picked up something in the way it

136

was asked that put her on the alert. 'Interesting.'

'That's it?'

'They talked about a lot of things that don't apply to us.'

'Like?'

'New advances in facial reconstruction.'

'Oh.'

Catherine leaned over and took Lynda's hand. 'What is it you're really asking?'

'I was wondering what happened to Tom. Didn't he go with you?'

Had she known Lynda was headed in this direction, she wouldn't have asked. 'I would imagine he's home by now,' she answered truthfully, if evasively.

'He doesn't like being here, does he?'

She took a deep breath. 'No, he doesn't.'

'Is it me?'

'Is what you?'

'Why he stays away.'

Lynda was beyond being satisfied with easy answers; still, Catherine wasn't ready to tell her the complete truth. 'He doesn't like hospitals.'

'I don't either, but if someone I loved was in one, I'd be there for them.'

Plainly Tom's absence had been bothering Lynda for some time. 'It seems Tom is not the man I thought he was.'

'You had a fight, didn't you? I could tell something was wrong.'

'It was more than a fight, Lynda. Tom and I broke up tonight.'

'It was because of me, wasn't it?'

'Yes — and I don't know if I'll ever be able to thank you enough. You kept me from making a huge mistake.'

'I thought you loved him.'

'So did I. Shows you even I can make mistakes.' She forced a smile. 'Not many, and certainly not often, but in this case quality made up for quantity.'

'I'm sorry.'

Catherine reached for Lynda's other hand and looked her daughter in the eye. 'You have nothing to be sorry about, do you hear me? If none of this happened I would have married Tom. We might even have made it work — for a while. Until I needed him. Then I would have been on my own. You kept me from making the biggest mistake of my life.'

'I thought Daddy was your biggest mistake.'

'You are the best thing that ever happened to me. And since I wouldn't have you without him, there's no way he could have been a mistake.'

'That's what parents always tell their kids.'

'Because that's how parents feel.'

Lynda sat up straighter in her chair. 'Now what?'

'I don't know. I haven't had a lot of time to think about it yet. I guess the first thing I should do is cancel the reservations at the church. And then there's the invitations . . . and the caterer.'

'Didn't you tell me Tom arranged all that?'

'We did it together.' At the time she'd thought he was doing it for her, but now she understood he was doing it to make sure the arrangements were to his liking.

'But wasn't he going to pay for it?'

'You're obviously leading up to something.'

'It's his money — let him take care of it. If he doesn't cancel in time, he'll forfeit his deposit.'

'You don't seem very upset about this.' Certainly not enough to justify Catherine's concern.

'You liked Tom, and I didn't hate him, so I never said anything. I hate him now, so I sure hope you aren't thinking about getting back together.'

'There's no way that's going to happen.'

'Good.'

Brian opened the door. 'They were having a special on banana splits. I got three. I hope that's okay.'

'We need to talk about this some more,'

Catherine told Lynda.

'Okay, but not now.'

'Want me to go away and come back later?' Brian asked.

Catherine almost said yes and then looked at Lynda. In the two and a half weeks she'd been in the hospital Brian had given Lynda more attention than Tom had the entire time they'd been engaged. Catherine made a snap decision, an alien action. She gave most things — like Tom — careful thought. 'I was just telling Lynda that Tom and I won't be getting married after all.'

'Mom,' Lynda wailed. 'He doesn't need to know that.'

'Maybe not,' Brian said. 'But I'm sure glad you told me. This way I won't wind up with my foot in my mouth because I said something I shouldn't have.' He opened the bag and handed Lynda a large container, spoon, and napkin. 'I know it's none of my business, but I think Tom's an idiot for letting you dump him.'

She liked that he assumed she'd done the dumping, or that he pretended he did. It shouldn't have mattered, but with her ego as battered as a heron in a hurricane, it did.

The door opened again. Rick looked through and smiled. He was in uniform, his appearance so startlingly different, he took all of them by surprise. 'Looks like a party.'

Rick Sawyer was the last person Catherine wanted to see. Well, almost the last. 'I thought you were working today.'

'I am.' He looked at Lynda. 'We were on the way back from a call and I thought I'd look in on you and Ray. I like the hat, by the way.'

'We were with Ray earlier,' Lynda said. 'He was okay then.'

'He told me you'd been by.' Rick checked out the container of ice cream. 'He also told me you'd been giving him a lecture about food and how to work the system.'

'He's a nice guy,' Brian said. 'Having his family die like that really sucks.'

'And his hand,' Lynda added.

'He told me,' Rick said.

Catherine stood on a mental sideline while they were talking. This was the first time she'd seen Rick in uniform. He seemed less approachable somehow. Too good-looking. Cliché or not, there was something about a man in uniform.

'Now that I see you're being well taken care of,' he told Lynda, 'I'm outta here. Enjoy your ice cream.' He looked at Catherine. 'Want to walk me out?'

When she hesitated, he added, 'I have a

new hat in the rig that I forgot to bring in with me.'

Confused, she played along because it was Rick, and in the time she'd known him, he'd never done anything without a purpose. 'Sure — that would be nice.' She put her ice cream container on the tray table and said, 'I'll be right back.'

When they were in the hallway, Rick took her arm and guided her into an empty examining room. 'I just got a call from the captain at Station Thirteen. Tom's been in an accident. He's fine,' he added quickly. 'It was just a fender-bender kind of thing. The air bag didn't even deploy. The ambulance crew said they couldn't find anything wrong with him, not even a bruise, but he kept insisting they take him in so he could be examined by a real doctor. He also insisted that someone call you to tell you that he was on his way to the emergency room.' The next he added reluctantly. 'He kept mumbling something about the accident being your fault.'

Catherine leaned back against the wall and closed her eyes. The day just kept getting worse and worse.

'The captain at the scene is one of the counselors at burn camp and he made the connection between us when Tom told him where you were and then threw my name into the mix. He called me to let me know that Tom was — well, you get the idea.'

'We had a fight.'

'You don't owe me an explanation. I almost didn't come, but then I thought maybe you'd want a little forewarning so you could keep Lynda out of it.'

'Thank you.' She put her hand on the door-knob. 'Did this captain happen to say if Tom was with anyone?'

'He was alone.'

She frowned. 'What kind of car was he driving?'

'A green Lincoln Navigator.'

She exploded. 'That son of a bitch! He waited until I was inside the hospital and then took my car.'

'I'll call the police when I get back to the station and see if I can find out where it was towed.'

Without her car, she had to arrange for a ride home. If she asked her mother to come and get her, she'd want to know why Tom wasn't available. Damn. She really didn't want to talk to anyone else about Tom that night.

Catherine jumped when she heard a knock on the door.

'Mrs. Miller?' The night nurse looked inside. 'There's a phone call for you. It's Mr.

Adams. He said he's at Sutter Hospital and needs to talk to you right away.'

'Thank you. I'll be right there.' To Rick, she said, 'And thank you. Again. For the hundredth time. I don't know what I would have done if Tom had blindsided me with this.'

'You would have rolled with it the way you have everything else.' He waited to follow her out of the room, but she showed no sign of leaving. Finally, he said, 'I'm out of my district so I can't hang around, but if you need me for something, you can reach me at the station.'

She nodded. 'Will you be here tomorrow?'

He'd planned to stop by for a few minutes on his way home and then spend the rest of the day taping and texturing wallboard. 'I'm free all day if you need something.'

'I hate to ask, but I don't want to involve the rest of my family in this until I absolutely have to and I'm going to need to get my car tomorrow. Do you know if it's still drivable?'

'No, but I'll ask when I call to see where it was towed.'

'Shit — something I didn't think about. I don't know any body shops. Where do I go to get it fixed?'

'Check with your insurance agent. They may want you to take the car to one of their

144

approved shops.' Sentence by sentence, he became more involved in her life. If he had any sense, he'd run like hell. Lyn had given him the option that morning. A female firefighter had become available to take Lynda's case. He'd declined the offer.

But he could still change his mind. He'd earned a free summer. His house needed him. Hell, Blue needed him. The dog was as neglected as the garden he'd started the week before he met Catherine and Lynda. If he didn't spend a little more time with Blue, he was going to move next door permanently.

Then he looked into Catherine's large brown eyes and saw the fear and confusion and pain. She'd lost the protective veneer of the belief that bad things happened to other people's children. She triggered a protective streak he had no business feeling, one he'd be crazy to act on. She had family to take care of her. She didn't need him.

She covered her face with her hands as if trying to close out the overwhelming onslaught of problems. Seconds later she dropped her hands back to her sides. 'I'd better take that call — I need to ask Tom who he's insured with if I'm going to get started on this thing tomorrow.'

'Do you have a way home tonight?'

'It's out of his way, but I'm sure Brian

would be willing to take me.'

He nodded. 'Let me know what time you need to be picked up in the morning.'

'You're sure you don't mind?'

'I'm sure.'

'Thank you.' She offered him an accompanying smile. 'Yet again.'

'It's nothing I wouldn't — '

'Don't you dare tell me you're only doing your job. What you're doing goes way beyond what you signed on to do. I know it and you know it. I promise I won't put you in this position again.'

He wasn't sure if he felt relieved or disappointed.

On his way back to the engine, Rick decided Tom was an ass, pure and simple. Someone who couldn't see what he had in Catherine and Lynda sure as hell didn't deserve them.

12

Janet stepped off the running board on the engine when she saw Rick come out of the hospital. 'Everything okay?' She climbed into the back with the rookie, Paul.

'Yeah, everything's fine.' As soon as he was inside the cab, Steve pointed to the computer.

'Dispatch called a couple of minutes ago. They wanted to know if we could take an animal rescue call.'

'What is it?'

'Cat in a wall.'

'What did you tell them?'

'That we'd be there as soon as you put us in service again.' He grinned. 'Figured we should make sure Paul has a full range of experience before he leaves us.'

Rookies spent six months at each of four different stations their first two years in the department. Paul was a week shy of two months on his first rotation. He was the only one of his graduating class of twenty to have actually fought a fire and the only one to go overboard on a white-water practice drill.

Rick put on his headset and pressed the

microphone button on the dash. 'Engine seventy-six responding.' He hit the Enroute button on the computer and the button on his headset that cut him off from his crew. He'd already sustained a significant hearing loss in one ear from the sirens and air horn, and he fanatically protected what was left.

Usually he enjoyed the enforced silence. It gave him time to think about whatever project he had going at the moment, especially if it was something that needed finessing. He tried concentrating on the half-finished texturing, but his mind kept drifting back to Catherine. He'd dated off and on in the ten years since his divorce, but never seriously. He kept waiting for the stars to spin, to hear a symphony in the wind, to know in his gut that he'd found someone who, when they were both eighty-five, would still tell jokes and take showers with him and lay on the grass to watch meteor showers in August. He refused to settle for the moment, or for someone who wouldn't stick through the hard times. He wanted a relationship, a lover, a friend to last forever.

He'd been through the death of love once; he didn't have the heart or the courage to go through it again.

Steve stopped in front of a two-story brick house and remained with the engine while

Rick and the two firefighters went up to the front door. A woman Rick guessed to be in her eighties opened the door seconds after he knocked.

'Oh, I'm so glad you're finally here. I'm so sorry about calling this late, but I didn't know what else to do.' She glanced up and saw the engine. 'Oh dear, I didn't know you would be coming in that. I told them it was only a little emergency. You could have come in a car. Now the neighbors are going to think I left something on the stove again.'

'Sorry — this is all the city gives us. We come in the fire engine or not at all. Now, why don't you tell me what you've got going on in here?'

She held open the door and stepped out of the way. 'Come in, come in.' When the three of them were inside, she closed the door and led them to a back bedroom. 'My son is out of town. He's the one who usually takes care of things like this for me — or my neighbor does. But he works at night, so he's not home, either. So you see I really didn't have any choice but to call you.'

'What makes you think you have a cat in the wall?' Rick asked.

She gave him a chastising look reminiscent of his mother's response to dumb questions. 'Listen for yourself.' She tapped the wall by the closet door and put her finger to her lips motioning for quiet. Sure enough, several plaintive wails followed. 'Well?'

'You're right,' Rick admitted. 'It sounds like a cat.' He went to the wall and tapped again to try to pinpoint its location.

'Would you like me to do that, Captain?' Janet said.

He chuckled to himself at her veiled attempt to cover for him. She'd picked up the results of his city-required hearing test a month ago and was convinced he was going deaf. 'I think I can handle it. You can get the saw and a couple of tarps out of the rig.'

'What are you going to do?' the woman asked.

'Cut a hole in the wall. The cat is too far down to try to reach it from above.'

'Oh dear, what am I going to do with a hole in my wall?' She put her hand to her ample bosom. 'Or were you going to fix it for me, too?'

'No, I'm afraid we don't do that.'

'Are you sure there's no other way?'

'Not any that I know of.'

'What would happen if we just left it there? Isn't it possible it could climb out by itself?'

'If there were any way that cat could get out of there on its own, it would be out by

150

now.' He could sympathize with her reluctance to see her wall damaged, but he wasn't about to walk away knowing an animal would starve to death because it was inconvenient to rescue it. 'Now, I can't force you to let us cut a hole in your wall, but I can promise you it's going to happen one way or another. If that cat dies in there, the smell is going to drive you out of the house. You won't be back until you find someone to tear down the wall and clean it up.'

'Oh dear. I had no idea.'

'I take it the cat isn't yours?'

She shook her head. 'I always wanted one, but my husband was allergic. Then when he died, I started going here and there — places he'd never go with me — and I was hardly ever home.'

Janet and Paul came back. Rick had them cover the bed and floor with the tarps. He found the studs by tapping and listening to the sounds change from hollow to solid. After marking the position with a pencil, he cut a straight line down the wall. Moving the saw to the second stud, he caught the look on Paul's face. His eyes were enormous, his mouth open, his expression one between horror and fascination. Clearly he expected blood to come spurting from the cut.

Rick made the second slice down the wall

sixteen inches from the first, and then one across the top. Wedging the tip of the pry bar into the third cut, he levered and pushed. The wall broke at the seam, two feet above the cat. He shined his flashlight into the hole. Two terrified eyes shined back. The cat was wedged upside down, its feet pointing toward the ceiling, its black fur covered in white dust. It started purring, the rumble loud enough for Paul and Janet to hear on the other side of the bed.

'Is it okay?' Janet asked.

'Far as I can tell,' Rick told her.

'May I see?' the woman asked.

Rick moved out of the way. 'Don't touch it,' he warned.

'Oh my, it's a pretty little thing, isn't it?' she said, the hole in the wall temporarily forgotten.

'Would you like me to get it out for you, Captain?' Paul asked. 'Cats like me.'

Rick had seen too many animals in crisis to trust one, no matter how loud it purred. But he was willing to give the rookie a chance. 'All right, but put your gloves on.'

'No disrespect, Capt'n, but if I go sticking a glove in there I'm only going to scare the poor thing. I do know what I'm talkin' about when it comes to cats. I tell you, they like me.'

There were some things you just couldn't teach; they had to be learned by experience. Rick shook his head and backed away. 'All right — have at it.'

'Hey, kitty,' Paul crooned softly. 'That's a good boy.' He slowly reached inside, talking the entire time. Everything went fine for about a second and a half. Then, as if on cue, the cat let out a high pitched snarl, spit, growled, and latched onto Paul's arm. Paul jerked his hand back and hit the dresser with his elbow. For a second, Rick wasn't sure whether the howling was coming from Paul or the cat.

'Jesus, *get him off of me.*'

Rick figured the cat no more wanted to be on Paul's arm than Paul wanted him there, so he stood back and waited. Sure enough, the cat used Paul for a launchpad, hitting the bed and then the floor.

'Ungrateful little — '

'Watch it,' Rick warned.

Janet couldn't hold back any longer and doubled over laughing.

The old woman went to the cat where it had settled in a corner. She spoke to it for several seconds, stroked its head, and lifted it into her arms. 'Cats like me, too,' she said to Paul.

It was too much for Rick. He roared.

'Look at this,' Paul said indignantly, holding out his hand. 'Look what that thing did to me.'

'Oh dear,' the woman said. 'You really should have a doctor look at that. I once heard that a man lost his thumb to a cat bite.'

'Is that true, Captain?' Paul asked, his outrage turning to concern.

'True enough,' Rick said. 'Once we get this place cleaned up we'll take you to the hospital and get you started on an antibiotic.'

When they were back at the rig, Janet went up to Steve. 'You missed a good one. The rookie got baptized.'

Steve grinned. 'And earned himself a new name in the process no doubt.'

'Aw, come on, you guys. I was only trying to help out,' Paul groaned.

Janet gave him a no-mercy grin. 'The long of it is — Paul 'Cats Like Me' Murdoch,' she told Steve. 'But I think plain old 'Cats' has a nice ring to it.'

'You're not going to tell anyone else about this, are you?' Had he been in the department longer, he would have known that the pleading tone in his voice would be his undoing. 'I'll never live it down.'

'Sure you will.' Rick slapped him on the shoulder. 'Ten or fifteen years after you retire, no one will remember anything about it.'

On the way to the hospital, Rick thought about his first house fire: how he'd gone inside so excited he never felt his feet hit the ground; how his captain had taken the hose and given him the nozzle; and how his heart had pounded so loudly he was sure everyone could hear. He'd spotted the fire right away — a deep orange glow against the far wall. He'd hit it with a smothering fog, but it hadn't been enough. He'd hit it again. And then again. Still it had burned as if fed by embers from hell.

He'd heard the truck crew cut into the roof. Someone had yelled from the back of the house that they'd found the fire. Confused, Rick had closed the nozzle handle, cutting off the water. The smoke had been drawn through the ventilating hole in the roof and the room had cleared as they'd backed out. Rick had stared slack-jawed at his fire: the neon light in a built-in fish tank.

His captain, a crusty man two years short of retirement, had told Rick that he'd just learned the most important lesson he would ever learn in the fire department. Never take anything for granted.

Rick had not entered a burning building since that day without reminding himself of that lesson.

13

Catherine leaned forward in Brian's Ford Explorer and waved to the guard at the gate. He smiled and pressed the button that started the heavy metal bars sliding along their tracks, letting them enter the Estates at Granite Bay. She glanced at the dashboard clock. They'd stayed at the hospital later than usual, and when Brian found out she'd decided to call a cab to take her home, he'd insisted on taking her himself. It would be two in the morning before he finally made it home.

'Did you call your mother and tell her you were going to be late?' She'd never asked Lynda's friends that kind of question. Just one of the differences three weeks with a daughter in the hospital had made. It seemed she worried about everything now, no longer leading a life where accidents always happened to other people.

He drove past the gate and started up the hill to Catherine's house. 'She's at the lake this week.'

'Don't you miss being there?' she asked carefully. She didn't know Brian well enough to understand his motives for being at the hospital every day, she only knew how grateful she was when she found him there. The last thing she wanted was to say or do something that might make him feel unwelcome. Lynda still wouldn't see any of her friends, including Wendy, her lifelong best friend. She even refused to talk to them on the phone. She said she wasn't ready and Catherine didn't push, confident that once Lynda was away from the hospital she'd start feeling more like herself again.

'Sometimes,' Brian admitted. 'But it wouldn't be the same.'

Her heart went out to him. 'It will be. You just need a little time.'

'You think that's all Lynda needs, too?'

She sighed. 'I wish I knew what she needs. I'd move heaven and earth to get it for her.' The one thing she knew for sure Lynda hadn't needed was Tom walking out on them.

'She's scared.'

'I know . . .'

'I keep telling her that no one is going to care how she looks, but she doesn't believe me.'

'She cares. When she looks in a mirror she doesn't recognize the girl looking back and she's afraid her friends won't, either.' She hadn't recognized what was happening until she'd gone to the meeting that night. She'd listened to other parents talk about their children and in bits and pieces heard them describe and explain Lynda's feelings.

'That's crazy.'

'To you and me maybe, but not to her. It's her head that was shaved, her body that's wrapped in bandages, her back that's scarred for life. We can't really know what she's going through, any more than she can know what it feels like for us to watch her going through it.'

'I thought about not coming so much.'

They were the words she'd feared hearing. 'But?'

'I couldn't stay away.' He pulled into the drive-way but left the car running. 'She keeps saying she doesn't want anyone there, but if I'm late, she always asks why.'

Brian comes because he feels sorry for Lynda. Catherine had hoped it was because they were friends. She felt a flash of protective, misplaced anger, but thankfully it was gone before she acted on it. Of all the men in Lynda's life, Brian had proved the most loyal; his motivation didn't matter. 'She'll be home soon.' The rest of her meaning — that he could move on with his life when that happened — was implied.

'Did you know she told me she didn't want me coming around when she left the hospital?' He ran his hands over the leather-covered steering wheel and stared straight ahead.

'No.' Catherine didn't know what else to say.

He turned and gave her a self-conscious grin. 'I told her I wouldn't be coming to see her, that I had a thing for older women.'

Another night, any other night, and Catherine would have laughed at the outrageous statement. Though she knew there wasn't enough truth in what he'd said for a con man to squeak past a lie detector, being dumped by Tom had left her just vulnerable enough to feel oddly flattered. 'And what did she say to that?'

'I don't remember.'

'That bad, huh?'

He laughed. 'She thinks you're pretty cool.'

'I think she's pretty cool, too.' Catherine reached for the door handle. 'Thanks for the ride.'

'Rick is picking you up tomorrow?'

She nodded. A month ago she'd barely known Brian and hadn't even met Rick. Now, with the exception of Gene, she counted on them more than men she'd known her entire life. Maybe she should stick to short-term relationships. They seemed to work out the best.

Catherine told Brian to drive carefully, said good-bye, and stood at the front door until he was out of the driveway. When his taillights disappeared around the corner, she sighed and went inside her empty, silent house. The security lights, a lamp in the family room and one in the back office, guided her to the hall closet where she put away her purse. A faint, lingering smell of cleaning products reminded her that it was Wednesday and that Juli, her three-times-a-week housekeeper, had been there to scrub and polish a house full of unused rooms.

Despite their decision not to live together until they were married, Tom was woven into Catherine's and Lynda's lives like the third strand of a braid. Everywhere she looked she saw him, from the humidor on the coffee table filled with his contraband Cuban cigars to the unread *Wall Street Journals* piling up by the sofa to the Bombay gin at the bar. She could feel his presence in the furniture he'd talked her into rearranging, the cupboards filled with his preferred brands of food, and even her own closet where his taste prevailed in the gifts he'd given her.

Seeking escape, if only for a moment, she grabbed her key and went to pick up the mail. Dry, warm air wrapped around her possessively as she stepped from her island of air-conditioning. Crickets, frogs, and air conditioning compressors created a familiar, discordant harmony. A full moon cast lurking shadows among the heritage oaks. As always when she ventured outside at night, Catherine felt a niggling warning. Her fear was more primal than reasonable, instigated and perpetuated by reports of yet another mountain lion being sighted in yet another foothill community, reports that became lead stories on slow news days.

Wild turkeys, brought to California and released by hunters, provided the lure for the half dozen sightings they'd had in their area. The turkeys freely wandered the manicured, acre-sized lawns during the day, a cross between curiosity and nuisance, tolerated by most, sworn at by others.

Catherine had never spotted the mountain lion that visited them periodically, but she'd seen his pawprints at the koi pond and secretly liked that something wild and free existed in her ordered life. Without the mountain lion she would enter the night without listening, look into the shadows without seeing, and never know the kind of wariness that made her forget, if only for the time she walked to the mailbox, that her ordinary, everyday life was falling down around her like windows in an earthquake.

She waited until she was back inside again to look at the inch-thick stack of mail. Most of it was for Lynda, cards and letters from friends determined to get through to her one way or another. The rest was an assortment of flyers and bills. The flyers went into the garbage, the bills into an ever growing stack she promised herself to get to one day. Soon.

She looked at the stack and decided it had better be damn soon. Right then, preferably. Instead she went to the refrigerator, took out the bottle of chardonnay she'd opened the night before, and poured herself a glass. She was headed for the back deck when the phone rang.

'Don't you ever pick up your messages?'

Her mother. Just about the last person she wanted to talk to. 'I'm fine, Mom. How are you? And what are you doing up at this hour?'

'The hour doesn't seem to bother Tom. He's called three times tonight looking for you. He said he left half a dozen messages on your machine. I know it's none of my business, but have you two had a fight?'

'Can we talk about this tomorrow?'

'So you did have a fight.'

'Mom — please. I really don't want to talk about Tom right now. I'm tired and I want to go to bed. I have a big day ahead of me tomorrow.' There it was. She'd given her mother an opening.

'Do you want me to come over?' she asked, her voice gentle with understanding.

The kindness nearly undid Catherine. 'No, I'm okay. I just need some time alone.'

'Well, I'm here if you need me. Anytime. Don't worry about waking me up. I'm in the middle of a great book that I can't seem to put down, so I'll probably be up all night anyway.'

As much as Phyllis Martin loved to read, there was no way she would ever let a book keep her up all night. She relished the daylight too much and would never give in to a nap. 'I love you, Mom.'

'Oh, baby, I love you, too.' She waited several seconds and added, 'This doesn't have anything to do with Lynda, does it? I'm sorry, I had to ask.'

'Lynda's okay. Actually, she's better than okay, she's fantastic. I think my daughter and I are on the path to becoming friends.'

'I told you it would happen. Wait long enough, keep the path clear, and mothers and daughters will find each other eventually.'

Catherine took a sip of wine. She let the liquid linger on her tongue, taking a second to savor the delicate flavors. Tonight it wasn't the flavor of the wine she was after. The sip was followed by a large swallow. She tucked the portable phone under her chin, took the bottle in one hand and her glass in the other, and went outside to sit on the deck.

Settling into a chair, she asked, 'Are you still leaving on Friday?' Her mother made a yearly pilgrimage to Washington where she and several of her old sorority sisters rented a house on Bainbridge Island. They took the house for a month with no set arrival or departure date.

'I thought I would — unless you need me here. I'm not staying as long this time, though. I want to be around for Lynda's homecoming. We should do something to make it really special.'

'Let's wait a while before we make any plans.' First the car and then a party. Catherine filled her glass again, leaned back, and stared at the flood of lights that filled the valley between her and Sacramento. Heat rose in undulating waves from the acres of concrete and asphalt that now blanketed rich farmland, distorting the lights, making them blink like distant stars.

'So what are you going to do instead?'

'I don't know,' she said, hearing the weariness in her own voice.

'What's wrong, Catherine? Is there something you're afraid to tell me?'

'I'm just worn down, Mom,' she said evasively. 'I'll sound better in the morning. After I've had some sleep.'

'I'm sorry. I said I wouldn't push. You'll tell me when you're ready.'

'Thanks.'

'Well, I guess I'd better get back to my book and let you call Tom.'

'I'll talk to you tomorrow.' Catherine pressed the Off button and put the phone on the table. At least she'd been warned that Tom was looking for her again. Now she knew not to answer the phone.

Later, as she put the last of the wine in the refrigerator and washed her glass, her gaze fell on the stack of unpaid bills. How could she have been so stupid to let Tom talk her into quitting her job? Her piddling paycheck — as Tom had called it — had made the difference between tight and comfortable for her and Lynda every month. They could make it without that money, but just barely.

In a moment of excitement over his upcoming freedom and guilt over her discovering him in bed with another woman, Jack had agreed to her attorney's wildly optimistic divorce settlement proposal with only minor changes. He'd regretted his generosity from the moment the first month's funds were transferred from his account to

165

hers, and had taken her back to court in an unsuccessful attempt to get it reduced. Of all the good wishes that had come her way with the news that she was getting married again, none had been more enthusiastic than Jack's.

If there was a silver lining to the day's events, it was the prospect of telling Jack that the wedding was off. Catherine let herself luxuriate in the prospect for a moment, aware it wouldn't last. She hated being dependent on Jack since their divorce, and had looked forward to the day the alimony would end almost as much as he had. It didn't matter that the settlement came wrapped with self-righteous claims that she deserved what she received from Jack; she couldn't escape the fact that he earned the money that paid her bills. When they were married she'd felt she more than earned her share of the income, the way she would have with Tom.

She lived in financial bondage. She'd talked herself into believing Tom represented freedom. But all he'd really offered was a new cell. Funny how the tarnish of facts diminished whatever glow of love still remained.

Alone in the dark, silent house with only her thoughts for company, Catherine struggled for answers.

How could she have fallen in love with a

man like Tom? What flaw in her personality, what deep-seated need, what compulsion had come into play to blind her to the real man inside the stunningly handsome package?

Of everything she'd lost that night, her confidence had suffered the most damaging blow. Twice she'd given her heart to men who'd abandoned her. Who bore the real blame for their actions — her or them?

One of her father's oft-used homilies came to her. *Fool me once, shame on you. Fool me twice, shame on me.*

She caught her breath in a quick sob.

She was alone. Again. The joy that came with knowing there was someone to share her day with was gone. For years she'd tried to keep *alone* from meaning *lonely* and had never found the formula, finally accepting that she functioned best as half of a pair. What irony that she lacked the ability to find someone who felt the same.

At least she understood her failings now. She wouldn't try again. Once she'd believed in love over self-preservation, but the pain demanded too much, stole too many years.

She would go back to work because she had to, but this time it wouldn't be just a job she went after; she would find a career even if she had to go back to school. She'd fill her days with the stimulation and challenge of making money the way Jack and Tom and Gene and every other man she knew did. To hell with the nights. She would find a way to get through them until the loneliness became as natural and unimposing as breathing.

Catherine turned out the lights and headed for the stairs and her bedroom. Her hand gripped the railing and she froze. She couldn't go up. Not yet. Tom had never spent an entire night in her bed, but she had imagined what it would be like to wake up and find him there so many times that it had become habit.

She went into the living room and curled up on the sofa. Her first test in the new independent world she planned to create for herself and she'd failed. Hardly an auspicious beginning.

She'd do better tomorrow. She had to. Broken hearts got in the way of everyday life, and Lynda needed her.

The telephone rang. Once, twice, three, four times before the machine picked up. Catherine listened as her own voice cheerfully announced the daily update on Lynda and then invited the caller to leave a message. She expectantly held her breath at the tone — waiting for Tom's voice to tell her he'd made a terrible mistake and beg her forgiveness — all the while knowing there was nothing he could say that could mend the tear in their relationship. Knowing how he felt, she couldn't trust him not to hurt her daughter, and Lynda came first. She always had, she always would. It wasn't sacrifice or commitment — it simply was.

The line stayed open for several seconds. Finally there was a click, a defining moment of finality.

Catherine turned her face into the pillow and silently wept.

14

Rick rang the doorbell to Catherine's house, then stepped to the side and stuffed his hands in the back pockets of his jeans. He studied the impressive double doors as he waited. They were made of hundreds of pieces of beveled glass leaded together in an art deco pattern and framed in a dark, rich mahogany. Stunning in concept and execution, the doors were museum-quality work that seemed oddly out of place in the modified ranch style house.

Without question, the easily breached entry came with an alarm system as impressive as the rest of the house. People who lived in gated communities with full-time guards placed a high value on security for themselves and their property. They believed they'd earned the right to flaunt the results of their hard work, but only to those of their choosing. Casual observers were not invited or tolerated.

The door opened just as Rick was about to ring the bell again. 'I'm sorry,' Catherine said. 'I was on the phone with the insurance agent. Please come in.'

She had on a pale blue cotton dress, sleeveless and simple, cut above the knee and fitted to her hips as if it had been made just for her. Her sandals were woven leather, her legs bare, and her hair done up in a twist with the ends sticking out. A narrow gold band circled her wrist, but the engagement ring she'd had on the night before was missing. Rick took it all in with a glance and then forced himself to look elsewhere — to the Persian carpet that protected the marble entry and the crystal chandelier that hung overhead at precisely the right height to reflect through the glass doors at night.

'Nice,' he commented.

'Yeah, it is,' she said without enthusiasm. 'I liked the view, Jack liked the house. Or so he thought. As soon as we moved in, he decided it wasn't what he'd wanted after all. Not big enough. Which is why I'm still here and he's in that hotel-like thing he had built in Carmichael.'

From the outside, Rick had judged the house to be between four and five thousand square feet. Jack must run with some crowd if that wasn't enough to impress them.

He followed her through the foyer and into the family room, which opened to the kitchen. A wall of windows overlooked the Sacramento Valley — at least what was visible through the haze. 'What did you find out about the car?'

'The radiator leaks, so it can't be driven. Tom's agent was going to have it towed to one of their contract garages but I told him I had my own mechanic.' She grinned sheepishly. 'And then I couldn't remember the name you gave me so I said I'd have to call him back.' She moved to the kitchen and took a cup out of the cupboard. 'Coffee?'

He shouldn't. He had a dozen things he had to get done that day and coffee with Catherine wasn't one of them. 'Please — black.'

She poured from a stainless steel carafe and handed him the cup. 'When I talked to Tom this morning I told him I either confiscated his car until mine was fixed or he made arrangements for me to pick up a rental car.' This time she smiled. 'He has a Corvette. Want to guess which option he chose?'

Rick sat on one of the barstools at the kitchen counter and tasted the coffee. It was good. Better than good — the best he'd had in a long time. He refused to consider it might be more the company than the brew.

'Considering the day you had yesterday, you're in an awfully good mood this morning.'

'I know, I thought the same thing. It's

amazing what a little self-righteous anger can do for you. I woke up so mad at Tom for what he's done that I couldn't think about anything else.'

If she'd slept at all, it hadn't been for long. Her makeup helped, but he could still see the dark circles under her eyes. 'He's an idiot,' Rick said without thinking. Seeing her surprised reaction, he quickly added, 'I'm sorry. I had no right to say that.'

'Why did you?'

'Because I can be tactless at times.'

'That's not what I mean. I want to know why you think Tom's an idiot.'

If he told her the truth, he'd be stepping over a boundary they needed to maintain their professional relationship. He was there to help Lynda. To go beyond that, to get involved personally, would compromise his work and the work of the Burn Association. 'He could have saved himself and everyone else a lot of trouble if he'd called a cab last night.'

'Oh . . . '

It was plainly not what she'd wanted him to say. She was in pain and looking for an analgesic, not rationale. He changed the subject. 'Has Lynda let any of her friends come to see her yet?'

'Brian's the only one.'

'It might be a good idea to start encouraging her to see one or two of them. The longer she puts it off, the harder it's going to be.'

'I'll talk to her about it today.' She picked up a sponge and wiped an already immaculate counter. 'I shouldn't be keeping you here like this. I'm sure you have a lot of things you'd like to get done today.'

'Nothing that can't wait.'

'I'll get my purse and we can leave.'

Rick took his cup to the sink, rinsed it out, and put it in the dishwasher. While he waited he went to the window and looked out at the acre-sized lot. The landscaping was as lush and expensive-looking as the house. A redwood walkway led to a free-form pool at the bottom of the hill. Fed by a moss-rock waterfall, the pool appeared more natural than man-made, an effect often attempted by the pool builders in the area, but rarely accomplished.

The maintenance on this place would take half his salary. Add taxes and insurance and there wouldn't be anything left for little necessities like food.

'I can get lost in the view,' Catherine said, coming up to stand next to him. 'Especially at night when you can't see the pollution.'

'I was admiring the pool.'

'They did an amazing job, didn't they? Lynda and her friends used to be in it all the time, but then she started high school and got into cheerleading and was hardly ever home. Maybe now . . . ' She looked up at Rick. 'I wish I knew what to expect. So far everything I thought she might do or feel has been wrong.'

'Such as?'

'Cutting herself off from her friends. I used to tease her that I wouldn't recognize her without a phone pressed to her ear.'

'Have you talked to the counselor?'

She shook her head. 'I wanted to see if she would come around on her own. But she's running out of time. She'll be home next week and there's no way I'm going to lie for her if someone calls or shows up at the front door.'

'Do you want me to talk to her?'

She looked at him. 'I'm desperate. I'll take all the help I can get.'

Just as Rick started to answer, he caught a hint of a faint, flowery fragrance. Catherine must have put on perfume when she went to get her purse. Drawn by the captivating smell, he had to consciously keep himself from leaning closer. For an instant his imagination led him where he had no right to be and he pictured what it would be like to hold her in his arms, to fill his lungs with her essence.

The transition of his thoughts startled him. He needed time to think, to reason through his feelings.

Time to get his head on straight again. If there was one sure way to screw up his work as a volunteer with the Burn Association, this was it. But it was more than that. The work and reputation of the entire organization was on the line with every volunteer.

He moved away from Catherine and folded his arms across his chest for added insurance. 'What Lynda's feeling is natural. All kids go through it to one degree or another. In her mind it doesn't matter how we see her, or how her friends see her, it's how she sees herself. Sometimes that image comes from a mirror, sometimes it comes from an unguarded look from a clerk in a store.'

'Thank God for Brian. At least she knows there's one person her age who isn't turned off by her burns.'

Rick felt her looking at him and chanced looking back. Her eyes were filled with the hope he'd come to recognize in parents of burned children. They desperately needed to believe everything would work out, that the scars wouldn't be as bad as they were told to expect, that the plastic surgeon would work miracles on missing noses and ears and eyebrows and lips, and that strangers wouldn't look at their child with dread.

Acceptance came in small, seemingly inconsequential miracles: the first joke, a tear shed over a sad movie instead of pain, anger at an injustice that had nothing to do with being burned. These were the moments when the scars became secondary to the personality, when the lost child was, at last, discovered again by her parents.

'Lynda thinks Brian comes to stay with her because he feels sorry for her,' Rick said.

'She told you that?'

'In a dozen different ways. Just like she lets me know that she thinks I'm there because it's my job and that you and the rest of the family come because you have to. Right now it's what she believes in her heart and there's no way we're going to convince her any differently.'

'Then how do I help her?'

'You keep doing exactly what you've been doing. When she's ready we'll arrange for her to talk to someone neutral — someone who's been through what she's going through, who she can spill her guts to or yell at or feel sorry for herself around and not have to worry about apologizing to later.'

Catherine studied him for a long time. 'I'm

embarrassed to say this, but I think I finally understand what you do and why I need you. More importantly, why Lynda needs you. Why we all do.'

Rick smiled. 'I told you it would take a while.'

'There's so much I don't know about helping her to become whole again.'

'I don't have all the answers, and some of the ones I do have could be wrong for Lynda. What I do know is how to find someone to help her or you if you need it.'

'I know you told me once, but I've forgotten — how long is your tour of duty with us?'

There was something about the way she asked that made him feel hopeful and concerned at the same time. 'A year.'

'That's a big chunk out of your life.'

'You'll be surprised how fast it passes.'

The phone rang. Catherine ignored it. 'I suppose we should get going. I had Tom arrange for a rental car in Roseville so you wouldn't have to take me all the way downtown.'

'You didn't have to do that.'

She looked at him, not the quick glance reserved for acquaintances, but one that was long and warm, for a special friend. 'Do you know the expression that nothing is ever taken away without something given in return?'

'I've heard it.'

'It was one of my father's. Not original. None of his sayings were. He collected them instead of baseball cards and had one he could whip out for any occasion.' She stopped talking long enough to smile. 'I'm not sure I understand it yet, but I believe you're our blessing, the balancing weight on the scale for me and Lynda and what she's going through.'

Rick had been called a lot of things in his life, but 'blessing' was a first. 'Thanks.' He hesitated. 'But if you don't mind, could we keep this blessing stuff between us? I wouldn't want something like that getting around the department.'

She flushed. 'Sorry — I was thinking out loud again. I didn't mean to embarrass you.'

'I'm not embarrassed.' But he was. Compliments always embarrassed him.

'No more so than a cat that misses a jump and tries to act cool about it?' she teased.

'Okay, maybe a little.'

She dug through her purse for her keys. 'After all the kids and parents you've taken through the program, I find it hard to believe you still blush when someone says something nice about you.'

This teasing was a side of Catherine he

179

hadn't seen before. 'It's just that I haven't had time to prepare. Most people save the outrageous compliments until they know me better.'

She laughed. 'That's encouraging.'

The phone rang again. Rick was amazed at how easily she ignored it. 'How do you do that?' he asked, following her to the front door.

'I gave the hospital my private number. It's the same one the family uses when they have to reach me. If I answered all the calls that come in on this line, I wouldn't have time for anything else.'

She locked the front door and, as they made their way to the truck, Rick asked, 'You're not going to set the alarm?'

'It isn't connected. It used to go off on its own all the time so I had it disarmed when Jack moved out. I'd rather take my chances with a thief than have that thing scaring me to death in the middle of the night.'

'I have a visiting dog that takes care of my place on a sometime basis. The way I figure it, I'm safe as long as the thief shows up in a rabbit suit and tries to steal dog food.'

Catherine laughed. 'We had a dog like that when I was growing up. My father bought her to take pheasant hunting. They went out one time and somehow that dog convinced a man who'd spent his entire life killing birds that it was a dumb idea. Dad stunned us all when he came home and sold his guns and kept the dog.'

Rick held the truck door for Catherine, then went around to get in his side. Where before he'd appreciated the truck for its heavy-duty springs, powerful motor, and large hauling capacity, all he saw now were the dents and scratches.

By the time he was backing out of the driveway he wasn't sure whether he was more upset with himself for caring how the truck looked or for caring what Catherine thought about it.

The traffic on Douglas Boulevard was worse than usual with boaters headed for Folsom Lake and an ambulance responding to an accident at one of the intersections in front of them. Rick cut off on Barton and then over to Olive Ranch. He pointed north on Barton as they turned. 'That's the way to my place.'

'How far?'

'Couple of miles. I'm off Laird.'

'I looked at some property up there a couple of years ago when I was thinking about moving,' Catherine said. 'I had it in my head that I wanted to be someplace where I could step outside and not see my neighbor looking back at me.'

'With me it's cars. I wanted to get away from the sound of them.'

'And did you?'

'For a while. But I knew it wouldn't last. Auburn's creeping down the hill and Roseville's creeping up. I'm right in the middle with large tracts of undeveloped land on all four sides. They just subdivided some high-dollar lots down the road, so it won't be long before we hear the sounds of building instead of birds.'

'Sounds ominous.'

'Yeah, I hate like hell to think I have to give up my little corner of paradise just so someone else can have theirs.'

She laughed. 'Well put.'

Rick turned left on Sierra College Boulevard and then right on Douglas again. The rental agency was behind a video store. Catherine had her door open before Rick turned off the engine.

She turned to him. 'Will I see you later?'

His immediate thought was to tell her yes. He had his mouth open to do so when it hit him that he had no reason to see her again that day — at least no reason that had anything to do with his work with Lynda. 'Probably not. I have some things I've been putting off that I should get done.'

If she was disappointed, it didn't show. She got out and lifted her purse strap over her shoulder. 'Tomorrow then.'

Hot, dry air swept through the cab, a giant hand stealing the air-conditioning, warning him it was not a day for a sane man to be pounding nails. 'I'm working.'

'Oh . . . I must have misread that calendar you gave me. I thought you didn't go back to work for four days.'

'Normally I wouldn't. I'm paying back a guy who took a shift for me last year.'

She looked confused. 'I just found out this morning that Lynda's friends are planning a surprise party for her when she gets home on Friday. I know she'd like you to be there. Can you come?'

He wanted to say yes, told himself to say no, and answered, 'Maybe. I'll have to let you know.'

She nodded. 'Well, thanks again.'

'You're welcome.' He waited until she was inside, a stupid, expectant smile on his face in case she happened to turn around one last time. Once safe, he let out a string of profanity that would have made his crew blush.

After ten years and more bad dates than he wanted to remember, he'd finally happened across a woman who made him smile just thinking about her, one who made him think of possibilities instead of roadblocks.

Shit, how could he have been so stupid? How could he have let this happen? Catherine Miller was less than twenty-four hours out of a relationship with a man she'd loved enough to agree to marry. There was no way she was ready to start dating again, even if it were possible for him to ask.

Which it wasn't.

She needed time. Lots of it. And he would have to be completely detached from the Burn Association before he could let her know how he felt. To do that now would mean leaving her and Lynda without the help they needed, just when they needed it the most.

Hell. Some choice. Walk out on Catherine now, on Tom's heels, and come back later telling her it had been so they could be together in the end; or stick it out for a year and try to pull off a cool, strictly professional interest. To do that he would have to back off — way off — her personal life. He'd already spent too much time at the hospital. His role in this process was as conduit for the parent, not interactive participant. At least that was the way it was supposed to be. The way it had always been. Until now.

Damn. A whole year? No way. He'd never pull it off. He was only a little better at hiding his emotions than Blue. Give him a tail and he'd be wagging it every time he saw Catherine.

15

Lynda stood in front of the mirror and adjusted the collar on her shirt for the tenth time that morning. When the collar stayed up, it hid the bandages at the back of her neck; when it fell down, it looked like she was wearing a really ugly turtleneck under her shirt. Only crazy people wore turtlenecks in the middle of summer in California. Or burned people. But who would know something like that?

She turned sideways to see how fat the tube bandages made her look. They went all the way around her, from her neck to her thighs, but the shirt and pants were so big she could have been a size twenty and no one would know the difference.

Leaning closer to the mirror, she pulled on one side of her bangs and fluffed the other. Then she adjusted her cap and her hair went back the way it had been. It was funny how fast she'd gotten used to her hair being short. Not the shaved part, but the bangs. The rest was past the spiky stubble stage and growing into a soft fuzz that her physical therapist said should be long enough to curl by Christmas.

She didn't care about the curling part. She just wanted her hair long enough to hide the scars on the back of her neck.

A now familiar double tap on the door let her know Brian was outside. He waited a few seconds, giving her time to cover up if she needed to, and then came in.

He had on a new shirt, at least one she'd never seen before, and was wearing chino slacks instead of his usual jeans. 'You look nice,' she said.

'Thanks. So do you.'

'Yeah, right.' She held out her arms to show him how big the shirt she'd borrowed from her father was on her. 'Straight out of *Cosmo*.'

He grinned. 'Maybe more *GQ*, but still pretty cool. Who knows, you could be starting a new fashion trend.'

She smiled back, which ruined her attempt to look put out. 'What are you doing here? I thought you were going to stop by the house later.'

He sat on the metal frame chair next to her, hanging one leg over the side, the other straight out. 'I had to drop some stuff off for my dad. His usual gopher moved to another hole — one with better benefits.'

'So you're working for your dad now?' she asked carefully. She knew he'd have to find an excuse for not coming to see her when she left the hospital and was curious what it would be. At least being tied up with a job was reasonable, something she could talk herself into believing.

'I tried that last summer. Mom said there was no way she'd ever let one of us kids work for Dad again. I'm just helping out until he can find someone else.'

'When did you say football practice started?' If he couldn't come up with a reason on his own, she would help. Anything was better than a lame excuse that she couldn't pretend was true.

'Not for a couple of weeks yet.' He stared at her, his eyes soft and warm, as if he could read her mind. 'You wouldn't be looking for a reason to get rid of me, would you?'

'Why would I do that?' she asked defensively.

'I don't know. You tell me.'

Postponing her answer, she arched her back and shifted her shoulders, going through familiar motions he understood. For days now her back and arms and neck felt as if she'd become the permanent food source for a swarm of mosquitoes. Everyone she asked told her it was part of the healing process and would go on for eighteen months or more.

'The itching thing bothering you again?' Brian asked.

'Driving me crazy.'

'You want me to get the nurse?'

She shook her head. 'They already gave me a Benadryl.'

He shifted forward, his hands on his knees. 'I got you a coming-home present.'

'You did?' She was more pleased than she should have been. Brian was always doing things like that for her, the way she imagined a big brother would do if she had one. Or a really good friend. Like Wendy. Only Wendy wasn't just a good friend, she was Lynda's best friend. Or at least she had been before Lynda had acted like such a shit and refused to see her or even talk to her on the phone. She missed Wendy. And she really, really needed to talk to her. There were just some things you didn't tell a guy, even a guy like Brian. Like how sometimes, when she was alone at night and all she could hear were the machines that spied on her and the nurses gossiping about stuff that didn't interest her, she let herself imagine what it would be like if Brian were more than a friend.

'It's in the car,' Brian said. 'I'm saving it for when you get home.'

'At least give me a hint.'

'It's round. And that's all I'm going to say, so don't even try to get me to tell you anything else.'

Her heart in her throat, she let herself believe for one sweet second that he'd bought her a ring. Not an engagement ring, she wasn't that desperate or dumb. But something simple, something that said they were more than friends. The impossibly crazy second over, she played along. 'Should I guess?'

'Guess all you want.'

'Will you tell me if I get it?'

'Nope.'

'Not fair.'

He laughed and reached for her hand. 'What wouldn't be fair is if I let you ruin the surprise.'

He'd never taken her hand before. He'd touched her cheek when she was crying, and messed with her hair when it was first cut, and he'd played around with her cap, helping her find where it looked best, but he'd never purposely done anything this intimate. Lynda didn't know what to do. Should she just stand there with her hand in his or take it back and mess with her hair and pretend it never happened?

Brian caught her gaze. 'I need to tell you something about today. I'm not sure — '

The door opened and her mother came in. Lynda let go of Brian's hand as if they'd been caught doing something wrong. She didn't know whether she was grateful or furious with her mother for the interruption.

'Ready to get out of this place?' Catherine asked cheerfully.

'I thought you wanted to say good-bye to everyone.' Her mother had spent half of last night telling her about the presents she'd bought for nurses, therapists, doctors, and social workers, describing them in detail and wondering aloud if she'd made the right choices. She'd asked a lot of questions like that since Tom had left, and Lynda didn't know what to do about it. Her mother used to think she had all the answers. For everything.

With all those deliveries to make, Lynda had figured they wouldn't get out of there before noon. It wasn't even ten.

'I did, but I cut the speeches short because I knew you were waiting.'

'I haven't told Ray good-bye yet.'

Catherine smiled at Brian. 'Do you think we could be making too big a deal out of this good-bye stuff when Lynda is coming back for physical therapy and a dressing change in two days?'

'My dad taught me not to answer questions like that.'

Catherine laughed. 'Smart man.'

The door opened again. Jack offered a

smile as big as the presentation bouquet of roses and orchids he carried in his arms. 'How's my girl today?' He swept into the room and gave Lynda a kiss. 'Ready to blow this joint?'

Catherine stared at the ostentatious display of flowers dwarfing her daughter and at the tight lines around Jack's mouth when he stopped smiling. They'd run into each other the night before when he dropped off one of his shirts for Lynda. Uncharacteristically, he'd been the one to suggest the shirt when Lynda told him she needed something light and loose to wear until her back was healed and the bandages gone. He'd started the strange turnaround the day after she and Tom broke up. She'd been suspicious at first, believing Tom and Jack had formed some unholy alliance. But Jack's reaction to her announcement that the engagement was off was too genuine to be fake.

Jack swore, as she'd known he would, and then grew quiet, which she'd expected, too. It was funny how well she still knew him, even after the transformation he claimed to have gone through when he hit forty. What she hadn't anticipated was the sincere expression of regret that things hadn't worked out for her and Tom. For once his feelings didn't come across as completely self-serving, which seemed to surprise him as much as it did her.

'I didn't know you were planning to be here this morning,' Catherine said.

'I didn't either,' he admitted. 'And then I realized there was nowhere else I would rather be.'

Catherine looked at her daughter. Lynda was fighting a smile, afraid to seem too pleased, too vulnerable to her father's capricious affection. 'Do you have to get back right away or can you stay for a few minutes? Lynda and Brian were about to say good-bye to a friend.'

He looked at his watch. 'I have some time.' To Lynda he said, 'You two go ahead. I'll be here when you get back — if you're not too long.'

Lynda seemed unsure what to do with the flowers. Catherine took them from her and laid them on the bed. 'They'll keep a while longer.'

'We'll be in Ray's room if anyone is looking for us.' At the door she turned to her father. 'Thank you for the flowers. And for remembering.'

When she was gone, Jack wiped his hands across his forehead. 'Am I really that bad, or is that just the way she sees me? How could she think I would forget this is the day she goes home?'

'She doesn't know what to think where you're concerned, Jack. You're an amazing, caring father one minute and then disappear from her life for weeks at a time. She's afraid to trust you.'

'I get busy . . . '

'Please — let's not get into this today. You're who you are. Nothing is going to change that.'

'What's this? No lecture on fatherhood? Not even going to tell me about all I'm missing by not being around more?' He put up his hand to stop her answer. 'I'm sorry. That was uncalled for. And unfair. You've never accused me of anything that wasn't true.'

Apologizing was not Jack's style. He'd come close a couple of times, but not once in all the years she'd known him had he come right out and said he was sorry for anything. 'What's going on here?'

He looked at her and then away, staring at the wall as if an original Monet had suddenly appeared. 'It seems I'm going to be a father again.'

She caught her breath. She hadn't even known he was seeing anyone seriously. 'When?'

'Six months, give or take.'

'How long have you known?' She didn't

know why it mattered, only that it did.

'A week or so. I went to Michelle's house after I left here.' His mouth curved in a smile filled with irony. 'I was looking for a quiet port in the storm after the bomb you dropped on me about you and Tom.'

'How do you feel about it?' she asked carefully.

'Trapped. At least that was the way I felt in the beginning. This morning . . . I don't know. I'm forty-two years old. I keep thinking how old I'll be when the kid graduates college. I'll look like his grandfather. Hell, I'll be old enough to *be* his grandfather.'

She didn't have it in her to feel sorry for him. Her first thoughts were for Lynda, and what it would mean to have to share what little time Jack had to devote to a child. 'I take it Michelle wants to have the baby?'

'She's ecstatic — said she's always wanted a baby and is willing to raise it alone if I'm not interested.'

Jack had an amazing knack for finding willing, malleable women. 'It's not as easy as the sitcoms make it out to be. You should tell her to talk to a few single mothers before she makes any more statements like that.'

He studied her for a long time. 'You and Lynda seem to get along okay.'

She snapped. 'By whose yardstick are you

measuring our lives? How do you know what your daughter feels when she's cheerleading at a football game and looks up in the stands and I'm the only parent looking back? What about the school play you missed last year? The soccer games? And that's the easy stuff, Jack. All the weekends you were supposed to take her but let 'business' get in the way, all the times you told her you would call when you were out of state and then forgot, all the generic presents you gave her because you had no idea what your daughter was really like — you can't even begin to imagine what you've done to her self-confidence through your casual, insidious neglect.'

She threw her hands up in frustration. 'I'm giving you the lecture I just said I wouldn't give you. How do you do this to me?'

He ignored her question. 'How am I supposed to know what she's like or what she needs when I never see her?'

'Precisely,' Catherine said wearily.

'We've had this discussion before, haven't we?'

'More times than I want to remember.'

'What do I say?'

It didn't surprise her that he didn't know. 'You promise to try harder.'

'Obviously I don't succeed.'

'Obviously.'

196

'There's no reason to believe I would be any different the second time around?' he said.

'None that I can think of.'

'Still — it's not like I have a choice whether I want to be a father again. Michelle told me she's going to have the baby with or without me.'

'This is crazy, Jack. I'm the last person you should be talking to about your impending fatherhood. I can't even find a generous spot in my heart to be happy for you.'

'No, but you will. You're the most generous person I know. Right now you're worried about Lynda and there's nothing I can say that will convince you I intend to be a better father to her from now on. But I will. You'll see.'

'Don't do that. I don't want to count on you. I'd rather go on thinking you're a son of a bitch and letting you surprise me the rare times you do something nice.'

'I'm sorry.'

Another apology? Twice in one day? She waited for the bolt of lightning, the clap of thunder. 'We're having a surprise welcome home party for Lynda.' She looked at her watch. 'It starts in an hour and a half.'

'I can't. I have a meeting. I have — ' He stopped and frowned. It was as if his words had been automatic and now, today, for the first time he actually heard how hollow they sounded. 'I'll be there.'

Catherine felt a flutter in her chest, a feeling she remembered but didn't recognize right away. And then she knew what it was: hope. She didn't welcome the feeling. All her adult life hope had led to disappointment. She'd learned to live without the first and she sure as hell didn't need the latter.

'Come if you can. I won't count on you. And I won't say anything to Lynda.'

'I guess I deserve that.'

'Guess?'

'All right. I do deserve it. But I'm going to change. From now on she's going to know that she can count on me.'

Catherine only looked at him.

'I've said that before, too, haven't I?'

Damned by his own words. Catherine almost sighed with relief. She wouldn't have to worry about hope dying again. It was already gone.

16

Brian tied the back of Lynda's gown and fitted her mask over her cap, adjusting the protective clothes they wore when they visited Ray. He started to reach for her shoulders to turn her around for a mock inspection when he remembered he couldn't touch her there. Or at her waist. Or at the small of her back.

After being in the hospital with her for three and a half weeks, knowing where he could and couldn't touch her should have been a given, automatic even. But he always forgot. At least for an instant. It was because she hardly ever complained. He'd overheard a nurse telling Catherine that Lynda was in constant pain, only the amount changed, depending on when she'd received her drugs. He liked to think he would be as strong, but he wasn't so sure.

He'd never known anyone like her. His friends, especially the ones on the football team, were always getting knocked around and hurt. They were babies compared to Lynda.

'You're done,' he said. His reward was a behind-the-mask smile that reached her eyes.

'Want me to do you?' she asked.

She was always saying things like that, stuff to which he had an immediate smart-ass answer, but there was no way he'd ever give one. Not with her. She might be one of the top students at her school, but she had a lot to learn about guys and how they thought.

He shrugged into the gown and turned his back to her. 'I rented some videos for tonight. Thought we could veg out on your mom's couch and eat popcorn and celebrate your freedom.'

'What did you get?'

'*Halloween* — one, two, and three.'

Her eyes widened in disbelief. 'You're kidding.'

He groaned. 'Don't tell me you're one of those people who don't appreciate *Halloween*.'

'Ugh.'

'None of them? Not even the first one where — '

'I'd rather watch the Three Stooges.'

He gave her a triumphant grin. 'As a matter of fact, they were all out of *Halloween* so I picked up five Three Stooges movies. We're gonna have ourselves a Three Stooges marathon.'

'You did not. No one really likes those guys. They just say they do.'

He loved her laugh. It was never forced or phony and always made him feel good about himself, especially when he was the one who'd prompted it. 'Okay — you win. You get to pick.' He leaned close. 'This time.'

'Anything? Even a chick flick?'

'You're pushing it.'

'I know the perfect one. No, make it two.'

'I can hardly wait.'

Again her eyes crinkled in a smile. '*While You Were Sleeping.*'

'And?' he asked warily.

'*There's Something About Mary.*'

He laughed. 'I think I could handle that.' He put his mask over his face and reached for the door, pushing it open and holding it for her while she went inside.

Ray glanced up from the television when he heard them enter. 'Hey — how's it going?' He spoke slowly, each word formed with effort and paid for in pain. 'Today's the big day, huh?'

Brian stood next to Lynda so that Ray could see them without having to move his head. They'd been dropping in on Ray for three weeks, and Brian kept waiting for him to show improvement the way Lynda had; not as dramatically, perhaps, but at least indicating he was getting better. But he always looked the same, no better, no worse. After his grafting surgeries, the drugs left him struggling to remember sentences he'd spoken only minutes before. Brian and Lynda would fill in the blanks later, adding dialogue that never happened until it became so outlandish Ray caught on and they all laughed.

Swathed in bandages that covered most of his body, he looked like a mummy in the making. In the beginning they'd talked about easy things — school and football and girls. Lately they'd talked about what would happen when Ray left the hospital, how he'd live with the aunt he hardly knew in a town he'd never visited and how hard it would be to make new friends looking the way he did.

Ray's girlfriend had come a couple of times and then told him her mother didn't want her making the long drive by herself anymore. Friends had come, too, but rarely more than once. When Lynda found out, she started dropping in several times a day. Brian always stopped by a final time before he left at night, sometimes only staying a minute or two, once staying over an hour.

He and Lynda tried to do what they could, but they weren't Ray's real friends or his family. They had no history, no shared memories, and Brian sometimes wondered if they made things worse. They were past visiting because they felt sorry for him, but there was no denying that's why they'd started.

Lynda gently laid her hand on Ray's arm, as she did every time she was with him. 'I can hardly wait to get out of this place and back to my own room at home.'

'Yeah, but she's coming back day after tomorrow,' Brian said.

'Three times a week. Can you believe it? I guess they don't trust me to do the exercises at home. At least I'll get to see you. And Brian said he's going to bring me once in a while so he can see you, too.'

Ray looked at Brian. 'You know those books on tape you were telling me about?'

'The textbooks or the novels?'

'Both. I was talking to the nurse about them and she said she'd see what she could find out. I was wondering if you would mind telling her about them again — in case she forgets.'

'I'll bring you the ones I have at home to get you started. That way you won't have to wait.'

'Thanks . . . I'm going crazy watching so much television.'

'I got hooked on one of the soaps,' Lynda sheepishly admitted. '*General Hospital.*'

'My mom used to watch that one,' Ray said.

Brian opened a sterile gauze packet and wiped the corner of Ray's mouth. It was something he'd hesitated doing when he first starting visiting Ray, not wanting to embarrass him. Then one day, the drool was just too obvious to ignore and he'd taken the chance. They'd gone on with their conversation that day as if nothing had happened, the only acknowledgment a single tear that rolled down Ray's unburned cheek and left a small, round drop of moisture on the pillow.

'It's not bad,' Brian said. 'I've been watching it, too. They have some great story lines, lots of intrigue, good writing. I'll probably keep — '

'What he's really trying to say is that they have some real babes on the show,' Lynda said.

Ray took a long time to answer, his eyes closed, his teeth clenched as he waited for a wave of pain to pass. Finally, he looked at Lynda and attempted a smile. 'Maybe I'll give it a try.'

'Do you want me to get the nurse?'

'No — ' He caught his breath. 'Yeah, maybe you should.'

Lynda pushed the button clipped to the sheet. 'I've got to go. My mom's waiting. But I'll be back. Day after tomorrow. Call me if you need anything. Or if you just want to talk.

I put my number in the drawer.'

'Mine, too,' Brian said.

'Thanks, you guys. You've been great.'

The nurse came in. 'What can I get you, Ray?'

Brian looked at Lynda and motioned toward the door. She nodded. 'Later,' he said to Ray.

Ray had his eyes closed again.

They went outside and took off their gowns and masks. 'I think he looks a little better today, don't you?' Lynda said.

Brian had been about to say he thought Ray looked worse. 'Yeah — sure. I guess.'

Lynda sighed. 'I know he doesn't. You don't have to pretend.'

'Why do you hold his arm like that?' He'd wanted to ask for a long time and finally had the nerve.

'It's just something I do.' She averted her eyes. 'It probably wouldn't make any sense to you.'

'Try me.'

'I want him to know that he's still worth touching, and his arm is the only place I can show him.'

She spoke so softly he had to lower his head to hear. 'You're right. I don't under-stand. Why would he think he wasn't worth touching?'

She looked up. Their faces were inches apart. 'Because I don't think I am,' she whispered. 'Not anymore.'

Simple words, but ones to break his heart. 'You're wrong.' He put his hands on the sides of her face and stared into her eyes. 'I've wanted to touch you for weeks now, but I was afraid I'd hurt you.'

She tried to turn away but he held on. 'Please,' she said, the word catching in her throat. 'Don't feel sorry for me. I couldn't stand that.'

Finally he did what he'd wanted to do all those weeks: He kissed her. At first she was too surprised to respond. Then her lips softened and he tasted a sweetness unlike anything he'd ever known. He'd wanted to prove a point and instead nearly drowned in the moment.

His forehead touching hers, he said softly, 'The last thing I'm feeling right now is sorry for you.'

She backed away. 'Why did you do that?'

'Because I wanted to.'

'I don't believe you.'

'Okay — I did it because there's a guy standing behind me with a gun in my back.'

Slowly, she smiled. 'Well, if it was the only way you could keep him from shooting you . . . '

The kiss had opened a door he hadn't known was closed between them. They weren't just friends anymore. He didn't have a name for what they were, but whatever it was, it had to be something synonymous with wonderful. 'What are you doing three weeks from today?'

'I don't know. Probably physical therapy or something just as bad. Why?'

'My dad has connections with someone on the Lilith tour and he said he could get me a couple of tickets if I wanted.'

'Oh, my God. I'd love to go. That's so cool.'

'You think you should ask your mother first?'

'Why? She never tells me — ' She stopped, remembering. 'Oh, you mean because I might still be in bandages. She can't keep me locked up forever.'

'I'll tell my dad to get the tickets and if you can't go, we'll do something else.' He held out his hand. 'If we don't get back, your mom is going to come looking for us.'

Tentatively, she put her hand in his. 'That's so cool about Lilith. Wendy is going to be so jealous.'

When they were outside Lynda's room, Brian said, 'I still have some running around I have to do for my dad so I don't know what

207

time I'll get to your house.'

'Don't worry about it. My mom will probably make me take a nap anyway.'

'See you later then.' He wanted to kiss her again, but it wasn't the time or place.

'Bye.' She looked at him for a long time before she put her hand on the door to go inside.

Brian waved, then turned and walked away. Later, he tried to remember how he got to his car, but his only memory was the way Lynda had smiled when she said good-bye.

17

'You're certainly in a good mood,' Catherine said.

Lynda smiled. Not even the intense itching that had started the minute she got in the car could spoil the ride home. 'I'm *free!*' she shouted. 'You can't imagine how it feels.'

'I think I have a pretty good idea.'

Everything seemed different: bigger, louder, dirtier, cleaner, brighter. She noticed things she never had before, like how many pigeons could sit on a billboard and all face the same way and how many cars were on the road even when it wasn't rush hour. She saw flowers she didn't recognize, but she knew they bloomed at the same time and place every year.

'When are we going to get our own car back?' she asked. 'This one stinks.'

'It's the air freshener they use to cover the cigarette smell.'

'Couldn't you make them give you another one?'

'They all smelled like this and I thought it was only going to be a couple of days before I got the Lincoln back. Now they tell me it will be at least another week.'

'It's going to be hot today,' she said, changing the subject. If they talked about the car anymore, they were going to end up talking about Tom. Yuk.

'The paper said we could hit a hundred.'

'I wish I could go swimming.'

'You're supposed to wait until you — '

'I know, Mom. I was just thinking out loud.' Her mother had something to say about everything lately, a warning from one of the doctors or nurses or social workers about being careful or taking things slow or what she could and couldn't do. The only person she never quoted was Rick, at least not about rules and restrictions. With him it was good stuff or funny things about his job.

Now probably wasn't the time to tell her about the concert, but Lynda had to tell someone. 'Remember last year when I told Dad I wanted to fly to Denver for my birthday and go to the Lilith concert?'

'And he said he couldn't get the time off to go with you.'

'Remember how I really, really wanted to go anyway and said I'd take the money out of my savings, but you wouldn't let me?'

'Just spit it out, Lynda.'

'What if I told you I had a chance to go this year? Not to Denver,' she quickly added. 'To

Concord. That's only a couple of hours away.'

'When?'

'Three weeks.'

Catherine didn't say anything right away. 'I suppose we could try to get tickets, but don't count on it. As popular as that tour is, I can't believe they aren't already sold out.'

Lynda's hopeful tone was impossible to miss. 'Brian has two tickets. He wants to take me.'

'You're kidding.'

'Why do you sound so surprised?' she shot back, her voice heavy with hurt.

'You've got to stop taking everything so personally. I found out a couple of weeks ago that Lilith was going to be in Concord and I've had Uncle Gene looking for tickets. I wanted to surprise you for your homecoming.'

Instead of feeling chastised, she was excited. 'That must mean you checked with the doctors and it will be okay for me to be in crowds by then.'

'As long as you keep improving the way you have been.'

'Cool.' She could hardly wait to tell Brian. And Wendy. She had to find a way for Wendy to meet Brian. Neither she nor Wendy had ever gone out with anyone the other didn't know. Half the fun of dating was talking about it the next day.

The first thing she was going to do when she got home was call Wendy. And apologize. And find out what she'd been doing. And tell her about being in the hospital. And about Brian. Mostly about Brian.

They were home. Almost.

Catherine pulled up to the gate, but instead of letting them in, the guard picked up the phone and made a call. He then leaned down and waved to Lynda and gave her a huge, conspiratorial smile. She returned the wave with a little too much enthusiasm and winced as she lowered her arm. It was unbelievable how fast the skin tightened where her back and arms connected and how much it hurt to keep it loose.

As soon as her mother drove around the corner, Lynda spotted the cars lining the roadway. Every space on both sides was filled. Dozens of oak trees sported red and white ribbons and dozens of her friends lined the driveway, all of them holding red and white balloons. A banner stretched from one side of the garage to the other. It said, WELCOME HOME LYNDA.

Catherine covered Lynda's hand with her own. 'I hope it's okay. They wanted to do this and I didn't know how to tell them they couldn't.'

Lynda nodded, terrified and excited, pleased but troubled, too. 'I thought they'd all be mad at me.'

Brian stood at the top of the driveway, a giant red-and-white stuffed bear in his arms, the bear wearing a duplicate, but smaller, welcome-home banner. Lynda started to cry. Catherine reached in her purse for a tissue.

Her friends surrounded the car when Catherine pulled to a stop at the top of the driveway, calling out greetings and good wishes, warm and loving words that melded into a swell of emotion. Lynda wasn't the only one crying. Even Brian blinked away tears when he opened the car door.

The only thing missing were the hugs. No one touched her. They didn't know how. She laughed at the awkward, funny things that were said and started crying again when she saw Wendy crying. When a natural lull occurred, Catherine suggested they head for the air-conditioning and start the party.

Anxious to let everyone know how much she'd missed seeing them, Lynda moved from group to group, trying not to miss anyone. No one asked about her burns. Not one person. It was as if they'd all gotten together and decided not to. At first, Lynda was grateful. She was exhausted with the subject of being burned and just wanted to be normal again, if only for a couple of hours and only in her mind. After a while she began to realize that ignoring the obvious didn't make her a part of the group, it separated her. They were like actors in some bizarre play with scripted lines that had nothing to do with reality.

She was in the middle of a conversation with the girl who'd taken her place on the cheerleading squad about one of their teachers when the doorbell rang. She knew her mother would answer, but used it as an excuse to get away. Being gracious to her replacement wasn't as easy as she'd thought.

She saw Rick through the glass before she opened the door. Having him there was what she needed. He always made her feel better. He bowed gallantly, and ceremoniously handed her a new, bright red cap for her collection. Embroidered across the front, in bold white letters, was something he'd told her on one of her particularly bad days at the hospital: SOMETIMES REAL COURAGE IS FOUND IN A SMILE.

She looked at him and purposely forced a smile.

'Not going well?'

Shaking her head, she admitted, 'It's not the same.' Damn. She was crying again.

He motioned for her to come outside. 'Tell

me what's changed.'

She stepped onto the porch and closed the door. 'Everything . . . me, I guess. They all stayed the same, but I didn't. I feel like an outsider.'

'You had something happen to you that none of your friends can understand. They can try, but no matter how much effort they give it, they will never know what you've gone through and why it's changed you. That doesn't mean you can't fit in again, it just means you have to give it some time, recognize the hard days for what they are, and remember you got through the last one and you'll get through this one, too.'

'No one cares what happened to me. They don't even ask. And if I try to tell them, they change the subject.' She'd finally tired of the awkward pretense and had tried to move past it, but no one would let her.

'Stop and think about that a minute. If they didn't care, would they be here?'

'You don't know my friends. They'll do anything for a party.'

'Feeling a little prickly, I see.'

She was never this way with Brian or her mother or grandmother, or even Uncle Gene. Only with Rick. With him she said what she felt.

'I'm tired.'

'It's been a big day.' He leaned his shoulder against the side of the house. 'Would you like me to get everyone to go home?'

'How?'

'I could tell them that the doctors just discovered you'd picked up a virus at the hospital that causes pimples and is highly contagious.'

She laughed. 'That would do it, all right. And I wouldn't have to worry about anyone ever coming back.'

'Do you want me to talk to them for you, explain a little about what you've been going through?'

He'd told her that part of the mentor program was going to school with kids on their first day back to explain about being burned. The mentors encouraged questions and usually got a lot, mostly about the pressure garments. At first the program had been geared toward the lower grades, but it turned out to be even more effective in high school. Like everything he did, Rick made it clear that the assembly wasn't a mandatory part of the program. She had the right to say no to whatever she wanted. He was the one person involved in her recovery who gave her that option.

'Thanks,' she said. 'But I don't think they're ready to hear all the gory details.'

'You could be underestimating them.'

'Maybe . . . '

'Let me know if you change your mind.' He pushed himself away from the wall. 'I'm going inside to say hello to your mom. And then I have to leave to pick up some hardware for the cupboards I installed yesterday.'

She didn't want him to go. Having him there was like having someone on her side, someone who understood without being told. 'It's only three thirty.'

'The store is in Florin. If I don't take off in a couple of minutes, I'm going to get stuck in traffic on Sunrise.'

'You should have called us at the hospital. We could have picked them up for you before we came home.'

He gently tapped the brim of her cap, forcing it lower on her forehead. 'Be careful — I just might take you up on your offer one of these days.'

She pushed the cap back into place, completing what had become a parting ritual between them. 'Thanks for the hat.'

'You're welcome.' He held the door. 'Coming?'

She shook her head. 'I'm going to stay out here a little while longer.'

'Not too much longer, okay? And not in the sun.'

'Yeah, yeah, yeah.'

He laughed. 'I must not be the first one who said that today.'

'The line forms to the left.'

'If I miss seeing you before I leave, you know where you can reach me if you need something.'

'Tell Mom I'm out here, will you? And tell her not to worry, that I know not to stay out too long.'

She waited until he was inside before she headed down the crushed-rock pathway that led around the house. She wasn't going to last outside much longer — she was already starting to get dizzy from the heat — but she wanted a minute to savor her freedom, and the side deck was the one place she figured she could do that alone.

But she'd figured wrong. She heard voices as soon as she neared the corner of the house. Frustrated, she took a second to consider whether she should join whoever was on the deck or look for someplace else for her moment of privacy. Or maybe she should simply give up and go back inside with the others. In that second she heard enough to realize she was the topic of conversation.

She knew it was dangerous to stand there and listen, and that she should walk away before she heard something she didn't want to hear, but the message failed to reach her feet until it was too late.

'I'll bet Shawn is glad now that they broke up when they did. He could be where that guy Brian is.'

'You mean stuck?'

Someone laughed. Someone else joined in.

'Hey, don't be so greedy,' a new voice protested. 'It's my turn.'

The words clicked when Lynda caught the faint smell of marijuana smoke.

Someone coughed.

'God, can you imagine having your head shaved like that?' a girl said.

'Is she going to have to shave her back from now on?'

That brought more laughter and, 'What an idiot. They didn't take the hair, just the skin.'

'What's with the fringe? She can't think she's fooling anybody.' This from a guy.

'It must be awful when she has to look in a mirror to comb it.' Again a girl.

'Maybe she doesn't. I know I wouldn't.'

'Don't you guys think it's sad?' Yet another female voice. 'She used to be so pretty.'

Lynda had heard enough. To stay for more was tantamount to sticking pins in her leg to see how much she would bleed. But before she could move, before she could protect herself from hearing more, she heard the words that broke her heart.

'I was listening to Wendy and Brian talking in the kitchen. He told her that he felt responsible for what happened to Lynda and that's why he's stuck around all this time.'

'Duh.'

They all laughed.

Lynda was going to be sick. She felt her stomach tighten and a burning feeling in her throat. Dear God, she couldn't let it happen. Not here. Not now. Not where they might find her. She couldn't let them know she'd heard. She put her hand to her mouth and swallowed. Hard. Again and again, until she was sure she'd stopped the spasms.

No one could see her. Not like this. But if she left, they'd only come looking for her. And then everyone would know.

Oh, God. Her back itched. And her arms. Worse than ever. She had to scratch. Just once, or she wouldn't be able to stand it anymore.

Her fingers dug into her elbow. She gasped at the pain. But it was a good pain, a blinding, searing pain that made her incapable of hearing or seeing or feeling anything else.

Someone came out of the house. She almost cried with relief when she saw it was Rick and not one of her so-called friends.

'Are you all right?' he asked as he came up to her.

She didn't know how to answer him.

He asked again. 'Are you all right?' When she didn't answer this time, he cupped her chin and made her look at him. 'Talk to me,' he insisted.

She shook her head.

'What's wrong?'

'My arm. It was itching so bad. I scratched it. I didn't think.'

'Come inside.' He moved to let her go first, then stopped her at the door, pulled his shirt from his jeans, and used the hem to wipe the tears from her cheeks. 'Blink.'

'What?'

'If you go in there looking like you've been crying, you're going to have everyone asking what happened. I don't think that's what you want right now.'

Somehow he knew her tears weren't because she'd hurt herself. She did as he told her and blinked, then took a deep breath. 'Now?'

'Now.'

She hung back. 'I can't.'

'Remember the hat.'

'*What?*'

'Real courage is found in a smile.'

'Screw courage.'

'Physically impossible, but point taken.'

He was right. She had to go in the house and she didn't want them to see that she was upset. She wiped her eyes, rubbed her cheeks hard to give them color, and took a deep breath. 'All right. I'm ready.'

He followed her inside, not so close to make it obvious he was with her, but close enough for her to feel his support. Lynda went into the family room, picked up a glass, and tapped it with a coaster to gain attention.

'Hey, everybody. I want to thank you for coming — and for being such good friends.' If she could say that, she could say anything. 'I hate to admit this, but when the doctor told me I'd get tired easily, I didn't believe her. Guess what? She was right.'

She looked around the room, trying to figure out who was missing. But it didn't matter. Not really. If some of them were talking about her, they all were.

'I'm sorry to cut out before the party's over, but it's that or fall asleep while someone's talking to me. And if I did that, they just might end up talking *about* me. I certainly wouldn't want that to happen. Who knows what they might say?'

She could sense Brian when he moved to stand next to her and knew that he was concerned by how close he stood, but she also knew that she wouldn't make it through the rest of what she wanted to say if she chanced a look at him.

She looked at Rick instead. He gave her the courage to smile. 'Thanks again for the party, everybody. I can't tell you how great it was to come around the corner and see all of you standing there waiting for me.'

She had to get away before she started crying again. She could feel the tears tightening her throat and burning her eyes. 'I'm going upstairs now. I'll see you all later.'

As if on cue, the doorbell rang. She used it as an excuse to leave before she had to acknowledge all the phony statements about how good it was to have her back.

When she opened the door her father thrust another huge bouquet of flowers in her arms and leaned forward for a kiss. 'I hope I'm not too late,' he said, beaming.

She turned to Rick, a pleading look in her eyes.

'You're just in time to cut the cake for Lynda while she goes upstairs to take a nap.'

Jack ignored Rick. 'You okay, baby?'

'I'm just tired,' she told him. She gave the flowers back. 'Would you please have Mom put them in water for me?'

'Sure, okay, whatever you want, baby.'

She came forward to kiss him on the cheek.

'Thanks for coming.'

She started up the stairs to her bedroom. Wendy moved to follow. When Lynda saw her, she turned and spoke just loud enough for Wendy to hear. 'Go away. I don't want to see you. Ever again.'

Wendy looked stunned, then devastated. 'What did I do?'

'Find another friend. One who can stand to look at herself in the mirror in the morning.'

'What's that supposed to mean?'

'Ask Brian. With you two being such good friends he should be able to help you figure it out.' She should have felt good that she got the last word. Instead, she felt a terrible, echoing emptiness.

18

The granite was incredible. Exactly what he'd had in mind for the countertops — reddish brown background, charcoal gray, cream, mauve, and brown specks throughout. After five years of planning, of preparing to scour the country for just the right color, Rick had started and ended his search on the same day.

And, best of all, saved over twenty-five hundred dollars of the eight thousand he'd budgeted for the project.

No, the best part was the pressure he'd put himself under to get the cabinets stained and varnished and up before the counters were ready to be installed. A whole afternoon could pass without thoughts of Catherine taking over and leaving him useless and unable to concentrate on anything else.

In the week and a half since Lynda's homecoming party, he'd put in three shifts at work, completed the base for the new sink, painted the dining room, and ordered the new flooring for the kitchen — a terrazzo tile that perfectly matched the reddish brown in the granite.

Rick checked his earplugs and put on his

protective ear coverings before starting the table saw for the final cut on the face frame for the pantry.

Although he'd stayed busy purposely to keep from thinking about Catherine, nothing could completely erase the errant connecting thoughts that would take him from the smell of sawdust to trees to ribbons tied around trees to Catherine's eyes lighting up with welcome when she saw him at the party. Or from the stifling afternoon heat to the sweat trickling down his back to the sundress she'd worn the last time he saw her to the way the soft hair at the nape of her neck clung to her moist skin.

He'd accepted that there was nothing he could do to keep from thinking about her at night. A year was a long time to wait when he'd waited his entire life to find someone like her. At odd moments in his day he had an insane desire to talk to her about a hundred inconsequential things — her favorite season or restaurant, whether she was a morning or evening person, if she liked to read, if she had to see certain movies in a theater rather than on video, whether she was a dog person, if she would like Blue . . .

But Lynda came first. After her party, he'd called a couple of the female firefighters who worked with the association and asked them about the dramatic mood swings Lynda went through and what he could do to help. They'd given him a better understanding of her mental turmoil, her loss of confidence and frustration, but not what he could do to make it easier. She needed time to find her own way and to realize the people she cared about would be there when she reached out to them.

Rick finished the cut, turned off the saw, and looked up to see Blue standing in the doorway to the kitchen. He stayed in the house when Rick ran the saws, only making his presence known when he wanted something.

Rick lifted one of the earmuffs. 'What's up?' he asked.

Blue barked once. The telephone.

Twice would have meant someone was coming up the driveway.

He made it to the phone just as the machine was about to pick up.

'Rick, it's Catherine. I'm sorry for chasing you down at home, but I was wondering . . . would you mind stopping by . . . if you happen to be in the area, that is.'

No one was ever 'in the area' where Catherine lived. You went there purposely or not at all. 'I'm covered in sawdust at the moment, but I can be there in half an hour

— give or take a few minutes.'

'I wouldn't ask, but I really could use your help. Lynda isn't doing very well.'

'Mentally or physically?'

After a long pause, she said, 'Mentally. Something happened at the party, but I can't get her to talk about it. She's refusing to see her friends again — even Brian. Ray is the only one she talks to and she only sees him when she goes in for physical therapy. I was hoping you could get her to tell you what's going on.'

'How is she doing otherwise?'

'You mean her burns?'

'Is she up to going for a ride?' He wasn't sure how he was going to get her to talk, just that it would be easier in a neutral environment.

'She seems to handle the trip to the hospital fine. At least she never complains. Doctor Randolph told me she thinks Lynda will be ready for her pressure bandages in another week, which means she's ahead of where they thought she'd be.' She lowered her voice to a whisper. 'I think she can handle a ride without any problem.'

'Have any meds she needs to take in the next couple of hours ready to go when I get there. But don't tell her I'm coming.' Since he didn't know where they were going, he had no idea how long they would be gone. 'If we do this fast, she won't have time to come up with a reason for not coming with me.'

'I keep an extra set in my purse. I'll give you those.'

Rick thought she was going to hang up when she said, 'We've missed you.'

He gave too much meaning to the casual remark and only allowed the flush of pleasure to remain a moment before dismissing it. 'I've been working on my kitchen.'

'I don't understand. Why would you be working on your kitchen? Did something happen?'

'I bought what was laughingly called a fixer-upper eight years ago and I've been working my way through the place room to room since. I saved the kitchen and dining room for last.'

'You do the work yourself?'

'When I have the time.' He knew immediately it was the wrong thing to say.

'I'm sorry. See how dangerous it was to tell me you were always available? I should have asked if you were busy.'

'I would have told you I wasn't, so it wouldn't have made any difference.' Blue came up to be petted. When Rick ignored him, the dog leaned against his leg, and then sat on his foot.

'I'd love to see this project of yours someday. That is, if you allow tours.'

He laughed. 'Whenever you have five minutes free let me know. That's about how long it will take.'

'I'll look forward to it.'

Rick would, too. More than he wanted her to know.

* * *

'Where are you taking me?' Lynda asked, just a note shy of belligerent as Rick backed out of the driveway.

'To visit a friend of mine.' He'd come up with the idea on his way there and called Sandra to see if she was willing.

'I get it — you want me to see what life is like after being burned. If you'd warned me, I could have told you not to bother. The social worker had a whole parade of burn survivors come to see me in the hospital. I don't know what makes everyone think being burned is like joining some big sorority. I'm me. I'm not like anyone else. You can't — '

Rick pulled over to the side of the road and stopped.

'What's the matter? What are you doing?'

'I'm looking for your off switch.'

'Why? Can't take it when someone talks

back? Or are you calling it quits, too?'

'Too?'

'Never mind.'

Rick shifted in the seat to look at her. 'I'm not a quitter, Lynda. And you're not close to being obnoxious enough to make me even consider it. Now why don't you tell me who you think has quit on you?'

'Everyone.'

She was hiding behind a wall of anger. If he pushed any harder the wall would crack. 'That must be a hell of a way to feel.'

That was all it took. A little sympathy, a little understanding, and she was crying. He reached in the side pocket of his door and dug around until he found a fast-food napkin. 'Sorry, this is the best I can do.'

She wiped her eyes, blew her nose, looked at him, and asked, 'Where are you really taking me?'

He pulled back onto the road and waved at the guard as they went through the gate. 'Like I said, to see a friend.'

'I know — a burned friend,' she said flatly.

'You couldn't be more wrong. Well, maybe if you invested in *Titanic, the Sequel*. Sandra has never been burned and doesn't have a clue what it's like to be burned. But she's one hell of a nice woman.'

'Your girlfriend?'

He laughed. 'Not even close. Sandra Brahams is one of the most happily married people I've ever known.'

'Then I don't understand why you want me to meet her.'

'I figured you could use some time off from hospitals and doctors and dressing changes and therapy and talk about dressing changes and therapy and doctors and hospitals.'

'What does she do?'

'She's a teacher.'

'Oh, I get it. She handles problem kids and you think she'll know what to do with me.'

'Have you always been this suspicious?'

She thought about the question before answering. 'No — at least I don't think so.'

'What happened? It had to be more than being burned.'

'It was lots of things.'

'Like?'

'Tom dumping my mom, for one.'

He hadn't expected that and was at a loss how to answer.

'He did it because of me.'

'And was his dumping her — as you put it — necessarily a bad thing?' He was taking a chance. He had no idea how Lynda felt about Tom.

She shifted position, smoothing a wrinkle on the synthetic sheepskin pad he'd put across the seat to cushion her back. 'She doesn't think so, or at least that's what she wants everyone to believe.'

'What do you believe?'

'She's *soooo* much better off without him. He's such a loser.'

'Then it would appear that if Tom did leave because of you, you did your mother a favor.' He pulled into a turn lane and waited for traffic to pass. 'I'm not sure I see the problem.'

'That's what Mom said, too.' She eyed him. 'How come you're not married?'

'I was once, but it didn't work out.'

'Why?'

She was testing him, seeing if the information highway ran both ways. 'I wasn't ambitious enough to provide the lifestyle she wanted and she was too ambitious to take time off to do things with me. It was your classic under- and overachiever match that neither of us recognized until we were years into the marriage and mired in the process of tearing each other apart.'

'Where is she now?'

'Houston. She has her own computer consulting business.'

'Do you ever see her?'

'We Email every so often, and when she comes to town to see her family we try to get together for lunch or dinner, but we're starting to discover it's not as easy to find things to talk about as it used to be. I'm not sure how much longer we'll keep it up.'

'I think my dad is trying to get back together with my mom, now that Tom is gone.'

Not exactly the best news he'd had that day. There were a dozen things he wanted to say, but none that he should, so he kept his mouth shut.

'He's been coming over a lot. Every day, as a matter of fact. Mom said it has nothing to do with her, that he's trying to learn how to be a father, but that doesn't make sense.'

Rick spotted a deer and slowed the truck. 'Look — ' He pointed to a stand of scrub oak, saying a silent prayer of thanks for the distraction. 'See the doe?'

'Cool,' she breathed. 'Oh, look, there's another one.'

A second doe gingerly stepped forward, its ears cocked, listening, ready to spring at the slightest provocation. Rick knew if he brought the truck to a complete stop they would bolt, so he simply cut his speed to a crawl and passed slowly.

'They used to come around the cabin when I was little but there are too many people up there now,' she said. 'At least that's what

Uncle Gene says. Now we get bears. But they come around at night so we never actually see them, just the stuff they do.'

'I understand Gene invited you to visit him in Japan.' Gene's bank had talked him into a six-month stay to work out the final details of the merger.

She looked at him. 'How did you know that?'

'He stopped by before he left to borrow one of my ocean fishing reels.' As soon as they were past the deer, he sped up again.

Lynda picked up a CD case off the seat and absently looked at it. 'How come you never stop by to see me anymore? You used to come every day when I was in the hospital, or almost everyday. Did I do something wrong?'

Shit, she'd done it again — blindsided him and left him scrambling for an answer. 'I can see why you might think that, but you got it wrong this time.' He needed a way to tell her the truth without telling her too much. 'I backed off because I was getting too close to you and your mother to do my job the way I'm supposed to do it. I was getting too involved in your life to maintain any objectivity. And that wasn't good for you or me.'

'So you can't be my friend?'

'I can be your friend, I just can't be your

best friend. That's Brian's job. Or Wendy's.'

She was instantly angry. 'You've been talking to my mother about me. I hate that. What did she tell you?'

'She's worried about you.'

'So that's the real reason you came to see me today? Because she called you?'

'Yes.'

'Take me home.'

'No.'

'Then stop the truck and I'll walk.'

She was crying again. 'Tell me what happened, Lynda. What did Brian do?'

'I don't want to talk about it.'

Rick pulled into Sandra's driveway and stopped the truck. Sandra would know not to come out until they were closer to the house, so they had time. 'I'm going to tell you something about men and women that has taken me forty-two years to figure out. It will make your life infinitely easier if you pay attention.'

She wiped her cheeks on her sleeve and looked at him, a challenge in her eyes. She was willing to listen, but not for long.

'My wife's heart was broken when we lost our baby. I broke it a second time when I brought her pink roses. I knew Barbara loved yellow roses, but I chose the pink because pink is for girls and our baby was a girl.

Barbara thought I forgot what she liked, or possibly that I didn't care enough to find yellow roses for her. She never said anything and I never knew why she didn't talk to me for two days until three years after we were divorced.'

'She should have said something. That wasn't fair.'

'That's easy to say when it involves someone else. A lot harder to deal with when it's you. Whatever happened between you and Brian might not be the same kind of misunderstanding, but you'll never know if you don't talk to him to find out.'

She was quiet for a long time. 'If only I hadn't worn that damned sweater . . . '

'But you did and there's no way to go back and change it.'

'If only I hadn't run.'

'You did what your subconscious told you to do. All of us run from danger.'

'Not Brian,' she said softly. 'He ran after me.'

'Give him a chance. If he doesn't deserve it, then at least you'll know.'

'Do you think it would have changed things with you and your wife if she had told you about the flowers?'

'Not in the end. We were too different to make our marriage work. But it would have saved a lot of heartache and misunderstandings.'

She smiled tentatively. 'My mom's not ambitious. Did you know that? She's always saying she doesn't care where we live as long as we have a roof over our heads.'

Rick leaned his head against the back of the seat, closed his eyes for a second, and tried to pretend he hadn't heard that. Lynda as a troubled burn survivor struggling to understand her place in a world turned upside down was something he could deal with. Lynda as matchmaker was more than he could handle.

'There's a dog sitting in the middle of the road staring at us,' Lynda said.

Rick opened his eyes to see an obviously confused Blue looking back at him. This was the first time Rick had ever used Sandra and Walt's driveway, and it had created disorder in Blue's orderly life. Disorder for Blue, a desperately welcome change in conversation for Rick.

19

Catherine opened the gas and electric bill and sucked in her breath in surprise. She'd known it was going to be high — they were near a record run on the number of consecutive hundred degree days and she'd been keeping the house cooler than usual for Lynda — but she'd had no idea it would be this high. Another two hundred dollars and it would be the same as her house payment.

This couldn't go on. She had to find a job. Soon. Or sell some stock. Or cut back on some of the extras, like the housekeeper who came in three times a week and the twice-a-week gardener. Then there was the pool service. How hard could it be to test the water and add chemicals herself? She'd watched the guy when he thought no one was home and he'd been there less than ten minutes. Two hundred dollars a month for ten minutes a week? If she could find a job like that, she wouldn't have to worry about paying her bills.

She'd drop the country club if it weren't for Tom. He was desperate to be a member and she'd be damned if she'd give him the opening to buy in. At her lowest point — when he'd been gone for two and a half weeks, when Lynda had slipped into another depression, when her brother had taken off for Japan for another six months, when Jack had informed her his business was in a slump and that he might have to take her to court to lower her alimony payments, when she'd pulled a pair of slacks from the closet that she couldn't get zipped — she'd seriously wondered whether Tom had asked her to marry him because he wanted her or her membership in the country club.

She'd recovered nicely when the cleaners called and told her they'd made a mistake and had given her someone else's pants. Someone who was obviously far too skinny for her height, Catherine decided.

'I'm home,' Lynda called from the front door. 'Where are you?'

Catherine almost wept at the upbeat tone she heard in her daughter's voice. 'Thank you, Rick,' she said softly as she pushed back her chair.

'I'm in here,' Catherine called in reply.

'Where's here?'

'My office. But hold on, I'm coming out.' She didn't want Lynda to see the stack of bills sitting on the desk.

Lynda was at the refrigerator looking for

something to eat when Catherine found her. 'Where's Rick? Didn't you invite him in?'

'He's doing something with some cupboards and had to get back. But he said to tell you he'd try to stop by next week. I invited him to dinner so he'd have to come.'

The idea startled Catherine. She'd never even considered asking Rick to dinner. 'And he said?'

'That we didn't need to feed him to get him here. But I told him you loved playing Martha Stewart.'

She groaned. 'You *didn't*.' She wasn't sure how she wanted Rick to see her, but that wasn't it.

'Maybe not in those exact words, but whatever it was worked. You're supposed to call and tell him it's okay and when he should come.'

'Lynda . . . ' Catherine knew no matter how she phrased it, what she was about to say would make her sound like a snob. 'I'm not sure it's a good idea to encourage Rick to see us on a social level.'

Not finding anything to her liking in the refrigerator, Lynda opened the freezer. 'Why not?'

'It could put him in a difficult situation with the association. As much as you feel he's your friend — and I like that you do — '

'He's your friend, too, isn't he?'

'Yes,' she said equivocally.

'Then I don't see the problem.'

Catherine could stand there and argue or enjoy her daughter's remarkable mood. She decided to put off the discussion until later. 'I take it you had a good time today?'

'The best. I met a terrific woman. You'd love her, Mom. She's Rick's neighbor. Who, by the way, thinks he's the most fantastic guy in the whole world — other than her husband, of course.' She spotted ice cream. 'Yum — my favorite. You must have gone shopping while I was gone.' She turned to Catherine. 'Want some?'

Catherine thought about the scare she'd had with the pants not fitting and knew it was only a matter of time and birthdays until it happened for real. But that was in the future. This moment with Lynda was real and it was now. 'Sure, why not?'

Lynda opened the refrigerator again. 'We have any chocolate sauce?'

'On the door.'

Lynda picked it up and looked at the label. 'Is this that stuff Tom bought with the rum in it?'

'I threw that out already.'

'Good job, Mom. Now if you could just get him to pick up his things in the garage.' She handed two bowls to Catherine before she put the chocolate in the microwave.

'I left a message on his machine telling him he had one more week and then I was making a very nice charitable contribution in his name.'

Lynda smiled. 'Let me do it. Please.'

'Be my guest. But he still has a couple of days.'

'That's so like you, Mom. Worried about being fair to a guy who treated you like shit.'

'Watch your — '

' — language,' Lynda finished for her.

'Forget Tom. Tell me about this woman Rick had you meet.'

Lynda poured the chocolate sauce over the ice cream, licked a drop from her finger, and dug two spoons out of the drawer. 'Her name's Sandra. She's old — older than you, but she doesn't act old. You know what I mean?'

'Like Aunt Eva.'

'Yeah, exactly.' She rotated her shoulders and leaned her back against the refrigerator, seeking relief from the constant itching.

'When did you last take your medicine?'

'I'm due, but I want to tell you about Sandra first.' She picked up her bowl and started eating with her back pressed tightly against the stainless steel. 'She's so cool,

Mom. You're not going to believe what she showed me how to do. I actually had a wild bird eating sunflower seeds out of my hand. Sandra feeds them that way all the time. They just come to her.'

'What kind of birds?'

'House finches. But that's not all. Wait till you hear this — she puts tubes in her hair that have red stoppers on the ends and sugar water inside and hummingbirds actually come to drink out of them.'

'This is what you were doing all afternoon?'

'That and talking. I helped her clean the feeders — she has dozens of them. She said the sugar water for the hummingbirds has to be changed every day in the summer or it gets a bacteria that can kill them. Did you know that?'

'No,' Catherine admitted. 'I just thought you refilled the feeders when they were empty.'

'I'm going to put one up outside my window. They have ones that stick to the glass so you can watch the birds up close. And I thought we could get a couple of regular bird feeders for the yard.'

For the first time since Lynda was burned, Catherine saw a glimpse of the happy, carefree girl she had once been. Her chest tightened with joy to know that girl was still inside the emotionally bruised young woman.

Finishing her ice cream, Lynda put the bowl in the sink. 'I'm going upstairs.'

'It's early. Why don't we rent a movie?' Catherine said, not wanting the moment to end. 'Better yet, how about a game? It's been a long time since I let you beat me at Scrabble.'

'Ha. I could wear a blindfold and still beat you. You're a terrible Scrabble player, Mom.'

'Then what about Monopoly?' Lynda had come too far that day for her to end it alone in her room.

'Maybe — after I call Wendy and Brian.'

Catherine sent Rick a mental hug of gratitude. He'd accomplished something she'd worried might be impossible. It would be so easy to say the wrong thing to Lynda, so Catherine didn't say anything and simply nodded.

Lynda smiled. 'Surprised you, didn't I?'

'That doesn't begin to describe it.'

'If Daddy comes while I'm on the phone, do you think you could tell him I'm busy without hurting his feelings?'

'I could try.'

'Thanks, Mom.'

Catherine made a dismissing motion with her hand. 'Yeah, yeah, yeah.'

Lynda headed for the stairs, remembered she was due for her pills, and went back for them. She didn't want anything to interrupt her phone calls, and the itching was getting bad again.

Alone in her room, she propped pillows against the headboard and settled on the bed, the portable phone on her lap. She'd tried to rehearse what she would say but couldn't come up with anything past the fact that she was sorry. With Wendy she knew what to expect. She'd be mad, but she'd listen. And she'd forgive. Eventually.

Lynda wasn't so sure about Brian. She'd given him enough time to figure out he was better off without her and all of her problems.

Needing to talk *about* Brian before she talked to him, she decided to call Wendy first.

Wendy's mom answered on the second ring.

'Hi, this is Lynda. Is Wendy home?'

'Lynda — how are you? I've wanted to come by to see you and your mother but Wendy said you weren't up to seeing anyone yet.'

'I'm feeling better now.' Obviously Wendy hadn't told her mom what really happened. 'You can come over any time you want. Just don't bring food. For some reason the neighbors keep bringing things to eat and there's no more room in the refrigerator.'

'I'll try to stop by tomorrow. Wendy will be sorry she missed your call.'

'She's not there?' Lynda should have known. It was Saturday, and Wendy was never home on Friday or Saturday night.

'She went to the lake with a couple of friends. I don't expect her until late tonight. But I'll tell her you called.'

'Thanks.'

'You take care of yourself now.'

'I will.' Lynda hit the Talk button to hang up. She had her finger poised to dial Brian's number but held back. What if he didn't say anything after she said she was sorry? Should she tell him how much she loved his present? Or that she'd listened to the Kate Wolf CD over and over again since the party and that he'd been right, she loved the music and songs as much as he had told her she would? Would he even care anymore?

Realizing she was about to talk herself out of calling him, Lynda dialed the number and held her breath as she listened to it ring.

A woman with a German accent answered.

'May I speak to Brian?' Lynda asked in a rush.

'I'm sorry. He's not here.'

This was the first time that she'd called him and he hadn't been the one to answer.

'I'm a friend of his, Lynda Miller. Can you tell me when he'll be back?'

'Oh, Miss Miller. I know who you are. Are you feeling better now?' She spoke in short, carefully enunciated sentences.

'Yes, I'm fine. Thank you for asking.'

'Mr. Winslow left for the lake early this morning. The whole family is there. He took a friend with him. I thought maybe you were his friend.'

'The lake?' she repeated numbly, her heart in her throat.

'Yes. But he said he would be back tonight. Would you like me to have him call you then?'

'Yes — no, I'll call him. Tomorrow.' She wouldn't, but she had to say something.

'He says such nice things about you. All the time he says these things. You must be a very nice girl. I'm so happy for you that you are not in the hospital anymore.'

'Thank you.' Lynda said good-bye, dropped the phone on the bed, and covered her face with her hands.

She'd lost them both and it was all her fault. She'd convinced herself what she'd heard at the party about Brian and Wendy wasn't true. At least not then. But now it was.

She didn't know how to be a friend anymore. Not to anyone. Not even Ray. She'd skipped going to see him the last time she was at the hospital because she was afraid he would ask about Brian again and she was fresh out of lies for why he never came with her anymore. All she wanted to do was get home and hide in her room. At least she had a home. He didn't have anything or anyone.

No wonder Brian didn't like her anymore. She was selfish and self-centered and ugly. Her whole back and her arms looked sickening to her. She could just imagine what it would look like to him. She was bald and had to wear stupid hats. What guy in his right mind would want to have anything to do with her?

She understood now what it felt like to have a broken heart and why it was called that. She really did feel as if her heart had broken, or if not broken, been crushed. It even hurt when she tried to breathe.

And it was all her fault. Just like being burned was her fault. If only she hadn't run.

How could Brian have kissed her the way he had at the hospital? That was the worst part. He'd given her hope, made her feel good about herself. She was so pathetic. All it took was a kiss and she'd believed in miracles. She'd even let herself believe he'd kiss her again when they were alone that night, that he wanted to kiss her again.

She sat on her bed, unmoving, for over an hour. The sky turned pink and then orange, casting colored light into the room, making it seem warm. But all she could feel was a cold inside her heart that left it empty and her soul devastated.

Her mother came to the door to ask her about dinner. Lynda told her that she was still on the phone and would get something to eat later when she was hungry. The shadows lengthened, the room grew dark.

Catherine came to say good night at eleven. Lynda told her she'd already been asleep.

At ten minutes after eleven the phone rang. It was Wendy.

'I just got home,' she said, her tone cool, reserved. 'Mom told me you called.'

'It wasn't anything important.' She didn't know how to sound normal or even casual anymore. 'You could have waited until tomorrow.'

'She tell you I was at the lake?'

'Yes.'

'It was nice. Hot as hell, though.'

Wendy was trying. Lynda had to give her that. 'Then you freeze when the sun goes down.' Which is why you put on a sweater and how you get burned.

'Not tonight. Even the ice in the ice chest

melted. Shawn had to go all the way into Folsom to get more.'

'Folsom?' That didn't make sense.

'The store at the lake was out.'

'You were at *Folsom* Lake today?'

'Of course. Where else?'

'I thought you were at Rainbow with Brian.'

'Why would . . . oh, my God. Is that why you've been acting like such a jerk? You thought I was after Brian?'

It was useless to deny it. 'I overheard something at the party — '

'Something I said?'

'No.

'Who then?'

Lynda could actually feel Wendy's anger. 'I don't know. I was outside and they were on the deck. I couldn't see who it was.'

'Why didn't you say something to me? Wait a minute. As I recall, you did say something. You told me to go away, that you never wanted to see me again.'

'I was wrong. I'm sorry.'

'You should be. Damn it, Lynda, I'm so mad at you I could spit.'

'If you think it would help, go ahead.'

'Don't try to make me laugh. I want to stay mad at you. At least for a while. You deserve it.'

'How long?' Wendy would stretch it out until she was spent, but the worst was over. They would talk about what had happened for days to come, examine every mistake and misunderstanding until it was laid open like a frog in biology class, and then they would go on, best friends again.

'I don't know. I haven't decided yet.'

'So, what do you think about Brian?'

'I like him. And I'm jealous as hell. Everyone is. Especially Lisa. He's all she can talk about. Wait until I tell you what happened today when she — '

Lynda settled against the pillows, using one to prop up her telephone arm. She had a feeling it was going to be a long conversation.

She listened to Wendy's story about Lisa's top coming off when David tried to teach her to ski barefoot. She smiled. She might not have her life back where she wanted it, but she had this, and for now, for this moment, she was happy again.

20

Catherine answered the door with a heart-felt smile, thinking it was Brian. Tom responded with a huge smile of his own.

'What are you doing here?' she asked, her good mood shattered.

'After that message you left on my machine I thought I'd better pick up the rest of my things before you gave them away to that fireman. He was the charity you were talking about, wasn't he?'

'Trust me, there's nothing you have that Rick would want.'

'Not even you?'

The problem with glass doors was that you couldn't slam them for effect. 'First of all, I'm not yours. I never was. Had I known you thought of me as a possession, I would have had sense enough to get out before I did.'

'Indulging in a little revisionist history, aren't you? As I recall, you weren't the one who wanted out.'

'What did I ever see in you?'

He held open his arms. 'I would assume it was the same thing Adriana Petersen sees in me now.'

Catherine leaned against the doorframe and folded her arms. She knew Adriana socially, and had never had any desire to have it go beyond that. 'So you've already found a replacement?'

He smiled seductively. 'One with a bigger house and in a better location.'

'And membership in the club. I'm sure you took that into consideration when you went looking. She must not have mentioned that her husband has asked for the membership in the divorce settlement.' Catherine had no idea if that was true, but the look on his face was worth whatever she'd have to pay for the lie.

'She didn't tell me,' he stammered. Quickly recovering, he added, 'But nothing's been finalized. There's still time for her to negotiate and Adriana is the kind of woman who will do whatever it takes to please her man.'

'But what a nuisance. How much better it would be if you started interviewing your women a little more carefully before you committed.'

'How's Lynda?' he asked, dismissing her sarcasm with a change of subject.

'Fine,' she said cryptically. And then decided he needed to hear more. 'Actually, she's fantastic. Better than anyone expected.'

'And Brian's still coming around?'

She could tell he expected her to say no. 'He's due any minute. You'll probably pass him on your way out.'

'Would you tell her I'm happy for her? And that I wish her all the best.'

'I will, but she won't believe it. Any more than I do.'

He shifted position, moving from one foot to the other, while he avoided looking at her directly. 'What did you tell her about our breakup?'

He was after something. She played along to find out what it was. 'The truth.'

'And that was?'

'That you're a self-centered, egotistical son of a bitch who didn't deserve us.'

Strangely, he seemed more relieved than angry. 'Then you didn't tell her I left because of her?'

She studied him, looking for clues. 'No.'

'I'm glad.'

'She figured it out for herself.'

Now came the panic. 'You changed her mind, though.'

'Why should I?'

'Because you don't want her going through life thinking she's not good enough.'

'She won't. Luckily you're a rare breed, Tom. She knows not to take anything you say or do seriously.'

He ran his hand through his hair and stopped to rub the back of his neck. He was too savvy to wear clothes that purposely showcased his build, but clever enough to move in ways that accomplished the task for him. Rubbing his neck pulled his sleeve taut and exposed his biceps. Wearing his pants a half size too large gave him reason to fiddle with his waist and draw attention to how narrow and flat it was. He would be mortified to know raising his arm had exposed more sweat ring than muscle.

In addition to these physical techniques, he had a dozen calculated self-effacement ploys to point out his mental attributes should anyone happen to miss them when left to their own powers of observation. How could she see this so clearly now and have missed it for all the months they were together?

'I think I should talk to her. I overreacted when she was in the hospital and I owe her an apology.' He gave her his most practiced smile, the one that had shattered her better judgment and put her in his bed on their second date. 'I owe both of you an apology.'

He wanted something, was desperate enough to humble himself for it — but what could it be? 'There's no way I'm going to let you talk to Lynda. You've done enough damage.'

'Damage only I can repair.'

He was good. 'What Lynda needs is time and distance from you and I'll do whatever it takes to see she gets it.'

'You're being unreasonable.'

'And you're being a pain in the ass and I'm through talking to you. Now, if you want your things, meet me at the garage.' She started to go back inside.

Tom caught her arm. 'What do you want? Name it — it's yours.'

She glared at him. He released her arm, his hands curling into fists. She'd loved him and hated him, but she'd never been afraid of him. Until now. 'What makes you think I want something?'

'You wouldn't be acting the way you are if you didn't.'

'How am I acting?'

'Jealous, vindictive — you're alone and you can't stand the thought of me being with someone else. Especially not this soon.'

Her mouth opened in surprise. Of all the things he could have said to her, this was the most bizarre. He actually believed she still cared what he did and who he did it with. She'd never known anyone like him. His ego —

No, that wasn't right. It wasn't ego she saw in his eyes, it was fear. He was afraid of her.

And Lynda. But why? What could they possibly do to him that would make any difference in his life?

Then the curtain opened, the fog lifted, the sun came out from behind the clouds, and she was hit with a blinding flash of logic. He was afraid Lynda would tell her friends about him, and eventually, even though she went to another school, it would reach Adriana's daughter.

'You're too late,' she said. 'Wendy already convened court and tried you in absentia. She hand-picked the jury, twelve of Lynda's friends. All of whom have known her since preschool.' If she'd only known seeing him again would give her this much pleasure, she would have felt better about opening the door and finding him on her doorstep. 'You were found guilty, by the way.'

He pulled himself up to his full height, towering over her. 'Thanks for the warning,' he said smugly. 'You have no idea how good I can be when I'm prepared.'

'If you were as good as you think you are, you would already be where you want to be.' She went through the house to the garage to open the garage door for him. Instead of hanging around to watch, she went back inside.

The doorbell rang again five minutes later.

This time she didn't answer with a smile. She'd thought about some of the things Tom had said and was prepared for a second go-around.

Jack took a step backward when he saw the expression on her face. 'Have I come at a bad time? Should I have called first?'

'I thought you were someone else.' She stepped out of the doorway to let him come in.

He hesitated. 'I could come back later.'

'Lynda won't be here. She and Brian are going to visit Ray and then they're stopping by someplace for a hamburger.'

'Really? That's great. I'm glad she's getting out again.'

Finally he came inside. 'Actually, it's you I wanted to see anyway. I need your advice.'

'This is turning into a red-letter day.'

Again he hesitated. 'I don't need to do this today, Catherine. If you've had a bad morning I don't mind making it another time.'

'You just missed Tom. I thought he'd come back when I opened the door just now.'

'Is he still trying to patch things up?'

'What makes you think he wants to do that?' she asked suspiciously.

'He'd be an idiot not to.'

'What's this? A compliment from the man

who found me so lacking he started looking for other sexual partners six months after we were married?'

'That had nothing to do with you. It was me. I understand that now and you should, too.'

'Are you in counseling again?'

'It's that obvious?'

'Remember, I've been through this with you once. I'd have to be asleep not to recognize the road signs.' She led him to the family room and indicated a chair for him to sit in. Before she sat in the opposite chair, she asked, 'Would you like something to drink? There's iced tea, and I think there's some lemonade left.'

'No, thanks.'

She sat down and tucked her legs under her. 'Okay, I'm all yours.' She smiled at the irony. 'For the moment.'

He leaned forward, resting his elbows on his knees. 'I've decided to ask Michelle to marry me.'

Catherine didn't know what to think or how to feel. She didn't love him. Why would she care that he was getting married again? 'You're telling me this before you tell her?'

'If I'm going to do this thing, I want it to last this time. I don't want this child to have to go through what Lynda did. And I want to try to make up for some of the harm I've done to Lynda by including her in my life now — the way she should have been included all along.'

'How do I fit into this?' she asked.

'I don't know how to tell Lynda. How do I convince her that she's important to me? I can say the words, but how do I make her believe them?'

'Don't tell her, Jack. You've told her too many times already. She doesn't listen anymore. You're going to have to show her.'

'How?'

She felt a flash of righteous anger. Jack was repeating a pattern established in their marriage. He would screw something up and then look to her for the easy answer to extricate himself. He wanted her to give him a roadmap to his daughter's heart, a menu where he could order one item from caring, one from attention, one from listening, and one from loving discipline and end up with a complete, satisfying relationship.

'Think of all the things you haven't done with her or for her in the past and start doing them. Sacrifice to be with her but never tell her when you do. She has to reach the point that she takes you for granted before she can trust that you will be there for her. That is a child's right, not a privilege.'

He seemed to fold into himself, as if overwhelmed by the prospect. 'I don't know if I can do all of that,' he admitted. 'How can I always be there for Lynda and Michelle and the new baby, too?'

How he worked things out with Michelle and their new baby was his problem. Lynda was hers. 'Your entire life you've put yourself and what you need and what you want first. Nothing else is going to change until that does.'

'Well, I asked.'

'And I answered,' she said.

'I want Lynda to be in the wedding. Do you have a problem with that?'

'Aren't you moving a little fast? You haven't even asked Michelle to marry you yet.'

'She'll say yes. And I want to get it over with before Michelle starts showing.'

'It's going to be impossible to find a formal summer dress that will hide Lynda's pressure garments. Everything that's in the stores now is sleeveless.'

'Why does she have to hide her pressure garments?'

If asked, Catherine would have sworn that not an ember remained of the love she'd once had for Jack Miller. But there it was, ready to

262

be rekindled. Not into the love she'd once felt, but into something more important. In that simple statement he'd created in her a willingness to do whatever it took to help him become Lynda's father.

21

'All right — what's going on here?' Catherine said, propping her hands on her hips and glaring at her daughter.

'Nothing,' Lynda insisted. 'Brian just reminded me that we promised Ray we'd come by to watch a movie with him tonight and that he'd invited Wendy to come with us. It's all arranged. And I know you wouldn't want me to disappoint Ray.'

She didn't believe for a minute that Lynda had forgotten anything, but the story was too good for Catherine to win the argument. 'You're the one who invited Rick to dinner. How is it going to look if you're not around when he gets here?' She decided to try a little of Lynda's own strategy. 'You wouldn't want to disappoint him, would you? Not after everything he's done for us.'

'You're good, Mom. But I'm better. Rick would never ask me to break a date with Ray to keep one with him.'

The oven timer sounded, signaling the cake was done. Catherine reached for an oven mitt and a toothpick. After inserting the toothpick in the center of the cake and checking it, she decided to give it another five minutes. She turned to see Lynda leaving.

'Oh, no you don't. I'm not through with you.'

Lynda blinked several times, feigning a wide-eyed innocence. 'I was just going to get the cream so you could rub my back.'

Catherine smiled despite her frustration. It was so good to see how far Lynda had come emotionally that at moments like these she had trouble staying angry for long. Still, she had to draw a line where Rick was concerned and insist Lynda didn't cross it again. It wasn't fair to lead him on this way, no matter who was doing the leading.

When the cake was out of the oven and cooling, Catherine went upstairs for the fifth of Lynda's six daily massages. According to everything they'd been told and had researched for themselves, the more Lynda's scars were manipulated with deep massage, the better the final outcome. They had eighteen months. After that, the scarring was set.

Lynda was too young to fully appreciate how important it was to keep to the schedule Catherine had set up as soon as her back was healed enough to begin the massage. She saw her future through the eyes of a teenager, unable to focus more than a month or two ahead. Reality was something she could touch or feel or talk to on the phone.

When Lynda was a woman and looked back on this summer with questions about her care, Catherine wanted her to know they had left no road untraveled, no potential solution untried.

If accomplishing that meant postponing her search for a job and using her savings to pay bills, then that's what she would do. Jack had agreed to cut back on his own expenses rather than ask the court to lower her alimony, at least for the next six months, while Lynda still needed so much of her mother's time and attention.

Not once in her thirty-eight years had Catherine been independent. She'd moved from her parents' home to a college dorm and then back home again while she planned her marriage. Jack had wanted her to be a homemaker, believing she could better help him socially if she was always available, and she'd agreed. The job she took after the divorce was more for pride than income. Her skills were limited, her degree in English literature limiting.

She'd earned 'play' money to cover the impulse purchase, the Italian shoes, the florist bill for the fresh flowers she ordered weekly to try to make their enormous house seem more like a home.

Reaching the top of the stairs, Catherine shook free of the dark thoughts that lately had nipped at her heels like a high-strung miniature poodle. Lynda had enough on her plate without a serving of financial concerns from her mother.

Lynda was already out of her pressure garments and on the massage table they'd bought the week before, her head over the end, slowly, rhythmically swinging her arms out to the side and overhead, stretching the skin and muscle where her arms connected to her back. She looked up from the fashion magazine she'd been reading when she heard Catherine come in.

'I hope we have an early winter.'

Catherine set the timer for twenty minutes and spread the cream across Lynda's back and arms and buttocks where the additional skin had been harvested for transplant. 'Don't tell me the designers have finally come up with something worth buying this year.'

'As if.' She flipped the page. 'Actually, I was just thinking about my sweaters and how well they'll cover my pressure suit. No one will even know I have it on — they'll just think I've gotten fat.'

'I thought you were okay with the suit,' Catherine said carefully. The custom-made garment was flesh-colored and fit like a second skin. Worn to further reduce scarring, it was the passive partner to the active massage. Lynda only took it off to shower or during a massage.

'Come on, Mom. If it was you, would you be okay with it?'

'I don't know,' she said truthfully. 'If I've learned nothing else these past couple of months, it's how insulting it is to tell someone you know what they're going through or how they feel when you've never experienced anything like that yourself.'

'Did you know Rick was burned?'

'Yes.' Lynda had slipped into the habit of abruptly changing subjects in the middle of a conversation. As disconcerting as it was, Catherine usually just went along.

'It doesn't bother him. But then, he's old.'

'I know — my age. Ancient.'

'That's not what I mean. He doesn't have to worry about girls being turned off by how his arms look.'

'Why not?' Instead of looking at Lynda's back, Catherine focused on the rectangular patch of sunlight bleaching the flowered wallpaper behind the dresser. There were times she couldn't bear to see the evidence of the pain Lynda suffered. The parents in her support group had told her that eventually

268

she would be able to separate the scars from the memory, but she couldn't imagine it happening. How would she ever be able to look at the imprint on Lynda's back and not remember the crimson camisole that had melted into the flesh?

'Jeez, Mom. Have you ever really looked at Rick? He's gorgeous. Who cares about his arms?'

'We need to talk about this, Lynda.'

'My hair should be out by Christmas, don't you think?'

'I'm serious. You have to stop trying to push me and Rick together.'

'Why?'

'I don't know where to begin.'

'What's wrong with him?'

'Nothing. He's a very nice man. So was Tom. At least I thought so in the beginning.'

Lynda pushed up on her elbows and twisted to look at her mother. 'You can't be comparing Rick to Tom.'

'I don't know Rick well enough to compare him to anyone. What I'm trying to get through to you is that a man — any man — is the last thing I need, or want, in my life right now.' She grabbed a towel and wiped the remaining lotion off Lynda's back. 'You have to promise me you'll stop this match-making. It isn't fair to either of us.'

Lynda sighed. 'Brian thinks you're perfect for each other, too.'

'It just keeps getting worse.' She moved to let Lynda sit up, then stood in front of her to get her full attention. 'I know you think you're doing me a favor, but you're not. Rick is going to wind up hurt if you keep this up and I'm going to be furious with you if that happens.'

'Okay, I'll behave.' She hopped down. 'But I still can't stay for dinner,' she added from her bedroom door.

Catherine considered calling Rick and giving him the option to cancel the evening. Once he found out Lynda wouldn't be there to fill the awkward silences, she had no doubt he'd come up with an excuse to bail. She dialed his number.

He wasn't home. Deciding it wasn't the kind of message she wanted to leave on his machine, she went back to preparing the meal.

* * *

Convinced he'd put on too much cologne, Rick ran his hands over his cheeks and down his neck as if he could remove a layer of fragrance. Half an hour was too long to still be smelling the stuff. The cologne was a brand he didn't know, something expensive his sister had given him for his birthday. She'd picked it up at Nordstrom and, after letting it sit on the shelf in his bathroom for four months, he'd stupidly decided to try it that afternoon. He'd liked it a lot when he first put it on, but was having second thoughts.

Now he pictured himself ringing Catherine's doorbell surrounded by an invisible bubble of odor that would knock her out cold when he walked by.

This was insane. Surely he could find something better to worry about — meteors striking the earth or oil being discovered on his land. He stopped and waved to the guard who opened the gate without leaving his air-conditioned cubicle.

Catherine must have been watching for him, because she opened the door before he had a chance to ring the bell.

'Hi,' she said, and smiled.

'I'm a little early. I hope that's okay.'

'Of course. Come in.'

He entered the foyer and handed her the bottle of wine he'd been saving to inaugurate his new kitchen.

She looked at the label. 'Randle's Roost — I love their wines, especially their merlot. I've never met anyone else who's ever heard of them. How did you?'

'I was wandering around the foothills looking for the lumber to make my kitchen cabinets and they had an old barn that wasn't going to see another winter upright. We made the deal — the lumber in exchange for some cabinets they wanted for the showroom. In the process of hauling and building we became friends. They gave me a couple of cases of wine out of their private collection and add to it every Christmas.'

Catherine seemed flustered. 'I'm afraid the wine is more special than the meal. Maybe you should save it for another time.'

'Any homecooked meal that I didn't have to help prepare is a special occasion. The way I figure it, if I come bearing gifts and behave myself while I'm here, you just might ask me back.' She stared at him as if he'd announced he was a visitor from another planet. 'It was a joke, Catherine.'

'I'm sorry.' She made a quick, helpless gesture with her hand. 'I don't know any way around it so I might as well just tell you straight out — Lynda isn't here. She never had any intention of being here. This whole evening was a setup to get us together.'

'I thought as much.'

'You did?'

'I could see her mind heading in that

272

direction when I took her to see Sandra. And then when she called and told me you'd asked her to invite me to dinner, I just hoped she'd at least warned you I was coming before I showed up on your doorstep.'

'You shouldn't have let her get away with it.'

Obviously she knew as well as he did that he had no business being there. She couldn't know how he felt about her, but she was aware they had a line they shouldn't cross. Which made it safe for them to be together, at least for that night.

He smiled to put her at ease. 'And give up a chance for a homecooked meal? Not a chance.'

She returned his smile. 'If I'd known you were so passionate about the homecooking part, I would have made meatloaf and mashed potatoes.'

'Instead of?'

'Marinated flank steak, green salad, Harvard beets, and baked potatoes.'

He put his hand to his chest. 'Be still my heart.'

She laughed. 'Keep that up and you'll be invited to eat with us every night.'

'You cook like this all the time?'

'Well, maybe not quite this elaborate. I've been pushing my culinary skills since Lynda came home from the hospital. I don't want her going back to her rabbit food until she's well enough to get along without the calories.'

'And it's working?'

She held up crossed fingers. 'So far. I even made her favorite dessert — thinking she was going to be here. If I'd known it was just you and me, I would have made something different.'

'And her favorite dessert would be?'

'Yellow cake with chocolate frosting.' She led the way to the kitchen, where she took a double-pronged bottle opener out of a drawer to uncork the wine.

'Sounds good to me. But just so I know what I'm missing, what would you have made?'

She put the wine on the table to give it time to breathe before dinner and removed the bottle of burgundy she'd put there earlier. 'Oh, probably something lighter, like Grand Marnier sauce over fresh raspberries.'

'Hmmm, that's a tough one, but I think I'd have to go with the cake.'

'Only because you've never tasted my Grand Marnier sauce. I guarantee you'll change your mind when you do.' Catherine was stunned at how easily she implied a future invitation when only hours earlier she'd insisted to Lynda that it would never happen again.

She looked at the elegantly set table, the linen and crystal and sterling, and decided it was all wrong. Not for Rick, for her. 'Would you mind if we ate on the deck?'

'That's fine with me.'

'My father always said you invited friends to an elbows-on-the-table meal and saved the fancy stuff for people you wanted to impress.'

'Wise man.'

'More a simple man, I think. He grew up poor and never accepted or understood the rules that come with having a lot of money. He was so oblivious to the social obligations that come with running a company like his that it became a full-time job for my mother.'

'What kind of company was it?'

'He looked for businesses that were failing because of poor management and turned them around. Along with everything my mother did for my father, she made sure Gene and I went to the right schools, had the right friends, and were invited to the right parties. When my dad died, she dumped every club and organization she didn't enjoy and then did the same thing with friends. She said she was through spending time with people she didn't like when she didn't have enough time for the people she loved.'

Catherine looked at Rick and frowned. 'I don't know why I told you that. I hardly ever talk about my family.'

'Why?'

'It's boring — like telling someone about your dreams.'

'Not to me. I'm always on the lookout for people with crazy relatives so I'll know I'm not alone.'

'You have crazy relatives?'

'On both sides. It can get kind of scary at family reunions.'

She took two plates from the cupboard and put them on a wooden tray, then added knives, forks, and spoons, place mats and napkins. 'I don't believe you.'

'How about a grandfather who built a house out of the hubcaps he found on the side the road?'

'So he's into recycling. What's wrong with that?' She added salt and pepper and salad dressing to the tray.

'All right, how's this: I have an aunt who insists she's Howard Hughes's love child.'

'It's possible. I hear he used to get around a lot in his younger days.'

'How about a great-uncle who wears a metal helmet to keep the Martians from stealing his secret salsa recipe?'

She thought a minute. 'I'm afraid I'm going to have to give you that one.'

'*Finally*. I should probably quit while I'm

ahead. Although . . . '

'Yes?' She handed him the tray and pointed to the French doors that opened onto the deck.

'There is this second cousin on my mother's side who lives in a cave and only comes out at night.'

'Thinks she's a bat, I suppose.'

Rick's eyebrows rose in surprise. 'Oh — so you've heard of her. Funny how things like that get around.'

It was everything Catherine could do to keep from laughing. 'It must be a terrible burden to be the only sane one in the family.'

'Oh, it's not as bad as you might think. The Sawyers and McCormicks measure sanity by a different yardstick. That helps. A lot.'

She laughed. 'You're so full of — '

'Careful. I'm a sensitive kind of guy.'

'And I'm the Queen of Sheba.' She let him hold the tray while she set the table, glancing up to see the mischievous look in his eyes despite the straight face.

'I don't think so,' he said after several seconds.

'Why not?'

'I distinctly remember Grandma telling me that my Aunt Margaret was the Queen of Sheba.'

She stopped, put her hands on her hips,

and glared at him. 'I'm not going to play anymore if I can't be the queen.'

Rick stared at her, openmouthed, and then burst out laughing. 'Good one.'

She gave him a prim smile. 'Thank you.'

★   ★   ★

They talked as much as they ate that night, about everything from books they'd both read to movies they hadn't had time to see. Catherine said she'd always wanted to visit the penguin colonies on Antarctica; Rick told her he thought she was nuts but admitted he could be talked into going if pressed. He told her he'd always wanted to climb Mt. McKinley; she said he was out of his mind and that she couldn't be talked into going even if promised a month in Hawaii in exchange.

The sun disappeared behind the Coast Range, leaving the sky a palate of oranges and pinks. Rick poured the last of the wine and stole a glance at Catherine. She looked thoughtful and a little sad, as if the sun had taken her joy along with the daylight.

'Are you okay?' he asked gently.

'I was just thinking about that night on the lake.' She turned to meet his gaze. 'I never know what's going to trigger the memory. It just happens, and it always catches me off guard. Sometimes it's a sound, or the way the air feels against my skin, or finding one of Lynda's pressure garments in the laundry or one of the bands she used to use on her hair.'

'You need a break. Get out and do something crazy. When was the last time you went to the State Fair and got sick on the rides? Better yet, spend a day doing whatever you would have been doing now if none of this had happened.'

Catherine thought a minute and smiled wryly. 'I'm not sure that's such a good idea. People might be a little confused to receive a wedding invitation from me and Tom when he announced his engagement to another woman last weekend.'

He couldn't have put his foot in his mouth more effectively if he'd aimed. 'Not one of my better ideas.'

'I'm long past caring what Tom does or who he does it with.' She hesitated long enough for a decidedly mischievous smile to form. 'As a matter of fact, I'm so far past caring, I think I'll offer to let him buy my membership in the club as an engagement present.'

She lost Rick with that. 'By club, I assume you mean the country club?'

'Sorry — I was thinking out loud.

Somehow Tom has managed to position himself as next on the list to buy a club membership. The only problem is that no one wants to sell, so he's been forced to try to marry his way in.'

'Why would anyone go to that much trouble to belong to a country club?'

'Over half the business done in the area is done at the club, either on the golf course or in the bar. Tom feels he's being held back by not being a member.'

'So now you're going to give up your membership to keep him from using someone else the way he tried to use you?' He was trying hard to understand something that was as far from his world as little green men rowing the canals of Mars. 'Is she a friend of yours?'

'Not even close. However, she has provided the one bright spot in all of this. If she's anywhere near as demanding with Tom as she was her first husband, his life is going to be a living hell.'

'Then it seems there's only one real option for selling your membership.'

She tilted her head to one side and studied him in the waning light. 'And that is?'

'Wait until the day after they're married.'

She smiled. 'You're my kind of guy, Rick Sawyer.'

What was it about her smile that made his mind turn to mush and his heart do a tap dance against his ribs? 'Anytime. I'm at your service — day or night.'

22

Lynda waved to Wendy one last time as Brian backed out of the driveway. Her face hurt from the phony smile she'd kept in place the past two hours. But it was that or put up with a ton of questions she didn't want to answer. It hardly took anything anymore — she only had to be quiet for five minutes or want to be by herself for a little while, and someone was asking her what was wrong.

'You want to talk about it?' Brian asked when they reached the corner.

'No.' She should have known she hadn't fooled him.

'Want to get a mocha?'

'Where?' She didn't want to go anywhere they would run into anyone they knew, but she wasn't ready to go home yet, either.

'I heard about a new place in Folsom.'

A lot of her friends hung out in Folsom. 'What about the Java City in Gold River?'

'All the way — ' He glanced at her. 'Uh, sure, that's fine.' Brian pulled into a driveway to turn around and head back the way they'd come.

They hadn't gone three blocks when Lynda

broke down. She didn't just want to talk about what was bothering her, she *needed* to talk about it. 'Did you see what happened?'

'You mean with Wendy at the hospital?'

'I wanted to die. God, I felt so bad. But I was afraid to say anything. I kept thinking maybe Ray didn't see the way she looked at him and if I said something I'd be the one who made it into a big deal.' She leaned her head back and stared out the moonroof at the barely visible stars. 'How could I have been so stupid? Whatever possessed me to invite Wendy to come with us tonight?'

'What made you think Ray didn't notice?' Brian asked carefully.

Because she was willing to grab at anything that would make the sick feeling go away, even if it was a piece of straw in a windstorm. 'He was so nice to her.'

He didn't say anything for a long time. 'Ray's nice to everybody. Even the physical therapist.'

'Damn it, it's just not fair. Ray can't help the way he looks.' All her life she'd been able to change things she didn't like or find a way around them or bargain them away. Until now. 'He wouldn't even be burned if he hadn't tried to save his sister.'

'If Wendy reacted the way she did even after we told her what to expect — '

'What's going to happen when Ray moves to Kansas where no one knows him?' she finished for him.

Brian turned right onto Madison Avenue. 'Did you see his aunt when she was here last week?'

Lynda shuddered. 'I didn't like her. She reminds me of Cruella De Vil — all skinny and pinched-nosed. The whole time I was in Ray's room all she talked about was how much time she'd had to take off from work to come there and how she couldn't come again until the doctors were absolutely sure he was ready to leave. She acted like it was his fault the graft didn't take.'

'What did he say?'

'Nothing. He just sat there and listened and watched her pace back and forth across the room.'

Brian stopped at a red light and turned to Lynda. 'Does he have to go with her?'

'Where else would he go?'

'My place. I was just thinking — we had an exchange student living with us last year and it worked out okay. I don't know why it would be any different with Ray.'

'Oh, Brian. You're brilliant and fantastic and wonderful and every good thing I can think of. When can you ask your mom?'

'She won't be back from the lake for a

couple of days.' He looked at her. 'We could drive up there tomorrow . . . '

Lynda was blindsided by a wave of panic. She opened her mouth to say something but nothing came out.

'Are you all right?' The light changed. Someone behind them honked when Brian didn't immediately move forward. 'Lynda?' he asked anxiously.

She nodded.

The horn sounded again. Brian started to raise his hand to gesture but brought it down again and simply drove through the intersection without comment. 'Are you afraid to go to the lake with me?' he asked when they were back in the flow of traffic.

'It isn't you,' she said, dumbfounded by what had happened. 'It's the lake. I don't want to go there.' She stared at him. 'I didn't know I felt this way.' She put her hand to her throat. 'When you said we could drive up there it was like I couldn't breathe. I felt like I was choking.'

'I'm sorry.'

'Why? It wasn't your fault. You didn't know. I didn't even know.'

'What are you going to do? You and your mom go up there every summer.'

Her mother loved the lake. So did her Uncle Gene and her grandmother. What if she could never go there with them again? 'I don't know. I need to think about it some more.'

'It won't hurt if I wait a couple of days until my mom and dad come home to talk to them about Ray.'

'What if his aunt comes back before then? Don't you think we should get going on this as fast as possible? If we wait until she's made more plans she could turn stubborn just for spite.'

Brian turned onto Sunrise. As usual, the traffic made the posted speed limit a joke on a weekend. It took two stops to get through every light. 'You know, it was just an idea,' he warned. 'I don't want you to be disappointed if my folks don't go for it.'

'Your parents are super. And smart.' She grinned impishly. 'After all, they think I'm wonderful. I bet they say yes once they understand how hard it would be for Ray to move away from here. Ray doesn't know anyone in Kansas. No one there cares about him. Here, at least he has us.'

'All right, all right. You convinced me. I'll go see them tomorrow.' He gave Lynda a serious look. 'I promise I'll do everything I can, but I don't want you to fall apart on me if it doesn't work out.' He stopped for another red light. 'I probably shouldn't have said anything until I talked to them first.'

Lynda unbuckled her seat belt and leaned over to kiss him. 'You're the best thing that ever happened to me.'

He kissed her back. 'No fair — that's what I was going to say to you.'

She saw the light turn and scrambled to get her seatbelt back on. Ten minutes later they were at the coffee shop. When she started to open the door, Brian put his hand on her arm to stop her. She turned to look at him and he took the bill of her cap and gently pulled her forward for another kiss. He opened his mouth and touched his tongue to hers, and in seconds what had started as tender affection became breath-stealing excitement.

'Wow,' she murmured as heat spread through her body, a tingling sensation curling her toes. 'What brought that on?'

He put his cheek to hers and whispered, 'I'm sorry.'

Lynda sat very still, her heart in her throat, her mind examining his words as if they were glowing rocks from another planet.

Brian leaned back and looked into her eyes. 'I've been meaning to tell you that for a long time, but I didn't expect it would be here and now. It just came out.'

'Why are you sorry? What did you do?'

He swallowed and blinked sudden moisture

from his eyes. 'I didn't run fast enough. I should have gotten to you sooner.'

His pain lay between them like an offering. She cupped his cheek with her hand. 'It isn't that you didn't run fast enough — it's that I ran too fast. I'm so lucky that you were there to save me. What if you'd been in the house? Or out on the boat? No one, not one single person, made a move to come after me, Brian. Only you.' Slowly, deliberately, she kissed him again. 'You're my hero.'

★ ★ ★

Catherine left the book she'd been reading on the sofa and got up to answer the telephone. Her greeting was answered with, 'You know that old saying, a friend in need is a friend indeed?'

'Karol?'

'I'm amazed you recognized my voice. It's been ages since we last talked.'

'You must have forgotten all the messages you left on the machine when Lynda was in the hospital. By the way, a very belated thank-you is in order. Knowing we were in your thoughts meant a lot.' She and Karol had been close friends for years and then drifted apart when Karol gave birth to triplets and Catherine started her job. They'd made and broken luncheon dates for a year before they finally gave up trying to get together. Hearing from her now brought a wave of good memories.

'I wish I could have done something to help but every time I asked, Tom insisted you wanted to handle everything by yourself.'

'He never told me he'd talked to you.'

'I kind of figured as much when I found out you weren't together anymore and I never heard from you.'

'I'm so glad you called. It's so good to hear from you.' Better than she could have imagined. 'Now what's this friend-in-need business?'

'Oh that — I foolishly let myself be talked into cochairing the Brand Name Rummage Sale this year.'

'And?' Catherine asked, already guessing the answer.

'I started thinking about all the fun we used to have all those years ago when we did the sale together and wondered if Lynda had reached a point in her recovery that she didn't need you quite as much as she had and you were ready for a distraction and I might be able to talk you into cochairing with me.' She laughed. 'Whew. Can you tell I'm a little nervous about dumping this on you?'

The proposal was so unexpected Catherine

didn't have an immediate answer. The years she and Karol had been in charge of the sale they'd taken it from a small charity function that benefited two local animal welfare groups to a half-million-dollar event that boasted contributions of items from the governor and half the legislators. Their stated goal was a completely no-kill county patterned after the animal shelter in San Francisco.

'Can you give me a couple of days to think about it?'

'I can give you a whole week if you need it.'

'I won't. I just want to make sure I can work it out before I commit.'

'Please try. I'd really love to work with you again. We used to have such a good time and I miss seeing you.'

'I miss seeing you, too,' Catherine said.

'Even if you can't be cochair, let's get together. As soon as possible.'

'I'd like that.'

Catherine hung up and went back to her book, excited about the prospect of doing something she knew she was good at again.

Minutes later, the headlights from Brian's car reflected through the glass front door, alerting her that Lynda was home. She put aside the book again, and waited, anxious to hear how Lynda's evening had gone.

'I'm home,' Lynda called from the front door.

'In here,' Catherine called back from the family room.

For a second, as Brian's headlights again swept through the room, Lynda's body was backlit and almost seemed to glow. As she had since she was an infant, Catherine wondered at her daughter's remarkable features and how they had combined to form such innocent beauty. There was nothing calculated or aloof about the way Lynda looked. When her eyes sparkled, they were filled with invitation to join in her happiness; when her full lips formed a smile, they invariably enticed a return smile; when she looked sad or forlorn, she broke the hearts of those around her.

'So, how did your date with Rick go?' Lynda asked, breaking the spell.

Catherine let out a long-suffering sigh. 'It was not a date.'

'Okay, how did your non-date with Rick go?'

'It was all right.'

'Nothing with Rick is just *all right*. Come on, Mom. I want details.'

'He brought a bottle of wine. We ate on the deck. He helped with the dishes and he went home.'

Lynda groaned melodramatically as she plopped down on the opposite end of the sofa. 'You made him do dishes?'

'No — I didn't make him. He insisted.'

'What did you talk about?'

'Crazy relatives.'

Lynda let out another groan. 'You didn't tell him about Uncle John, did you? Please say you didn't.'

Damn, she'd forgotten all about her mother's brother and his spitting camel. She'd have won their crazy relative contest hands down with Uncle John. 'You're safe.'

Lynda looked at the ceiling. 'Thank you, God.'

'How did it go at the hospital?'

The smile in Lynda's eyes disappeared. She kicked off her shoes and put her feet on the coffee table. 'Not good.'

All it took was a lost smile to remind Catherine that the ground she walked on with Lynda these past few months was filled with unexpected peaks and valleys and she never knew when she might stumble on one of them. 'What happened?'

'Wendy freaked out when she saw Ray.'

'I was afraid that might happen.' She should have followed her instincts and tried to talk Lynda out of taking Wendy to the hospital. Brian and Lynda had become blind to Ray's appearance, seeing the person trapped inside the terribly burned body and forgetting how they, too, had reacted in the beginning. 'Did he notice?'

'He didn't say anything, but I don't know how he could have missed it. He was looking right at us when we came in.' She drew her legs up, tucking them underneath her. 'I felt so awful, Mom. I know it hurt him and I don't know what to do to make it better.'

'Sometimes life just stinks.' Catherine said, putting her book aside. 'And there's not a damn thing we can do about it. As sad as it is, as unfair as it is, Ray is going to have to find a way to deal with all the good-intentioned people who are going to break his heart.'

'You mean me?'

'No, I mean people like Wendy.' Automatically accepting blame was something new with Lynda and it always caught Catherine by surprise. 'She would never hurt anyone on purpose. And I'm sure if she visited Ray on a regular basis, the way you and Brian do, she would stop seeing what the fire did to him and start seeing the wonderful young man he is inside.'

'She doesn't want to go back,' Lynda said, a catch in her voice. 'Not ever. She won't even give him a chance.'

Catherine only had Band-Aid words for her

daughter, and it would be an insult to use them on a wound this deep.

Lynda reached for a tissue. She blew her nose and looked at her mother with a corner of her mouth lifted in a sad, ironic smile. 'Well, at least there's one good thing that came out of all this. At least, I think it's good.'

'And that is?'

'It's pretty hard for me to feel sorry for myself when I'm around Ray.' She pulled off her Roseville Fire Department cap and ran her hand over the downy stubble that covered her scalp.

'I'm so proud of you,' Catherine said.

'Because I feel sorry for Ray?'

'Because you care.'

'Well, I guess if we're going to get all sloppy and sentimental tonight I suppose I should go ahead and tell you how much I love you and how glad I am that you're my mother.'

'Thank you — that's nice to hear.' She would tuck Lynda's words away and keep them to savor during the weeks ahead. School was less than a month away and Catherine had a feeling Ray wouldn't be the only one who needed unconditional and non-judgmental support. When Lynda needed to vent, Catherine had no doubt who she would vent to.

She stood and held out her hand. 'Come on. It's time for one of my incredible backrubs.'

Lynda followed Catherine upstairs. 'I forgot to tell you that Grandma called. She wanted to know if we'd made plans for your birthday.'

'What did you tell her?'

'That I wasn't sure, but you might have a date.'

'*What?*'

'Well, I thought you might let it slip that it was coming up and Rick would ask you to go to dinner with him. I checked his calendar and he has the day off.'

Catherine stopped on the landing, turned, and glared at Lynda. 'Did you listen to one thing I said about this matchmaking of yours? Rick and I are friends. That's it. End of story. If you keep trying to make something out of it that it's not, you're going to ruin the friendship. *And that would make me very unhappy.*'

'Wow, chill out, Mom. I'll call Grandma tomorrow and tell her we'll be there for dinner.'

Catherine started up the stairs again, then turned to face Lynda. 'How many are you going to tell her to expect?' she asked suspiciously.

'Uh . . . two?'

'You know that new CD player you wanted me to look at?'

'Yeah?'

'Think about it before you change your mind and decide to invite Rick without telling me first.'

'Blackmail? My own mom? I can't believe it.'

'Believe it.'

'Can I invite Brian?'

'I'd rather you didn't. I don't want to make a big deal out of this and you know Grandma would if we started inviting a whole bunch of people.'

'Brian isn't a bunch. He's one person.'

'All right.' Catherine didn't mind Brian being there but knew if she made Lynda fight to invite him, she would back off inviting Rick. 'But tell him he's not allowed to bring a present.'

'You can't go to a birthday party and not bring a present. How about if we go in on something together?'

'You're pushing.'

Lynda held her hands up in surrender. 'That's it. I promise.'

'Nothing over fifty dollars.' She'd decided the lavish presents had to stop. Along with club dues and fresh flowers that didn't come from her own garden.

'You're kidding.' When she didn't get the response she expected, she added, 'Aren't you?'

'Consider it a challenge.'

'But I already picked something out.'

'What?'

She hesitated. 'A St. John sweater I found when I was at Nordstrom trying on dresses with Dad for the wedding.'

She loved St. John knits. And Lynda had a perfect eye for what looked good on her. But the last thing she needed was a fifteen-hundred-dollar charge on her credit card for another sweater to add to her collection when she had to sell stock to make the house payment. 'It sounds lovely, but I think the fifty-dollar present would be a lot more fun. And fun is important when you're turning thirty-nine.'

'You want me to get you a joke gift? I thought you hated that kind of thing.'

Catherine knew it was going to be hard to make the changes she had to make to keep them afloat financially, she just hadn't realized how hard. Lynda had never wanted for anything. There had never been a reason not to give her what she asked for or needed. She didn't just expect a car for her sixteenth birthday, she believed she would be given the car of her choice.

'How about getting me . . . ' Catherine couldn't even come up with anything to suggest. The thought stunned her. It seemed they both had a long way to go.

'Never mind. Brian and I will figure it out.' She motioned for Catherine to move upstairs. 'I want to talk to you about something else anyway. What do you think about Ray staying here instead of going to Kansas?'

'What do you mean by 'here'?' Catherine asked carefully.

'I'll tell you about it while you're rubbing my back.' She grinned. 'Brian's going to call when he gets home.'

'Oh, now I understand the sudden rush.'

'What can I say? I'm in love.'

Catherine blinked in surprise. 'Well — congratulations.'

'Thank you.'

'When did this revelation take place?'

'It's been creeping up on me for a long time and tonight I figured I might as well give in.' Responding to the look Catherine gave her, Lynda blushed and quickly added, 'I don't mean give in like in *give in*. That's a long way off yet.'

'I'm glad to hear it.'

'Come on.' Lynda put her hands on

Catherine's shoulders to turn her around. 'Let's go.'

Catherine found she was suddenly as anxious as Lynda to get through the massage and be alone. She had some thinking to do. Lynda in love? She'd known the day would come. She just hadn't known it would make her feel left behind.

Could her life get any more complicated?

23

'You might as well lie about how old you are.' Phyllis stuck the last candle in Catherine's birthday cake and stood back to study the symmetry. 'Pick an age you really like. No one believes you when you tell them you're thirty-nine, anyway. It's a terrible age. One of those in-between things. You spend the entire year knowing it's the last one in your thirties and that old age begins in just a few months.'

'Thanks, Mom,' Catherine said. 'I can always count on you to cheer me up when I'm down.'

Phyllis stopped fiddling with the cake long enough to look at Catherine. 'I didn't know you were feeling down. Is there something you haven't told me about?'

'I wasn't serious.'

'Sounded pretty serious to me. Is Lynda having problems again?'

'Lynda's fine. Actually, there are times when I think she's almost doing too well. When she and Brian went to the Lilith concert she wore a short-sleeved linen shirt and never said a word about anyone noticing her pressure garments. It's as if she's become

300

oblivious to people staring at her with a questioning look in their eyes.'

'Maybe they aren't anymore.'

'Oh, it still happens. Every time we go out. I think I've finally convinced her that it's not rudeness so much as curiosity.'

'Well, then maybe she's become more accepting of that.'

'She hasn't gone through any of the stages they talk about in the support group. Or if she has, they've been so minor I haven't recognized them.'

Phyllis ran her finger over the frosting knife and popped the chocolate-coated digit in her mouth. 'I seem to remember she had a number of incidents in the hospital when she was less than cooperative. And she was a real handful that week she came home. Couldn't those have been stages?'

'I don't count them.' Catherine took the sponge from the back of the sink and began wiping the counter. She loved working in her mother's kitchen. There was a warmth here that was missing in hers, and she'd never been able to understand why. She was sure part of it was knowing that if she opened the pantry door she'd find a stair step of pencil marks with her and Gene's names attached, but her feelings ran deeper than tradition. Because she hadn't looked in a while, she opened the door to see that they were, indeed, still there. The marks followed hers and Gene's growth from the time they were old enough to stand up by themselves until they left for college. She closed the door and looked at the woman who loved her without question, half of the pair who had built the foundation for a childhood full of good memories. There was more, but she couldn't put a name to it, things she only felt, things that made her feel special.

'There has to be a reason you're worried about Lynda.'

'I guess I'm waiting for the other shoe to drop. At first I thought she was doing as well as she is because she comes from a good background and has always had lots of love and support. Then I looked around at the other parents in the group and realized I was being the worst kind of snob. Lynda isn't loved any more or any better than the other kids. Money and position have nothing to do with how much someone cares.'

Catherine rinsed the sponge and put it away. 'Did I tell you she's even decided to go to the fire-fighters' burn camp at Lake Tahoe after all?' This was Lynda's one chance to attend the camp; the cut-off for participants was sixteen. The parents in the support group insisted the interaction with the other seventy-five burn survivors at camp was the best medicine their children received every year. Catherine had done everything short of ordering Lynda to go, with no success.

'Now that does surprise me. When did this happen?'

'She just came out with it the other night when I was massaging her back. I think Brian might have had a part in it — both the not wanting to go and then changing her mind. Turns out he's going to be tied up with football that week and they wouldn't be able to see much of each other anyway.'

'When does she go?'

'In two weeks.'

'And she's going to be gone for a week?'

'Sunday to Saturday.'

'Want to do something fun?'

'Like?'

'We could drive up the coast, eat seafood until we get sick, and then meander home through the Napa Valley.'

She couldn't believe how tempting getting away sounded, even if only for a couple of days. 'I can't. What if something happened at camp and they couldn't reach me?'

'Ever hear of a cell phone?' Phyllis moved the cake to the opposite counter and checked the roast in the oven. 'Come on, Catherine. It'll be good for you to breathe some ocean air. And you couldn't ask for better company.'

'True.' Catherine put her arm around her mother's shoulders and gave her a hug.

'Well?'

'I think my time would be better spent job hunting.'

'What? You're going back to work? When did this come about?'

'Lynda's therapy is just about over, so she won't need me to drive her to the hospital three times a week anymore. And she's going to be back in school in another month, so we'd have to adapt her massages to her new schedule anyway.' If her mother found out job hunting was a necessity, not an outlet for boredom, she'd jump in with advice and help, neither of which Catherine wanted right then. 'Even if it's only part-time, I want to get back to doing something productive with my life. Which is one of the reasons I told Karol I would cochair the rummage sale with her.'

'Did you talk to Rick about it?'

Catherine shook her head in wonder. Even her mother had succumbed to the Rick mystique, believing him to be all-knowing, all-caring, all-powerful. 'No, I haven't. Believe it or not, there are some decisions I still make all by myself. Besides, we already take more of his time than we should and I don't know why he would care whether I get a job or what I do in my spare time.'

'I don't think he sees it that way.'

'Mother — you hardly know the man. What makes you think — '

'I do too know him.'

'How?'

'I met him at the hospital. Several times. And you and Lynda never stop talking about him.'

Catherine's eyes widened in surprise. 'I hardly ever talk about him.'

Now it was Phyllis's turn to look surprised. 'You should stop and listen to yourself sometime. You talk about Rick almost as much as you do Lynda.'

'I may mention him once or twice in the context of the conversation, but — '

Lynda came into the room. 'Mention who?'

'No one,' Catherine said.

'Rick Sawyer,' Phyllis said at the same time.

Lynda brightened. 'Is Rick coming? I thought you told me that I couldn't invite him.'

'No,' Catherine said. 'Rick is not coming.'

'Then why were you talking about him?'

Phyllis focused on Catherine. 'Why didn't you want to invite him? Is something wrong? Did you two have a fight?'

Catherine looked from her mother to her daughter and then back again. 'No, we did not have a fight — and I do not talk about him all the time.' She shifted her gaze back to Lynda. 'Yes, I did tell you that I didn't want to invite him and that I will take phone privileges away from you for the rest of your life if you ever even think about trying to fix us up again.'

'Oh . . . now I understand what's going on,' Phyllis said. 'You and Rick are — '

Catherine felt the ground slipping away beneath her. 'Rick and I are *friends*.'

Lynda held her hands up and began backing out of the room. 'I can see I'm not needed here. I'm going to go outside and wait for Brian. If you should decide I'm worthy company after all, you know where to find me.'

'I'm sorry,' Catherine said. 'You don't have to go.'

'While you're out there, would you check the mail?' Phyllis said. 'Gene said he sent a package a couple of weeks ago and it hasn't arrived yet.' She opened a drawer and tossed Lynda a stuffed toy lion with a key attached.

When Lynda was gone, Phyllis turned to Catherine, a mischievous smile lighting her eyes. 'Okay, now tell me what's going on with you and Rick.'

Catherine sighed. She could either tell Phyllis outright or put up with a dozen circuitous questions that would get it out of her eventually anyway. 'Lynda's been trying to play matchmaker, and I can't seem to convince her that it's a bad idea.'

Phyllis was quiet for several seconds. 'I don't know. Seems like a pretty good idea to me.'

'Oh, Mother, please — not you, too.'

'All right. Tell me what you think is so wrong with dating Rick Sawyer.'

Catherine had purposely avoided this conversation because she knew her position wasn't one her mother would understand. That didn't make it any less valid, just harder to defend. 'It isn't Rick, it's me. I've given this a lot of thought, so I want you to promise me you won't start reasoning with me or try to get me to change my mind.'

'I can't promise something like that until I know what you're talking about.'

'I'm through with men. With dating. With all of it. It's pretty obvious from the choices I've made in the past that I can't tell a good man from a rotten one, and I'm not willing to go through that kind of pain again.'

'Did you tell Lynda this?'

'How could I? It just so happens one of those rotten men I'm talking about is her father.'

'Rick is nothing like Jack.'

'That's what I thought about Tom, too. I didn't go into that relationship blindly. Or at least I thought I didn't. I looked for someone who believed what I did, who liked the same kinds of things I did, who had the same goals and dreams and ambitions, and you can see what happened. I couldn't have wound up with anyone worse if I'd thrown a dart at the telephone book.'

She pulled out a chair from the kitchen table, sat down, and started folding napkins. 'I don't know. Maybe someday I'll have enough confidence in myself that I'll be willing to get involved with someone again, but first I need time to get over what I almost did with Tom.'

Phyllis sat next to Catherine and picked up one of the napkins. 'Tom fooled us all. He's charming and thoughtful and as phony as the smiles on the faces of the losers at the Academy Awards.'

'The only answer I can come up with is that I was so caught up in the idea of not being alone anymore that I refused to see anything bad about him. Now I can see it all. Especially the way he listened to my dreams and turned them into his promises. He was so good, Mom. When he talked me into quitting my job, I didn't hesitate for a second. Here was someone who wanted to take care of me in every way possible. How could I not see how dependent that would make me? Tell me, how dumb is that?'

'Well, I can see you've got a ways to go before you stop beating yourself up and hit your emotional bottom. I'm just afraid that when you do and you're ready to start climbing out of that hole, Rick's going to be long gone. What a shame he came into your life when you can't appreciate him.'

'It doesn't matter when Rick came into my life, we would be wrong for each other.' The instant it was out she knew she'd made a mistake. Instead of letting the subject die, she'd added fuel.

'Why is that?'

'We have nothing in common.' Nothing that counted anyway. Family trees studded with fruits and nuts made for good conversation, but did little to build a foundation for a long-term relationship. 'We come from different social backgrounds.' She wasn't explaining it very well. 'If you invited his friends and my friends to a party, they would have nothing to say to each other. I know it sounds petty, but in the long run, things like that matter.'

'You may not have friends in common, but you have Lynda. That's a lot more than you could say for Tom.'

'Lynda is his job, Mom. As soon as his year with her is up he'll move on to someone new.'

'Well,' she said, and sighed. 'At least you've considered your options.'

A stray thought hit Catherine and she laughed unexpectedly. 'Can you imagine how horrified Rick would be if he could hear us dissecting him this way?'

'Poor guy, we've all but put him in a box and tied it up with a bow.' Phyllis stood and gave Catherine a meaningful look. 'It would have been nice if you had at least looked inside before you stamped it 'return to sender'.'

'We're friends.' It was turning into a mantra. 'As a matter of fact, I consider Rick one of the best friends I have right now.' When she thought about it, she was a little hurt by how most of her long-time friends had drifted away that summer. A couple of them still called, but it had been weeks since she'd received any of the invitations to dinners or parties that she'd told Tom were her prerogative. If not for Karol, she would have felt completely forgotten. 'He even laughs at my jokes. And the last time — ' She frowned, brought up short by what she was about to say. What would her mother think if she told her that the last time she was with Rick, she'd been struck by how much her father would have liked him.

'Yes?'

The front door opened. 'Brian must be here,' Catherine said when she heard voices. 'We can talk about this later.'

'You think I'm going to forget, but I'm not,' Phyllis said.

Catherine smiled. She had no doubt her mother would remember, but it was more likely to be in the middle of the night when Catherine was safely home in bed.

24

Catherine stood at the back door and watched Brian and Lynda as they walked across the lawn hand in hand. They'd said they were going outside to work off dinner and make room for cake and ice cream, but it was plain their real interest was in being alone.

'He's such a nice boy,' Phyllis said, coming up beside her.

'Remember how wild his father was at his age?'

'Wasn't he the Winslow brother who wound up in jail?'

'Yes, but that came a little later. I was thinking about the summer he and his brothers stole that big plastic chicken from the restaurant in Tahoe City and glued it on top of the sheriff's car.'

Phyllis laughed. 'I'd forgotten about that.'

'Now he's doing the most remarkable thing. Brian and Lynda have decided Ray should stay in Sacramento. They think he'll do better here with them than somewhere where he doesn't know anyone. Brian asked his parents if Ray could stay with them

— and they said yes. Can you imagine?'

'Ray wants to stay here? Considering he lost everyone in his immediate family I would have thought being with his aunt would be more important than being with friends.'

'They haven't said anything to him yet, but they know he doesn't want to live with his aunt. Brian's father talked them into waiting until his lawyer could investigate the legal end of having Ray live with them. He didn't want Ray to get his hopes up and then find out it couldn't be done.'

'I don't understand.'

'Ray is going to need ongoing medical care for a long time. He'll still be going to Shriner's, so there's no financial problem, but since he's still a minor, the Winslows would have to be his legal guardians to get him the care he needs until he's of age.'

'It would be like adopting him.'

'Almost.'

'They're willing to do this just because Brian asked them?'

'Pretty amazing, huh?'

Phyllis looked at Catherine. 'And these are the people Tom wanted to sue.'

Lynda saw them standing at the door and waved. 'Time to open presents?'

Catherine couldn't remember Lynda ever being as excited about a gift she'd bought.

She'd been bubbling with enthusiasm for days, demanding Catherine try to guess what was inside the large box she'd put in the middle of the dining room table and then laughing with pleasure when she guessed wrong.

Catherine opened Gene's first. It was a full-length black evening coat made out of raw silk. Elegant in its simplicity and cut, it all but shouted money. Catherine did some quick mental calculations and figured she could cover the gas and electric bill for three months on what she estimated the coat had cost.

'Obviously Uncle Gene didn't have to follow the new rules on presents,' Lynda said. 'Or was that rule just for me?'

'I forgot to tell him,' Catherine admitted.

'What new rule?' Phyllis asked.

Catherine looked at Lynda. 'Okay, this time it was just for you, but from now on, it's for everyone.'

'I don't care,' Lynda said. 'Open mine next.'

She'd wrapped the box in the comics section of the Sunday paper, topping it with a bow made out of a roll of hospital gauze. 'Very creative,' Catherine said.

'And cheap,' Brian added with a grin.

'I didn't know whether the wrapping

counted and I didn't want to take any chances.' Lynda leaned forward in anticipation.

'Go on, open it.'

When Catherine saw the illustration on the box, she didn't make the connection that it was a picture of what was inside. After all, she'd never expressed any interest in birds or in feeding them. But then she saw that it was indeed as advertised — a humming-bird feeder.

'I know you're not into the nature thing,' Lynda said. 'But just wait. You're going to love it, Mom. The hummingbirds are so cool the way they hover and dive around the feeders. I figured we could put it on the deck outside the family room window. That way you can see it from the kitchen.'

'It's the most incredible feeling when they buzz by your head,' Brian said. 'They sound like some giant bumblebee that's about to have a piece of you for lunch.'

'We asked Sandra about the best kind to buy and she said it had to be one that could be taken apart to be cleaned. I was going to get you one of those long skinny brushes, but then I remembered we already had one.'

Catherine examined the feeder, doing her best to look interested. 'When did you talk to Sandra?'

'The other day when we went to Rick's house.'

'You saw Rick? At his house? Why didn't you tell me?' She could feel Phyllis looking at her. So much for ending the discussion about Rick.

'He called and said he had a present for you and wanted to know when would be a good time to drop it off. We were on our way to see Ray, so Brian offered to stop by and pick it up. I didn't know I wasn't supposed to go to his house.'

'It's my fault,' Brian said. 'I'm the one who — '

Catherine stopped him. 'You didn't do anything wrong. I was just surprised that you and Lynda went to see Rick and didn't mention it.'

'Well?' Lynda prompted. 'Do you like it?'

'Yes — I do.' She smiled. 'This very well may be the best present you've ever given me.'

'Now you have to open Brian's.' She was grinning again.

'You really shouldn't have gotten me anything, Brian. I told Lynda not to let you.'

'Don't worry, it's not anything — '

Lynda put her hand over his mouth. 'You'll give it away.'

Catherine could hardly lift the package to

put it on her lap. She tore through the wrapping, popped the tape on the box with her fingernail, and looked inside. When she saw the thirty pounds of sugar, she laughed out loud. 'I assume this is for the hummingbirds and not a hint that you'd like another batch of brownies.'

'Brownies? It didn't even cross my mind,' Brian said innocently. 'But now that you mention it, I suppose there's enough sugar to take care of me and the birds.'

'And the whole thing came to less than forty-nine dollars,' Lynda chimed in. 'I saved the receipts. Want to see them?'

'I believe you.' She shifted the sugar off her lap.

'Now Rick's,' Lynda said, and handed her mother a beautifully wrapped package a little longer than a shoebox but not as wide.

'Do you know what it is?' Catherine asked her.

'He wouldn't tell me.'

She glanced at her mother and saw that Phyllis was still watching, this time with one of her cat-in-the-cream smiles. 'I wonder how he knew it was my birthday?'

'Maybe it was in the papers you filled out at the hospital,' Brian suggested.

She fingered the bow and looked at Lynda. 'This makes me very uncomfortable. I really wish he hadn't bought me a present.'

'I'll bet now you're sorry you wouldn't let me invite him,' Lynda said.

Catherine started to put the box aside. 'Maybe I should wait until — '

'Oh, just open the damn thing,' Phyllis interjected. 'I'm ready for cake and ice cream.'

Catherine removed the iridescent bow and set it aside. It seemed a shame to destroy the matching paper, but it was taped so securely, there was no other way to get to the box.

Feigning a casualness she didn't feel, she looked inside and found a bottle of Randle's Roost Reserve merlot nestled in a bed of pink tissue paper. 'Oh . . . ' She sighed. 'How perfect.'

'What is it?' Lynda asked.

'A bottle of wine,' Phyllis answered, plainly confused at Catherine's misty reaction.

'Wine?' Lynda said. 'You got all sloppy on us over a bottle of wine?'

'It happens to be a very good wine,' Catherine protested.

'Yeah, maybe,' Lynda said. 'But it's not nearly as impressive as the flowers Dad sent.'

Phyllis whipped around to face Catherine. 'Jack sent you flowers?'

'Thirty-nine roses.' Any hope for a personal touch was lost, however, when the flowers came with Jack's business card. She'd spotted handwriting on the back and turned it over to find instructions to Jack's assistant on which florist to use and the price range to stay within.

'White ones,' Lynda said. 'They're my favorite, not Mom's. Dad must have gotten us mixed up.'

Catherine surreptitiously dug through the tissue looking for a note from Rick and was disappointed when she didn't find one. She glanced up at her mother and smiled nonchalantly. 'Cake, anyone?'

Brian stood and offered his hand to Lynda. Catherine put the wine on the coffee table and moved to follow.

Phyllis caught up with her, leaned in close, and said softly, 'Just friends, my ass.'

25

Catherine looked up from the Sunday newspaper when she heard Lynda coming down the stairs. 'Ready?'

'I couldn't find my Tweety Bird beach towel.' She brought her canvas sports bag into the kitchen and dropped it by the back door. Dressed in navy blue shorts, a long-sleeved white blouse, red cap, and tennis shoes, she looked crisp and nautical and, until you looked closer, perfectly normal. Only the pressure garment peeking out at the top of her blouse gave her away.

'Did you look in the linen closet down here?' Lynda had waited until the last minute to finish her packing for camp despite Catherine's two days of prodding. The only thing that had stopped Catherine from stepping in and taking over was the knowledge that it was more important for Lynda to be responsible for her decision to go to camp than it was for her to show up with every item on her list.

'I took the Superman one instead.' She poured herself a glass of orange juice and sat next to Catherine at the kitchen table.

Glancing at the newspaper that lay open in front of her mother, she looked closer and frowned. 'You're reading the want ads? How come?'

'I've been thinking about going back to work when you start school again.'

'Why?'

'Something to do.'

'What about the club? I thought you'd want to get back to work on the projects you had going there.'

Catherine got up to pour herself a fresh cup of coffee and glanced at the clock. She didn't want to start something she couldn't finish and send Lynda off for a week worried that there was a problem at home. They had an hour and a half before they were to meet the van in Rancho Cordova.

'That's something I've been meaning to talk to you about,' Catherine said. 'The club doesn't seem all that important anymore. To either of us. Do you realize we haven't used it once this summer?'

'I never did like going there. It's just a bunch of women with nothing better to do than sit around and talk about whoever isn't there. And don't even get me started on the dirty old men who think they could have been golf pros if they'd just had a little more time to practice.'

Catherine looked at Lynda over the rim of her cup. 'Dirty old men? Is there something you haven't told me?'

'Didn't you ever notice how they look at girls my age when we walk by? It's disgusting.'

'Then you wouldn't care if I sold our membership back to the club?' She tried to make it sound as if it were an option instead of a necessity.

'Like you said, we never use it anymore.' She finished her orange juice, filled the glass again, and grabbed a bagel to go with it. 'So, what kind of job are you going to get?'

'Something in human resources probably. It's the only thing I have any experience doing.'

'Why not go back to Husbey's? You said you liked it there. And they gave you that big party when you quit, so it's obvious they liked you, too.'

'They don't have any openings.'

Lynda eyed her mother. 'I thought you said you were just thinking about going back to work. But if you already checked on your old job, you must have already made up your mind. When were you going to tell me?'

How could she not have known Lynda would expect to be included in this kind of decision? They were at a stage in their

322

mother-daughter relationship where Lynda felt entitled to know everything her mother did and felt, but was fiercely protective of her own privacy, impatient and stubborn when she thought she was being asked too many questions. Thankfully, Catherine remembered going through this same stage with her own mother and most of the time managed to handle Lynda's lopsided demands with a tolerance she didn't always feel.

'When you got home from camp. I figured we could work out our schedules together. I want to be home when you are so we can keep up with your massages.'

'Maybe I should just stay home.'

'Getting cold feet?'

'A little,' she admitted unexpectedly. 'The camp is only a couple of miles from Rainbow Lake.' She took her cap off and put it on the table, then ran her hand over her head. 'I can't stop thinking about going back there. I'm even dreaming about it. Awful dreams where Brian doesn't catch me and I just keep running and running until my whole body is on fire. And then I wake up.'

'I didn't know . . . ' Catherine put her cup aside and leaned forward to touch Lynda's hand. 'Maybe you shouldn't go. Maybe it's too soon.'

'I talked to Rick about it and he said he

would come and get me if I decided I didn't want to stay.'

'I thought Rick was going to be there.' She hadn't asked, she'd just assumed.

'He usually is. But when he thought I wasn't going, he told a firefighter whose wife has cancer that he would work a couple of shifts for him.'

'When did you talk to Rick?' She tried to make the question seem casual.

'He called the other night when you were in the shower. I think he was hoping you'd answer, but when I asked if he wanted you to call him back, he said no.'

She couldn't question Lynda without giving the call too much importance, so she let it drop. 'Did you leave your dress out?' The flower girl at Jack and Adriana's wedding had knocked over the punch bowl when she lunged for the bridal bouquet. Lynda and Brian had gotten the full force of the flow. 'I'm going to the cleaners tomorrow.'

'I think it's a lost cause, Mom.'

'Oh, I don't know. We managed to get the stains out of your pressure garments.'

'I can't see myself wearing that dress again anyway. It isn't very comfortable.'

Catherine had purposely not asked Lynda about the wedding, hoping she would talk about it without prompting. Obviously that wasn't going to happen. 'Okay, so how was it?'

Lynda grinned. 'I was wondering how long you could hold out.'

'Do you know I changed your diaper twice as often as any other mother I knew just so you'd never get a rash? And this is the thanks I get?'

'Funny, Mom.'

'Well?'

'Let's see ... where to start. I guess Adriana's as good a place as any. She wore a Vera Wang knockoff, simple lines and no train.' She thought a second. 'At least I think it was a knockoff, but maybe not. She's always flying to New York. She could have picked it up there. Anyway, she didn't have a veil, just some flowers in her hair that matched her bouquet. Dad got her a gold band. He said she doesn't like diamonds.'

'Did Jack look happy?' Selfishly, she wanted this marriage to work. She believed that fulfilling his promise to be a better father to Lynda hinged on whether he and Adriana could build a stable home life with their own child.

'I'd say he looked more accepting than happy. He smiled a lot but he wasn't bouncing all around the room talking to everybody the way he usually is at parties.'

'He's trying,' Catherine said. 'I think he really wants it to work this time.'

'Does it bother you?'

'What?'

'His getting married again when it didn't work out between you and Tom?'

'That's a complicated question,' she answered honestly. 'All I know for sure is that I would have answered it differently a couple of months ago. Then I might have cared. I don't think I do now.'

'You don't *think* you do, but you're not sure?'

'No, I'm sure. I just don't know whether I'm neutral or I sincerely wish him well. I'd like to think it's the latter.'

'Pretty heavy stuff for nine o'clock in the morning,' Lynda said.

'Is it nine already?' She folded the newspaper and added it to the stack she'd already read. 'We should get going.'

A moment of uncertainty flashed through Lynda's eyes.

'There's still time to change your mind.' Only at that moment did Catherine realize she wanted Lynda to change her mind. She was as nervous about having her leave as Lynda was about going.

'I told Rick I would give it a couple of days. If I don't go, he'll be disappointed in me.'

Catherine came around the table and put

her arm across Lynda's shoulders. 'I used to think I knew what bravery was all about, but I was wrong. There are times, like now, when I'm so proud of you I want to shout it from the rooftop.'

Lynda hugged her back. 'I love you, too, Mom.'

★　★　★

For an indulgent minute Rick let the hot water run across the shoulder he'd strained in the fire that afternoon, and then squeezed a circle of shampoo in his hand and spread it in his hair. Using his fingers to scrub his scalp hard, he worked the lather until he was sure the soot and ash and smell of smoke were gone. Just as he stuck his head under the shower spray he heard the alarm sound.

'Damn,' he said aloud, although no one was around to hear. His crew took their showers in the dorm while he enjoyed one of the few privileges of rank in the fire department, at least at his firehouse: a private bathroom.

He shut off the water, grabbed a towel, and hurriedly dried off, missing more than he hit. Tossing the towel over the shower door, he grabbed the clean blue T-shirt and Jockey shorts he'd taken from his locker, put them on, and stepped into his still-wet turnout pants and boots. Not only were the pants and boots still wet from the fire, they still smelled. Even with his nostrils coated with smoke he could detect the acrid stench on the heavy, once-yellow canvas.

Glancing at the address as he pulled the report from the computer, he let out a groan. A patient down at the Haversmorning Care Facility. Their shift responded to the care home an average of once a month, and the calls invariably left the entire crew depressed and determined to do anything not to wind up in a care facility at the end of their lives. If he'd heard one firefighter tell another that they'd rather be shot than go to a place like Haversmorning, he'd heard a hundred.

'Where to?' Paul asked.

'Haversmorning,' Rick answered.

Even Paul knew enough to swear.

'I knew it had to be bad,' Janet said, standing beside the button to close the apparatus room door. 'This is number thirteen.'

Rick looked at Steve across the front seat of the fire engine. 'Thirteen? We've rolled thirteen times today? It's only four o'clock.'

Three of the calls had been false alarms, some smart-ass kid pulling boxes at the local grammar school. The cops caught him on the last one, which came in just as they sat down to eat lunch. Before they made it back to the house they were dispatched to a fire at Capital Nursery. Now Haversmorning.

Shit.

'Should have grabbed some bananas for the ride home,' Steve said. 'I'm starving.'

'We'll stop for something on the way back,' Rick promised. 'There's that sub shop on the corner we all liked last time. My treat.'

After the call, for the first time since arriving at their firehouse, Paul was quiet on the ride back. When they were in the kitchen getting drinks and chips to go with their sandwiches, Rick overheard him talking to Janet.

'I hope when I'm that old there's someone who loves me enough to shoot me before they allow me to be put in a place like that.'

Janet reached for the glasses. 'Cats — you just officially joined the ranks of every firefighter in this department. There's not a one of us who doesn't think the same thing when we go to a place like Haversmorning.'

Rick took a bag of Ruffles out of the cupboard, poured them in a bowl, and put the bowl on the table. The dog-tired camaraderie of the earlier fire had disappeared into a depression at the futility of a call they knew would be repeated.

A man put in a wheelchair in the morning and ignored while he quietly died, his lunch untouched, his personal needs neglected, his dignity forgotten, was not something any of them would ever get used to, no matter how many times they went out on the call.

Rick looked across the table at Steve and saw that he, too, was lost somewhere in thought. It wasn't hard to imagine where. Rick picked up his sandwich and took a bite, chewed and swallowed and did the same thing all over again, forcing the food down, aware that with a full moon that night, he might not get another chance to eat.

The captain's phone rang. Rick got up to answer, taking a handful of chips with him.

'Captain Sawyer,' he said.

'Rick — it's Catherine. I hope I'm not calling at a bad time.'

He leaned his shoulder into the doorframe, the dragon of depression chased from the castle by the mere sound of her voice. 'No, it's a good time.'

At least it was now.

'I was wondering if you'd heard from Lynda. She hasn't phoned in a couple of days and I don't know if it's because she's having such a good time or she's miserable and doesn't want to let me know.'

'I called up there yesterday to see how

things were going and Carol told me that Lynda's doing great. Seems she's really good with the crafts stuff, so they've put her to work helping the little kids paint bird feeders.'

'She's always loved that kind of thing,' she said, relief in her voice. 'And speaking of bird feeders, I had my first hummingbird this morning.'

'Lynda was pretty proud of herself for coming up with that idea.'

'I know. She told me.' Catherine paused in such a way that it was plain she had something else she wanted to say. 'Did you get my note about the wine?'

'Not yet. But then I haven't been home for a couple of days. I worked a shift for a friend yesterday.'

'I know,' she said. 'Lynda told me about that, too.'

They were like a courting couple with a chaperone, stilted and awkward, careful with everything they said. Only they weren't a couple and they weren't courting. 'I hope it was all right. The wine, I mean.'

'Perfect. All I need is someone to share it with.'

Was that a comment or an invitation? He wasn't sure how to respond. 'It holds pretty well if you're thinking about having a glass tonight. Up to a couple of days if you get the cork in nice and tight.'

'Oh — I'll be sure to remember that.'

The disappointment in her voice told him he'd guessed wrong. Damn. Why was he always a step off with her? 'Of course, if you're looking for someone to share — ' The alarm sounded. 'I'm really sorry, Catherine. I have to go.'

'Thanks for telling me about Lynda.'

'Anytime.' He hung up, his depression gone, frustration slipping into its place.

26

Catherine spotted Brian from across the hospital's parking garage as she pulled up the ramp. He waited until she found an empty spot and then came over. The first thing she noticed when he was close enough for her to get a good look was a thin line of moisture on his eyelashes.

'What's wrong?' She'd promised Lynda she would stop by to visit Ray while her daughter was at camp and wanted to give her a report when she called that night. 'Has something happened to Ray?'

'She won't let him stay with us.'

'Who?'

'Ray's aunt. She said he has to live in Kansas with her. I tried talking to her, and so did Ray, but she won't listen. She says she owes it to her sister to take care of Ray, but I don't believe that's the reason.'

'Ray knows that you wanted him to stay here with you? Lynda said you weren't going to tell him until your father had everything worked out.'

'He got everything worked out — everything but Ray's aunt. She's been a real witch about it. There's no way he wants to go with her. He doesn't even know her. You should have seen how he reacted when I told him my mom and dad said he could stay with us. It was the happiest I've ever seen him.'

'Then I don't understand why she — '

'My dad said it's because she thinks Ray has money coming that no one has told her about and that we're trying to steal it from him.'

Catherine's heart sank. She'd known people like Ray's aunt, and the more you tried to convince them that no one wanted their money, the more convinced they became that they had something worth stealing. 'Money from where? Did she say?'

'She was rattling off a whole bunch of stuff. Life insurance, fire insurance on the house, she even said something about a story she heard that crime victims could collect money if they caught the person who hurt them.'

'Is she here now?'

'Yeah — she's in Ray's room packing his stuff. They're flying out in a couple of hours.'

So soon. Lynda would be devastated she hadn't been here to say good-bye. Catherine felt the shoulder strap on her purse start to slip and impatiently hiked it back in place. 'Do you think it would do any good if I talked to her?'

'I don't know how it could get any worse.' He stopped to take a deep breath. 'Ray begged me to help him . . . ' He looked at Catherine. There were fresh tears in his eyes. 'I never should have started this. I only made things worse.'

She opened her arms and he moved into them. Catherine held him until they heard a car coming up the ramp and he released her to wipe his eyes.

'I'll see what I can do,' she said. 'Probably nothing if she's as intractable with me as she was with you, but it's worth a try.'

'Would you mind letting me tell Lynda about this?' he asked. 'She doesn't even know Ray's leaving.'

'She's supposed to call me tonight around dinner. I'll tell her that I met you at the hospital and that you're anxious to talk to her. But you have to promise me you'll have her call me back before she goes to bed. I want to know that she's all right.'

'Thanks — I appreciate you letting me do this.'

She thought about his thanking her for something so easy to give, and about everything he'd done for Lynda, and how if she told him thank you every day for the rest of her life she would never be able to say it enough. 'You're welcome, Brian.'

They said good-bye and Catherine left the relative comfort of the shaded garage to walk the short distance to the hospital in the intense, ugly sunlight. Some of their summer days were blessed with a crisp blue sky that boasted an occasional cloud. The majority were like this, as if the sky had been washed in a cheap bleach, not blue, but not white, either. And hot. Breath-stealing, dizzy, mirage-on-the-pavement hot.

The door swung open and a cool rush of air escaped to be instantly absorbed and forever lost. The thin sheen of moisture on the back of Catherine's neck amplified the effect of the air-conditioning, and for a second she was almost cold.

The woman at the desk looked up and smiled. 'It's been a while since I've seen you around here. How is Lynda doing?'

'She's at camp having a wonderful time.'

'All the kids do. It's a great program. The firefighters really go all out for them while they're there.'

Catherine pressed the elevator button and the door opened immediately. 'Thank you for asking about her.' Before words like that would have been automatic and meaningless. Now she'd learned to appreciate people who showed interest, even if only peripherally.

The door to Ray's room stood open and

his aunt's voice was the first thing Catherine heard when she came around the corner. High-pitched and nasal, it put Catherine on edge and lured her into snap judgments about its owner.

'Excuse me,' she said from the doorway.

The woman turned. The face didn't match the voice. Catherine couldn't believe this woman, pinched and coarse, with unshaped eyebrows and hooded eyes, was a blood relative of Ray's. Only then did she realize she had no idea what Ray had looked like before being burned. The image she had in her mind had nothing to do with the way he looked now, but came from what he'd said and felt and expressed since she'd known him. She pictured the old Ray with tender, expressive eyes and a quick, mischievous smile, his skin smooth, hair thick and dark.

'Yes?' the woman asked, more suspicious than curious.

'Hi, I'm Catherine Miller.' She held out her hand. 'Lynda Miller's mother.' She offered Ray a quick smile.

The woman gave her a blank stare. 'Is that supposed to mean something to me?'

'Lynda's a friend of mine,' Ray said defensively.

Catherine's hope died an inglorious death. She'd believed adherence to social graces would provide a common ground for conversation. 'I'm so glad I had this chance to meet you. I had no idea Ray was leaving today and I know Lynda will be devastated that she didn't get a chance to say good-bye. They've become such good friends. She's really going to miss him.'

'Look, Mrs. Miller — '

'Please, it's Catherine.'

'If you're here to try to get me to let Ray stay, you're wasting your time. I already told that Winslow boy the same thing I told his father. Ray is family and we take care of our own.' She reached for her purse and tucked it under her arm. 'You people out here seem to have a real problem hearing what you're told.' She looked at Ray. 'I'm going to see about those papers I have to sign. I want you ready to leave when I get back.'

'I'm sorry,' Ray said.

Catherine sat on the bed next to him when his aunt was gone. 'No, I'm sorry. I didn't do a very good job of pouring oil on troubled water.'

'She didn't give you a chance.' He was still weeks away from being fitted for his pressure garments and was encased in protective bandages for the trip. He looked like a half-finished mummy and was sure to bring long, curious stares he wasn't prepared to handle.

'Brian's dad hasn't given up, you know.'

'He'll never get her to change her mind.'

'Don't count him out too soon. The Winslows are known for their stubbornness. I'm sure he plans to make direct, frontal attacks every time you come back to Sacramento for surgery and follow-up.'

'But I'm not coming back. The Texas Shriner Hospital in Houston is closer, so I'll be going there from now on.'

The news left her reeling. Brian and Lynda would be heartbroken. She had to give them something, even if it was only hope. 'Do you think she'll let you come for a visit? What about over Christmas break?'

'I don't know. I doubt it. Not the way she feels now, at least.'

Catherine reached for his hand, curling her fingers into his gauze-covered palm. She tried to imagine him on a football field, his hand clutching a football, his skill at throwing so accurate that there were college recruiters sent to watch him his junior year. 'When do you turn eighteen?'

Curiosity in his eyes at the peculiar question, he stared at her. 'In May.'

'Then we'll see you in May for sure. Once you're eighteen, she loses control.'

'I don't know if I can last that long,' he said softly.

The words sent a cold chill through her, raising goosebumps on her arms. 'Of course you can.' He needed something more concrete than words to hold onto. To a seventeen-year-old, May was a lifetime away. 'How about this — if your aunt won't let you come to see us for Christmas, we'll come to see you. All of us.' Finally, she saw a spark of hope. 'And Easter, too. May is right around the corner. We'll all be wearing birthday banners and carrying balloons when you step off the plane.'

She felt a little squeamish making promises for Brian's father, but if he changed his mind, she would figure something out, even if it meant Ray moved in with them. 'I'm going to use a cliché on you, but only because it's true and it works. Keep reminding yourself that all you need to do is take this one day at a time. Don't count the months or weeks ahead. If you have to count the hours and days, look at the ones you've put behind you.'

'I'll try.'

She gently squeezed his hand. 'Can you use the phone by yourself yet?'

'They set up a special one here that I get to take with me.'

'Then call me when you need to talk. If you need something and I can't get it, I'll find someone who can.'

The aunt came back. 'Ray, *please*. The plane leaves in two hours.'

'I can't get dressed by myself,' he finally, painfully admitted.

She had enough sensitivity to blush. 'No one told me.'

All you had to do was look, Catherine felt like shouting. 'I'll get the nurse to help him.' If she could do nothing else, she could give him this last dignity.

She stood without letting go of Brian's hand and looked down into his eyes. 'You will get through this,' she said softly, desperately seeking a way to give him the willpower he would need to get through what was ahead. 'And you will come back to us.'

His eyes filled with tears that spilled onto his cheeks. 'Thank you.'

Twice that morning she'd been thanked for giving hope that wasn't hers to give. She had no real control over what would happen, only words that lost their meaning in the harshness of day-to-day reality. She wiped his tears the way she imagined his mother might have and leaned down to kiss the corner of his eye, the one part of his face where the skin and feeling had survived intact, the one place where she knew for sure that he could feel her touch.

★ ★ ★

Catherine headed for Fair Oaks Boulevard when she left the hospital, thinking foolishly that she could distract herself with shopping. She'd gone to the hospital to fulfill her promise to Lynda, nothing more. Until today she'd stood in the wings while the drama of Ray's fate played itself out on a stage not her own. Now she was one of the players, but without a script to follow or anyone to direct.

First she went to Pavilions, a small upscale shopping center with exclusive high-end shops and restaurants. The center had been a favorite haunt for years, a place she came to buy presents when the wrapping counted as much as the gift inside. She perused the wine at David Berkely's, looking for something from Randle's Roost, wondering if Rick had ever come there for a sandwich from the deli, whether he liked the bitter Italian olives she always bought to take home with her, and if he ever drank sherry. Was he a meat-and-potatoes man, or could he be content with an occasional meal of champagne and crackers and cheese and fruit by the fireplace?

Had he ever shopped at Pavilions or did he simply drive by, believing it held nothing of interest to him? Did it make a difference?

She wandered to the florist and then Williams-Sonoma to see what was new in their kitchenware. She left with a nutmeg grinder, unable to remember the last time she'd used nutmeg in a recipe, but caught up in the idea of fresh nutmeg in pumpkin pie.

At Ann Taylor she tried on a dress, decided it made her look slimmer than she'd felt in a long time, and had it at the counter before she bothered to look at the price. Her behavior had been automatic. Now it struck her that the casual fall dress could pay for a round-trip ticket for Lynda to visit Ray in Kansas.

She returned the dress to the rack, to her surprise feeling neither deprived nor constrained.

She left the shopping center and on impulse stopped in to see her friends Cary and Joe at the Duck Stamp. Cary was one of those people who saw spring flowers in a raging winter storm. She brought an unbridled enthusiasm to the art shop that made her customers feel as welcome when they came just to browse as they did when they came to buy.

Cary was home with a cold.

She visited with Joe for several minutes and then left. As she got in the car, she remembered that he had contacts in the secondary art market. The week before when she'd called her broker to sell another block of stocks, he'd suggested she hold off until

343

the market rebounded from the current low, or she'd lose almost a third of her initial investment. His manner and tone made it clear he assumed she wanted the money for something frivolous. Her pride stood in the way of telling him the truth.

Catherine returned to the gallery and told Joe that she'd been thinking about selling some of her signed and numbered prints and asked how she should go about doing it. He looked up their value, told her what she could reasonably expect someone to pay, and warned her that it could take months to years for a sale to come through. She gave him her all-too-familiar, I-wasn't-really-serious smile, asked him to give her best to Cary, and told him she'd be in touch when she made up her mind about the prints.

Disheartened, she headed for Tower Books to see what she could find on writing résumés.

27

Lynda knew. Or at least she guessed the outcome without knowing the details. Either she'd picked up something in the tone of Catherine's voice or had figured it out by her unwillingness to give details about her visit with Ray. Whatever tipped her off, she was angry and then contrite, demanding details and then saying she was willing to hear them from Brian.

Catherine refused to let her go until she'd received a promise that Lynda would call her back that night before she went to bed. She even made her set a time. Ten o'clock. No matter what was going on, no matter who she had to coerce, either the call came or Catherine would show up at camp in the middle of the night.

She wouldn't, of course — having her mother show up at camp was a sure way to draw attention to herself, something Lynda didn't want. But Catherine was fairly sure Lynda didn't recognize the threat as bluff.

She looked at her watch. It was only five. She would go out of her mind if she sat around the house five more hours waiting for the phone to ring.

Needing some of the mothering she wanted to give Lynda, Catherine grabbed her purse, got in the car, and headed for her own mother's house.

Phyllis wasn't home.

Catherine considered going to see a half dozen friends she'd neglected that summer, but wasn't up to explaining the chain of events that had put her on the road looking for company when the rest of the world was concentrating on dinner. She still had another month at the club before her membership expired, but the prospect of running into Tom ranked a rung below being in a plane with engine failure.

Instead she drove aimlessly, sticking to the back roads to avoid commuter traffic, turning her air conditioner to high, and the radio to a conservative talk show that never failed to make her rethink her belief in the basic goodness of her fellow man. Not even a woman on a tirade about her right to kill any animal that crossed her property line, no matter what the State Fish and Game said, was enough to distract her for long. She switched to public radio. Organ music by Bach. Hardly something to lift her spirits.

She came to an intersection and glanced at the road signs. She was on Laird Road. Rick lived on Laird Road. Coincidence or subconscious need? She knew if she tried to analyze her behavior, she would reach a conclusion that made her turn left or right, any direction to take her away from yet another complication in her life. Instead, giving in to need instead of intellect, something she'd sworn she would not do again, she went straight and sought something, anything that would lead her to him.

A half mile later, she spotted his truck. She glanced in the rearview mirror and saw a car coming up behind her, fast. She could either drive by or turn into his driveway. Gut instinct told her if she passed, she would not turn around. It would seem too planned that way, too calculated.

Again, she glanced in her rearview mirror. The car was closing in. She had to make up her mind and do it quickly. If only he'd asked her there, even casually. Just a hint, a simple comment that she should stop by sometime. She had no business being there.

She turned.

⋆   ⋆   ⋆

Rick stopped pulling weeds in his vegetable garden when Blue lifted his head and cocked his ear toward the front of the house. For

Blue to expend that much energy with the temperature still in the hundreds, it had to be serious. Someone had pulled into the driveway.

Rick put the hoe aside, lifted his cap, and wiped the sweat from his forehead. He was expecting a package from UPS, but they usually made their deliveries to his area in the morning. He waited several seconds to see if it was someone using the driveway to turn around or someone who would come close enough to rouse Blue to a sitting position.

Blue skipped sitting and actually stood, his tail wagging with a surprising show of enthusiasm considering his previous lethargy.

'Must be someone special,' Rick said, giving the dog's ear a scratch as he passed on his way to the side of the house. Blue followed on his heels.

'Well, I'll be damned,' he said under his breath when he saw the Lincoln Navigator pulling to a stop. Blue sidled up beside him, plopped down on his foot, leaned against his leg, and let out a soft whine. 'The snowball made it through hell.'

She hadn't spotted him yet when she started walking toward the house, and Rick had a chance to observe her unnoticed. She looked as she always did: impossibly beautiful. She was the kind of woman who could wear the linen suits his sister favored and have them wrinkle just enough to look fashionable instead of as if she'd slept in them. Rick glanced down at his bare chest and dirt-encrusted jeans with the holes in the knees. He'd pass on being able to leap tall buildings with a single bound if he could just manage to hop in a shower, put on clean clothes, and meet her at the door before she had to ring it a second time.

She saw him. The look on her face was somewhere between surprise and dismay. When she threw a quick smile in the mix, Rick didn't know what to think.

'You're busy.' She stopped and made a nervous gesture with her hand. 'I should have called before I came.'

'How did you know where to find me?' It was something to say while he tried to think of something better. Something short of telling her his heart was beating so loudly he had to concentrate to hear her voice, or that he'd imagined her there so many times he was having trouble convincing himself it had finally happened.

'The day you took me to the car rental you told me you lived on Laird Road.'

'I'm surprised you remembered. That was months ago.' Now he was really reaching. While clever dialogue might be beyond him at the moment, he could at least get her out of the sun. He wiggled his foot free of Blue's rear end. 'I made some iced tea this afternoon. Would you like to come in and have a glass?'

'You're not even going to ask why I'm here?'

'I figure you'll tell me when you're ready.'

She started toward the door he indicated. 'I've never known anyone like you.'

'Then we're even. I've never known anyone like you, either.'

She laughed. 'You must run with an interesting group. I'm the most ordinary person I know.'

Rick reached around her to open the front door. He took a moment to brush the dirt off his jeans, step out of his boots, and point at Blue. 'Shake,' he commanded.

Blue dutifully shook himself, bits of leaf and grass flying into the air. 'Again,' Rick said. Blue patiently obeyed. 'Okay.' Rick stood aside and let Blue come in the house. He stopped in front of Catherine and looked up at her.

'Hi there.' She leaned down to scratch his head. 'Don't tell her I told you, but my daughter thinks you're really special.'

'The feeling's mutual. Blue fell in love the first day she came over.' He crossed the room.

'How do you take your tea?'

'Straight.'

'I'll be right back. Make yourself at home.'

Catherine took the opportunity to look around the room when he left. His house was nothing like she'd expected. Operating from a prejudice she hadn't known she possessed, she'd taken his description of the half-burned house he'd purchased eight years ago and turned it into a very ordinary dwelling with tasteful but ordinary furnishings. Not only hadn't she imagined what she now saw, she never could have imagined it. What Rick had done with his house made everything about hers appear pedestrian. The sterile look she'd inherited from Jack's favorite decorator, the one he'd left her to live in after the divorce settlement, was cold and pretentious compared to this.

The floor and molding and doors were made from a honey-colored wood she didn't recognize even after a childhood spent in her father's woodworking shop. The finish had been applied as painstakingly as the crown molding had been fitted. Built-in bookshelves flanked a floor-to-ceiling fireplace, the wood hand-rubbed to a deep shine.

The end tables and matching coffee table showed the same degree of craftsmanship and care. Only the sofa and chair appeared commercially made. They were covered in a forest green and burgundy fabric, comfort colors that invited tucking up feet or sprawling with book in hand.

Rick returned, a glass in each hand, wearing a smile and a clean T-shirt. Putting the shirt on brought attention to the fact that he hadn't been wearing one when she drove up. She'd known he was in shape — that much was evident when he was wearing clothes. Where her imagination had let her down was in how hard and lean and strong he really was. She would not forget now. The image of him standing bare-chested in the early evening light would be a familiar one from then on, both waking and sleeping.

He handed her a glass. 'Now, as glad as I am to see you, I know you must have had something on your mind to wind up here. I said I wouldn't ask, but why don't we get it out of the way?'

'It's Lynda.' She took a drink. 'I'm worried about how she's going to react to Ray's leaving today.'

'Ray's gone?'

'There was some mix-up and his aunt thought she was supposed to come today instead of next week. Ray's doctor reviewed his chart, wrote a bunch of instructions to the doctor who's going to be taking care of him in Kansas, and said he could go.'

'How did Ray take the news?'

'He was crushed. I think he was hoping for a last-minute miracle that would let him stay with Brian.'

'Wasn't the plan not to tell him about staying here until it was set?' He led Catherine to the sofa and then sat on the raised fireplace hearth facing her. 'I can see I've got some catching up to do.'

She filled him in with everything she knew.

'I'm afraid you're right to be concerned about Lynda. She made Ray her responsibility and she's going to feel as if she let him down.'

'She's been doing so well until now.'

Rick didn't comment.

His silence disconcerted her. At the very least, she'd expected an affirming nod. She tried again. 'After listening to the other parents, I expected her to fight wearing her pressure garments. But she's never even complained about them — not that they're uncomfortable, or hot, or anything. She's accepted them as if they were cutting-edge style.'

'She's hiding,' Rick said gently. 'It's the way some of the kids react. It's perfectly normal, but can bring some real headaches down the line when it comes time for her to stop wearing them.'

'What do you mean, 'hiding'?'

'From her scars. As long as she's wearing her pressure garments, no one can see what's under them. She has a ready-made excuse for not going swimming, or dressing down for gym, or doing anything that would expose her to curious, hurtful stares.'

The answer was so obvious. How had she missed it? She'd seen and believed what she wanted to see and believe. Somehow, Catherine had convinced herself that because Lynda came from a loving, extended family, enjoyed a standard of living that only ten percent of the population attained, and was bright and beautiful and popular, of course she would be different, would react differently, would accept her scarred back intellectually as well as emotionally and move on with her life.

How could she have been so stupid? So ego-driven? So blind to reality?

'I'm scared, Rick,' she admitted as the impact of the door he'd opened hit her. 'If you're right, and I have no reason to believe you aren't, then she's holding in a lot of other stuff, too. She accepted Jack's marriage as a matter of course. I thought it was because she'd been through so much herself that

354

she'd learned to put other things in perspective.'

'He'll always be her father. She must have felt something about losing a part of him to another woman, even if it was a part that wasn't hers to lose.'

'That's what I expected, what I looked for. But she actually seemed happy for him. And when I told her she was going to have a little sister or brother in a few months, I thought she was excited.'

'Maybe she was. Maybe we're wrong and she really is happy for him and — ' He paused. 'Sorry, I can't remember her name.'

'Adriana.'

'Adriana has to know how important Lynda is to Jack. She probably went out of her way to make her feel comfortable.'

'I hope so. I can only take one crisis at a time.'

'Why don't I call the camp and ask Rachel how she's doing?'

'Can you do it without Lynda finding out?'

'Rachel won't say anything if I ask her not to.'

'Then yes, please. I really need to know that she's all right.'

'You want to come with me or wait here? The phone's in the kitchen.'

'With.' She followed him down a short hall,

rounded a doorway, and stopped cold, as if she'd run into a glass wall. She stared, unbelieving, questioning a reality she could see and touch and feel.

Rick's kitchen was the one she had created in her mind when she and Jack had decided to design their own home. From the countertops to the practical gourmet stove — a stove so ugly only someone who loved to cook could appreciate its true beauty — to the built-in refrigerator and tile floor, everything was as she'd imagined it. What she'd wound up with was Jack and the architect's idea of a showplace kitchen, one that sacrificed function for form.

She innately knew where everything was stored in this kitchen, she could find the plates and glasses and pots and pans with her eyes closed. The only thing that threw her was a double row of drawers beside the stove, each a little over a foot wide and less than eight inches tall. Her curiosity aroused, it was everything she could do not to open them and look inside.

'Rachel, it's Rick. Lynda Miller got some bad news this evening and I was wondering how she's doing.' He listened for several seconds. 'Is she okay now?' He glanced at Catherine, his expression neutral. 'Uh-huh . . . yeah, that's my take on it, too.'

The kitchen forgotten, Catherine concentrated on Rick's conversation, filling the silences with frightening scenarios, knowing it was foolish but unable to stop.

'You have any problem with us taking a drive up there tonight?' He gave Catherine a questioning look. She nodded. 'Good. We'll see you in a couple of hours, then. Do me a favor, don't tell Lynda we're coming.'

He hung up. 'Give me a couple of minutes to shower and we can leave.'

'What's wrong?' Catherine asked anxiously.

'One of the counselors noticed she was upset, and when she asked if she could help, Lynda broke down and started crying. The counselor took her to the nurse's office and they finally got her to tell them about Ray.'

'How could I not have known how much he meant to her?'

'I think it's a little more complicated than that. Nothing that happens to Lynda stands alone anymore. When she gets upset about one thing, she loses the ability to handle everything else. She's like a traffic cop who stops to tie her shoe and looks up to see cars headed toward her from every direction.'

'How do you know these things?' She didn't doubt him, she simply wondered how he could be so perceptive with someone he'd only known a couple of months.

'Experience. And I've learned not to take anything at face value. If one of my kids — one of my burned kids — is getting along better than they should, or is always on their best behavior, I get suspicious. Lynda's a remarkable young woman, but she's not as different as she wants all of us to think she is. You don't go through what she's been through without getting hurt on the inside, too. Our job is to make sure whatever she's carrying around gets the exposure it needs to heal properly.'

'No matter how many times I say thank you to you and the people at the Firefighters' — '

'When I said *our* job, Catherine, I meant you and me.'

Blue came into the kitchen, his toenails clicking on the tile floor, providing a distraction that Rick ignored but Catherine couldn't.

He sat in front of a cupboard and twisted his head to look at Rick, a pleading expression in his eyes. 'He knows I'm leaving,' Rick explained. 'It's his version of a guilt trip.'

'You keep his treats in that cupboard,' she said with confidence. Along with assorted canned goods, crackers, cereal, and pasta, she could have added just as confidently.

'Would you mind getting one for him? I'd like to get out of here as soon as possible.'

'Is there something you're not telling me?' She'd had no idea such random fears hung around so close to the surface and could be aroused so readily.

'I just thought it would be better if we got there before the campfire skits start. Lynda's cabin is putting them on tonight, and I don't want her to miss it because of us.'

Her relief left her eager to give something back. 'Have you had dinner?'

'Not yet.'

'Why don't I make us some sandwiches to eat on the way?'

'You don't have to do that.' He smiled. 'But it would be nice if you did.'

'Go on, get in your shower. I'll take care of everything out here.'

'The bread is in — '

'I know where the bread is. And everything else. Trust me, I can handle this.'

Blue let out a soft whine. 'Oh, and don't let him talk you into giving him more than one dog bone.'

'From the look on his face I don't think one is going to be enough.'

'Break it in half,' Rick said from the doorway. 'That way he'll think he's getting two.'

Catherine looked at Blue when they were alone. 'That's not going to fool you, is it?'

Blue thumped his tail and woofed.

'I didn't think so.' She took the box from the cupboard and found two pieces that weren't whole, but more than half. He took the first one and looked at her expectantly as he chomped it down. The second one he held in his cheek until he was curled up on the rag rug by the back door.

Catherine washed her hands and without thinking reached for the towel hanging off a hook on the side of the cupboard, knowing it was there. She was headed for the refrigerator when she spotted the double row of drawers and gave in to the temptation to snoop.

She smiled in discovery and appreciation as she opened and looked inside the drawers. Rick had solved the problem of what to do with the odd utensils that invariably created junk drawers in most kitchens. Everything that grated or minced was in one drawer, if it cut or sliced, it was in another. Large spoons and ladles were combined with salad tongs while meat forks were in with a set of crab crackers and picks.

She thought about her mother's kitchen and how easily the drawers could be installed if she took out the cupboard where she kept her cookie sheets. But in order to tell her about it she'd have to tell her where she got the idea. That was bound to lead to questions about why Catherine had been in Rick's kitchen in the first place. Questions she'd begun to ask herself. Questions she either wasn't ready to or couldn't answer.

28

Rick parked next to the administration building, set the emergency brake on the truck, and turned to Catherine. 'This is it. Camp Cassidy in all of its military-green glory. Come on, I'll introduce you to everyone.'

She hesitated. When they'd crested the summit and she'd caught sight of Lake Tahoe shimmering gold in the waning light, she'd been hit with doubt about what she was doing. If Lynda had wanted her at camp, she would have called. Catherine had checked the answering machine at home and nothing was on it, not even a message from Brian.

'Second thoughts?' he asked gently.

'Second, third, and fourth. I promised Lynda more freedom. Now here I am, chasing her down at the first sign of trouble.'

'It was my idea, remember? You're just along for the ride.'

'She'll never buy that. She knows me too well.'

'We can still turn around and go back. No one has spotted us yet.'

Catherine looked up and saw someone

waving to them. 'Oh, yeah?'

Rick followed her gaze, smiled, and waved back. 'That's Rachel. Even if we don't stay, we've got to take a minute for you to meet her.' He opened his door and came around the truck to open hers.

'I've been watching for you,' Rachel said. 'I was hoping you'd get here before campfire.' She opened her arms for a hug. Rick obliged, lifting her off the ground and planting a kiss square on her mouth.

Catherine experienced an insane moment of jealousy so intense she could only laugh it off. To say or do something would be the real insanity.

Rick put Rachel down, but kept his arm around her waist. 'Rachel Issenberg — Catherine Miller.'

They shook hands. Catherine even managed a smile. 'How is Lynda?'

'Still a little quiet, but I put her to work helping Sandi get ready for tonight's skit.'

Rachel was nothing like Catherine had expected — someone she'd mentally patterned after a boot camp instructor. Not only was she tall and slim with long black hair pulled back into a bouncy ponytail, she had the glow and confidence that came with being in superb physical condition. She had flawless skin, large, expressive eyes, and fashionably full lips. She was beautiful, sophisticated, and at least fifteen pounds lighter and five years younger than Catherine. Most of all, she had a thing for Rick that he either didn't see in his expansive friendliness for everyone or chose to ignore.

'Catherine's concerned about being here,' Rick said. 'She's afraid Lynda will think she's intruding.'

Rachel directed her answer to Catherine. 'Then instead of introducing you at campfire, we'll take our cues from Lynda and keep you low-profile.' She glanced at Rick and smiled. 'Besides, we can always blame it on Rick. I knew he'd show up sooner or later. There was no way he could stay away the whole week.'

When Rachel turned her smile on Catherine, it was filled with such genuine warmth, she, too, fell under the woman's spell.

'Come on.' Rachel took Catherine's arm. 'I'll show you around the place while we're waiting for Lynda to finish with Sandi.'

They headed for the dining room, which, Rachel informed her, was also the arts and crafts area. 'Wait until you see what the kids did with the bird feeders, Rick. I think we have a couple of budding artists in the group.' To Catherine she said, 'I assume Rick told

364

you about the feeders?'

'No, he didn't.' The innocent question had effectively put her on the outside of his circle of friends. She knew what she had to know about him as Lynda's mother, little more. She had to fight an urge to tell Rachel that she might not know about the feeders but she'd been to his house and she knew about his part-time dog and his incredible neighbor who had taken Lynda under her wing just because Rick had asked her to. But she only knew these things peripherally; they weren't hers to claim or share.

'He conned some man he met at a crafts show into donating the plastic bubbles that hold the seed and then Rick made all these bird and squirrel and fire-engine cutouts that hold the bubble. The birds sit on a dowel and pick seed out of a hole in the bubble. When he first showed it to me, I told him there was no way any self-respecting bird was going to stick its head in that hole. Guess who won that argument.'

'Lynda mentioned she was helping out with them,' Catherine said. 'She said she was bringing one home with her. A fire engine, I think.'

'*Rick* — ,' a high-pitched voice squealed from across the green. He turned just as someone else yelled, 'Hey, look everybody. Rick's here.'

A short, stocky boy in a bright yellow T-shirt came running toward them. He was followed by a girl wearing a long red scarf around her neck. The volleyball game stopped and the teams set off at a sprint.

'We'd better stand back,' Rachel warned Catherine, her eyes brimming with humor. 'This could get ugly.'

The boy in the yellow T-shirt never slowed down. He hit Rick at full speed, wrapping his arms around his waist as Rick laughed and braced himself to stay upright. 'How are you doing, Danny?'

He looked up and grinned. 'Good. I can use my fingers now.' He held his hand up and wiggled the three fingers that still remained. 'See?'

The girl arrived, growing shy as she neared. 'Melinda — you look fantastic,' Rick exclaimed. 'Who did your nose?'

'Dr. Wiggins.'

'Turn sideways,' he said. She did. 'Out-standing.' He held his hand up for a high five.

She beamed at his approval.

The volleyball team arrived. Rachel motioned for Catherine to follow her. 'We might as well go on without him. He could be tied up here for a long time.'

Catherine watched from the window when they were inside the dining room. 'They seem to like him. A lot.'

'It goes deeper than that. He works magic with these kids. He's the perfect father or big brother or uncle that a lot of them don't have. Half the time when I find a kid in tears at the end of camp it's because he knows he won't get to see Rick for another year.'

'I'm surprised he could stay away. He must have known how disappointed the kids would be.'

Rachel gave her a puzzled look. 'He didn't tell you?'

Again, the feeling of being on the outside. 'Tell me what?'

'Why he didn't come this year?'

She shook her head.

'Sorry. That was a dumb question. Of course he wouldn't tell you. He stayed away because of Lynda. He thought it was more important for her to gain the confidence that comes from knowing she can make new friends on her own than it was for him to be here. He knew she'd never believe she'd done it by herself if he was around for her to lean on.'

'He didn't tell me. Or Lynda. She thinks he

stayed to work for a friend whose wife is sick.'

'He didn't have to take the shifts he did. Someone else would have worked them this week. Firefighters always take care of their own. It's one of the things I admire most about them.' She took Catherine over to a table lined with paint-splattered newspaper and half-finished bird feeders.

She saw bright-blue-and-orange squirrels, as well as some that were gray and brown. There were pink-and-green loons and even a couple of black-and-white ones. Every fire engine was red, however.

'This is Lynda's,' Rachel said.

Catherine shouldn't have been surprised. Lynda had always shown an artistic streak. But she'd had no idea her daughter had this kind of talent. The engine was painted with painstaking detail, from the lettering on the side to the firefighters on board. 'It's wonderful.'

'She's incredible with the little kids,' Rachel added. 'But then, you already know that. I told her she should be a teacher. She has a real gift.'

'She's going to be a business major,' Catherine answered automatically. She and Lynda had discussed it for the past two years and agreed business was the one degree that would give her financial freedom. Unspoken but understood was the need for Lynda to protect herself should she have inherited her mother's skill at choosing men.

'I never would have guessed that. She seems more the English lit or history type.'

Out of the corner of her eye, Catherine saw someone walk by outside. She looked closer and saw that it was Lynda. She was dressed in a gathered skirt, an off-the-shoulder white blouse, huge ear-rings, and rows of plastic beads around her neck. All of this set off by a Bakersfield Fire Department baseball cap.

Rachel spotted her, too. 'I'm not supposed to know this, but their skit involves fortune-telling. They've made up wild stories about what the counselors are going to find waiting for them when they get home.'

Catherine was on her way out the door when she heard another loud squeal and realized Lynda had spotted Rick. Decorum abandoned, she, like the others, ran into his arms. He lifted her the way he had Rachel and swung her around, her skirts swirling like a square dancer's.

'We do a lot of hugging around here,' Rachel said. 'Touching is important to these kids. For some of them, this is the only place they receive any physical contact at all.'

Instead of immediately going outside, Catherine stood at the door and observed.

The genuine warmth between Rick and Lynda went deeper than camp routine. They liked each other. Lynda looked at him with an adoration she'd never shown another man, not even her father.

'What are you doing here?' Lynda asked, her voice brimming with surprise and happiness. 'Never mind, I'm just so glad you came. Wait until you see our skit. It's *soooo* cool. We've been working on it all week.'

'I heard it was going to be something special. It's one of the reasons we came up tonight.'

'We?' Lynda turned, her gaze going to her mother as if drawn there by the force of her need.

Catherine knew a moment of sickening fear. What if Lynda didn't want her there? The fear melted — along with her heart — when she saw a look of raw love and sheer joy come over Lynda's face.

Lynda ran to her and they hugged, longer and harder than Catherine could ever remember the two of them hugging.

Rick and Rachel gathered the kids surrounding them and herded everyone off to campfire, leaving Catherine and Lynda alone.

'I'm sorry you didn't get to tell Ray good-bye,' Catherine said.

'At least you and Brian were there. He got

to say good-bye to someone.'

'I told him you would call when you were home again and he was settled. The hospital gave him a phone he can use by himself so he'll be able to call you, too. I even checked into getting an eight-hundred number for Ray to use when he wants to call us. That way he wouldn't have to worry about his aunt getting upset over the telephone bill.' First thing tomorrow morning she would have to send out her résumé. And keep sending it out until she had a job.

Lynda brightened. 'That's a great idea.'

'And I told him that if his aunt wouldn't let him come to see us over Christmas break, then we'd fly out to Kansas to see him.' When Lynda didn't say anything, Catherine cupped her chin in her hand and looked her square in the eyes. 'One way or another, this will work out. I promise.'

She saw Rick signaling them from behind a green building that held an enormous homemade sign that said, SPICE GIRLS CABIN. 'I think they're waiting for you.'

Lynda slipped her hand in Catherine's and led her across the quad. Catherine followed, a contented smile on her face as her gaze locked on Rick's. She couldn't remember the last time she'd held hands with her daughter, or the last time she'd felt as comfortable being watched by a man.

★ ★ ★

Catherine sat next to Rick on the wooden bench in the small amphitheater. They were in the last row, higher than everyone else and able to see everything, including the audience.

The kids sat in groups with their counselors, laughing and clapping their approval at punch lines that made little sense to Catherine. Her pleasure came in recognizing Lynda's hand in the composition and direction of the short play and in watching the unaffected way Rick joined in on the fun. Periodically, he would lean in close and explain one of the running jokes, usually directed at the kitchen staff — firefighters from Sacramento, Chico, and Bakersfield, all longtime camp veterans and favorites of the kids.

When a light breeze moved in, she crossed her arms and pulled into herself for warmth. Rick noticed and put his arm around her, drawing her into his side. For one brief moment she let herself believe she belonged next to him, that they were more than friends, that she'd finally found the soul mate she'd dreamed of when she was an impressionable young girl.

She was filled with a longing so powerful she knew her only escape was to get away before she did something that would embarrass them both, like touching his cheek or kissing him, or asking him to touch or kiss her.

As soon as Lynda's portion of the skit ended and another group took over, she stood and said, 'I'll be right back. I have to use the rest room.'

Instead, she went to the truck, got her jacket, and walked around until she was sure her foolish yearnings were under control.

She returned to see the final bows being taken. With shouts of excitement, everyone headed for the kitchen and the traditional mile-long ice cream sundae. While it wasn't a mile long, Catherine guessed the rain-gutter trough used to hold the ice cream, bananas, marshmallow cream, chocolate sauce, nuts, and whipped cream was a good sixty feet long. Spoons and napkins were handed out, chairs and benches dragged up, and the order to begin eating shouted out.

Rick insisted she join in. They took their positions on the end, sitting opposite each other. When he saw how daintily she ate, he began feeding her, catching a drip of chocolate with the spoon and a smear of whipped cream with his finger.

'Stop,' she laughingly protested when she saw a mound of ice cream twice as big as her mouth headed in her direction. 'I'll explode if I eat another bite.'

He grinned and put the spoon down. 'Okay, since we're done here, you can lick your lips.'

She did but could see by the look he gave her that she hadn't gotten everything.

He picked up his napkin and wiped the corners of her mouth. 'Stick out your tongue.'

'What?'

'Just do it.'

She did. He touched the napkin to her tongue and finished wiping her chin. 'This is the first time I've been this messy,' she said suspiciously.

He leaned forward until their noses were only inches apart. For one sweet, heart-pounding second she thought he was going to kiss her. Instead he looked deeply into her eyes and said softly, 'It's a perfect night for first times, don't you think?'

The implication was his, the decision was hers.

29

Catherine glanced at the dashboard clock as they turned into Rick's driveway. It was almost one, but she was so energized it could have been the middle of the day instead of the middle of the night. Even though they'd been together longer than they ever had before, even though they'd talked and laughed nonstop and she'd finally had the chance to tell him about her crazy Uncle John, she still wasn't ready to say good night.

She liked being with Rick. She wanted to tell him clever anecdotes because she felt good when her story elicited his smile. And she loved listening to him. He had a deep, resonating voice that, at times, was like a caress.

'Want to come in for a cup of coffee?' Rick asked when he'd turned off the engine.

The look that accompanied the words told her that he didn't want the evening to end, either. 'Coffee sounds good.'

'Or I could open a bottle of Randle's Roost merlot . . . '

'A man after my own heart.' The tired cliché came across more serious than she'd intended, but she let it go. Rick wasn't the kind of man who looked for encouragement in casual comments.

Blue whipped his tail in greeting when Catherine came around the truck, including her in his welcome as if she were a member of the family. She stopped to scratch his ears. 'How does he know which days you'll be home?'

'I've never been able to figure that out, but he's never wrong. He has full-time access to both houses through our garages, but if I'm off-shift and just gone for the day, it doesn't matter what time I come home, he's here waiting for me. He's even got a system for figuring out when I've been called in for overtime or I'm working a trade, and he stays with Sandra and Walt.'

She thought about going home and how empty her house would seem that night. She missed Lynda. But it was more than walking into an empty house alone — it was wanting to be exactly where she was.

Rick offered to let her wait in the living room while he went to get the wine, but she followed him into the kitchen instead. He gave her the bottle and opener and got out crackers and cheese. They worked together as if they'd done so a hundred times before, Catherine taking down the wine glasses and then a plate for the snack while Rick took out the cutting board and sliced the cheese.

'You must like to cook,' Catherine said, watching him.

'Why do you say that?'

'This kitchen. It's fantastic.'

'All show. I'm the king of soup-label recipes. Just ask my crew.'

'I don't believe you. No one owns a stove like this for show.'

He chuckled. 'I bought it because we have one just like it at the firehouse and I like the way it cooks.'

'You cook at the firehouse?'

'And mop floors and mow lawns and wash windows.' He held out a piece of cheese for her to taste. 'It's part of the job.'

The cheese was spicy, with a hint of garlic and a touch of heat she attributed to the green specks liberally sprinkled throughout. A perfect choice for the merlot. 'So you're busy cleaning toilet bowls and cooking meals in between rescuing people from fires and performing CPR on heart-attack patients?'

'Keeps us humble.'

'Are all firefighters like you?'

He opened the crackers and scattered them across the plate. 'In what way?'

'So self-effacing.'

He considered her question. 'I don't know

377

if I'd call it self-effacing. I think it's more a sense of being grateful for having a job that lets us do what we do.'

'How can you be so cavalier about risking your life?'

'It's my job.' He struggled for a better answer. 'It's what I do. Besides, not all calls are life-and-death situations. Sometimes it's a kid with a finger stuck in a pipe or a pan someone left on the stove.'

'And sometimes it's a man who's drowning in a swollen river or a propane tank that exploded because someone tried to use a barbecue to heat their house.'

Rick eyed her suspiciously. 'Who have you been talking to?'

'Brian.' How had she missed the small scar on his chin or the way his eyes narrowed when he was deep in thought?

'Of course. I'd forgotten he did a sleepover with us.' He chuckled. 'Steve said Brian kept them up half the night asking questions.'

'He talked about it for days afterward. Every time he came to see Lynda.'

'Did he also tell you how boring it is around there between calls?' Rick asked.

'You're talking about a young man who idolizes you, Rick Sawyer. Boredom isn't in the equation.' She poured the wine and handed him a glass. 'Now if I could just find a job that interests me half as much as yours does you, I'd be a happy woman.'

'You're job hunting?'

'It's that or go stir-crazy when Lynda goes back to school.' Not exactly a lie, but not the complete truth either. 'I'm only going to go part-time for now and then switch to full-time when she's out of her pressure garments.'

'What kind of job?'

'My background is human resources, but I'm looking at everything.'

'I know of a part-time job that's opening up at the union office. Shirley and Pam have worked there for years and could fill you in on the details if you're interested.'

'You mean the firefighters' union?' The way she felt about organized labor, she couldn't imagine working for a union, but to be polite, she showed interest.

'They're in the city,' he added. 'So it might be a longer commute than you wanted to make.'

He was providing her a way out. Obviously she hadn't been as subtle in her question as she'd intended. 'I'll call tomorrow. Pam was the woman's name?'

He gave her a knowing smile. 'Or Shirley.'

'Did you know Brian has decided he wants to be a firefighter?' She held up her glass and brought it to his. 'His father is going to have a fit when he finds out.'

He touched his glass to hers, the crystal making a crisp, bell-like sound. 'Why is that?'

'Peter has such high hopes for Brian. He made almost perfect scores on his SATs and — ' She almost choked on the words when she realized what she was saying. 'I'm sorry. I didn't mean that the way it came out.'

'Yes, you did,' he said without judgment. 'I'm not color-blind, Catherine. I know my shirt has a blue collar. And I know the kind of baggage that color brings with it.'

'I'm sorry.' If she could have arranged for a hole in the floor to open right then and there, she would have gladly jumped into it.

'Forget it,' he said easily. He took a sip of wine.

'Never.' How could she have been so insensitive?

'Look, you said what you feel. Would it help if I told you it doesn't come as a surprise?'

How did he know? Had she said something? Acted some way? 'I really am sorry. I feel like such a snob.'

'You need to understand something here, Catherine. I don't need outside opinion to confirm my worthiness. I carry that inside. For me, knowing that what I do makes a difference is a lot more important than how other people might see me or how much money I might have in the bank at any given moment. I know you find this hard to believe, but money isn't important to me. It never has been.'

She put her glass on the counter. 'I think that's my cue to go slinking off into the night.'

'Only if you let it be.'

'First I have to tell you something I've been meaning to tell you for a long time now. I'm well aware that Lynda wouldn't be where she is without you. Neither would I. I will never be able to thank you enough. You came along — '

'I appreciate what you're trying to do, but it isn't necessary.' He settled in close and gave her a small, intimate smile. 'I know what I'm up against and I'm not the least bit worried I can't handle it.'

She could see the flecks of gold in his eyes and smell a hint of smoke from the campfire. The top button on his shirt was open and there were gray hairs at his temples. Her heart did a funny little tap dance against her ribs as she took all this in.

She would have been all right if she hadn't looked at his lips, if she hadn't wondered how they would feel against her own . . . but most of all, if she hadn't tilted her chin up and swayed forward and let out a sigh of longing.

The kiss opened the door she thought she'd barricaded. Reason, rationale, determination were like dandelion seeds in the wind. Her mind yielded to her senses and she was swept away by a deep yearning.

He took control with the second kiss, bringing her into his arms and holding her as if he'd held her a hundred times before. She fitted herself to him, becoming instantly, almost unbearably aroused. 'This is insanity,' she murmured against his lips.

'Too soon,' he agreed.

'We shouldn't be doing this.' She opened her mouth, tasting, testing, taking him in. Her hips moved against his, gently and then harder.

'It's going to complicate things between us.' He put his hands on her waist. 'That's the last thing I want.'

'Me too.' Her breasts swelled with the need to be touched.

He cupped her buttocks and brought her tight against him. 'I want you, Catherine,' he whispered into her ear. 'More than I've ever wanted anyone or anything.'

She pulled back to look at him. 'I feel the same way. It's wrong . . . it's insanity,' she repeated. 'But I don't care.'

'Then you're sure?'

'Yes . . . oh, yes.'

He took her hand and led her to the bedroom. She stood next to the king-size bed as he undressed her, removing the layers of her clothing the way she had opened his present. He touched her skin as if it were silk and he had on a work-roughened glove — gently, so very gently. She caught her lip between her teeth to keep still when he softly lapped at her nipple with his tongue. Wave after wave of desire and need spread through her body.

Unable to stay still any longer, she impatiently pulled his shirt from his jeans, unbuttoned it, and ran her hands over his chest and down his arms. Her fingers slowed as they lifted and dipped over the ridges and valleys of his scars. He caught her hands with his own and ran his thumb over her palm, kissing her ear, the hollow at the base of her throat, and the narrow, flat spot between her breasts.

'I've imagined you like this,' he admitted. 'A hundred times. Only I never got it right. Not once.' He looked into her eyes. 'You are more beautiful than I could ever conceive. You take my breath away, Catherine.'

Suddenly self-conscious, she surreptitiously tightened her stomach to hide what she knew to be an imperfection.

'Don't do that,' he said in response. 'Can't you feel how perfectly we fit the other way?' He put his hand flat against her belly. 'I like knowing I could rest my head here and not hurt you. Your softness, your curves are more erotic than hard angles and bone could ever be.' His hand moved lower, and lower still, until his fingers were pressed into her moistness.

She let out a small cry of surprise that turned to pleasure as he moved a finger against the hard nub he'd unerringly found.

She was already near a climax. When she felt herself at the edge, she tried to pull away, to wait for him, but couldn't. Instead she tumbled uncontrollably into a series of rapid contractions that sent a hot burst of intense, coiling pleasure deep inside her belly and left her gasping for air.

She wanted more. She wanted to feel him inside of her, needed to feel him. She reached for the button on his jeans but couldn't get it open. 'Help me,' she told him, a small plea in her voice.

He lifted her onto the bed, slipped out of the rest of his clothes, and joined her. He made love to her with a tenderness and understanding that had nothing to do with show or technique or locker-room bravado, never mentioning the constriction of using protection or complaining about its necessity. She didn't understand at first, and kept expecting the mechanics that modern male experts had dictated were necessary to please a woman. Instead, Rick tested and waited and pursued and whispered his own excitement and pleasure into her ear, making her feel like a true partner in lovemaking for the first time in her life.

He didn't wait until they were finished to ask her if she'd climaxed again; he sensed when she was close, and moved to make the peak more intense and long-lashing.

Afterward, sated and pleasantly exhausted, they lay curled in each other's arms. Rick kissed her forehead and then each closed eye. 'Do you have anything to do today that can't be put off?'

'Today?' she repeated sleepily.

'Yes, today — the sun's going to be coming through this window in a couple of hours.'

She tried to remember her schedule, but nothing stood out. 'I can't think of anything. Why are you asking?'

'We need to work out what we're going to tell Lynda.'

She opened her eyes and frowned. 'About what?'

'About us.'

Catherine propped herself up on her elbow and looked down at him. 'We're not going to tell her anything. Why would we?'

'Because I'd rather be up-front with her than have her think something is going on behind her back. There's no telling what she'd come up with on her own.'

'But nothing is going on. Or at least nothing will be going on when she gets home.' The nebulous fear that they were making a mistake tonight had found its focus. They'd each known they were crossing a line. What they hadn't known was that their lines were different. Rick believed they'd gone somewhere together; she'd accepted they were ending a friendship.

He sat up, his back against the mission-style headboard. 'This is it, then? Is that what you're saying? We're not going to see each other anymore?'

Feeling more naked than she had when they were making love, she pulled the sheet up to cover her breasts. 'I thought you understood.'

'The only thing I understand is that I love you.'

She recoiled at the words. 'You can't. How could you? You hardly know me.'

He caught her moving hands and held

them still. 'I've loved you almost from the moment we met.'

'You never said anything.' Her panic was like a weight in her chest, growing heavier with every word.

'I was waiting for Lynda to grow stronger,' he said simply. 'She had to come first.'

Catherine was the only one who had ever put Lynda first. It was something Jack had never considered, let alone managed. She didn't — she couldn't — believe Rick, even though she knew he was telling the truth. 'What happened to make you change your mind?'

'Nothing complicated. It was selfishness — pure and simple. I wanted you.' He held her tighter when she tried to pull away. 'I'm only sorry that you're sorry.'

'If I'd known how you feel I never would have let this happen tonight.' Tears of regret burned her throat. She didn't want to hurt him, but she had no choice. 'I am sorry, Rick,' she said in a choked whisper. 'More sorry than I can say. I don't love you. I can't.'

'But you do, Catherine. You just don't know it yet.'

'You're wrong. It would never work out between us. We're too different.' She looked deeply into his eyes. 'And I'm too worn-down to try to change who I am . . . even for you.'

'I would never ask you to change.'

'Then you'll have to let me go, because it wouldn't work any other way.'

Finally, nodding, he released her hands. 'I'll find someone else to mentor Lynda.'

The weight in her chest turned to regret. She would give anything to go back, just a couple of hours, to erase the words that had set them on this path, to forget his exquisite, selfless lovemaking. 'She won't understand,' she said, struggling to breathe against the regret.

'I'll find a way,' he promised.

'I'll miss you.' Unshed tears sent the words out in a rush and stripped them of their true depth of feeling.

He leaned forward and brought her to him for an infinitely sad and tender kiss. 'Having you in my life gave me more happiness than I'd ever known. I let myself believe it was only the beginning, and forgot that belief had to be shared.'

'I'm sorry.' She managed to turn her back to him before he could see her tears. Still he touched her, offering her comfort when she'd just broken his heart. Desperately she wished it could be different, that she could take another chance, that she could trust herself one more time.

It would be so easy to give in. Rick loved

her. What did it matter that they had Lynda in common and nothing else? So their relationship only lasted a year or two. Couldn't she glory in the good while they were together and be philosophical about the bad when it ended?

So what that she would be a three-time loser. So what that her pride would be dealt a crushing blow. Surely she could pick up the pieces and go on.

But what if she couldn't?

30

The sky was the deep purple of false dawn when Catherine arrived home. More out of need for shelter and isolation than out of exhaustion, she crawled into bed and curled into a fetal position, her pillow a sponge for her tears.

Finally, she cried herself to sleep.

The phone rang, dragging her from unconsciousness into a world she wasn't yet ready to face. When she could no longer ignore the summons by incorporating it into a dream, she snaked her arm out from under the sheet and answered.

'Hello?'

'Catherine? Is that you?'

'Why are you calling this early, Jack? Is something wrong?' She gave up the hope she could go back to sleep, tucked her pillow against the headboard, and sat up.

'It's almost noon,' he said judgmentally. 'Late night?' he added.

'What do you want?'

'We need to talk. I was hoping you could meet me at Scott's Seafood for lunch.'

'Today?' She didn't feel like going any-where, let alone to lunch with Jack.

'Isn't Lynda coming home tomorrow?'

'Yes . . . ' She didn't like the way this was going.

'It would be better if she wasn't around for this.' He paused. 'It concerns her as much as it does us.'

'And it's something that can't be handled over the phone?'

'I'd prefer to do it in person.'

'What time?'

'One? Can you make it by then?'

She looked at the clock. That gave her an hour to get ready and a half hour to drive into town. She could make it if the freeway was clear. 'I'll be there.'

★　★　★

Grateful for the distraction that meeting Jack provided, Catherine managed to put aside her annoyance at being summoned. She spotted him the minute she entered the restaurant, bypassing the hostess with a quick smile.

'You're late,' he said when she was seated.

'Five minutes.'

'Must have been some night.'

He was fishing and she refused to bite. 'Have you heard the specials?'

'Salmon and some kind of chowder.' He motioned for the waiter. 'We're ready to order.'

She smiled sweetly. 'I'm sorry, I still need a few minutes.'

'Something to drink?' the waiter asked.

'Club soda with lime.'

'Hangover?' Jack asked when the waiter had gone.

She didn't bother looking up. 'Having trouble at home, Jack?'

He didn't say anything for several seconds. 'I'm sorry. That was uncalled for.'

The apology brought a reaction. She put the menu aside. 'Now that we have the small talk out of the way, why don't you tell me why you wanted me here?'

He moved forward in his chair. 'I've been going over my finances. I know I promised I'd hold off having your alimony reduced, but I don't see how I can any longer.'

'And you're willing to have my lawyer look at your financial records?' She knew how much the idea would upset him.

'Do I have a choice?'

'No.'

'Then I guess I am.'

Not even a full-time job would get her and Lynda through this. She was going to have to sell the house. 'Are you sure it has to be now?

You couldn't hold off a couple of months?'

'What possible difference would that make?'

'Lynda would be established back in school by then. I want her to have that much stability before I tell her she has to leave the house she's lived in all of her life.'

The waiter brought her drink and they ordered. He was barely gone when Jack said, 'You're making me out to be the bad guy in this. You always do that to me.'

'And you're putting me on the defensive, the way you always do. What happened to our détente? I thought we were going to work together to make Lynda's life better.'

He closed his eyes and rubbed his temples, hard. 'I'm trying, Catherine. I really am.'

'But?'

'I'm broke. Or damn near.' When he looked at her again, there were tears in his eyes. 'I went out on a limb with something that was supposed to be surefire and it wasn't. Adriana's income is the only thing that's keeping us afloat right now.'

She didn't know what to say. 'I'm sorry.'

'Yeah, me too.'

Their salads came. 'What are you going to do?'

'Start over. What else can I do?'

'Lynda's college fund?' She hated to ask but had to know.

'It's there.' He picked up his fork and put it down again. 'I assume you still have your savings?'

Not nearly as much as she'd started out with. Images of St. John knits, club dues, and the money she'd continued to spend after her paychecks stopped whirled through her mind. 'Some.'

'Enough to get by?'

'One way or another.'

'You know I'll resume paying you the full alimony as soon as I'm on my feet again.'

She believed him, but it didn't affect her the way she would have expected. She was scared about what lay ahead, but she was strangely exhilarated, too. Without the house, she could get by on a tenth of the income she'd needed. If she took the profit from the sale and bought something she could manage without outside help, she and Lynda could get by on what she made — even if it were only a part-time job.

'We'll talk about that later,' she said. She was suddenly ravenously hungry. 'Stop worrying, Jack. It will all work out.'

He gave her a surprised look. 'That's it? That's all you're going to say?'

'What did you expect?'

'I don't know. Tears? Panic? Threats? Teeth-gnashing?'

'That's how you see me?' She really wanted to know.

'That's how you've always been, Catherine. You've never handled crises well. Why would I think you'd behave any differently now?'

'I've changed,' she said. The why and where and how she would think about later. Right now it was enough to know she would get through this.

He studied her for a long time. 'I can see that now.'

Satisfied, she smiled.

★　★　★

Before Catherine left the restaurant, she looked up the address of the Firefighters' Union Hall in the telephone book, deciding she might as well get started on her new life as soon as possible. She went there figuring it wouldn't hurt to have a little practice applying for a job; she left employed.

She was to start a week from Monday, the same day Lynda would go back to school. Through the entire interview, she'd had a surreal feeling that she was exactly where she was supposed to be, that this was the way she was supposed to say good-bye to Rick and still see him occasionally. She would never be able to pay him back for all he had done for her and Lynda, but for once in her life, her actions would speak louder than her words.

Walking into the real estate office brought an unexpected lump to her throat. It seemed even something that had become a burden could be hard to let go.

The agent gave Catherine a rough estimate on what she could expect the house to bring, basing the figure on several similar houses that had sold in the area. She added that while spring was a better selling time, the demand for homes in Granite Bay seemed to hold steady throughout the year. With luck, the house could be sold and they could be out by Christmas.

The meeting was businesslike and friendly and the agent had the intuition or good sense not to ask Catherine why she had decided to sell. In the end, she only hesitated a moment before she signed the papers that would put the house on the market.

When she left the office and got in her car, her hands shook so badly she had to make three attempts to get the key in the ignition.

She was scared. And she was excited. And she was heavyhearted. How could she do so many things right and so many wrong in the same day?

31

'Your'e selling the house?' Lynda sat up from her massage and grabbed a towel to wrap around her. 'Why? Where will we go? How could you do this without telling me? Don't I get a say? It's my house, too, you know.'

Catherine wiped the lotion off her hands. Knowing it would be impossible to continue afterward, she'd waited until the massage was almost over before telling Lynda. Although Lynda had handled the news about the job better than Catherine had expected, she'd harbored no illusions that the same thing would happen when Lynda heard about the house. If she could, Catherine would have waited. Dumping news of both the job and the house on Lynda the first day back from camp was a lot for her to take in. But the last thing she wanted was for Lynda to come home from her date with Brian and find a For Sale sign on the front lawn.

'It wasn't a matter of choice,' Catherine said. 'I have to sell.' She tossed her towel into the hamper.

'Why?'

'Because we can't afford to live here anymore.'

'But you have a job now.'

'It doesn't pay enough to cover the taxes and insurance on this place.'

'Can't you get a better job?'

'I'm not qualified for anything better.' She took a clean washcloth out of the drawer, wet it, and wiped down the table. 'I'm not a career woman, Lynda. I'm someone who held a job for a couple of years. There's a huge difference.'

'I don't understand. What about Dad? Can't you get more money from him?'

She flinched at the suggestion. Lynda had learned that lesson by example. 'He's having problems himself. Until he gets back on his feet, he isn't going to be able to pay full alimony, or child support. Besides, I think it's time I started taking care of myself, don't you?'

'Where will we go? You're not going to make me change schools, are you?'

'No, I'm not going to make you change schools. As for where we'll go, I'm not sure yet. We have a lot of places we can explore — the entire city, the entire county. I was going to look for another house to buy, but I think we should rent for a while.'

'I don't want to live in an apartment.

Anything but that.'

'Good, neither do I. I was thinking more along the lines of a house. One with a big yard so we could get a dog.'

Finally something positive, something hopeful penetrated. 'Really? I thought you didn't like dogs.'

'I changed my mind.' Actually, it was Jack who hadn't liked dogs. She'd simply gone along. The way she had with so many other things in their marriage.

'Are we poor now?' Lynda asked. Before Catherine could answer, she added, 'Does this mean I'm not getting a car for my birthday?'

'Maybe,' she hedged. And then, 'Probably.'

'What about college?'

'That's taken care of.'

Lynda pressed her back into the wall and gently moved from side to side. The itching had started again. 'Everything has changed,' she said softly. 'I can't count on anything anymore.'

'You can count on me.'

'How do I know that, Mom?' When she looked up, there were tears in her eyes. 'I thought I could count on being a cheerleader and wearing tank tops and living in this house forever and being homecoming queen and having a father who loved me enough to want to see me once in a while, and I wasn't right about any of it. Why should I think you're any different?'

'Because you know I am. I might disappoint you sometimes, and I might not always be able to do things the way you want them done, but I will always be here for you.' She went to her and took her in her arms. 'I know you're not ready to hear this, and I know it's going to be hard for you to believe, but I know in my heart that someday we're going to look back at this year and remember the good more than we do the bad.'

'I hate it when you do that.' She propped her chin on Catherine's shoulder. 'I don't want to feel better. Not yet, anyway.'

Catherine closed her eyes against the overwhelming feeling of relief that washed over her. 'I know. But it's bound to happen sooner or later, so it might as well be now. You don't want to mess up your night out with Brian worrying about something neither one of us can change.'

'There's no way we can keep the house?'

Catherine shook her head. 'I'm sorry.'

'Yeah, me too.' She adjusted her towel. 'I better get ready. Brian's always early.'

'Where are you going?'

'His house. It's his brother's birthday.'

'You didn't tell me. Did you get him a present?'

'Brian took care of it.' She was halfway through the door when she stopped and turned back. 'You went to Rick's house, didn't you?'

The question took Catherine off guard. 'What makes you think that?'

'The dog thing. You want one because you saw Blue.'

'I was there the night we came up to see you,' she said.

'And?'

'And what?'

'What did you think?'

'Blue's a terrific dog. Everything you said he was. I'd take him in a minute, but I don't think we could get Rick or his neighbor to give him to us.'

'Not Blue. What did you think about the house?'

'I loved it.' That didn't begin to describe her feelings. Rick's house was a home, the very thing she'd tried so hard to make for her and Lynda.

'Do you think we could rent one like that?'

'I don't think there is another house like Rick's.' And if there were, it would be out of their price range. No one in their right mind would trust that kind of craftsmanship to a renter.

The doorbell rang. 'That *can't* be Brian,' Lynda said, clearly believing it was. She flew to the window. 'Oh, my God. It is.' She sent Catherine a pleading look. 'Tell him I'm almost ready.' She ran down the hall to her bedroom. 'Fifteen minutes. No, make that ten.'

Catherine opened the door with a flourish and a broad smile. The smile faded when she saw the look on Brian's face. 'Something's wrong. What is it?'

He came in and stood in the foyer. 'Where's Lynda?' he asked softly.

'Upstairs getting ready. We were talking and lost track of time.'

He shoved his hands in his back pockets. 'Ray's in the hospital. I tried calling him before I came over and his aunt said he has some kind of kidney infection. I asked for the number at the hospital and she said he was out of it most of the time and couldn't talk.' He glanced up the stairs toward Lynda's room. 'I don't know how much I should tell her. She was so upset about not being here when Ray left, I'm afraid she'll freak if she finds out he's sick.'

'How bad is it?'

Brian shrugged. 'All I know for sure is that he's bad enough to be in the hospital. I don't think his aunt would put him there unless it was serious.'

'She probably didn't have a choice. It's my understanding that kidney problems are fairly common with burn patients. Lynda was checked constantly when she was in the hospital.'

'But shouldn't Ray be past that kind of thing by now?'

He wanted reassurance that she couldn't give him. 'I don't know. His burns were so much worse than Lynda's.'

'Should I tell her?'

To ask him to wait would make his burden heavier, but Lynda had already been given enough to deal with. 'Can you wait a couple of days? She could use a breather.'

'Sure.'

She was touched by his easy acceptance. Her incredible, beautiful, thoughtful daughter deserved someone like Brian, just as he deserved someone as wonderful as Lynda. She was so glad they had found each other.

'Lynda's going to be a few more minutes. Would you like something to drink?'

'You have any lemonade?'

'Coming up.'

He followed her into the kitchen and stood at the window where she'd hung the hummingbird feeder. 'You get any birds yet?'

'A couple. I haven't been home to watch for them lately.' She no sooner had the words out than an Anna's hummingbird swooped in to land at the feeder.

'I bought a feeder for my mom, too. The hummingbirds found hers right away. Now she's going to get one for up at the lake. Dad said she'll have them hanging everywhere in a couple of months.'

Catherine handed Brian his lemonade. 'Rick tells me you're thinking about becoming a firefighter.'

'Me and ten thousand other guys.' He sounded discouraged. 'And ten thousand women, too.'

'I'm sure if you're still interested after you finish college, you won't have any trouble getting a job.'

He gave her a disbelieving look. 'Rick must not have told you how hard it is to get into his department — or any fire department. In the bigger cities there are hundreds of applicants for every job opening.'

'Why?' The question was automatic — and insulting. She'd done the same thing to Rick. Would she never learn? 'I'm sorry, Brian. I just don't understand the allure, and I'm afraid your parents won't, either. Why would you want to do something that hard and dangerous when it pays so little?'

'Because it matters. How many people can say that about what they do?'

The words were an echo of Rick's, but she innately knew they were Brian's. She should have known. Take away the years and circumstances and Rick and Brian were as alike as leaves from the same tree.

'I'm ready,' Lynda called, bounding down the stairs. She beamed when she saw Brian and turned in a circle, her long, flowered skirt swirling sensuously around her legs. With her hand on top of her head to hold on a hat with a turned-up brim and matching flowers, she did a quick curtsy and asked, 'How do I look?'

'Awesome,' Brian said appreciatively. 'Wait until my brother sees you in that dress.'

Lynda grinned and looked at Catherine. 'Jimmy has a little crush on me.'

''Little,' hell. It's more the size of a boulder,' Brian said. 'One he'd hit me over the head with if he thought he could get away with it.'

Jimmy was the youngest of the Winslow boys, ten years old and running hard to try to catch up. 'Sounds a little like your father when he was that age,' Catherine said.

'That's what Mom tells him.' Brian took Lynda's hand and turned to Catherine, a sudden thought sparkling in his eyes. 'Hey, you want to come tonight? It's nothing formal, just a barbecue in the backyard.'

Catherine smiled. 'Thanks, but I have some things I have to get done around here. Closets to clean, that kind of thing. We're having an open house next weekend.'

'Open house? Isn't that what you do when you're — '

Lynda tugged him toward the front door. 'I'll tell you about it in the car.'

Catherine walked them out and waved good-bye. It was a perfect night for a barbecue, hot but not suffocating. The mosquitoes would be out, but not in numbers so great that they couldn't be controlled with citronella candles and a little yard spray.

Now that she was alone again, her plans for the evening seemed as empty as she felt. Without the distractions she'd used to keep from thinking about Rick, she had to deal with what had happened between them.

She wasn't ready for another relationship. At least not a serious one. How could she be, when she was struggling to learn how to stand by herself for the first time in her life. Rick wanted more than she had to give. She couldn't love someone casually. Loving required commitment. A commitment she owed to Lynda.

Lynda came first. She had to. And while Catherine was prepared to let Rick walk out of her life, she couldn't let him walk out of Lynda's.

Before she could find a reason to change her mind, she went back inside and dialed the number at Rick's fire station. Her stomach did a quick roll with every ring.

She was about to hang up when he answered. 'Captain Sawyer.'

'Rick, it's Catherine.'

There was a long pause. 'Great minds, I guess. I was going to call you later.'

'Is this a bad time?' She was acutely aware that he could be called away at any moment, and she always felt the need to talk fast.

'We just got back from a fire and I don't like to leave all the cleanup to the crew, but I have a few minutes before they miss me.'

'Was it bad?'

'Garage. The people lost their Mercedes but we got the dog out, so the kids were happy. You didn't call to hear this, Catherine.'

She took a deep breath and let it out in a rush. 'It's Lynda. I'm sorry for asking. I know how hard it would be for you to keep seeing her, but is there a way you could — '

'I'm not going to find her another mentor, Catherine. What I said was a knee-jerk reaction, and I've felt like an ass ever since for letting it happen.' He paused. 'Okay, now it's your turn.'

There were a hundred things she could say, things she should say. The one she chose was the one from her heart. 'Don't give up on me. Not yet, anyway. I have a long way to go, but I'm trying hard.'

'I'm not going anywhere, Catherine. When you're ready, you know where you can find me.'

There wasn't anything else to say. She told him good-bye, replaced the receiver, and took out the bottle of Randle's Roost Rick had given her for her birthday. She poured herself a glass and went out on the deck. The sun set slowly that evening, painting the sky with a liquid fire that dripped onto the horizon.

Somewhere in the city, a man she didn't understand sat and waited for the call that told him someone needed him. He would answer the call regardless of its tedium or danger, do what he could to help, and then slip away to wait for the next summons. For the people who thought to offer thanks after their rush of adrenaline had settled, it would be too late. If they tried the next day, their rescuers would be gone, replaced by others of their kind on another shift.

She'd come to understand that firefighters were silent heroes in an age of role models who raged at each other on professional basketball courts and football fields. Their silence was a part of their basic makeup. Their bonus checks were hearts that restarted at their dogged insistence; their vacations were smiles elicited from children at camp; their country club dues were preschoolers who tramped through the fire station with stars in their eyes.

How could she expect to understand Rick when she'd never known anyone like him?

32

'So when are you going to hit the panic button?' Phyllis asked. 'Seems to me it better be pretty soon.'

Catherine leaned forward to wave to the guard at the gate and saw that it was someone new. 'You might as well stop. The new ones take their job seriously.'

Phyllis dutifully identified herself and waited for the guard to check the list of approved visitors. 'What is he doing in there? Didn't he see the grocery bags in the back seat? For all he knows we could have ice cream melting back there.'

'Goodness!' Catherine exclaimed. 'I had no idea you were operating with such a short fuse today.'

'You know how I feel about all this business. Who are you people trying to keep out of here, anyway?'

'Girl Scouts. You should see them. Every year they storm the gates to try to sell us their cookies.'

Phyllis laughed. Finally the guard came back, but instead of simply opening the gate, he saluted first. 'What nonsense.' Phyllis couldn't resist adding, 'You'd think he was letting us into a top secret military compound.'

'You won't have to put up with it much longer,' Catherine said cheerfully. Her house had sold the first day it was officially on the market, at the asking price. Which, of course, convinced her that they'd priced it too low. She spent five minutes stewing over the possibility before calling her mother to celebrate. They'd gone to lunch at Cooking with Linda, Catherine's favorite restaurant, the one place she allowed herself to indulge without a moment's hesitation or guilt.

In the week and a half since then, Lynda had started school, Catherine had started her new job, and Rick had missed Brian's first football game when he was called in for overtime.

'Have you at least decided where you're going to look for a new house?'

'Lynda and I talked it over. She wants to stay in the area while she's still in school and then doesn't really care where I move when she starts college. I have a list of places the woman from the rental agency gave me. We're meeting her when I get home from work tomorrow. There's one in Johnson Ranch that looks promising, but I don't know about the others.'

'Johnson Ranch is nice.'

Nice, certainly, but nowhere near what they were accustomed to. Catherine had never lived in a tract house and didn't know what to expect. The idea that she could walk into a neighbor's house that was just like hers was a disconcerting novelty.

'More important,' she said, 'it's somewhere I can afford. And small enough that I can take care of it myself.'

'I promised myself I wouldn't do this . . . the last thing I want to do is interfere . . . '

Catherine smiled. 'What is it?'

'Do you need money? I have more than I'll ever spend and I'd rather give it to you now than make you wait until I'm gone. I certainly don't see any fun in that.'

'I'm fine.'

'I don't see how you could be. I know it's none of my business, but — '

'By renting another house instead of buying one and investing the money I'm clearing on the sale of this place, I'll be able to support myself and Lynda on the income from the interest and my job.'

'You're handling this thing a lot better than I thought you would.' Phyllis pulled into the driveway and set the parking brake.

'I know. It's a little surprising to me, too. I

keep waiting for depression to set in. Instead I wake up every morning with this incredible sense of freedom. I love my new job and Lynda loves being back in school. I'm excited about the direction our lives are taking. For the first time ever I'm completely on my own. Life couldn't be better.'

'Now all you need is a good man to keep you — '

'Don't even start,' she warned. Phyllis had been asking pointed questions and dropping decidedly unsubtle hints about Rick since the birthday party. 'Whether you want to believe it or not, what I told you about Rick and me being friends is the way it is.'

'I understand why you're moving slow. I thought about what you told me and I can't say I blame you for thinking you're a pretty poor judge of men. But you have to have figured out by now that Rick is nothing like Jack or Tom.'

'I don't need a man in my life right now. I'm doing fine on my own.'

Phyllis was halfway out the door when she said, 'That's your problem, Catherine. You get need and want mixed up. You needed the other two to define and support who you thought you were. There was a time when you thought having a guard and a gate was a good thing, important enough that you let yourself get caught up in believing what a man could provide was somehow related to what he was inside.'

'That's a terrible thing to say. You make me sound like — ' *Like the woman she was.* Or at least the woman she had been.

Phyllis came around the car, carrying a bag of groceries in each hand. 'Now I suppose you're mad at me and I'm going to have to stick around until you get over it.'

'Why didn't you tell me this before?'

'Because it took me this long to figure it out. Not every insight comes riding in on a lightning bolt, you know.'

'Is that why you married Dad?' With Phyllis, insight was often based on experience. She took the groceries from her side of the back seat, joined her mother on the porch, and, instead of digging through her purse for her keys, rang the bell for Lynda to let them in.

'I think that was part of it. In the fifties, girls were raised to be homemakers. No one ever told me I could take care of myself, so it was important I chose someone who could do the job right. I don't know whether I was smart or just lucky that I wound up with your father.'

Catherine looked at her mother, trying very hard to be serious when she said, 'So, what you're saying is that it's all your fault that I can't tell a good man from a bad one.'

Phyllis blinked in surprise. 'That's not what I'm saying at all.'

'Gotcha.' She rang the bell again. After several seconds, she tried the door and found it open. Puzzled, she glanced at Phyllis. 'Could I have forgotten to lock it?'

'No, I distinctly remember you checking.'

A feeling of unease crawled up her spine. She moved into the foyer. 'Lynda?' No answer. '*Lynda?*' she said louder. Still no answer.

'Maybe she's out back,' Phyllis suggested.

Catherine went into the family room and saw Lynda's backpack on the sofa. The magazines that had been stacked on the coffee table lay scattered across the floor. The portable phone was in the fireplace and the curtains had been torn from the kitchen window. The coin of her fear flipped to terror.

'*Lynda?*' she screamed. '*Lynda, where are you?*'

Phyllis dropped the groceries. 'I'll check upstairs.'

Her heart in her throat, Catherine ran to the sliding glass door, flung it open, and crossed the deck. Lynda wasn't in the backyard.

'She's not up here,' Phyllis called as she

hurried back down the stairs. She came into the family room and slowly looked around. 'My God . . . What happened?'

Frantically, Catherine began searching the room. 'Do you see her purse? She wouldn't have left without her purse.'

She flung open the closet and checked it top to bottom. Phyllis looked behind pillows and under cushions. 'Where could she have gone?' Phyllis asked. 'And why?'

'Damn it.' Catherine hugged herself tight. 'When I took the job, I promised her I would be here for her when she came home from school. I never should have gone shopping.'

'That's crazy,' Phyllis said. 'You can't be with her every minute.'

Catherine whipped around when she saw a movement at the front door. For an instant, less than a heartbeat, she felt profound relief. And then she saw that it wasn't Lynda, but Brian standing there. He looked pale and scared.

'Is she gone?' he asked.

His fear fueled Catherine's. 'What happened?'

'It's Ray. He's dead.'

The heat drained from her body. Her mind screamed a denial. Not Ray. He'd been through so much, fought so hard, had so much to give. 'How?'

'His kidneys stopped working. The doctors tried everything but nothing worked. It was like he just gave up. At least that's what his aunt told Lynda when she called to talk to Ray.'

Catherine's knees gave out. She reached for the sofa and collapsed on the arm. 'When did he die?'

'Yesterday. Lynda didn't even know he was sick. I was going to tell her, but . . . I didn't.' He caught his breath in a sob. 'Everything was going so good for her at school I didn't want to spoil it for her.' He held his hands out in a helpless gesture. 'I didn't know he would die.'

Phyllis reached for him and brought him into her arms. His sobs became tears. 'I'm so sorry,' she crooned softly. 'For all of you.'

Catherine could picture Lynda bubbling with excitement when she called to talk to Ray, full of news about school that she wanted to share, eager to find out how Ray was doing in his new school. How many times could Lynda come back from having her world shattered? Which time would be the one that stole her youth and turned her into an old woman at fifteen?

'We can't just sit around here,' Catherine said. 'How long has it been since you talked to Lynda?' she asked Brian.

He wiped his eyes on his shirtsleeve. 'Half hour — maybe a little more. I thought she was going to be okay, and then she totally freaked when I told her that I knew Ray had been in the hospital for over a week. She kept asking me why I didn't tell her, and nothing I said made any difference.'

'She couldn't have gone far.' Catherine tried to put herself in Lynda's place. Where would she go to cry? Someplace where she could be alone. 'She's probably headed for Folsom. The lake is only a mile from here by the back roads. I'll drive down and see if I can intercept her.'

'What do you want me to do?' Brian asked.

'Take the horse trail in case she went that way.' As far as she knew, Lynda never went that way because the path wandered through the hills a long time before it dropped down to the lake. But there had been too many first times in that summer to discount another one. Since he would have to travel by foot, she asked, 'Do you have your cell phone? I don't want you wandering around out there if she's already come home.'

'It's in the car. I'll take it with me.'

Phyllis started picking up magazines. 'I'll wait here in case she shows up before you get back.'

Catherine grabbed her keys and headed for the garage.

Seconds later she was back again. 'Catch Brian,' she told Phyllis.

He came back inside. 'The car's gone,' she said, fighting to control a rising panic. 'Lynda took the car. She doesn't know how to drive.'

'Yes, she does,' he said softly, a stricken look on his face. 'I've been teaching her. We go out behind one of my dad's warehouses. Actually, she's pretty good for only — '

'*Pretty* good?' Catherine glared at him, at last finding a target for her fear. She knew she wasn't being fair but couldn't stop herself. 'What is that supposed to mean? Does she know how long it takes to stop a car going sixty-five miles an hour? Can she merge into traffic at that speed? Can she defend herself against the commuter lunatics who are on the road right now?'

Phyllis dropped the magazines on the table. 'You're not being fair. This isn't Brian's fault.'

Catherine needed her anger. It gave her something to hang on to. But not when it was aimed at Brian. He deserved her loyalty, not her rage. 'I don't know what to do,' she admitted.

'I'm sorry, Mrs. Miller,' Brian said. 'Maybe I shouldn't have taught her how to drive, but

I swear I didn't know anything like this could happen.'

He was as terrified as she was. 'Do you have any idea where she could have gone?'

He thought about it for a long time. 'Anywhere.'

'I'm going to call Jack,' Catherine said. 'She was going to spend the night there tomorrow.'

'I could try Wendy,' Brian offered.

'Yes, of course,' Catherine told him. 'Thank you for thinking of it.'

'If she's not at Wendy's, maybe Wendy would have some ideas where to look,' he said.

'You can use Lynda's phone upstairs. Her address book is in the nightstand.' She knew there wasn't a whisper of a chance that Lynda had gone to see Jack, but she had to do something.

She dialed her ex-husband's number, waiting breathlessly while it rang. The housekeeper answered and informed Catherine that Jack wasn't home, and no one had stopped by.

'What about Rick?' Phyllis asked when Catherine struck out with Jack.

'He's at work. If she went there, he would make her call me the minute she walked in the door.' She didn't know how she knew this, she just did.

'The police?' Phyllis offered tentatively.

Even the suggestion was more than Catherine could bear. If she called the police, she accepted the possibility Lynda might need them. She couldn't lose her daughter. Not now. They'd walked through hell that summer and come out the other side. She couldn't go back. Not again. Please, God, not again. 'Not yet. Not until Brian comes down.'

The words no sooner left her lips than he appeared at the top of the stairs. In silent reply to her unasked question, he turned his head from side to side. Just once. It was enough.

33

Rick heard the captain's phone ringing as soon as Steve shut off the engine. He climbed down and made a dash across the apparatus room and down the hall to his office.

He snatched the receiver from the cradle. 'Captain Sawyer.' When no one answered, he assumed they'd hung up and was about to do the same when he heard Catherine's voice.

'Rick? Thank God. I was afraid you were gone and I . . . '

The desperate note in her voice raised the hairs on the back of his neck. 'What's wrong, Catherine? *Talk to me.*'

'It's Lynda. She's disappeared. She took my car and she can't drive — at least not well enough to be on the roads with other cars. I don't know what to do. I thought maybe she'd gone to see you. I knew you'd make her call if she had. But then I started thinking that you could have been out when she got there and if you didn't answer the phone she could be sitting in the parking lot waiting for you.' She paused to take a shuddering breath. 'I'm sorry. I know I'm not making sense. It's just that I don't know what else to do, who to call.'

'How long has she been gone?'

'I don't know — at least not for sure. Maybe an hour.'

She could be anywhere in an hour, including a hospital emergency room. 'Is anyone there with you?'

'My mother. Brian is out looking for her.'

'Why did she bolt? What happened?' He was hoping the answer would give a clue to where she'd gone.

'She called to talk to Ray and found out he died yesterday.'

'Jesus — I didn't know.' He wasn't as surprised as Lynda must have been, since he hadn't been as hopeful that the worst was behind Ray. He'd seen unexpected complications take too many kids just when everyone thought they were in the clear. 'Who have you called to help you look for Lynda?'

'No one yet. If she wasn't with you, I was going to call the police.'

'Let me see what I can find out first.' If something had happened to Lynda, he didn't want Catherine to hear about it over the phone. He grabbed a notepad and took down her license number and the year and make of the car. 'I'll get back to you as soon as I can.'

He hung up and immediately called the

423

contacts he had in the Placer, El Dorado, and Sacramento police departments, asking them to run Catherine's license for any routine stops or accidents. He then called the fire departments and asked for the readouts on all emergency calls for the past two hours.

Fifteen minutes later he was back on the phone with Catherine. 'Have you heard anything?'

'Only where she isn't. Brian and Phyllis call every time they go somewhere and she's not there.'

'There haven't been any police reports and she's not in any of the hospitals in the area,' he said. 'Wherever Lynda went, she managed to get there without receiving a ticket or wrecking the car.'

Catherine sobbed in relief. 'Thank you, Rick. I was so scared. I don't know what I'd do if something happened to Lynda again.'

'I told the people I contacted to get back to me if they heard something, but I don't think they will. Wherever Lynda was going, she's arrived by now. Once she calms down a little she'll realize she has no business driving your car and she'll figure out another way to get home.'

For the first time since discovering Lynda missing, Catherine felt as if the weight had been lifted from her chest and she could breathe normally. 'I'll call you the minute I hear something.'

'I'll see what I can find out about Ray. Sometimes just knowing helps.'

She reached for a tissue to wipe the tears running down her cheeks. 'I told him — I *promised* him, that he could come home with us.'

'Then he died knowing he was loved and wanted.'

'I should have found a way. I've been so wrapped up in my own problems that I put him to the back of my mind and — '

'Catherine, I'm going to hang up on you now. We can talk about this another time.'

Why should he listen to her when she hardly made sense to herself? She said good-bye and went to sit on the corner of the sofa, her legs drawn up, her chin resting on her knees, the phone by her side.

A half hour later the doorbell rang.

It was Rick.

'I thought you could use some company,' he said, as if he'd done nothing more than walk across the street to get to her.

Speechless, she went into his arms, his metal badge and captain's bugles cool against her warm skin. She knew if she tried to tell him how much his being there meant to her, she would start crying again. Instead, finally,

425

she tilted her head back and said, 'Thank you. From the bottom of my heart.'

'You're welcome.'

★ ★ ★

Brian didn't know where to look next. He drove around aimlessly, rechecking places he'd already been. He was headed back to the coffee house in Gold River when it hit him with sun-up certainty where Lynda had gone. As sure as he'd been that he wouldn't find her at Wendy's or with any of her other friends, he knew he would find her now. He didn't understand why he hadn't thought of it first.

Lynda loved driving through the foothills, especially in the evening when they would roll down the windows and let the hot summer wind blow through the car. Just when the heat was at its worst, they'd hit a pocket of cool, moist air from the lake or the river and it would be like a promise that the heat of summer would end.

When they stopped, it was always in the same place. Out on a point where they could watch the city lights start to appear at dusk. As the sun set, the lights formed a patchwork pattern, slowly filling in until the entire valley floor was a shimmering blanket in the rising heat.

He made a U-turn on Old Auburn, crossed over Folsom Dam, and turned left on Green Valley Road. A half hour later, he made the final turn on the narrow dirt road that wound around the hillside and felt a gut-punch of disappointment when the car wasn't there. He only had another hundred yards to go and should have been able to see her no matter where she'd parked.

Refusing to believe he'd been wrong, he went on.

When he reached the point where the road had been washed away by decades of rain, he stopped and got out to look around. A hot wind blew through the tall golden grasses, creating a lonely, whispering sound. From somewhere behind him came the hammering of a woodpecker as it slammed its beak into a dead tree. From everywhere came the low rasping of grasshoppers and crickets, and the call of the birds that made the foothills their home. Nothing out of the ordinary. Nothing he didn't hear every time they came here. Nothing to give him hope.

Instead of going back to the car, he walked another hundred yards, following a pathway marked with deer droppings. He stopped to look around and saw nothing that would lead him to believe Lynda had been there. In frustration and fear he yelled her name.

'*Lynda* — where the hell are you?'

'Over here.'

His heart in his throat, he whipped around, thinking she had come up behind him. 'Where?'

'Here,' she called. She came out of a stand of oak halfway down the hill and waved to him. 'Right here. Can you see me? I'm here, Brian. Please, please see me.'

He waved back and started down the hill at a run, slipping on the tall grass, falling, getting up and falling again. When he reached her, he took her in his arms and kissed her over and over again, the volatile combination of fear and joy finding voice in touch. Her shirt and shorts were torn, her pressure garments covered in dirt, her knees scraped and bloody, her face tear-streaked.

'I knew you would find me,' she said. 'No one else could. Only you.'

He cupped her face with his hands and looked deeply into her eyes. 'I would have searched forever.'

Fresh tears glistened in her eyes. 'I love you, Brian.'

'I'm sorry I didn't tell you about Ray.'

'You were only trying to protect me.'

He kissed her again, tenderly, with pent-up passion and longing, tasting her tears, her heartache. 'I should have tried harder to keep him here,' he said, tears burning the back of his throat. 'It's my fault. If he hadn't gone with her — '

She put a finger against his lips. 'Don't say that. It's not true.' Tears spilled onto her cheeks. 'You were his friend. You gave him hope.'

He tried to swallow his own tears, but the hurt ran too deep. With a soul-wrenching sob, he told her, 'I should have done more. He was counting on me and I let him down.'

Lynda cradled him and cried with him. 'I never told him good-bye,' she said, her heart breaking all over again. 'I should have called when I got home from camp. He must have thought I didn't care.'

'He knows you cared,' Brian said with absolute conviction.

She leaned back to look at him. 'How can you be so sure?'

'Because his family told him when he was with them again.' Brian wiped his eyes and then gently wiped hers. He kissed her cheeks and lips and whispered into each ear that he loved her, then gathered her in his arms and sat down with his back to the ancient oak that gave them shelter from the sun. He held her without saying anything for a long time.

He believed what he'd told Lynda, the

same way he believed the universe owed its creation to a Higher Being. He hadn't known that Ray was with his family until he heard himself say the words aloud. Now he knew those words were a parting gift from a friend who somehow felt their sorrow and wanted them to know he was all right.

'I think we should plant a tree for Ray,' Lynda said. 'Somewhere safe where we can watch it grow and never have to worry about it being cut down.'

'An oak tree that will live a couple of hundred years,' he said.

'And be home to birds and squirrels and in the autumn drop thousands of acorns to feed the deer and raccoons.' She sat up and looked at him. 'How will we make it safe?'

'I don't know yet.' She was so beautiful. He could tell her every day for the rest of their lives how much she meant to him and still not say it enough. 'But we'll find a way.'

'I love you, Brian.' She offered him a smile. 'I wish this hill was ours and we could stay here forever.'

It was the forever part that made him remember why he was there. 'What are you doing down here? And how come your knees are all skinned up?' He looked around. 'And where's the car?'

She pointed down the hill to the bottom of

the ravine. 'My mom is going to kill me.'

'Holy shit. Your mom. I promised I'd call her as soon as I found you.' He jumped up and reached for his back pocket. It was empty. 'I must have dropped the phone when I fell.'

'She's going to kill me,' Lynda repeated.

'Maybe — but my guess is you've got a couple of days. She's going to be too happy to see you to do anything before then.' Brian took Lynda's hand and brought her to her feet. 'Are you okay? Can you walk?'

'I made it this far.'

'How did you get down there?'

She didn't answer right away. Then she said with a sigh, 'I was trying to turn around and I must have gotten too close to the edge, because the car started going downhill. Backward. I stepped on the brake as hard as I could, but it didn't do any good.'

He stopped to look at her. 'Are you telling me you slid all the way down there from up here?'

She nodded.

'Did you roll over?'

'I thought I was going to a couple of times, but I didn't. I don't know how we're going to get it out. There aren't any roads down there. I looked.' She kicked something, glanced down, and said, 'I found the phone.'

'Good. Now call your mother.'

'I thought you said you were going to call her,' she said hopefully.

'No way. This one's on you.'

She sat on a rock and dialed the number. Catherine answered on the first ring.

'Hello?'

'Hi, Mom,' Lynda said, a sudden catch in her voice. 'It's me.'

34

Catherine sat with her head in her hands, paralyzed with relief. Finally she looked up and gave Rick a trembling smile. 'Now all I have to do is figure out a way to get my car out of a canyon.'

'After what you've been through today, that should be a piece of cake.'

Her heart did a funny little skipping beat. He'd come there without being asked, quietly supplied the strength she desperately needed, and expected nothing in return. 'I couldn't have made it without you,' she said with stark honesty.

'Sure you could.' He stood and stretched. 'You're a lot stronger than you think you are.' He moved toward the door. 'Tell Lynda to call me when she gets a chance.'

'Can't you wait? She'll be here soon.' Catherine didn't want him to go.

'I promised the chief I'd get back as soon as possible.'

She nodded. 'Will you come to dinner?' she asked, surprising them both. 'Let me do at least that much.' She wasn't being fair. She'd told him that she couldn't love him, that a relationship was impossible, and yet here she was, opening the door again. 'At the new house. As soon as we move in.' She smiled nervously. 'As soon as I know where the new house is, of course.'

'You don't have to cook dinner for me. And you sure as hell better not send a thank-you note,' he said. 'We moved past that stuff a long time ago. Or at least I hope we did.'

She couldn't let him go. At least not this way. 'I want to see you again,' she blurted out. 'And it has nothing to do with Lynda or thanking you for staying with me.'

He ran his knuckle over her chin and touched her lip with his thumb. 'You're an emotional basket case right now. Give it a couple of weeks and see if you still feel the same. If you do, call me. I'll meet you anytime, anywhere.'

Slowly, pausing to give her the option of refusal, he came forward and brushed her lips with a whisper-soft kiss. She closed her eyes and swayed toward him. She opened her mouth when he kissed her again, a soft moan in her throat.

Rick broke the kiss, looked at her, and smiled. 'I can see you have some serious thinking ahead of you. Just remember, I'm on your side. Always have been. Always will be.'

She walked him to the door and waited

while he backed out of the driveway and her mother drove in.

'Where's Rick going?' she asked, carrying a bag of Chinese takeout in one hand and a suitcase in the other. She'd insisted she was going to stay until Lynda came home, even if it took all night.

'He had to get back to work.' Catherine took the suitcase.

'But I bought all this food.'

'I'm sure Lynda and Brian can handle it.'

Phyllis spun around, almost dropping the bag. 'You found her? Where?'

'Brian found her. Some place up in the foothills where they go to watch the sunset.'

'And she's all right?' Phyllis went into the kitchen and put the food on the counter.

'Surprisingly, yes.'

'That poor girl. She's had one bad thing follow on the heels of another all summer long.'

Catherine thought about her mother's statement. 'Maybe, but I'll bet if you asked her, she'd tell you that she doesn't see it that way.'

'You mean Brian?'

'And Rick.'

Phyllis shook her head. 'He's become such an important part of this family, I have to remind myself that he hasn't always been here.'

'Did you know that he and Gene were in the same fraternity at USC?'

'I was wondering how they knew each other.' She turned on the faucet to wash her hands, then stood frozen in place while the water ran unattended. She stared at Catherine and burst into tears.

'What is it?' Catherine asked.

'I don't know what I would do if something happened to you or Lynda.' She turned off the water and grabbed a tissue. 'When I lost your father I swore I would never take another day for granted, but I slipped right back into the same old complacency. How could I ever think I would be happy in Arizona with all of you here?'

'It breaks my heart to think what Ray will miss,' Catherine said. 'What was stolen from him.'

'Do you want me to call Ray's aunt to find out about the funeral and where we should send flowers?'

Flowers . . . she'd forgotten. Of course they should send flowers. But what kind? Mums to represent the football games Ray would never play? Orchids for the corsage he would never buy another prom date? Roses for the boutonniere he would never wear in his wedding tuxedo?

'Why don't we wait and find out what

Lynda and Brian would like,' Catherine said, sadness threatening to overwhelm her.

'It's too bad the funeral is so far away.'

'Why?'

'Oh, I know the modern feeling is that funerals are too expensive and overdone. I agree that things have gotten out of hand, but I think people get the trappings and the need for closure confused. There's a tendency to throw one out with the other. What gets lost is the fact that when someone leaves us, we all have a need to say good-bye one last time.'

There it was, the answer to what she had to do. Simple, but absolutely necessary for Lynda and Brian to begin their healing process. She reached for the phone book.

'What are you going to do?'

'See if I can get Lynda and Brian to Kansas in time for the funeral.' Catherine hesitated. 'Remind me to call the rental agency to cancel tomorrow.'

'What about work?'

She'd been on the job such a short time, it was easy to forget. 'They're wonderful people. I'm sure they'll understand.' No matter how wonderful, they'd hired her because they needed her. She hated to let them down.

'Is there any reason I couldn't go for you?'

It was the perfect solution. 'You wouldn't mind?'

Phyllis waved away the thought. 'I like feeling needed. And this way you can use my car while I'm gone.'

★ ★ ★

After getting lost in the maze of new parking lots at the airport, Catherine had to run to get to the terminal on time. She arrived just as the plane taxied up to the ramp. Phyllis was the first one off, explaining that Brian had stepped forward to volunteer her to be moved to first class when it was announced the plane was overbooked.

'I think he's a keeper,' Phyllis said. 'I've always wanted to fly first class and could never bring myself to part with the money.'

'I think he's a keeper, too.' Anxious to see Lynda, Catherine searched the steadily moving stream of passengers. For a moment she was sure she'd spotted her, and then decided it had to be someone else. The blonde with the short-cropped hair wasn't wearing a cap, and Lynda hadn't been without one since leaving the hospital.

But then the blonde glanced up, saw Catherine looking at her, and smiled.

Catherine caught her breath at the glimpse of the beautiful young woman her daughter had become over the past summer. She wasn't a child anymore. While Catherine experienced a swell of pride, there was also a poignant sense of loss.

Lynda worked her way through the flow of departing passengers and threw her arms wide for a hug. 'I'm so glad to be home. I missed you, Mom.'

'I missed you, too.' She gave Brian a hug. 'And you,' she added. 'It got a little lonely around here without the both of you.'

'You were right,' Brian said. 'We needed to go. For a lot of reasons.'

'For one — we found out Ray's aunt isn't the witch we thought she was,' Lynda said. 'She really did care about him. She just didn't know how to show it.'

Brian hitched his backpack over his shoulder. 'We knew him a lot better than she did.'

'She asked a million questions after the funeral when we went back to her house.' Lynda looked up at Brian. 'I think she was really happy we came.'

'I know she was,' Phyllis said, joining them. 'She told me so.'

'I probably shouldn't ask,' Lynda said. 'But what did you find out about the car?'

'The insurance company decided it wasn't worth fixing.'

'Does that mean we get a new one?' Lynda said, excited.

'A nice little economy model.'

'I was thinking more along the lines of that new little BMW.'

'Well, *new* and *little* apply.' She put her arm around Lynda's shoulder. 'Two out of three isn't bad.'

★ ★ ★

On the way home, Catherine drove by the house she'd rented the day she'd gone out with the agent. She pulled to a stop out front. 'I wanted you to see it first,' she said to Lynda. 'But there was someone right behind me who was going to take it if I didn't. This was the best one I looked at — by far — and I didn't want to chance losing it.'

Lynda rolled down the window to get a better look. 'Can we go in?'

Catherine asked Phyllis, 'Do you have the time?'

'I have all the time in the world.'

'What about you, Brian?'

'I told my folks not to expect me before dinner.'

The house was three years old, two stories,

half the size of the one they were leaving, and located in the middle of a cul-de-sac that backed up to a large tract of undeveloped land. At least they had the illusion of property, even if that property belonged to someone else.

Catherine opened the front door, praying Lynda would keep an open mind. She didn't know what she would do if Lynda didn't like the place.

A small tile entranceway led to a sunken living room. The walls were white, the carpet beige, the curtains and miniblinds cream. To the right was an oak stairway that led to a wide landing. Oak floor-to-ceiling book-shelves lined the back wall.

'Where's my room?' Lynda asked.

'Upstairs. You decide which one you want.'

'Come on, Brian. You can help me.'

Catherine and Phyllis went into the kitchen. 'I like it,' Phyllis said.

'I do, too. Or at least I think I will when I get used to it. It's a big change.'

Phyllis unlocked the sliding glass door off the family room. 'Just look at this view. You're going to love being outside in this backyard.' She turned and looked at Catherine. 'A little paint, a little wallpaper, and we'll have this place looking like a million dollars.'

'The paint and wallpaper are going to have

to wait. The movers are coming next week.'

'Why so soon?'

'I want to get in and get settled before I have to start work on the rummage sale with Karol,' Catherine said.

'I decided which one I want,' Lynda called from upstairs. 'The closet's a little small, but the whirlpool bath makes up for it.'

Catherine went to the bottom of the stairs and called up, 'Where are you?'

Lynda came out of the master suite. 'Right here,' she said innocently. 'In my new bedroom.'

Catherine was at a loss for words.

The look on her mother's face was too much for Lynda. 'Gotcha,' she said gleefully.

When Lynda and Brian left to continue their exploration, Catherine folded her arms across her chest and leaned against the wall. It had been months since she'd heard Lynda laugh with such honesty and abandon.

The fears she'd carried like hoarded coins were spent. She had no idea what was ahead for her and Lynda, only that the journey would be a joy.

35

He had a bad feeling about the fire the minute he pulled the address from the computer. The house was on a block of old Victorians, many of them beautifully restored, but none able to pass modern building codes for fire suppression. The balloon construction meant there were no firebreaks in the walls. The spaces between the lath and plaster became runways for the flames to travel unimpeded from the basement to the attic.

No matter how quickly they responded, they faced sudden death overtime, with the other team in possession of the ball. Their normal second-in engine and the truck assigned to accompany them to fires in their district were both tied up fighting a warehouse fire. Help would be a good five to seven minutes later than usual.

As soon as they rolled out of the firehouse, Rick gave Steve the hydrant location and checked the late afternoon sky for smoke. A single, dark gray plume rose like an exclamation point in the windless October sky. Even Paul sensed the urgency of the situation and kept his banter to questions about what to expect when they arrived.

Steve drove with his usual caution and confidence but pushed a little harder, giving an air horn blast to thoughtless drivers who refused to yield or pull to the side of the road to let them pass.

'Serve 'em right if it was one of their houses,' Paul said, expressing a rookie frustration over something he would learn to take in stride as a veteran.

For Rick it wasn't the lack of respect for the red lights and siren that bothered him; it was the disregard for the equipment. Empty, their engine was a formidable vehicle. Filled with the thousand gallons of water they carried for immediate fire suppression, it was a behemoth. To race it to a corner or dash in front of it at a turn was tantamount to playing Russian roulette with a fully loaded gun.

Rick began assessing the fire as soon as the house came into view. He read the situation as if it were a familiar book sporting a new cover, determining his plan of attack. In a glance he took in how close together the houses were, the intensity of the fire, and the number and demeanor of people standing around on the sidewalk and street.

Thick black smoke poured from the front door while thin gray wisps escaped through the weathered siding. The only immediate visible flame was from an air vent near the peak. Like a playful child trying to touch its tongue to its nose, the flame reached for the tinderbox eaves, its efforts growing stronger with each attempt.

As they drew closer, Rick saw the fear that comes from understanding in the faces of the observers. These were neighbors who recognized their vulnerability to a fire that only need send a second tongue of flame to taste the house next door to spread the destruction and loss.

One woman stood out from the rest, her fear a raw, gaping wound, her jeans and T-shirt gray from the smoke and ash. Rick focused on her as Steve pulled to a stop in front of the house. 'We've got a rescue,' he said with gut-deep certainty.

She ran to them, screaming, 'My little boy is in there! You have to help him!' Reaching for Janet as she climbed from the backseat, the woman clung to her, begging, 'Hurry. Oh, God, please hurry. He's in there all alone. I couldn't reach him. I tried. I kept going back, but I couldn't find him.'

'How old is the boy?' Rick asked, drawing her attention. Janet left to get the airpacks.

She turned pleading eyes to Rick. 'Seven.'

'Is there any chance he could have gotten out by himself? Have you checked the area?'

'The window in his room doesn't open.'

'Where is his room?'

'The back of the house.'

'First floor?'

She nodded.

'Left or right?'

She paused to think as if the question were too much to take in on top of everything else. 'Left,' she finally said.

'Lead the tank line,' Rick called to Steve. Although it would restrict their ability to fight the fire by limiting the water they could put on it to the thousand gallons in the engine, they didn't have the extra five minutes it would take to connect to the hydrant. With a child inside, time was the paramount concern, the structure was expendable.

Steve pulled the inch-and-a-half hose from the engine and dropped the nozzle at the front door. He then went back to the pump panel on the side of the engine and turned the dials that controlled the flow of water to charge the line. Too much pressure and he could knock Janet off her feet when she opened the nozzle.

'Please hurry,' the woman pleaded. 'Please, you have to get in there. He's only seven. He can't save himself.'

Rick nodded to the woman as he contacted the com center on his portable radio, telling

446

them they were leading a tank line to perform a rescue and to dispatch a code three ambulance. 'Have our second-in company drop a wye, and a feeder line. The hydrant is a block down on the right side of the street.'

Janet came up behind Rick and handed him his airpack. He heard the faint cry of sirens as he loaded the forty-pound tank onto his back and tightened the straps. Moving toward the house, he shouted one final instruction into the radio before slipping it into his pocket. 'Tell the second-in captain to assume incident command.'

By going in with his firefighters he relinquished control of the fire scene to the captain of the responding engine. Two seasoned firefighers could have handled the rescue by themselves, but Paul was still too green to recognize the subtle warning signs that came with house fires. Rick wasn't about to let them handle it alone.

Thick black smoke rolled and curled from the front door. There was heat, but no visible flame. Janet picked up the nozzle and opened it to spray wide, creating a wall of mist, trying to force the smoke backward. But without the truck crew there to cut holes in the roof and break windows for ventilation, the smoke had nowhere to go. It enveloped them in a menacing false night devoid of stars.

Paul took the hose three feet behind Janet. Rick brought up the rear several feet behind Paul. Once inside, they dropped to a crouch, hugging the floor, where the smoke and heat were most forgiving. Pops and squeaks and groans accompanied the soft roar of the advancing fire as the house shouted in futile protest over its imminent death.

They came to an open door and made a quick sweep of the room. As convinced as the mother was that her son was at the back of the house, they couldn't count on that fact. He could have moved. Too many victims were found where no one believed they would be.

Rick's ears began to burn when they returned to the hallway. Despite department regulations that dictated they wear Nomex hoods under their helmets, Rick went without. He wanted to feel the heat. His ears were like the miner's canary. If they were too hot, it was too hot for everything else and time to get out.

The black smoke cleared to a thick fog and took on an orange cast. Five more feet and they discovered flame hungrily consuming the kitchen, tasting the table, devouring the cabinets, spitting out the curtains. Unwilling to leave the dragon behind them, Janet ended its meal with a thirty-second fog that stole the oxygen and created dense roiling smoke. She

448

hit the window with the nozzle wide open, shattering the glass outward, sucking smoke out while pulling more into the room from the hall.

Heated water rained on Rick, soaking his turnouts, creeping down his neck and onto his back. Again there was claustrophobic darkness as they crawled further into the house, searching for another doorway, another room.

They found two. Both bedrooms. They swept the closets, under the beds, in the corners and behind dressers. Children hid from fire. They had to think like a child.

Nothing.

Frustration, fueled by failing hope, kept them there for a second sweep. The heat grew unbearable. Rick's ears blistered. Finally, defeated, he tagged Paul and then Janet on the shoulder and motioned for them to fall back.

It was then that Rick heard the sound he'd only heard once before in all his years of firefighting, an ominous staccato cracking: the fire's victory dance. Instantly he was back at the warehouse fire. The horror of catching his best friend as he fell through the roof, the struggle to pull him free of the consuming flames, the defeat when he could only hold on and watch him die.

'Out!' Rick shouted, knowing the word reached Paul and Janet as little more than a muffled cry. He jumped to his feet and started backing down the hall, pulling the hose with him, forcing them to follow.

They made it to the kitchen doorway before the ceiling collapsed. The force of the impact threw Rick backward, the top of the airpack hitting him in the back of the head. Dizzy, fighting to stay conscious, he scrambled to his knees and dug through the flaming debris, looking for Paul.

Paul put up a hand. Rick snagged it. The other hand appeared, frantically clawing the air. Rick clasped it and leaned back to give himself leverage to pull Paul free of the burning weight that sat on his body.

'Goddamn it, don't you die on me!' Rick shouted. Slowly, too slowly, he inched down the hallway to the front door. 'We're going to make it. We're almost to the door. You fucking hang on, Paul.'

A painting dropped through the opening and fell on Paul's legs, the landscape bubbling, searing, and then bursting into flame. Rick strained to pull harder, faster, praying Steve had heard the thunder of the collapsing ceiling above the roar of the fire.

Rick hit something he wasn't expecting and fell over backward, losing his grip on Paul. He swung his arm in a wide arc and made contact with Steve, who had come in on his hands and knees to look for them.

Righting himself, he pointed to Paul, got up, and headed back through what had become a wall of fire to look for Janet. Blinded by the flame and smoke, he reached down, found the hose, and picked it up to use as a guide.

He found her, unconscious, the nozzle still clutched in her hands. Adrenaline shot through him. For a moment he was invincible — for that second he could do anything, and then it would be all over.

For both of them.

He acted now, or not at all.

Grabbing the nozzle, he shot a narrow fog at the flame, opening an escape window that could last from ten seconds to one. When it closed, it would be with deadly fury. From the moment he dropped the hose and grabbed Janet's airpack harness, they would be at the mercy of the dragon.

The hallway cleared. A tunnel of light opened and Rick saw through to the outside. Paul was stretched out on the lawn. Steve stood over him, directing the ambulance crew. Firefighters from the second-in company appeared, shouting, pointing, running.

The bell sounded on Rick's airpack and

then Janet's. Five more minutes and they would be out of air.

Five minutes.

A lifetime.

He dropped the hose and reached for Janet's harness. A deafening roar raced through the dying house.

The window closed.

36

Catherine smoothed the shelf paper in the linen cupboard and stood back to admire her handiwork, a part of her amused at how little it took to please her nowadays. They'd been in the new house two weeks, and she was finally through unpacking and putting things away. The boxes still in the garage were headed for storage. What she didn't use or miss in a year she would give to the battered women's shelter she'd already overwhelmed with a truckload of furniture.

Lynda came up behind her. 'I'm going downstairs to watch *General Hospital* and then do my homework.'

'Did you check to see if it recorded today?' Yesterday, the tape had been blank when Lynda went to watch it, and Catherine wasn't sure if she'd made a mistake setting it up or if the VCR was on its way out.

'Not yet.'

'Let me know.' Lynda started to walk away and Catherine called her back. 'Want to see the shelf paper I bought today?'

Lynda's eyes widened with disbelief. She

shook her head. 'Mom, you have got to get a life.'

'It's really pretty. And smells good, too. It was on sale at William Glen.'

'Oh . . . *William Glen*. You should have said so.'

'Sarcasm gives you pimples,' Catherine told her.

'And pizza clears 'em right up.' With exaggerated reluctance, she came back, looked in the cupboard, and sniffed. 'Incredible. The best shelf paper I've ever smelled.'

'And?'

'Oh, the most beautiful by far.'

Catherine laughed. 'Go watch your soap.' Alone again, she picked up a stack of bath towels and put them in the cupboard. Next came the hand towels and washcloths and then, on the next shelf, the sheets and pillowcases.

She broke down the empty cardboard box and was on her way to put it in the garage when she heard Lynda scream. The wrenching sound tore through the quiet house like a spear through silk.

'No . . . no, no, no — '

The heat drained from Catherine's body.

'*Please* no.'

She tried to move, but the message was lost somewhere between her mind and her legs.

454

'*Not Rick*. He can't be dead.'

Her knees buckled; she slid down the wall to the floor.

★ ★ ★

The hospital was organized chaos, with two ambulances in the bay and another pulling in. Medical personnel stood to the side as the patients were unloaded, then moved in to begin their assessments.

The firefighter paramedics yielded their precious cargo but stuck close as they rolled deeper into the emergency room, reciting the field reports taken at the scene — blood pressure, pulse — desperate, determined steps taken to make sure one of their own did not die.

'Let me off of this thing,' Rick said as he struggled to remove his oxygen mask.

A stern-looking nurse with yellow pencils behind both ears glared at him. 'You're mine now, big boy. You will do what I say. Do you hear me?'

'Yes, Sergeant.'

She smiled. 'Glad you got the picture.'

Rick had no intention of obeying. As soon as they left him alone, he would be on his feet and off to find Paul and Janet. He had to see for himself that they were all right. No one would tell him anything except that they'd all made it this far.

When they were in the examining room, a male nurse picked up a pair of scissors. 'What are you going to do with those?' Rick asked him.

'You know the routine. I'm going to cut off your clothes.'

'Do you have any idea how long it takes to get a set of turnouts replaced? It could be six months. Even longer. And while I'm waiting, I'll have to use a loaner set from the tower, and then — '

'All right, all right.' He put the scissors down. 'If you can sit up, I'll help you get this stuff off. If not, it's back to the scissors.'

'Fair enough.' Rick started to roll to his side. For an insane moment he thought someone had come in behind him and punched him in the ribs. The pain wasn't so bad he couldn't work through it, but it wasn't anything he wanted to have to live with for long. As soon as he was upright, his personal, invisible boxing champion started throwing punches at his head.

He was sitting up, but the way the room was swaying, he knew he wasn't going to stay that way for long. He shrugged out of his jacket and shirt. When he was prone again, he unsnapped his suspenders, lifted his hips, and the nurse tugged his pants off.

With more patience than he felt, he went through the triage exam — the flashlight to check his pupils, the taps and scratches to test his reflexes, the pokes and prods for pain — knowing they wouldn't find anything serious.

The doctor ordered Xrays and bloodwork. 'Looks like you're going to get away with a couple of cracked ribs and a mild concussion. The head wound is going to need a couple of stitches. I hope you're a side sleeper.'

'What about the others?'

'I'm going to check on them now. As soon as I find out anything, I'll let you know.'

'Thanks.' Rick settled against the pillow, too tired to pay attention to the pain it caused. Sounds from an examining room down the hall drifted to him in unrecognizable snatches. He concentrated and picked out a voice asking for a name, over and over again. 'Can you tell me who you are? What's your name? Hey, fella, can you give me your name?'

Fella? It had to be Paul. He was either unconscious or unresponsive. Rick turned his good ear to the voices, sending a silent message to his rookie, urging him to wake up. He focused so intently, he didn't hear the nurse come in to take his blood, wasn't even aware of her until she reached for his arm.

She started to say something and he cut her off when he heard one of the distant nurses say, 'What did he call himself?'

'I'm not sure.'

'Tell me again,' the nurse urged. 'What is your name?'

This time, as clearly as if they were lying side by side, Rick heard the answer.

'*Cats* . . . ' Paul said with unmistakable pride.

★ ★ ★

'They won't tell me,' Catherine said, turning to Lynda as she hung up the phone. 'They said they won't release the names or any information about their condition until the families have been notified.'

'I know it's him,' Lynda said. 'I saw him when they were putting him in the ambulance.' She broke down again. 'He had . . . he had blood . . . all over his face.'

Desperate, Catherine tried the firehouse. No one answered. She didn't know who else to call. She took Lynda's arm and steered her toward the front door. 'We're going down there.'

'They won't let us in. We're not family.'

'The hell they won't. Just let them try to stop us.'

When they were in the car, Catherine turned the radio to an all-news station. They were in the middle of a report on rising interest rates when the local newscaster broke in.

'Three firefighters were taken to the hospital this afternoon after being trapped in a house fire. The firefighters, one of them female, were attempting the rescue of a seven-year-old boy reported inside.

'The mother of the boy told reporters she'd gone next door to visit a friend while her son — who had stayed home from school with an upset stomach — was taking a nap. The boy was found later by police hiding in the backyard of a nearby house.

'The source of the fire is under investigation.

'Stay tuned for updates as they happen. Now back to our regularly scheduled program.'

'That stupid woman,' Lynda raged. 'This is all her fault. She had no business leaving — '

'Rick's okay,' Catherine said.

'How do you know?'

'I can feel it,' she said with absolute conviction.

Lynda turned to her. 'I know you love him. When are you going to do something about it?'

For thirty-nine years she'd planned and thought and considered, following the dictates of her mind. It was time to let her heart take the lead.

She looked at Lynda. 'I do love him. And I think it's time I told him that.'

★ ★ ★

Janet winced as she turned her head to look at Rick. She was still in the examination room, waiting to be transported to the orthopedics floor. An expert on joint surgery was on his way in from the golf course to look at her shattered knee. 'Did anyone say how long Paul's going to be off?'

'No one has said anything to me.' Rick sat forward in his chair, looking for what had become an oxymoron — a comfortable position. 'Having the burn on the same leg that's broken is going to present some problems.'

'Did they get your X rays back yet?'

'Two cracked ribs,' Rick told her.

She nodded. 'What about the head?'

'A couple of stitches. Nothing to get excited about.'

'Shit — ' She pinched the bridge of her nose, trying to hold back tears. 'I just get you guys doing things the way I like around the firehouse and look what happens. Now someone else is going to come in and get the benefit of all my hard work.'

Rick accepted the bravado for what it was — a potent mixture of fear and regret. Janet loved her job and was facing the possibility of never going back. 'I'll do what I can to make sure there's no backsliding.'

An awkward silence followed. 'Steve told me what you did. I suppose now you'll be expecting me to bake you a cake or something.'

He laughed. It hurt like hell. 'If you're looking for a way to thank me, one of your cakes isn't it.'

Steve came in. He touched Rick's shoulder. 'There's someone out there looking for you.'

Rick didn't feel like moving. 'Who is it?'

'Trust me, it's someone you want to see.'

Puzzled, Rick stood and stiffly moved past him. He pulled the curtain aside and barely had time to brace himself before Lynda was in his arms. He let out a soft groan at the impact but the pain wasn't near what he would have expected. She felt good where she was.

He looked into Lynda's face and could see that she'd been crying. 'I'm sorry if I scared you,' he said softly.

'Scared doesn't begin to cover it,' she said.

'When I saw you on television, I thought for sure you were dead. Thank God Mom was there. I don't know what I would have done if I'd been by myself.'

'Where is your mother?' Rick asked carefully. Before she had a chance to answer, he looked up and saw Catherine watching them. She was crying, and smiling, and walking toward him.

'She's in love with you, you know,' Lynda said, stepping aside.

'Yeah,' he said. 'I do know.'

Catherine looked up at him, her eyes filled with the wonder of finally knowing what it was to be in love and to be loved for the first time in her life. She touched his face gently, longingly, and then kissed him. 'I've come to take you home.'

He looked deeply into her eyes. 'It's your home, too. As soon as you're ready.'

'I already feel as if I belong there.'

He brought her closer, the pain in his ribs forgotten in his need to feel her, to smell the perfume of her hair, to mark the moment that their life together began. 'I'm a forever kind of guy, Catherine. You can have as much time as you and Lynda need. I'll be right here waiting when you're ready.'

She lifted her chin, touched her lips to his, and whispered, 'I love you.'

'You're going to have to tell me again,' Rick said. 'I've waited too long to hear it only once.'

She kissed him again. 'I love you . . . I love you . . . I love you.'

'That's a fine start,' he told her. 'Now you can take me home and tell me again.' He held an arm out to Lynda.

They left the hospital together. A family.

★ ★ ★

Thirty-five miles away, Blue awakened from a deep sleep. He stood and stretched, looked at Sandra and Walt for several seconds, whined softly, and let himself out through the garage door. Pausing for one questioning, backward glance, he trotted across the lawn and through the opening in the fence that separated what had been his two homes.

Innately, he knew his wandering days were over. With long, purposeful strides he made his way through the abandoned vegetable garden, past the heritage oak, and around the house to the driveway.

There he sat and waited, his tail slowly, steadily sweeping the dust in a wide, welcoming arc.

We do hope that you have enjoyed reading this large print book.

Did you know that all of our titles are available for purchase?

We publish a wide range of high quality large print books including:
Romances, Mysteries, Classics
General Fiction
Non Fiction and Westerns

Special interest titles available in large print are:
The Little Oxford Dictionary
Music Book
Song Book
Hymn Book
Service Book

Also available from us courtesy of Oxford University Press:
Young Readers' Dictionary
(large print edition)
Young Readers' Thesaurus
(large print edition)

For further information or a free brochure, please contact us at:
Ulverscroft Large Print Books Ltd.,
The Green, Bradgate Road, Anstey,
Leicester, LE7 7FU, England.
Tel: (00 44) **0116 236 4325**
Fax: (00 44) **0116 234 0205**

BLACKBERRY SUMMER

Phyllis Hastings

Debbie converted a wing of the old farmhouse into an Academy for Young Ladies. She hoped this would enable her to make provision for her children's future careers. But she could not foresee the disastrous fire or the regret and guilt she would feel for giving her youngest son to be reared by her twin sister Dolly. Next to the farm, Dolly's wealthy husband Christopher built an imposing mansion in the Gothic style, and planned to run a racing stable, but his schemes were doomed to end in tragedy.

NOVEMBER TREE

Ann Stevens

Rowena and Phyllida are both sixty-something, and both on their own — so what better than sharing their declining years? They have known each other for fifty years — and there's something to be said for the devil you know. But who said that retirement would be peaceful? Amidst demanding relatives and with a new suitor on the horizon, it looks as though the future is far from predictable, bringing past resentments and a festering secret to the surface. As the tension rises and tolerance falters, the long-suppressed truth threatens to erupt in a most unpredictable way.